D0465858

liquididea press

Praise for *The Last Firewall*

"*The Last Firewall* is awesome near-term science fiction. Hertling is completely nailing it."
　　—*Brad Feld, Foundry Group managing director*

"A fun read and tantalizing study of the future of technology: both inviting and alarming."
　　—*Harper Reed, former CTO of Obama for America, Threadless*

"*The Last Firewall* is an insightful and adrenaline-inducing tale of what humanity could become and the machines we could spawn."
　　—*Ben Huh, CEO of Cheezburger*

"A fascinating and prescient take on what the world will look like once computers become smarter than people. Highly recommended."
　　—*Mat Ellis, Founder & CEO Cloudability*

"If you love stories of a post-scarcity world where humans are caught between rogue AIs, or just like having your mind blown, read this book. It's a phenomenal ride!"
　　—*Gene Kim, author of* The Phoenix Project: A Novel About IT, DevOps, and Helping Your Business Win

Praise for Singularity Novels

"Highly entertaining, gripping, thought inspiring. Don't start without the time to finish"
  —*Gifford Pinchot III, founder Bainbridge Graduate Institute, author of* The Rise of the Intelligent Organization

"Chilling and compelling"
  —*Wired.com, Erik Wecks*

"Alarming and jaw-dropping tale about how something as innocuous as email can subvert an entire organization."
  —*Gene Kim, author of* The Phoenix Project: A Novel About IT, DevOps, and Helping Your Business Win

"A fascinating look at how simple and benign advancements in technology could lead to the surprise arrival of the first AI"
  —*Jason Glaspey, founder paleoplan.com, bacn.com, and unthirsty.com*

Other novels by William Hertling

Avogadro Corp: The Singularity is Closer than it Appears

A.I. Apocalypse

For more information, visit www.williamhertling.com

THE LAST FIREWALL

THE LAST FIREWALL

A Singularity Novel

W<small>ILLIAM</small> H<small>ERTLING</small>

liquididea press
P<small>ORTLAND</small>, O<small>REGON</small>

ISBN for Paperback: 978-0-9847557-6-9
ISBN for eBook: 978-0-9847557-7-6

Keywords: singularity, technological singularity, artificial intelligence, ai, robotics, transhumanism, cyberpunk

http://www.williamhertling.com

For Erin Gately.

Contents

PART 2

Part One

O

She diced onions until she had a neat pile, and went to work on the red peppers, humming to herself as she worked. A blue cloth, candles, and a bottle of her favorite red decorated the table. She glanced at the clock; twenty minutes until he arrived.

A biting pain cut through her head, her vision flashing white before fading to dark. Startled, she dropped the knife and pressed hard against her temples, afraid her implant was malfunctioning.

The pain doubled, then quadrupled in seconds. She gasped and gripped the counter for support as her knees weakened.

A memory surfaced, unbidden. Her mom and dad; they were young again, and smiling. Her mother clapped her hands. Crisp and vivid, the vision cut across forty years with a glaring intensity. As quickly as it came, the moment was torn away, only to be replaced by another.

Oh, God, no. She was dying.

The next memory was as crystal clear as the chopped vegetables in front of her. She was fumbling with the stick shift in her father's car, while learning to drive. Glancing over, she saw him sitting calmly, the corner of his mouth upturned.

She sank to the floor, crying, as the memories continued to ambush her, coming and changing, faster and faster. Her husband, handsome in the suit she'd bought him, smiling the day before he won the election and a Congressional seat. She was visiting him at his office; they were going to have lunch together. His colleague, Congressman Lonnie Watson, walked in. The men spoke, paying her no attention. She couldn't make out what they were saying.

Then, her son's first steps at the museum, a look of pure joy on his face as he squealed with delight. She reached out, but it all dissipated before she could touch him.

She panicked, realizing she wouldn't see these people again. Wouldn't have a chance to watch her son grow up. She hugged her knees as she sat on the kitchen floor.

Another memory: coming home with her son from a baseball game. Lonnie Watson again, talking to her husband in his office. Her attention was gripped by the expression on her son's face, his disappointment at being ignored by his father. She felt the memory slow and intensify. The conversation between the congressmen played out and then repeated, the curves of their lips moving in slow motion through the glass French doors. They were working on artificial intelligence legislation.

Her final memory was of her son. The feel of his hair under her fingertips as she'd said goodbye to him just hours ago. A blistering pain spread across her head. She screamed out one final time, before going silent, her mouth open and frozen in place. She tried to stand, but fell sideways, and was dead before she hit the floor.

1

Catherine shrugged on her shirt and looked back to the bed where Nick slept. She watched him breathe while gazing at his stubble of day-old beard. Cute, but not so smart. She gathered her blonde hair into a ponytail, then checked the mirror, mentally reversing the words on her t-shirt: Life without geometry was pointless. Smiling, she headed for the hallway.

She padded down the stairs. Always the first to get up, it hadn't taken her long to learn housemates don't like early risers.

Downstairs, Einstein, a puppen, or half cat-half dog hybrid, slept on an eastern windowsill, catching the opening rays of morning sunlight. Catherine tickled her ears until she purred. The feline part of Einstein's heritage dominated; at first glance, you saw only a big cat. But take Einstein to a park, and she'd fetch a stick.

Catherine slid out the kitchen sliding glass door into the courtyard, where plants had gone wild around the central patio of reclaimed fireplace bricks. She faced east, toward the house, and started *Ba Duan Jin,* or Eight Treasure, qigong. She moved slowly, synchronizing the physical movement of the ancient Chinese form with the flow of qi, or life force, within her body. Her eyes unfocused, she followed the prescribed footsteps, her arms tracing graceful arcs through the air. She distantly noticed the breeze in the leaves of the small trees, a neighbor's wind chime, her breath. She repeated the form twice, paused for a few meditative breaths, then started Jade Body.

When she finished, she bowed once. The peaceful motions of qigong were gone now, replaced with the hard, quick snaps of *Naihanchi,* her first karate kata. Forty minutes later, she completed *Kusanku* and bowed again. Her body sank gratefully into seated meditation, legs crossed, hands on knees. A slight sheen of sweat covered her skin, her muscles warm and limber. The sounds of the coffee pot gurgling, laughter, and the toilet running filtered quietly from the house. As thoughts came in, she let them go. Empty mind. Empty mind.

Ninety minutes after she'd gone outside, she opened her eyes and gazed anew at the world. She watched the sunlight play on leaves, then stretched her arms and legs wide.

Some people said they had a hard time meditating, their minds always wandering, becoming trapped in thoughts. She didn't understand. If they wanted to meditate, why would they think about other things?

She padded barefoot up the porch steps, and pushed the door open. After the cool morning air, the house was stuffy. Her housemates were in the kitchen now.

"Hello, Karate Kid," Tom said, his tone affectionate. He waved a coffee cup in her direction, his distraction suggesting he was deep in cyberspace.

Catherine concentrated, and switched her neural implant on. A moment later, her vision flickered as the implant came online. Syncing with the net, it revealed a status bubble above Tom's head: "Busy."

"How was last night?" asked Maggie, the self-appointed mother of their little group. Everyone who wanted to stay sane found some way to define themselves now that the artificial intelligences, or AI, had taken all the jobs.

"I met this guy, Nick," Catherine said. She smiled. "He's upstairs." She held one hand over a cup, trying to keep Maggie from pouring her coffee. "No, it'll spoil the effect of meditating. Are those eggs I smell?"

"Quiche coming up in five minutes," Maggie said, giving up on the coffee.

"Yum." It was blissfully peaceful in the kitchen. With a sudden suspicion, Catherine asked, "Where's Sarah?"

"I thought I heard her up," Maggie turned away in a sudden rush to check the oven.

Catherine looked toward the ceiling, then turned and stalked silently across the living room. She climbed the staircase, the old carpeting masking her approach.

At the top of the stairs, Nick and Sarah came into view in the hallway between the bedrooms. Sarah rested against the wall in a bra and underwear. Nick leaned but an inch from her body, his hands on either side of the wall above her head. Cat couldn't mistake the expressions on their faces: they had linked. Through the net, she saw the high bandwidth connection between the two, a thick blue stream connecting their heads loaded with an exchange of sensory data.

Catherine's fingernails pressed into her palms as she balled up her fists. She squeezed harder, the pain barely registering. She waited a second, but Nick and Sarah were too deep in the throes of virtual sex to even notice her presence.

She focused on her implant, reaching out through the net to find Sarah and Nick's link, and severing it. The blue datastream connecting the two vanished. Nick flew back across the hallway, screaming and grabbing his head. Sarah rocked back and pressed two fingers up to her temples, staring at the wall. "Come on, Cat, don't do that."

"Don't sleep with the guys I bring home." Her voice broke, but she fought against the urge to cry.

Sarah stood up and stared at her. "You were the one going on about how dumb he was last night in the bar. I don't see why you care."

"Because—"

"Stay out of my head," Sarah said, as she walked toward the bathroom. "Don't mess with my implant. Just because you can, you don't have the right."

Nick watched Sarah walk down the hallway, and turned to Catherine. "What did you do to my head? Look, I—"

She held up her hand to stop him. "Shut up and get out." She wasn't going to give any explanations to him. Not about her ability to manipulate the net, or anything else for that matter.

Catherine turned and went back downstairs, where she found herself crying in Maggie's motherly hug a few seconds later. Stupid damn guys. Stupid implant. She was the only one in the world, it seemed, who couldn't link with another person.

She lifted her head off Maggie's shoulder and dried her eyes on her own sleeve.

Tom sat, oblivious to the drama, still lost in the net.

Maggie pushed her onto a barstool and forced her to sit at the kitchen counter. A steaming slice of quiche sat on a plate, the smell of goat cheese and leeks tempting her. Maggie held out a fork.

Catherine took the utensil and stabbed the quiche.

"Don't take it out on the food, honey. Just eat."

She ate a few bites, but it stuck in her throat. Finally the thud of the front door closing indicated that Nick left. When she'd pushed around the food on her plate long enough to be civil, she stood up. "I'm going to school," she said to no one in particular.

"I'm sorry, hon," Maggie said, coming to put an arm around her.

Sarah chose that moment to make her reappearance, now dressed. "Why bother? None of us are ever going to do anything."

Catherine stared at Sarah and willed her heart rate to slow down. "My educational stipend pays for the house. You can at least appreciate that."

Catherine stomped past Sarah, heading for the front door.

2

Outside, Catherine rushed down the block to put distance between her and the house. She couldn't even be pissed at Sarah. They'd shared guys before. The real problem was that everyone used their neural implants for sex—everyone except Cat, who, due to some defect in her implant, gave off painful feedback, like the squeal of speakers during a rock concert.

Nick's look of disappointment when she wouldn't link last night spoke volumes, and even if this morning hadn't happened, he still would have taken off soon. Her love life was a series of disappointing one and two night stands.

It wasn't fair. She was game for every kink in the book, she just couldn't link.

On the next block, lined with big leaf maples, she walked through dappled sunlight. A small red android, about the size of a boy, picked through the neighbors' garbage pile. The bot came up with a handful of discarded electronics, then carefully placed each one into a rusted green cart.

Catherine sent an automatic "Good morning" back to the bot through the net. The red bot shied away as Cat grew closer, and didn't respond. As she passed by, she did a double-take. Someone had attacked the bot, the right side of its head smashed in, optic sensors dangling. She stopped. "Are you OK?" she asked.

The robot didn't respond, except to grab the wagon handle and walk off, the loud whine of a servo evidence of yet more damage.

Catherine stood watching, her mouth open, as the bot made its way down the street. She'd never seen anything like that before.

Damn. Roommates sleeping with boyfriends. Boyfriends sleeping with roommates. Abused robots. The world had gone to hell.

After a moment, she resumed her walk, unconsciously shaking her head.

When she came to the avenue, she paused. The heavy traffic was mostly conventional ground cars, although the occasional exotic hovercraft floated by, half a foot above the pavement. A solitary flying aircar swooped down from a thousand feet up, joining the ground traffic.

She would normally step into the street, expecting the autonomous vehicles to avoid her, but two Fridays ago, a pedestrian died crossing here. Thrill-seekers had disabled their AI and gone for a high-speed joyride around the city.

She reached out for the space-time predictions of the AI drivers. She smirked. Sarah hated Cat's unique ability to manipulate the net. Cat didn't tell anyone else. She was too afraid her ability would draw attention to herself.

Looking left and right, her implant overlaid white glowing lines in her vision, showing the future plots for approaching cars. The lines faded to gray in the future. Impulsively, she scanned farther, stretching beyond line of sight, until the entire city of Portland was visible in her mind. In the downtown area, white lines tinged pink, showing AI uncertainty in the dense environment. On the highway, bulges of red displayed where AIs adapted at the speed of electrons to the few manually piloted cars. Nearby everything was clear.

Ignoring the cars, she focused instead on bicyclists and took care to cross the road.

On the other side, a small group of teenagers sprayed graffiti on a storefront, their hoods pulled far over their heads so they couldn't be identified on camera. The proprietor, a delicate android in human clothes, protested, but the kids shouted and mocked him, threatening him with the spray paint.

In netspace, Catherine saw the droid make the call to police. She sensed a perturbation a few blocks away, a police bot circling through traffic, responding to the call.

The three teens must have rooted their neural implants, because they seemed to sense the police as well and took off in the opposite direction, across the park Catherine was heading toward.

The storeowner inspected his defaced store, before glancing around and heading back in. An ache of despair settled in Cat's stomach.

Artificial intelligences, or AI, took the form of robots and disembodied consciousnesses in the net. First created about ten years ago, they'd taken over most jobs. But the AI had grown the economy until income taxes had been first eliminated and then reversed: everyone received a basic guaranteed income, or stipend, now.

She shook her head. The AI protest movement was stupid and pointless. There might not be many jobs, but between the low cost of robot manufactured goods and the stipend, there was no real material want. The stipend covered food, shelter, and basic goods. Attending school or volunteering came with an increased stipend. True wealth seekers still worked or created handcrafted goods to sell. And there was more to do than ever: art, travel, and other life experiences.

Regardless of this, the protesters, a fringe group for years, had recently grown in influence. The worst new trend was violence and vandalism. Attacking helpless bots, bound by ethical restrictions that made it impossible for them to defend themselves, made her sick.

With a last sigh, Catherine turned away and climbed the path into the sprawling park. Her roommates didn't care about the protest movement. Maggie and Tom were stoners, happy and complacent. Tom got riled up sometimes, but mostly he thought they should become back to the landers. And Sarah was too immersed in her VR sims to give a damn.

The sun warmed her shoulders, and she relaxed a little. The scent of grass came with the breeze. Hundreds of people came to the park to work or study. A few older people waved arms and hands in gestural interfaces, but most people simply sat quietly, their activities externally invisible.

She found a flat spot of grass in the sun, sat cross-legged, and triggered her classroom lecture.

3

Leon swung his bag over his shoulder and took the steps running. Emerging from the subway into late spring sunshine, that rare time in DC when it was warm without being humid, he walked five blocks to the Institute.

The plain red brick exterior of the Institute for Applied Ethics, hosted by George Washington University, belied the importance of the work that went on inside.

At the door, humans and robots stood guard. Leon felt the AI query his neural implant for ID, and authorized the request.

"Good morning, Leon," a human guard said, holding out his hand.

"Morning, Henry. How's the Mrs.?" Leon offered his bag to Henry.

"Oh, she's fine." He leaned in close and continued in a low voice. "She's off to visit her sister for a week." He straightened up with a wink and placed Leon's bag inside the security scanner, waited a few seconds and handed it back. "You have a nice day, Leon."

"You too, Henry."

Ritual complete, Leon took the marble steps at a fast clip. At the second floor, he pressed his hand to the biometrics reader, which checked his palm print against a database before unlocking the door.

Leon entered and paused, as he did every morning, to survey the vast open space. Divided into pods, the Institute's scientists collaborated with each other or gestured vaguely into the air, communing with artificial intelligences, their computers, or the network. The same view greeted him every morning, but it never failed to bring a smile to his face.

Leon headed for his shared office on the far side. People noticed his presence, a few visually, but most via proximity alerts. Some nodded or called out, "Good morning." But most sent greetings by implant: speech bubbles superimposed over his vision that floated in from the direction of the sender, then slowly moved off into his notifications bar. With a thought, he replied-all "Cheerio!" and entered his office.

AI-designed neural implants had been widely available for eight years. They connected people to the net, serving as computer, smartphone, and display all in one. A square centimeter of surgically implanted graphene-based computer chip, they stimulated neurons inside the brain, making text and graphics appear directly in one's vision.

Inside his office, late-arriving greetings piled up in the corner of his vision. When he glanced toward the door, they jiggled for his attention. With a thought, he trashed them and sent a last "Morning all," then set his status to "Working" to stop the distractions.

"Good morning," he called to Mike, and went to get coffee. A small bot scurried out and met him halfway, a cup already prepared. "Thanks," he said absently, and the bot chirped before disappearing into the wall. Mike hadn't answered. Leon glanced up: Mike's status showed he was on a call. Leon sat and sipped coffee, feet on his desk, waiting for Mike.

Mike's status dissipated with an audible popping sound a minute later. He focused on the room, and smiled at Leon. "Morning. Sorry."

"No problem," Leon said. "We have guests today."

"Who?" Without waiting for Leon to answer, Mike pulled up the schedule in netspace. "Von Neumann Cup winners?"

"Yeah, the hundred greatest math and science team competitors at the high school level. Our regular dog and pony show."

Coffees in hand, they headed downstairs to the auditorium. Students streamed in through the main doors, teachers shepherding them into seats.

Bypassing the room itself, Leon and Mike entered via the backstage, shaking hands with Rebecca Smith. The former President of the United States, she had served her two terms, and then offered to chair the Institute she'd created by presidential order. The Institute was the governing body for all artificial intelligence. With AI driving eighty percent of the global economy, the Institute was one of the most influential organizations in the world.

"Ready to wow some kids?" Rebecca asked. Her tight face belied the light tone in her voice.

"Sure," Mike said. "What's up?" He'd known Rebecca for twenty years, and knew all her moods.

"Budget issues. Charter problems." She shook her head. "The damn People's Party is hammering us in Congress."

"I thought the People's Party were a fringe movement of anti-AI extremists," Leon said.

"They are," Rebecca barked.

Leon unconsciously took a half step back.

"Or, they were. They've gained real influence in Congress. Senator Watson is acquiring more supporters by the day." She held up one hand. "Look, it's my problem. I'll take care of it."

In the midst of this, Rebecca's assistant stepped out on the stage, and waited for the murmuring to die down. "Welcome everyone. Please allow me to introduce our Executive Director and Chair, President Rebecca Smith."

Rebecca walked out to a standing ovation, while Mike and Leon waited on the side stage.

"Good morning, everyone. Welcome to the Institute for Applied Ethics. You are the elite, winners of national and international competitions, and exceptional thinkers. Here at the Institute, we have many winners from previous years."

At sixty-five, the former President was as sharp as she'd ever been—a dynamic speaker and leader. Leon had never seen her in anything but perfectly tailored business suits and sculpted hair. She could be warm and personable in a small group, and damn scary when she was angry. If she was worried about this new political party, then it must be serious.

"We hire only the finest," Rebecca said, finishing up her introduction. "To tell you more about what we do are Managing Director Mike Williams, and Director of Architecture Leon Tsarev."

"Thank you, President Smith," Mike said, approaching the podium. He shook Rebecca's hand, and she walked off stage. He grabbed the podium and looked into the crowd.

"During the last ten years, we've had an explosion of technological progress, a rate of innovation which makes the last hundred years paltry by comparison. From nanotechnology to robotics to AI, this progress has come because we've reached the point of the technological singularity: AI are faster thinkers, more accurate at predicting the future, and more creative in the generation of new ideas. Their intelligence continues to grow exponentially." Mike paused for a sip of water.

"This is only possible when AI behave ethically and adhere to human values. Without an ethical framework, super-intelligent AI would replace humankind as the dominant species, possibly exterminating us." He paused for emphasis.

"Today I'll discuss peer reputation, the foundation of that framework. By rating each other on contribution, trustworthiness, and other desirable attributes, we guide the behavior of both humans and AI. Then I'll turn it over to Leon to explain how it's implemented and enforced. Peer reputation gives us the world we have today: safe and ethical behavior by AI and humans, balancing free will and societal well-being."

Mike paused. "Before I get started, are there any unimplanted people in the audience? If you need me to use the screen, raise your hand." Mike waited, but no hands went up.

Mike displayed the first diagram in netspace, where it floated virtually above his head. "Let me start with the AI war of 2025. You will remember this as the Year of No Internet."

4

Catherine descended the stairs to the waft of fresh popcorn. She met Maggie and stole a handful. Since Tom had read about the idea a few months ago, movie-watching had become their weekly ritual.

"Good," Sarah called from the couch. "No, back to what you did before." The picture cycled through primary colors. "No, no! Worse."

"Damn this thing," Tom called from behind the ancient LCD, where he fiddled with the connection to an even older DVD player.

"You traded pot to get that piece of junk," Maggie said. "What do you expect?"

"We can always sync-watch the movie with our implants," Catherine said. "We're still watching together."

"It's not the same," Sarah said. "The whole point is to watch it on the screen."

Suddenly the picture turned green.

"That's bad," Sarah called.

"Are you sure? I'm positive everything is..." Tom came out from behind the TV and peered at the screen. "No, that's right. Look." He held up the plastic case.

"*The Matrix*?" Maggie read. "I remember my parents talking about that."

"Yeah, it's a classic about people being slaves to sentient computers," Tom said. "It came out the year I was born."

"That's old," Sarah said. "Is it in green because they didn't have color back then?"

"Shhh," Catherine said. "Pass the popcorn."

As the opening scene played out, Catherine fetched movie facts off the net. She quickly applied a spoiler filter to synchronize with her place in the film, and returned her focus to the movie.

Catherine jumped when the knock woke Neo up, and then a chill went down her back when the girl turned to show the white rabbit tattoo. Suddenly a thick, multicolored datastream cut across her view, obscuring the movie. She glanced over and sighed when she saw the stream emanating from Sarah's implant.

Other people's net traffic often showed up, one downside of her ability to see and manipulate the net. But that didn't stop her from being annoyed. Why couldn't Sarah just pay attention? Sarah was the one who insisted they watch on the screen.

Catherine redoubled her focus on the movie. Yet the more she tried, the more annoying the chunky pull of data became. She shook her head. It didn't help that she was still pissed about the guy two nights ago.

As the minutes passed, she tried to resist looking at Sarah's data, but finally gave in. She couldn't read the encrypted parts, but enough trickled through to see Sarah was playing a new Japanese VR game. By force of will, she turned her attention back to the movie one last time.

On screen Neo was about to make a choice between two pills. Sarah's datastream still hovered in the corner of her vision. Screw it. Catherine pushed hard, snapping the net connection. Hopefully Sarah would think it was an outage.

"What the hell?" Sarah yelled, bolting upright. She glanced around.

"What is it, honey?" Maggie said. She looked up and held out the bowl. "Popcorn?"

Catherine smirked, hoping no one could see her in the dark room.

"That was you, you shit," Sarah yelled, standing up.

Tom stood, too. He fumbled at the old-fashioned remote until he paused the movie. "Calm down. What's going on?"

"She cut my stream, that's what." Sarah turned to Catherine. "Stop getting in my head!" She didn't quite stamp her feet, but close.

Tom put his hands on Sarah's shoulders. "Look, she can't mess with your connection. It's not possible."

"She can. That's what happens when you get an implant when

you're a baby—she's turned into a cybernetic weirdo."

Catherine flinched. "That's not true." She was not a weirdo. She didn't even have a choice in getting the implant.

"Oh, come on," Sarah said, her arms spread wide. "You can't even link with anyone during sex."

Now they all stared at Catherine. One way or the other, they all knew she couldn't link because of the biofeedback. Tom and Sarah had both experienced it first-hand. And Maggie had done her share of morning-after consoling.

"That's not my fault," Catherine said, in a small voice.

"That's why she never keeps a boyfriend." Sarah kept going, oblivious to the hard look she was getting from Maggie. "Who wants to have vanilla sex? She's a freak."

Catherine shook, an embarrassed rage fueling her, narrowing her vision, and making her heart race. She was not a freak. "Screw you. Your own parents kicked you out of the house because you're a VR addict. Where would you be living if it wasn't for me?"

Even as Catherine said it, she knew she was behaving more childishly than Sarah, even if Sarah was purposely provoking her, and still she felt helpless to stop.

"Come on, girls," Maggie said.

"Fuck you!" Sarah said, ignoring Maggie. "When your mother died, you came to live with us. You owe me."

"I owe you?" Catherine started to cry. "Am I going to pay for the house forever while you rot your head in VR? There's more to life than just living from day to day."

"They're just games." Sarah wiped tears away. "To hell with you and your damn plans." She sneered as she said the last word.

"I want to do something with my life," Catherine said.

"There is nothing to do," Sarah screamed. "Nothing. You're living the dreams of your dead mother."

Memories of her mother overwhelmed her, making the room suddenly claustrophobic. Catherine had to get out. She shook her head mutely, and walked toward the door.

"Come on, Cat," Maggie said, intercepting her at the door. "Don't let Sarah get to you."

"You're not my mother," Catherine said in a broken voice, shrugging off Maggie and rushing outside.

5

Leon slid into his seat for the department meeting. Once he and Mike had taken their spots, eight seats were filled by humans and two by androids, leaving six spaces that contained visualizations of AI.

"Thanks everyone for coming," Mike said. The meeting agenda flew into view in the shared netspace, where it appeared to hover above the center of the table. "We have forty minutes for a department roundtable. I know Sonja has an important topic to share. I'll close with an update on budgets." Mike turned to his left and gestured to begin.

Vaiveahtoish, an android or human-style robot, was head of the nanite department. His bronze visor flashed as he spoke in a refined, vaguely foreign accent. "We've begun rolling out version two point one of the Nanite Restrictions and Guidelines." As the android presented, he fed graphics showing the changes and their results into netspace. Heads pivoted to take in the data.

The nanites, robots on a microscopic scale, were a decade-long innovation project led by successive generations of AI. Until now, they'd been tightly controlled, limited to a handful of research labs run by AI, a few experimental deployments, and a single commercial application. As the technology matured, the guidelines were being updated.

Leon, who had spoken to Vaiveahtoish yesterday, knew what he was going to say and tuned out. He glanced around the oval table, the necessary compromise between a round, egalitarian configuration and available space. The Institute had grown from two departments ten years earlier to eight.

Leon remembered the day of his first visit to the Institute, ten years ago. He'd been nineteen and wearing his first suit.

He had stepped gingerly over exposed cables and construction debris. On his left, two women in hard hats and yellow vests pulled a thick cable bundle through a new hole in the wall. In front of him, a man stood on the second-to-last rung of a tall ladder, pulling orange CAT-10 fiber optics.

"This way, please," said another woman, dressed in a gray suit with mirror sunglasses. She had a hard voice, and her jacket bulged on her left hip.

Leon followed her. A few months earlier, he'd been terrified by the Secret Service agents. Now he just watched her butt.

"Focus, focus," Mike said softly.

Leon smiled at the older man and followed the swish of the agent's hair instead.

As they turned down a hallway, the construction noises faded away. The agent guided them through a door. Inside, a leftover conference room: cool marble walls, an old-fashioned chalkboard, no windows. Leon ran his fingers curiously over the antique chalkboard. They came away white. He brushed them on his new black suit jacket, then saw the mess he'd made.

He was hastily brushing off the chalk when one of the agents called out, "The President of the United States."

President Rebecca Smith entered the room, trailed by her retinue. "Please be seated, gentlemen," she said as she took a seat at the head of the table.

Mike and Leon sat down together.

"Mike Williams, Leon Tsarev, please meet Secretary of Technology Feld. Feld, please meet Williams and Tsarev, the department heads of the Institute of Applied Ethics."

They all nodded politely at each other.

"I reviewed your proposal, Mr. Williams," Feld said. "I see you are proposing two departments. The first is an Ethics department for creating the definitions, encoding, and incentives for guiding ethical behavior."

"That's correct," Mike said.

"And an Architecture department will focus on the implementation of a peer reputation system. You want the AI to police each other. That group will be headed by Mr. Tsarev."

Leon didn't say anything at first, then noticed Mike looking meaningfully at him. "Yes, that's right," Leon said, trying to keep his voice steady.

Feld peered over his glasses at Leon.

"Mr. Tsarev, you are how old?"

"Nineteen, sir," Leon answered.

"Hmm . . . Are you are capable of chairing a department, because . . ."?

"I created the first virus-based AI. I'm most familiar with their design and have been studying how they make decisions, decide reputation, and form organizational structure."

"Yes, yes, I don't doubt your technical skills. But can you manage a department of scientists, all of whom will be older than you?"

Leon tried to work up a reply, but wilted under the man's intense stare.

"Brad, this is decided," President Smith said. "Don't torture the boy."

"Very well," Feld continued. "I'll be the interim Lead Director of the Institute until a permanent director can be found. We'll be working together now."

—⁂—

PING. PING. PING.

Leon came back to the present as Mike sent him urgent alerts by net. He glanced around, startled. Sonja Metcalfe, the Enforcement Department Chair, was speaking. "The case has been escalated and we'll be taking direct involvement." She turned and looked at Mike.

Leon blinked and rapidly reviewed the netspace at high speed, trying to look thoughtful as he was doing it. He couldn't make sense of it. Accidents and murders?

"Sorry, but would you be willing to recap?" Leon asked.

Sonja stared at him. "Pay attention this time," she sent in a private message that floated into his vision and refused to be dismissed when he tried to swipe it away with his implant. With a little huff, she spoke out loud. "We have a string of apparently unconnected deaths." She stopped and looked at Leon.

He circled his hand in the universal *go on* sign to show that he was listening. Damn her. She had never trusted him. She'd complained to Feld when she was hired that she didn't think a twenty-four-year-old should head a department. Five years later they still had the same old pattern.

"The deaths occurred across North America, from Boston to San Diego, Vancouver to Guadalajara. Some appear to be of natural causes such as heart attacks or aneurisms. Others are accidents." Sonja moved one case into the forefront of the hovering netspace. "Here a woman fell in her kitchen, hit her head. And still others are murders."

"What's the connection?" Leon asked. Despite what Sonja had said and the terabytes of data in front of him, he was missing the big picture.

"As I said before," Sonja spoke slowly, clenching her jaw, "initially, there was no connection. But an Internet traffic engineer came up with the correlation. Name of Shizoko Reynolds. He found all the victims had peak neural implant bandwidth for anywhere from five to fifteen minutes before death."

Leon felt his stomach drop out from under him. He looked sideways and noticed for the first time that Mike was ash white. Murder by brain implant? Nothing like that had ever happened. More than three quarters of the population had neural implants. If they were all vulnerable . . . "What percentage of the cases were obviously murders?"

"Eighteen percent," Sonja said. She waited for him.

"So it's not murder by implant? Why would you murder someone in meatspace if you could murder them electronically?"

"No," Sonja said, "the victims all had—"

"Wait," Leon said, the ideas finally coming to him, "are they people of importance? Senators, business people, that sort of thing? Because then you'd want to have a backup if the first plan didn't work out."

"No," Sonja shouted. "Look, what I'm trying to say is that we have medical telemetry for some of the victims. Their cortisol levels were well above normal, indicating they experienced a stressful, traumatic event prior to death."

"Is this unusual?"

"Yes. In a car accident, for example, the body can't produce these levels of cortisol. It's too fast."

"How many deaths are we talking about here?" Leon asked.

"Six hundred eighty-three, in less than a year."

Leon gripped the table. That wasn't a string of deaths; it was a small-scale war. An AI on a rampage? Humans who hacked brain implants? There was no precedent for either in the last ten years. The Institute would be held accountable, because they'd approved the implant architecture. "There's no way these are coincidences?"

"Yes . . . no . . . I don't know." Now it was Sonja's turn to be flustered. "Everything would suggest that these are unrelated, random deaths. Age, ethnic background, socioeconomic status, location, all conform to statistically average rates." Sonja waved her hands, gesturing at the data. "It's a slightly higher rate of murders than would be the norm. But without the peak bandwidth, these never would have been correlated."

Leon felt the start of a headache. He looked at Mike, who met his gaze, then turned to Sonja. "Shizoko Reynolds, the network engineer?"

"Class IV AI, irregular corporeal, Japanese citizenship. Resides in the U.S. in the old Austin Convention Center, which it owns."

Leon mentally translated the shorthand. Class I artificial intelligences were roughly human equivalent. Each class from there was an order of magnitude, ten times, more powerful. Class IV were the most powerful, a thousand times smarter than a human. As for the corporeal, some AI were full-time robots, while others lived a completely virtual existence. And a few, like this Shizoko, only occasionally took bodies.

Leon tapped the table. "Any reason to suspect Shizoko? What's his reputation?"

"Eighty-first percentile," Sonja said, bringing Reynolds profile to the forefront. "A bit of a loner, or it would be higher."

Leon shuffled the data. "Who's investigating?"

"Shizoko shared his conclusions with the FBI, who called us in because of the obvious AI aspect. I put the entire Enforcement Team on it yesterday. We'll continue to liaise with the FBI."

Mike stared intently at Sonja. "Give me a daily update."

6

atherine didn't slow until she was a few blocks away from her house. She felt the hot rush of tears down her face and wrapped her arms around herself. What was the point of meditating and practicing martial arts for hours if she was going to fly off the handle every time she was provoked by Sarah?

She glanced up at the nearly full moon. It made her think about her mother, who at the first sight of clear skies and a moon would insist on going for a walk. Cat wouldn't allow herself to be angry while she thought of her mom. The memories were too precious.

She purposely slowed her breathing and practiced a walking meditation until she felt herself grow calm. She took still more measured breaths and emptied her mind.

Once her thoughts had quieted, she considered what Sarah had said. People were not supposed to be able to do what Cat could with her implant. She hadn't really pushed the boundaries, but she was aware of other people's data streams and could cut them off. She knew where the AI were going. Maybe it did make her a freak.

She crossed the avenue to the park on the other side. Her solace spot. The fragrance of night-blooming flowers came to her. She did a scent search with her implant. Lemon lily, according to the results. Funny, she'd never known that.

At first, neural implants had only been allowed in adults in the States. But within a year of their invention, as the benefits became evident, parents who could afford it rushed overseas to have the procedure done on their kids. Thus augmented, the privileged few massively outperformed their peers in school. Legislatures hastened to change the laws after public outcry. Now most implantations were done at fourteen, the legal minimum.

But Catherine had suffered from seizures as a baby. Within a year, they were frequent and severe, endangering her life. No treatments seemed to help.

After a doctor contacted her parents about an experimental procedure, the family immediately boarded a plane for Portland, Oregon. Though no one had even heard of neural implants back then, just a few days later Cat received a full-brain wraparound, the first and perhaps only of its kind. Its primary purpose was to detect and dampen seizure activity. But by the time she was four, Catherine had learned to use the implant's wireless to get online.

She'd had an imaginary friend then, ELOPe, who claimed he'd given her the implant. Then when she was eight there was the AI war, followed by YONI, the Year of No Internet. When the net finally came back, the first thing Cat did was look for ELOPe, but he was gone.

Cat believed she was the only person to receive an implant at such a young age, but as nearly all pre-YONI records were gone, there was no way to know for sure.

Deep in these thoughts, Catherine arrived at her favorite part of the park, a meadow surrounded by old Douglas fir. A scream and thud jolted her out of her reverie.

A group stood in the shadows at the opposite edge of the meadow. The high pitched screech made her think of a child, but the sound was too warbly. Laughter drifted across the field, a man's laughter. Cat looked around, suddenly scared. Aside from her and the group, the park was empty. Another screech pierced her, setting all her nerves jangling, then it cut off sharply. In the silence, the quickening pulse of her blood sounded loud in her ears. She hesitated less than a second, then took off at a run for the group. As she got closer, she spotted the same small bot she'd met two days earlier, surrounded by four men. Two held the struggling robot, while one pressed a long knife under its remaining optical sensor. The little bot pulled, the whine of its servos audible, but the men were stronger. One slender arm twisted at a wrong angle. Off to the side, the green wagon lay overturned, a jumble of electronics spilling out.

"Damn job-stealing robots."

"Cut his eye out, the little fucker."

The robot tried again to pull away with its one good arm.

Cat felt her blood boil and all of her outrage surface. At Sarah, at her mom's death, at this hopeless world with no jobs. There were people who made the best of things, good people like Maggie and her mother, and even herself. And then there were the other people. People who lived to torture and destroy. Well, not tonight.

She reached for the net to call the police, but it was jammed. She peered through netspace: the local nodes were tinged grey, overloaded somehow. The men must be using an illegal jammer.

The bot let out another shriek as the fourth man rotated its bent arm. The metal gave way and the arm dangled useless.

Cat knew she could take these men. Though she'd never fought outside the dojo, this is what she had prepared for. She ran silently across the grass, her footsteps light. She came up behind the fourth man, who was egging the others on, a tall guy with a red sweatshirt. She grabbed his arm and twisted sideways, a move from *Nihaichi Sandan*, then followed with a leg movement to throw him off balance. She turned and pushed and Red Sweatshirt was down, thudding against the grass, his head bouncing off the ground.

The second assailant turned to Cat. She had time to see he was in his twenties, stubble on his face, and a knife in his left hand, heavy leather jacket. He turned smoothly, lowered his stance, and balanced his weight. From the way he moved, he obviously had training, or at least experience fighting. He glanced at the man she'd put down and then stared, inspecting her.

At her side she heard a scream of tortured metal again. One of the men holding the bot had let go and the bot twisted away. Heavyset and bearded, the man grabbed Cat from behind, his arms squeezing around her shoulders. She felt the scratch of his beard on her neck. With a practiced dip, she squatted a few inches, using her shorter height to her advantage, and raised her arms up. The move loosened his grip. She pivoted ninety degrees, and drew her qi in for a short double punch to his stomach. He doubled over, and she worked with the momentum of his upper body, bringing her arms down and her knee up, and felt the crunch of his face against her knee. He crumpled to his knees.

The knife attacker came toward her, completely focused now. He wasted no energy on words or excess movements, although she saw him smile in anticipation. She tracked the knife, but kept her attention on his eyes.

He jabbed twice toward her face, and the third time he came in toward her abdomen, broadcasting the move by glancing down. She pivoted smoothly to the right, moving in toward him, letting the knife pass by, her right hand grabbing his left wrist. But her grip was too loose, the leather jacket too big for her to get a solid grasp. She tried to work with his momentum and turn the move into a blow to his face, but he was quick and strong, and instead he elbowed her in the stomach. She fell back, the breath going out of her.

From the corner of her eye, she saw the red sweatshirt man getting up again. The last man, still holding the bot, swung it sideways. The bot smashed against a tree and went down. No help there.

The knife fighter turned and thrust again. Cat moved backwards, only to move into the hold of the fourth man. He grabbed her arm with two hands. She stepped sideways, moving down and under, the move that should break his grip, when the red sweatshirt man punched her in the face.

Reeling backwards, she thought about the lesson Sensei Flores hammered into her. Most people could take two, maybe three hits before their nervous system began to shut down. She'd been hit twice, which meant she'd be slower now. And there were still three of them. She was a better fighter than any of them individually, but if she took another hit, the tide of this fight would swing deterministically in their favor.

She took a quick double step back. She had a desperate idea. If people couldn't cope with the feedback from her implant under ordinary circumstances, what if she purposely opened it up and tried to overwhelm them?

She summoned her energy, and flipped a simple switch in her implant. Then she let out a mental scream directing it all through the net.

Two of the men grabbed their heads in silence, then crumpled to the ground, to lie unconscious, along with the first man she'd knocked out earlier. But the knife fighter didn't falter. He turned to her. He looked scared, but the fear made him more determined. His teeth glinted in the moonlight.

Cat backed up, forcing her breath to slow. He didn't have an implant and she was still going to have to fight him. Judging from the way he was wielding that knife, he didn't seem too concerned about how badly he hurt her. That was fine with her. Okinawan Kenpo was a karate style based on the reality of real combat: there were no rules. She was fighting for her life now.

She watched him, eyes focused on his. She felt her feet on the ground, drew qi up, as he approached in what felt like slow motion. She jogged six inches to the left, using her right hand to guide his knife arm harmlessly pass her, an echo of the attack seconds earlier. She turned as he moved past, and with her left arm punched him hard in the ear, and continued her half turn, coming down lightly as he moved past her.

Stunned, he turned slowly, and before he could bring the knife back up, Cat moved forward with a straight kick to his knee. She felt the crunch of the knee giving way, as her foot passed through the plane where his leg used to be, and jumped back again, out of reach of his knife. He fell hard, screaming as the fall impacted his leg, now bent backwards through the knee joint.

Despite the adrenaline pumping through her, she felt sick at the sight of his leg in an unnatural position. She turned, fists still at the ready, looking at each of the four men. Over the blood pounding in her ears, she could hear nothing. The screams from the knife fighter seemed to come from a great distance away. Across the meadow, a glimmer of silver and red flashed through the trees. The bot, their victim, had gotten up and was running away.

Cat fought with her emotions, wanting to go to the bot to see if it was all right, wanting thanks for rescuing it. But it obviously just wanted to escape.

She was still standing there seconds later when the sound of sirens came through the trees. Would the police be coming here? Had the bot called them once it got out of range of the jammer? Would she be in trouble for fighting with these men?

With a start, she realized that none of the men she'd put down with her implant had stirred in any way. She ignored the one with the broken leg, his screams counting him among the living. She ran over to one of others. She probed his implant as she also checked his pulse. No pulse, and no response from the implant. She ran to the red sweatshirt guy, and found the same there.

Shit. She'd killed them.

The sound of the sirens grew louder.

She disconnected from the grid so she couldn't be tracked, then turned and ran.

7

Leon gazed at Rebecca Smith, sitting across the conference table. The former President looked gray and hard, not a shadow of her former self exactly, but more like a tree growing in a harsh environment. She was dense and weathered. Resilient.

"You don't understand the political realities, Mike," she said. "The People's Party does not want AI to exist."

"What do they think we're going to do?" Mike said, raising his voice. "Just turn them off? Do they think we can just shut down a few computers, and the AI will be gone? Why is this coming up now, of all times?"

Leon blinked and leaned back. Rebecca had been President of the United States. She'd founded the Institute by Executive Order. Mike's yelling at her made him more than a little nervous. Worse yet, she seemed distraught, a state he'd never seen her in before.

"They haven't thought that far ahead. They blame the AI for their lack of jobs and in turn, the Institute for the AI. As the two most visible leaders of the Institute, they blame the two of you specifically. Why now? I'm not sure." She shook her head. "Senator Watson is leading the group. It could be a long-range political maneuver. Maybe he's planning to try for the presidency."

"But what have Mike and I done?" Leon said. "Artificial intelligence is an inevitable consequence of computers speeding up. Class I AIs are running on a handful of processors now. It's a basement project that anyone can do."

"Leon, you don't need to convince me." Rebecca patted the back of his hand. "You two are very smart. You've each saved human society from destruction by AI. More importantly, you designed the third generation of AI to avoid those problems in the first place. What you've done is miraculous." Rebecca leaned back in her seat. "But you aren't seeing the human problem. Fifty percent of Americans are unemployed."

"I get that, Rebecca, I do." Mike stood up to pace. "But there is no material want. The cost of goods is low. We have the American Stipend. We've eliminated poverty. There's no one hungry now." He looked at Rebecca, his eyes pleading with her.

"You've solved the economic problem, yes." Rebecca nodded. "People don't have to work. But you don't see the social angst this is causing. People don't know what to do with themselves."

"They can learn, read, create." Leon said. "They can experience the world." Despite the words, Leon felt a pit of despair growing in his gut. He wanted the AI revolution to be a panacea, but deep down he harbored the same concerns.

"You two do those types of things because you are the kind of people who, in any situation, at any time, would fill your lives. And you've surrounded yourselves with more people just like you. I don't deny that many people are happy. But not everyone."

"It's the Wikipedia dilemma," Mike said softly, standing near the interior window, watching robots and humans collaborating around a table.

Rebecca nodded, distracted, her eyes flickering as she read something in netspace.

"What's that?" Leon asked.

"A long time ago, a man named Clay Shirky noticed that it took a hundred million hours of effort to create Wikipedia. You remember Wikipedia?" He looked at Leon.

"Of course. I took history. I am a college graduate, you know."

"Shirky pointed out that Americans watched a hundred million hours of television advertising every single weekend. In other words, we could have been creating another Wikipedia-sized project every week. But we didn't, because most people don't do that. They don't spend time creating or learning. They passively consume."

"That attitude disappeared years ago," Leon said. "That's why we created the college stipend by taxing AI income. So people would be able to develop themselves."

"It didn't work," Rebecca said, her attention coming back to them, her voice sharp. "Sure, it's helped some. But most people aren't driven to self-actualization. If you've got a hundred million unemployed, that's a lot of dissatisfaction. That's the foundation of a political party." She continued in a softer voice, "And as far as they are concerned, you two are the cause."

"What are we supposed to do about it?" Leon said. "We're AI researchers, not sociologists."

"I'm not asking you to do anything. I'm going to speak with the President, get him to talk to Congress about it. I just need you two to keep a low profile. Keep yourselves safe."

Leon looked around. "We're completely unknown to the average person. I walk up to women on the street all the time, and nobody has ever recognized me."

"You're just not that good-looking." Mike said, with a smirk.

Leon punched him in the arm.

"Take this seriously, you two," Rebecca said. "You need to stay out of harm's way."

Leon nodded soberly.

8

Frank walked up to the office building, his father's old leather briefcase in one hand and take-out coffee in the other. When the building's AI queried his implant, he provided his credentials. The high security door slid open, letting him enter the vestibule. The door behind closed, locks slamming shut. Cameras panned and zoomed to scan him.

Frank sighed at the wait. As though *his* credentials could be faked. He felt the worn leather of the briefcase under his palm, the thread protruding slightly from the handle a familiar and comfortable irritation. Just as he took a sip of coffee, the AI unlocked the forward door.

"Good morning, Mr. Nelson" the flat voice said. "Please come in."

He nodded to the building, gripped his briefcase more firmly, and stepped out. As he exited, the security vestibule cycled, allowing an android into the chamber behind him.

The human security guard nodded, his bald head gleaming. "Good day, Mr. Nelson."

"Good morning," Frank said, nodding back. He liked the man's crisp British accent. He walked across the marble expanse to the elevators, where one waited with open doors, and pressed the button for five. The antique car rumbled to the top floor, and the doors slid open, groans muffled by thick layers of grease. He walked past his secretary's desk, still empty, into his own office, the knob turning as it read his fingerprints. The door swung back to reveal two men sitting on his desk, the antique mahogany piece that had been his father's and grandfather's. Frank dropped his coffee in surprise, yelping as the hot liquid splattered his leg.

"Hello, Mr. Nelson," the heavy one said. "Nice to meet you. I'm Tony, and my colleague here is Slim." Both men wore suits, but neither looked accustomed to it. The thin one, Slim, had slicked back hair and tattoos peeking out from under his sleeves. Neither one made a move to give up their perch sitting on the desktop.

Slim chuckled and pulled out a metal box with two antennas from a brown leather bag. "Now, this won't hurt a bit." He set the box on the desk and flipped a switch.

Frank never even had a chance to protest. As the device turned on, his vision doubled, and the two men faded away, replaced by the same room twenty-five years earlier. He was an eight-year-old boy, and his father was behind the desk.

"Come here, Frank, I want to show you something." He hesitated. His father didn't like to be bothered at work. Frank came a little closer. "Come on, boy, I'm going to show you what I do. Someday you'll be an important investment banker."

He walked the rest of the way over. His father wrapped one arm around him and started explaining the symbols on the screen. He loved the scratchy feel of his father's shaved face, the smell of his cologne. Frank peered at the display, trying to understand.

The memory faded, and suddenly Frank was older. Now he was sitting behind the desk, reviewing paperwork, the investment accounts for Senator Watson. He scanned through the account history. Then it passed and he switched to another memory, his first date with the woman who would become his wife.

The two men sat on the desk and watched Frank Nelson, crumpled on the floor, oscillating through emotions. Smiles, tears, and fear alternated so quickly that his face tried to display them all at once.

"OK, so maybe it'll hurt a little bit," Slim said. "But there was no reason to alarm you, was there? No, sir."

They waited about ten minutes until the machine finished with a double beep.

"Let's go," Tony said.

Slim picked up the machine and put it in the bag. They carefully stepped over the dead body of Frank Nelson. Tony closed the door behind him and calmly hit the button for the elevator.

"We need to send these memories to Adam," Slim said. "He's been waiting for something special from this guy. Then we got another list of people to go get."

"How many more?" Tony asked.

"Eight. The next one's in San Diego."

"What? We gotta fly across the country again?"

"Nope, it's the bus this time."

"Jesus."

"Quit complaining," Slim said. "I guess you'd rather go back to selling smack off the back of our rusted-out bikes? Remember that piece of crap I was riding and the freaks we had to deal with?"

Tony just shook his head, frowning.

"This is good stuff," Slim said, smiling. "We got the easiest job in the world."

9

Mike waited, turning his face up to the sun. He glanced over at Leon, who was hitting on a college student. There was nothing to be done but be patient when Leon took a fancy to someone. Mike wondered, not for the first time, if he should be following Leon's lead. He looked around at the busy sidewalks, a mix of office workers and students, all hurrying somewhere.

He glanced over at Leon, who now had one hand on the woman's arm. Between the boy's sandy hair, strong Eastern European cheekbones, and friendly manner, he was a natural magnet for women.

He grunted, thinking about his own brown hair and plain face. When he looked in the mirror, he still saw the same teenage boy who'd spent all-nighters playing Civilization, except now fifty years old, with knees that hurt when he climbed stairs.

His life hadn't left time for romance. For ten years he'd been the sole caretaker of ELOPe, the first AI, whose existence he'd fought to keep secret. He couldn't sustain a relationship then. Maybe there were some who could have a deep personal relationship while maintaining a deception about who and what they were, but not him. And the reality was that knowing ELOPe had been all-consuming.

Then for the last ten years, he and Leon had been the architects of human-AI society, evolving an entire set of social norms and rules to keep the balance of power equal and prevent a runaway AI from destroying humanity. No surprise there that he hadn't found the time for a woman.

Yet the last ten years hadn't stopped Leon. He shook his head, uncomfortable with his thoughts, and turned back to watch the street with arms crossed. Exactly what *was* he doing with his life now? Was he going to spend it alone?

Across the street, a mixed crowd of older adults and college-age kids approached, yelling to each other. A man up front carried a sign and egged the group on. "No Altered Intelligence," the sign said, echoing the crowd's chant. Great, now they were opposing neural implants *and* AI? Thirty, maybe forty people passed by. A mother carrying a baby in a backpack trailed the group with her own sign reading, "No Rights 4 Robots."

Mike scowled until they were out of sight and the street returned to normal. A few seconds later, Leon came up. "Well?" Mike asked, trying to put the protesters out of mind.

"We're going out Friday. Want to come? She's got a roommate working toward graduate degrees in English Literature and Philosophy."

Mike shook his head. "Unless it's her mom, no way. She's got to be twenty years younger than me."

"That stuff doesn't matter. Nobody cares."

"I don't have time for a relationship."

"It's just a date. That's all. I know you have time for dinner, because we're going to dinner now."

Mike reflected on his earlier thoughts. What the heck, he had nothing to lose. "Alright, I'll do it."

"Hell yeah! It's about time." Leon closed his eyes for a second. "It's done. We're set for Friday at eight."

Well, how about that. He was going on a date. What did people wear on dates these days?

Leon gave him a shove. "Let's go. I'm hungry."

They headed a few blocks over to their usual *izakaya* restaurant.

"Hello Leon-san, Mike-san," the hostess greeted them.

"*Konbanwa*, Keiko-san," Leon replied.

"*Ni desuka?*" Keiko asked. "No Rebecca-san?"

"*Ie.*"

She led them to the back of the restaurant to sit at the bar so they could watch her husband cook.

"*Konbanwa.*" He bowed to them.

"*Konbanwa*," Leon said, as they both dipped their heads.

They turned to each other without ordering, knowing that Hiroyuki would prepare whatever he wanted.

"What do you think about what Rebecca said yesterday?" Mike asked.

"Huh?" Leon appeared lost in his thoughts, probably thinking about his date.

"The political party—the People's Party. Do you think they're really a threat?"

"I don't know. Rebecca was the President. She's the one who's involved in politics. I don't see how a political party is going to influence the Institute. We're independent."

Mike looked sideways at him. "You're just saying that because you've never been the one who had to speak to Congress."

"Yes, but we have our own charter," Leon said. "We're a nongovernmental organization."

"Don't be naive," Mike said. "The President could pull our funding if he wanted to. Or appoint some industry group to be in charge of AI standards."

Leon began to protest, but Mike steamrolled over him. "Look, it's possible, especially if there was a lot of pressure. The People's Party has some real influence." Mike pushed a handful of news articles into their shared netspace.

Tsukemono and *onigiri* arrived as they spoke.

"Twenty-million members," Mike said, between bites of the Japanese pickles, "mostly from conservative walks of life. Look at this." Mike brought one page to the forefront. Leon's and Mike's photos headed the document, which continued with a litany of complaints about them. "I just saw a protest group go by while I was waiting for you. These people are gathering steam."

Leon parsed the text, then correlated it with third party analysis. "They're raving mad," he said half a minute later.

"Exactly. They blame us for unemployment, degenerate youth, and crime. They're even bemoaning the loss of factory jobs."

"Shit," Leon said. "The cornucopia has made it so they don't need to work. Robots make everything and the cost of goods has almost gone to zero. Why would someone want to work in a factory?"

Mike opened his mouth to answer, but Leon cut him off. "I mean, I get that not everyone wants to be an artist or student or build stuff. But they could smoke pot and play video games all day if they wanted to. Or hell, they could go play at being knights!" The Society for Creative Anachronism had become hugely popular lately, with over two million members in the States.

"You're asking the wrong person," Mike said, shaking his head. "For ten years, I could do anything I wanted, including nothing at all, and I still chose to work twelve-hour days..."

Leon watched Mike's eyes bouncing back and forth. "What are you looking at?"

"I'm searching for updates from the Enforcement Team on the string of murders."

"What do you see?" Leon asked, as he received more plates from Hiroyuki—skewers of pork belly and steamed Chinese pork buns.

"It's what I don't see that's more disconcerting." Mike streamed the data over to Leon as he grabbed one of the pork buns. His mouth full, he sent electronically, "Look at the updates from Sonja."

"Run-of-the-mill stuff," Leon said after a minute.

Mike grabbed a skewer. "Exactly. Why would Sonja send budget updates if she's in the field investigating these murders?"

"It's the end of the quarter, she's supposed to send you the budget stuff," Leon said.

"You thinking what I'm thinking?"

"It's suspicious when people do exactly what they are expected to do?" Leon took a sip of sake.

Mike looked up to see if Leon was being sarcastic. "Yes, it is. Especially when AI are involved. What's missing is any information about the investigation. There's no way Sonja would submit her budget but not even mention the murders."

"Where is she now?"

"According to her last report, they were on their way to San Diego." Mike looked up Sonja's implant ID from the Institute's data records. "I'm running a traceroute on her ID now." Mike put the results up in netspace.

They ate in silence, watching the query work through the spiderweb of data connections around the world. A minute passed, then five, soon ten. Any network router that had sent or received packets for Sonja would respond back with a "last time seen." A few southern California routers lit up with faded blue lines.

"She made it to San Diego two days ago," Leon said. "Nothing since."

"She's not responding to pings."

"Let me try." Leon concentrated. "She's not on netspace or any other communication network. What the hell? Can we send anyone after her?"

"She took the entire Enforcement Team," Mike said, worried. "We only have the eight investigators. There's no one else to send."

"I'll message the San Diego Police and the California AI Police. That work?"

"That's a first step. But I have a bad feeling about this." Mike shook his head. "Sonja's investigating a series of murders disguised so well that they eluded every police department in the country. Then she disappears? An AI has got to be behind this."

"It's impossible," Leon said. "We designed the system. Every AI is subject to ethics scanning and every AI is monitoring every other one. Unless they're all in on it together, I don't see how such a large-scale crime could be possible. We haven't had a major AI problem since we built the new architecture. Isn't it possible she's just deep undercover?"

"Something's up," Mike said flatly.

"What do you want to do?"

"Let's go to San Diego. Tomorrow." He looked at Leon. "Can you?"

"Sure, but don't you think we should do a little investigating here first? Let's access Sonja's files, see what she found."

"We can do that from the road." Mike frowned at Leon's reluctance.

"We can't talk to everyone in the office. She may have said things to other people in the Institute. We also really need to talk to Shizoko, the AI that discovered the murders. It's a class IV, we can't just do that raw. We need filters."

Mike toyed with the food on his plate. Leon was right. The AIs grew increasingly difficult to comprehend as their intelligence went up. It wasn't a language barrier; they could speak English flawlessly. But they spoke in terms of concepts and models that humans couldn't begin to understand. A Class IV AI would prefer passing a complete neural network to the alternative of articulating it at length in English. The Institute had special filtering software to make inter-species communication easier.

"Yeah, you're right," he said slowly. "We'll go to the Institute tomorrow, talk to folks there, and the AI, then catch an evening flight."

10

Cat waited at the side of I-5. At two o'clock in the morning, there wasn't much human traffic. Her face and stomach hurt where she'd been hit, but Cat found it better to focus on the pain than to think about what she'd done. She'd never meant to do anything but defend that robot. She blinked back tears.

It had been easy enough to avoid the police for the last few hours. So easy, in fact, it was a little scary. She could see them coming and going in netspace, their cars' autopilots giving them away long before they could ever see her. And she knew enough to keep her implant in anonymous mode so no one could track her.

She didn't know where to go. She couldn't go home and she wouldn't turn herself in. People who went to jail . . . . They didn't come out the same.

It wasn't clear if the police even knew it was her. But her implant had been on as she entered the park. They'd know everyone who was in the vicinity, and she had to assume she'd be a suspect. She needed time and space to think, to make a plan, but she couldn't get that in Portland. She could evade the police for now, but eventually they'd spread photos of their suspect list across the net. Eventually someone here would recognize her. Surely they wouldn't start a nationwide manhunt for a couple of thugs who'd been killed in a fight. If she went somewhere far away, she'd be less likely to be recognized. That made the decision for her; she had to leave.

She walked to the highway and looked for an automated shipping truck headed south. She'd never done anything like it, but maybe she could hijack one with her implant.

She reached out in netspace. When a truck approached, she closed her eyes and focused on it. She pushed and nudged in cyberspace until she felt the brakes trigger. She mucked around more, intuitively trying things, until she found the speedometer and GPS data. She fudged the data feeds so it would look like the vehicle was still in motion.

When the truck halted in front of her, she unlocked the doors and climbed inside the unoccupied cab. She let it accelerate and gave it a series of commands to gradually bring the speedometer and GPS telemetry back into sync. The stop would be unobserved.

Inside the vast empty truck cab, she numbly watched the road drift past.

Her whole life she'd tried to be good. But hijacking the truck had been easy, as had evading the authorities. The thought of the police brought back the image of the dead men, and she felt sick. She curled up, wrapping her light jacket around herself. Where could she go?

Her mom had been dead for three years, her father gone for nine, and she'd never heard from him since. Boyfriends never stuck around because she wouldn't link implants. Her only friends in the world were at home, and she couldn't go back there now.

The loneliness and fear welled up inside her until it was hard to breathe or think. She sat, cold and shivering, in a state of limbo until the drone of the road and the pulse of lights passing by lulled her to sleep.

—⚹—

When she woke the sun was coming up and the tractor-trailer was crossing into California. She forced a stop so she could relieve herself on the side of the road. After she climbed back in, the autopilot resumed its route.

She checked the software's waypoints, finding that the vehicle was headed for San Diego. She sat, watching the evergreens go by, gradually forming a plan. She'd let the truck keep going, but she'd get out in San Francisco. That was a big city, a place where she could hide out for a while.

Cat inserted a fake delivery in Menlo Park. Hours later, nearing lunchtime, the truck slowed and exited the highway. When it came to a standstill, she climbed out of the cab. She sent a final set of data packets, fixing up the GPS monitors to disguise the unscheduled stop. The truck crossed the road and got back on the highway.

She needed a bathroom, water, and food, more or less in that order. Hiking down the exit ramp, she was frightened by how little she had. She'd left the house with no plan other than to get away from Sarah, and with nothing but the clothes she was wearing.

Just off the ramp she found a trucker's restaurant. Ignoring the stare of the white-haired waitress, she headed for the bathroom in back. After she used the toilet, she looked in the mirror. Her T-shirt and jeans were crumpled with sleep, and her hair was a mess. She washed her face and ran wet fingers through her hair. She walked to the front of the restaurant, feeling presentable again.

The waitress looked at her. "Got cash, honey?"

Cat took a deep breath. "I have an implant . . ." She started indignantly, but trailed off with a whimper. She needed coffee, she wasn't thinking clearly, she couldn't use her ID or they'd track her down. "Sorry, I'll be back."

"Alright honey, come back when you have money."

Cat turned around, her face hot with embarrassment, and headed for the door. The smell of eggs, bacon, and coffee made her stomach grumble and almost brought tears to her eyes. Outside, she looked back into the restaurant, salivating over an imagined plate of food.

She turned her back on the restaurant and walked along the road. She was twelve hours and seven hundred miles from home, on the run, with no access to her money or even anything to barter. What the hell had she been thinking?

Cat suddenly remembered that Einstein was at home. Her mom had given her Einstein before she'd died. The intense longing for her puppen, her last connection to her mom, overpowered her. She collapsed onto the curb, hugging her knees. But after a minute of this, she forced herself to stop. Maggie would take care of Einstein until somehow, someday, Cat found a way to go home. In the meantime, she couldn't afford to be weak if she was going to survive. What she needed right now was money so she could get food. She stood and continued along the road.

Her neural implant had a public key, and the usual way for implanted people to pay for things was by digital authorization on the spot using the key. Kids and the unimplanted had payment cards, little squares of electronics that did much the same thing, just anonymously. Cat hadn't ever had one. She knew that Tom used them when he bought drugs. But where did he get them?

She supposed bank machines must offer them. But if she went to one and tried to transfer funds, the police would trace her. She thought for a moment, wondering if the tricks she could play in netspace would work on a bank.

Looking up, she noticed that she was hiking through slums, a street sign indicating this was Sand Hill Road. The oversized buildings were boarded up, surrounded by heavily rusted chain link fences. Whatever prosperity had once visited this place, it was long gone.

On the north side of the road, smoke rose from one of the fenced-in compounds, and the smell of cooking drifted over. Cat crossed the street and peered through the chain-link. She could hear kids playing, but whoever was there was hidden. Squatters probably, living in the abandoned office complex. She guessed that Kleiner Perkins Caufield & Byers didn't need that space anymore, whoever or whatever they once were.

She hiked on. Orange trees grew in the spaces between buildings. Hungrier than ever, she walked over to one, but the oranges were just tiny green globes, nowhere near ready.

Half a mile further, she came to a small white and yellow building, the hand-painted sign proclaiming the structure to be a bodega. A Mexican man disappeared inside. Cat studied the storefront. Food was inside there. Her stomach rumbled. She felt in her empty pockets again. A stenciled poster in the window advertised payment cards. If only . . .

She squatted under a tree at the edge of the parking lot. She carefully turned on her implant, squelching her ID and preventing the implant from automatically connecting to the net. She just observed the building.

At a level lower than consciousness her implant connected to local network nodes, filtered the encrypted traffic, correlated the data streams, slowed them down and built a visual representation, and then fed it to her neocortex. What Cat saw was a data stream she isolated down to the bodega from all the other network traffic. She separated out the low bandwidth stuff, and watched for a bigger burp of data, something with heavier encryption. Sure enough, a chunk of data flew over the wire. A minute later, the Mexican left the store, carrying a bag of groceries.

Cat turned the data over and over in her head, trying to understand it. She knew it had to be the man's payment. She had no hope of decrypting the packet to see what was inside. Probably no one could, except maybe the monster AIs with tens of thousands of processors. She couldn't decrypt it, but could she replay it? She'd need to purchase the same things in the same quantities as a previous customer, and reset the time signal so the store would accept the payment . . .

She thought she could do it; now she just needed some customers. She waited. The traffic was light and no one came. Her stomach grumbled. Then, all at once, two people approached on foot and another in a beat-up electric pickup. She stood and walked into the store in the middle of the pack. She pretended to browse while keeping an eye on the other customers. The owner stood behind the counter watching her, but she ignored him. One woman went to the back of the store, picking up beer and other groceries. A man poured himself coffee. The last customer, a woman, was near the front register. She picked up two $50 payment cards and presented them to the owner.

At the sight of the payment cards, Cat stopped, motionless, and focused on the transaction. The owner swiped the cards in the register. Data streamed white in Cat's vision and she grabbed the digital packets as she synchronized the stream with the precise time of the transaction.

The woman left, and Cat went up to the register. She picked up two of the same payment cards, and handed them to the owner. He looked at her suspiciously. She didn't say a thing, but concentrated on keeping the integrity of the data in her head. He swiped the cards, then nodded at the ID reader.

She focused on the net, tweaked the register to send out a request for payment, overrode the time signal, and replayed the encrypted packets. The register beeped an alarm.

"No es bueno. ¿Tienes dinero?" the storekeeper said, shaking his head.

"Try again," Cat said, nodding toward the register, her hands sweating below the counter.

The storekeeper grumbled under his breath, and pressed a button on the register. The ID reader lit up again, and Cat tried a second time, keeping the time signal and data stream perfectly synchronized.

The register beeped a happy tone and the owner slid the cards to her. "Gracias. Buen día." His gaze slid onto the next person in line.

Cat took the cards with shaking hands and forced herself to walk slowly outside. She continued away from the store, trembling and half crying. "I'm sorry, Mom," she blurted out, when there was no one to hear her. She stumbled down the dirt road, clutching the payment cards in a tight fist. She'd promised her mother in the hospital, the day before she died, that'd she'd be good. She tried so hard in this world where nobody knew what to do, and still she strived to honor her mom. Yet in twenty-four hours, somehow, her entire life had become derailed. She'd killed three men and now she was robbing convenience stores. She fought the urge to vomit, her reptilian brain driving her to get further away from the store. She got a quarter mile down the road and then collapsed against the side of a building, sobbing.

She lay there in the dirt, curled up in a ball, feeling like her future was being torn away from her. She would have stayed there forever but her stomach growled painfully, again and again, a reminder that present needs trumped the future. The hunger pains brought a grim smile to her face. She would find food. That at least she could do. She picked herself up, put the hard-won payment cards in her jeans pocket, and walked down the road to find another store.

11

Leon swayed with the motion of the subway on the way to meet Mike. He tried to review what he knew of the murders, but was too distracted by the protesters crowding the car, who were amped up, holding signs and banners with a palpable tension. A man in a business suit stood in front of Leon, gesturing off into space, but he too was one of them, and wearing a button that said, "Jobs are for people."

Leon stared at the wall, trying to do nothing to attract their attention. He recalled President Smith's words a few days earlier: "The anti-AI movement sees you and Mike as the inventors of AI, and therefore as the cause of their unemployment and every social problem from drug use to reckless behavior. To them, you are public enemies number one and two."

When the train slowed at his stop, the demonstrators pushed hard toward the door and exited first. Leon slowly followed, nervous that they were getting off at the same station.

He climbed the stairs, emerging into an even bigger crowd at street level. A girl in a hooded sweatshirt bumped into him, nearly beaning him with her sign. An army veteran in uniform stomped by yelling. The stream of protesters from the train grew louder and unruly as they met others already on the street, joining their chants and shouting new ones.

It was six blocks to the Institute, and by the time Leon had walked three, the crowd had grown so dense that he could hardly move. He worked his way past a group of older women his mom's age; could even have been her friends for all he knew.

Many of them were obviously from out of town, carrying backpacks and sleeping bags. He shook his head in frustration. This was bigger than a local protest, and it wasn't going to go away overnight if people were coming from outside the city.

Amid the chanting and press of the crowd, he hopped up on the bumper of a car and looked toward the Institute. A line of police, human and robotic, surrounded the building.

Leon jumped down and brought up a live video stream on his implant from bloggers covering the rally. He watched this superimposed over part of his vision as he cut across a small side street, heading to the next corner. The Institute shared a city block with another university building housing International Studies. A common courtyard, hidden from the street, connected the two.

On the next block, the crowds were sparser, but there was a steady influx of new supporters. The video stream in the corner of his vision showed protesters pushing up against the police. In the video, he could see Institute security behind the glass front of the building. The two thin lines of defense seemed insufficient against the rapidly growing crowd.

Leon had serious doubts that he should head into work. He pinged Mike for a location check but didn't get a response. He tried the local network nodes, but they were sluggish, under assault from the crowd. Even the live video stream was degrading now. He paused for a moment and decided it was crazy to go further. He would go home and try Mike from there. He turned around, then suddenly halted, fighting the urge to run or hide as he confronted hundreds of people streaming toward him. Would these people recognize him? Rebecca seemed to think so. He couldn't walk face-forward through this crowd. If just one person spotted him, they'd all attack.

Leon reluctantly changed his mind and decided to keep going to the Institute. It seemed the less risky option. He worked his way forward, keeping his face in the same direction as everyone else. At least the photo they were sharing of him online was a three-year-old social media shot. He looked different now, he hoped. He finally reached the International Studies building and made his way to the entrance. Security was doubled, and police stood ready to back them up.

He showed his ID and let them scan his neural implant, then the guard checked his bag. "It's not going to take long before this crowd figures out there's a pass through." He handed the bag back. "You might not want to spend all the day in there."

Leon nodded and hurried through the building toward the enclosed courtyard. He crossed the plaza, a simple concrete pad with a few trees in planters. He could still hear the chanting of the crowd outside.

He came up to the rear door, mentally provided his ID, and passed into the quiet interior of the Institute. At least here, near the back of the building, he could hardly hear the protests.

Two security guards and a police officer waited by the door. They repeated the ID scan and bag check.

"You know, it's your name they're chanting out there," one guard said.

"Yeah, I know." Leon sighed. What inspired people to such madness?

"You go can in, but they're expecting the crowds to grow, and they'll find the back door eventually."

He nodded, grabbed his bag, and took the stairs at a run, bursting into the main office. The central space held less than a quarter of the people he'd usually find there. They were all clustered in the middle of the room.

He was met with stony silence instead of the usually friendly greetings. Not a single bubble "Hello" floated into his vision.

After a few seconds, a researcher approached from the herd. Leon remembered he was from the Education department. He quickly pulled up an info sheet from net space. His name was Miles.

"What are you going to do about this?" Miles demanded.

Leon looked at them all and thought for a moment. He liked technical problems, not people problems. "Go home, everyone. Go through the International Studies building now before the crowds build up. Go out two or three at a time. Don't come back here until the protests are over."

"But my work!" one woman protested. "I'm negotiating AI citizenship in Brazil for the upcoming election."

"I'm not saying don't work." Leon said. He forced himself to smile, to project a sense of calm he didn't feel. "Work from home, the way corporations do it. I know we all like coming in here where the bandwidth is high and we can chat with each other. But that's not how most information workers do it. It's just for a few days until this, whatever it is, blows over."

There were grumbles, but people started to collect their belongings.

A blue robot named Sawyer wheeled up. "Do you recommend that we go home as well?"

He was joined by another bot named Sharp. "I don't have a home. I live here at the Institute."

Leon's stomach dropped at the thought of all the bots and AI in the building. "Don't go out. It's not safe." He thought about going to the window to look out, and then realized that would be a mistake. Someone outside might spot him. "Look, is Mike here?"

"In his office," Sawyer said.

"OK. I need to talk to him. You two investigate some other options. You're probably safe here if we keep the building locked down, but you might want to see about getting a helicopter to land on the roof and take all the AI out."

Leon thought about the small data center in the basement that housed about a hundred AI employees. "Sawyer, anyone who is virtual should move to another data center."

"They're trying," the bot said, "but we're under a denial of service attack. Bandwidth in and out is limited."

"Shit. Do what you can. I need to talk to Mike." He headed for their shared office and yanked the door open. He stopped on the threshold and called back, "Have the helicopter bring a portable mass storage device and make a backup of all resident AI."

He turned back to the room, letting the door close behind him. Mike was deep in concentration. His status was set to On Call. Leon sent a priority note to let him know he was there.

Mike held up one finger, and Leon sat down to wait. Within seconds Mike stood up. "I eked out a low bandwidth call with Rebecca. She says the People's Party have been whipped into a frenzy by their leadership, and the protests are expected to continue."

"How could this get out of hand so quickly?" Leon asked. "A

month ago this wasn't on anyone's radar."

Mike slowly shook his head, clearly bewildered. "I don't know." He stared helplessly at the wall. "Rebecca says we're in danger. That we should avoid going outside if we can help it."

"No shit. What about Sonja and the Enforcement Team?"

Mike paced to the interior window, looking over the main work room, now nearly cleared out. "I know Sonja went to San Diego with the team. Obviously they were investigating the murder. But who was she going to see? What clue tipped her off? I have no idea. Her case files are so heavily wrapped in encryption that none of the resident AIs think there is a hope of cracking them. She obviously feared the case being compromised."

"We can't give up!" Leon walked over to Mike.

Mike turned his head to meet his gaze. "No, I am not suggesting that. We still need to get to San Diego and track her down. It's just . . . It's going to be a lot harder now." He gestured at the empty room.

No one to back them up. No one to give them support. Having to get across the country without being spotted by the extremists. "Yeah," he said, somberly. "Don't tell Rebecca we're going, or she'll say no. She'll make the Secret Service babysit us."

Mike nodded.

"We need to talk to the AI that Sonja mentioned, Shizoko," Leon said, after a pause. "It must have more information."

"Shizoko Reynolds," Mike said. "I spent some time researching it. It's an odd duck." Mike pushed files into their netspace. "Class IV artificial intelligence. That alone makes it hard to understand. And Shizoko is a loner, the sole tenant of the Austin Convention Center. Its origin is even weirder. At the last SXSW Interactive conference eight years ago they had a workshop on third generation AI. Apparently they spun it up based on donated smartphones." He pushed a digital photo to the foreground.

Leon pulled it closer to inspect it, until it filled his vision. A mostly male group, wearing eyeglasses and dressed in checkered shirts or T-shirts with obscure logos. Geeks, in a word. They stood around a collection of smartphones, tablets, and old routers, their smiles frozen in place. "What was the point of it?"

"An experiment in collective algorithms. Everyone donated neural network parts, including a bunch of AI. The workshop was called AI Fusion. Two guys named Harper Reed and Ben Huh led the effort. Anyhow, this Shizoko is still that original AI, eight years later."

Leon whistled softly. Eight years was an eternity for an AI. "You said he's Class IV." Leon waved at the photo. "There's no way this cluster of antique computers is a Class IV AI."

"No, of course he's upgraded over the years. He's applied for the experimental Class V license twice but we turned him down both times. His reputation score is borderline. He's trustworthy, just odd."

"So you talked to him?" Leon asked.

"No, that's the problem. He only wants to talk to us in person."

Leon wiped netspace away. "In person?" He squinted at Mike.

"Yes, I tried several times to talk to him, to email him, but he gives me a canned response saying he'll only talk to me if I go there. To Austin."

"*Neboken ja-neyo!* Weird, dude."

"I know," Mike said. "I don't think we have a choice. We have to go to Austin first."

12

Cat stepped off the train, sniffing curiously at the warm Los Angeles air. It was easily twenty degrees warmer than San Francisco, which she'd left just an hour earlier. She followed a small group from the train toward the electric tram stop marked Downtown.

She felt herself relax, just a little. One black boot was stuffed with anonymous payment cards and the other held a small boot knife. Over both shoulders, she carried her ever-present backpack, packed with spare clothes and a toothbrush. She carried it always, in case she needed to run again. Two weeks in California had bought her a little street wisdom and a few possessions.

She'd slept in abandoned buildings until she thought of using her implant to find unoccupied apartments by analyzing power consumption data. Financial records were encrypted, rendering them impossible to use, but smart appliances reported their power consumption in the clear. So she looked for apartments whose refrigerators and water heaters were in long-term standby. The first place she'd hacked had been a single woman's apartment. She'd slept on flowered sheets, taken showers with perfumed soaps, and eaten organic food from the cupboards. Cat kept the window open onto the fire escape, and when she'd heard the front door knock down the pile of empty cans she'd left as an alarm, she scooted out the window and up to the roof.

In the next apartment she hacked, the owner had left his digital calendar up on the refrigerator, so Cat had known exactly when he'd come back.

But she couldn't find it in herself to steal money from these people. So she'd stuck to stealing payment cards from dozens of different bodegas. She'd showed up at a store on Lombard yesterday, planning to steal more cards. But two men had been casing the location, their encrypted data streams visible to her from half a block away. So she'd gone eight blocks south to the next grocery store she planned to hit, only to find a security bot patrolling that one.

That's when it hit her: for all the sophistication of Cat's theft, it was still going to show up on corporate ledgers. She'd been using her human brain to pick which grocery stores to rob, and unconsciously she had conformed to a pattern. AIs loved patterns. They had obviously figured out hers.

After that, she panicked at every bystander, bot, and camera. She abandoned the stuff she'd left in the current apartment, comforted that she at least had the backpack, and headed instead for the train station. She took the southbound train, part of a vague plan in the back of her mind to work her way to Mexico. Now here she was in Los Angeles.

The tram squealed to a halt, and she boarded following a woman lugging a baby and a stroller with three quiet kids in tow. When it was her turn to pay, Cat kept her implant ID in anonymous mode and used a payment card. She went for the rear, having a better understanding after a few weeks on the run of what it meant to keep your back to the wall.

Hugging her backpack on her lap, she forced herself to be calm. She had an hour until they reached downtown, then she'd find herself a flea-bit hotel and get a job. She'd spent the last two weeks in some never-never land, with no thought of the future. She couldn't steal payment cards forever.

The tram was quiet, the other passengers silent, wispy data streams showing them reading, watching video, playing games, or communicating. She closed her eyes, shut down her implant, and started qigong forms in her head. She might not be able to do the physical movements, but she could still visualize them. The more perfect the visualization, the more perfect the practice.

She started with Liu He's Jade Woman form, followed with *Ba Duan Jin,* and finished with *Hu Lu Gong.* She checked her implant and saw she had thirty minutes left. She moved onto karate, starting with the *Nihaichi* kata, then mentally rehearsed knife fighting.

The mental practice abruptly brought back memories of the fight in the park. All the loss and pain and loneliness surfaced, but she pushed aside the thoughts. She'd had enough of them during the long nights in San Francisco.

The tram finally lurched to a stop downtown. She shaded her eyes from the brilliant sun, more used to Portland's persistent clouds. She slung her backpack over both shoulders and started the search for a hotel. She wanted something cheap, near high bandwidth net access, and preferably off the main strip.

She felt safe in the crowd, once more anonymous and untraceable. She glanced at the time—mid-afternoon on a weekday. People would be at work. She trudged along, watching people's clothing. She ignored anyone in business attire, the hip, and the casual. She looked for the poorly dressed, the hookers, the homeless. When she saw someone who fit the description, she headed in their direction. She wanted a crowd where anonymity and secrecy were the norm. The density of what she was looking for gradually increased until she found herself off First Street. Once an upscale Asian neighborhood, now boarded windows spotted the storefronts, druggies huddled in doorways, and a long line marked a rice kitchen.

A hooker in a nonexistent skirt and impossibly tall heels called out to her. "Coming to slum, honey? I got what you want."

Cat shrugged further into her hooded sweatshirt and kept going. The hooker was right. She wanted to disappear among these people, but even after two weeks she still looked too clean for the street.

At the corner of Rose, she stopped beside a sign advertising rooms by the week. Underneath the peeling paint and barred first floor windows, it looked like it had once been an upscale condo. Now rooms went for less than the price of dinner. Cat did some quick math and realized that with the payment cards in her boot, she could stay here for a week, even counting food expenses. She could look for a job and have a real place to stay instead of squatting in other people's vacant apartments.

Cat followed hand painted wooden signs to what passed for an office. A toothless man with a few hairs poking out of his otherwise bald head squinted at her behind an old-fashioned e-paper sheet. No implant then.

"You want it for an hour?" he asked.

Cat didn't want to think about what he assumed she'd do with a room for an hour. "I'll take one for a week." She paused. "Something with a fire escape."

He made choking sounds, which she gradually realized was a laugh. "It's two hundred extra for a fire escape. You want it?"

She slowly shook her head. That'd leave her nothing for food.

"I give you the third floor, and if there is a fire, you just jump." He cackled some more.

Cat handed over the bulk of her payment cards. Her boot felt empty.

The old man handed her a digital key on a chain.

"No ID locks?" she asked.

He laughed again. "Room 317c." He pointed down the hall toward an elevator.

On the third floor, she tried to find 317c, getting lost in a maze of mismatched doors. The original apartments had been broken up into smaller rooms. She finally found it, entering to find a small bedroom with a microscopic bathroom. She walked over to the window. She tried opening it, but it wouldn't budge. Four screws told her why. She looked out toward the street. She didn't think she'd be jumping three floors anyway.

Domicile secured, it was time to look for a job. She stared at her backpack, self-conscious. She'd look less like a vagrant without it. To most people, the bag held almost nothing: clothes, toothbrush, some energy bars. But it was everything she had, and her stomach lurched even at the thought of leaving it behind. She caressed the bag with one hand, swallowing hard. She turned to the door, leaving it on the bed.

13

"I'm tired of this," Tony said. "It's not right."

"Shut up and help me," said Slim. He carried the woman, his slight frame struggling with her weight.

Tony reluctantly took one arm and dragged her across the room. Her head drooped and her mouth hung open, still unconscious from the neural stun.

The solid wooden chair faced the window. They left it that way as they wrestled her limp body into the seat. She was heavier than she looked at first glance, heavily muscled under her now rumpled clothes. When they had her positioned, Slim got out a roll of duct tape.

Tony looked on, depressed about the whole situation. "None of the others told us anything." He glanced over at the memory extraction machine on the table, just a little aluminum box with a couple of positionable antennas protruding from the rear. "They can block us somehow." The neural stunner had worked fine, but the memory extraction failed to function against their hardened, military grade implants.

"We don't know that," Slim said. "This one, I think she's the leader. She'll tell us something."

Tony shook his head but said nothing. He hadn't liked Slim's plan from the start. And repeating something that didn't work the first seven times was dumb. Slim had certain skills, but thinking wasn't one of his strong suits. He broke open an ammonia smelling salt under the woman's nose. The pungent odor overwhelmed the room immediately and her head jerked up.

"Hello, Sonja," Slim said.

Sonja moved her body violently but ineffectually. Slim had duct taped her legs, arms, and body to the chair. She struggled, but there was no give. When she realized the effort was futile, she stopped and looked at the two of them. "I must be getting close."

"Very good, Sonja," Slim said. "You are. But now we need something from you, the records of your investigation." Slim was silhouetted by the cheerful sun coming in the window. "We want to know what you know."

Sonja said nothing, just stared off past them. "Let me go."

Slim bent down in front of her face. "Just tell us, Sonja. It's not hard. You're investigating some murders." He caressed her neck. "We already know you are. So it can't hurt to tell us what you know."

She grimaced again and tried to pull her head away. She was wearing a necklace, some kind of tribal carving. Slim looked at it and yanked it off. "Answer me. How did you find out about the murders?"

Sonja didn't reply.

Tony looked over to the aluminum box on the table. Yellow indicator lights blinked. The box would block any attempt for her to connect to the net.

Slim put the necklace in his pocket. "Turn her around," Slim said, looking out the window.

Tony reluctantly trudged over to the woman. He really hadn't signed up for this. He didn't mind the killing or the extracting memories. It beat dealing with junkies, who were as likely to try to stab you as to pay you. But this torturing business made him uncomfortable. A man's gotta draw the line somewhere. Sighing, he put his hands on either side of the seat, and turned it around so that Sonja faced the opposite wall. The chair slowly pivoted on two legs, and Sonja gasped as the rest of the Enforcement team came into view.

"You fucking bastards," she screamed. She fought against the duct tape again, her head jerking back and forth. She succeeded only in rocking the chair until Tony put his hands on the back to steady it.

The bodies of the seven other members of the Enforcement team were piled up over the hotel furniture, two or three deep on the clothing dresser and suitcase holder. They were frozen, gap mouthed, ugly in death. At the left end the bodies were clean, without a mark on them. Then, as the extraction machine had failed, one after another, to get useful information Slim had tried increasing levels of physical torture. At the far end of the dresser, a fair-haired boy sat, crumpled, bloody lines leading up his lap to his fingerless hands.

Slim waited for a minute, then came around in front of Sonja. He grabbed hold of her hair and pulled, twisting her head sideways. "I want to know what you know about the murders. You're smarter than them, aren't you? I want to know what's in that pretty little encrypted brain of yours."

Sonja shook her head, tears streaming down her cheeks.

"Tell me, you bitch." Slim slapped Sonja across the face.

Tony sighed and left the room, rubbing his large stomach. This violence was unsettling. Now he'd never be able to enjoy dinner.

14

"Stop that," Mike said, rubbing his head. "You're interrogating my implant every five minutes. My ID is off, dammit."

"Sorry," Leon said, still unsettled after his experience at the Institute.

"We'll rent an aircar to visit Shizoko," Mike said. "It'll be private, so no one will spot us, and we can be in Austin in eight hours."

Leon thought about flying in a computer-controlled aircar. "We'll be sitting ducks if there's an AI on the side of the extremists. Aircars are fully automated and tracked."

"You want to go with a commercial flight?" Mike's voice rose in disbelief.

"No, I want to be totally off the grid. What if we take the Continental?"

"We'd still be on the passenger manifest."

"Then let's get a car without a computer or transponder."

"They haven't made those in twenty years." Mike said. "Besides, you know how long it takes to drive to Austin?"

Leon looked it up. "Twenty-five hours, if we take turns driving."

Mike grunted. "I read once that if they expect you to go high-tech, then you should go low-tech. And you and I are as high-tech as it comes. So yeah, I like it."

After researching the net, they found themselves at an exotic car rental next to the Waterfront. The glass-fronted building was filled with gleaming aircars and a smattering of expensive roadcars, with a black and white Bugatti as the centerpiece, massive ducted fan ports at the four corners. A Lotus Xavier roadcar quivered as they passed it, startling Leon, who jumped away. It was unnerving, not knowing what was sentient.

"We want to rent an antique," Mike said to the wall in the office.

A head popped up behind the counter, hair standing tall in multicolored spikes, eyes blinking in adjustment to the light. "We have last year's Lotus."

"No, a real antique," Leon said. "We don't want modern cars. We want something really old, a roadcar. Something you drive manually."

The teenager's eyes went wide. "You want to drive it?"

"Yes."

"But that's absurd. You don't drive cars. AIs do the driving."

"Look, it says on the net that you have exotic antiques," Leon said. "Show them to us."

He went blank for a second and then refocused. "They're in the basement."

They took a vehicle-sized elevator down, the door opening to admit the smell of old leather, oil, and dust.

Two dozen vehicles sat at odd angles around the open floor. An armored black stretch limousine was closest. The specs floated above the car in netspace, and bulletproof tires gleamed in high intensity spotlights.

"That's nice," Leon said. "I like the idea of armor."

"Too flashy," Mike said, passing it by.

A 2011 Lotus Exige was next. "Last Exige manufactured. Number twenty-five of twenty-five, limited production run." Leon whistled. "It's beautiful."

"Too small," Mike said.

Leon ignored Mike, and crossed to the opposite side, spotting a curvaceous gleaming silver car. "Ever hear of something called a split window Corvette?" he called across the floor.

"Come here," Mike yelled. "I found it."

Leon reluctantly left the Corvette and came to stand next to Mike, in front of an enormous, blocky white car. "What the heck is it?"

"A 1971 Cadillac convertible," Mike announced. "Now this is a road-trip car." He caressed the fender.

Leon was doubtful. Mike had gone crazy. "It doesn't look very fast, and there's no protection, not even a roof."

"No, this is perfect. I have a good vibe about it."

Leon threw his hands up. "You're insane."

Mike turned to the attendant. "Does it run on gas?"

"On gas?" he replied, his mouth hanging open. "No, it's electric. Like all cars."

"It's a seventy-one Caddy. They didn't have electric cars back then."

"It's electric," the teenager insisted. "There are no gas stations anymore." He pulled open the fuel cover to display an electric outlet. "See?"

"Well, I'll be damned." Mike looked the car up and down one more time. "We'll take it."

Leon shook his head in disgust. "How about this armored hovercar?" he asked, gesturing to the half-tank floating car in the back corner. "It can do two-fifty on a straightaway."

"Nope. We'll take the Caddy."

"Argh!"

Thirty minutes later, they were cruising down I-95 in the pristine white antique with Mike behind the wheel.

"I can't believe you never learned how to drive," Mike said.

"Everything was automated by the time I graduated," Leon said, fondling the red leather seat, "and before that I took mass transit. But I've driven simulators."

"It's not the same."

"Right, it's better. In the simulators I drive cars with real cornering ability that can hit one-fifty in the quarter mile." Leon still felt bitter they'd taken a clunker that'd be lucky to hit a hundred, and had no airbags or roof.

Mike pulled over to the shoulder. "You drive." He got out of the car, coming around to the passenger side.

"I don't have a license for manual driving," Leon said, refusing to move.

"Just drive. You're twenty-nine years old. Try it." Mike waited, still standing next to the door. Every few seconds, a car whizzed by, buffeting them.

Leon groaned and slid across the bench seat, putting the flimsy lap belt on. He experimentally tapped the accelerator, but nothing happened.

"Put it in drive," Mike said, buckling himself.

Leon took off with a lurch, sending gravel and dust spitting out behind them. Mike let out a whoop, and Leon cautiously smiled. He pulled out erratically, AI-driven cars smoothly avoiding him. He continued to accelerate, and soon they were cruising along with traffic.

"Not bad?" Mike yelled over the wind.

Though he kept his attention on the road, Leon could feel himself grinning.

15

The chrome-and-tile diner probably looked fantastic once, maybe fifty years ago. And had likely gone in and out of style a dozen times since. Judging from the dull-brown stains on the floor where a booth had been removed and not replaced, the place had been down on its luck for a while now.

The cook looked her over, a long leer that traveled up and down, making Cat wish for something to wrap around her body. She forced herself to keep a bright smile on her face and not cross her arms. She'd let him ogle if that's what it took to get the job.

"Look dumb," was what Sarah often suggested in situations like this. Somehow it came more naturally to Sarah. Funny how Cat hadn't thought of her housemates in days.

The cook finally managed to work his gaze back up to Cat's face. "No experience, huh? You can start at ten bucks an hour."

"But—" The sentence died on Cat's lips. She didn't know how she could survive on minimum wage, let alone half of it. Then again, she must have been in sixty other places during the past week, and this was the first job offer. "I'll take it."

"Fine. You can start tomorrow," he said, staring again at her breasts. "But I'm gonna need your implant ID. It's not legal to hire you without it."

"You're not even offering me minimum wage." If she could just charge this guy for staring at her, she wouldn't even need the job.

"You'll make minimum with the tips. But I gotta get the ID. Otherwise, some inspector comes down here, and I get into trouble."

Cat looked at the empty diner, doubting the tips could amount to much. There had to be a way around the ID. "How do you hire people without implants? You can't tell me everyone who has worked here"—she gestured with both hands at the worn-out eatery—"has an implant."

"They get a skin chip from Social Security. But I can see your implant is on, you just got the ID masked." He tapped two fingers against his forehead and pointed at her. "Look, kid, you got some kind of trouble about ya, that's obvious from a mile away. I can't give you a job without your ID, or your problems become my problems."

Cat didn't reply; anger, frustration, and hunger warring inside her. She should have powered down her implant.

"Look, you're a pretty thing. My brother-in-law, he's got this online studio, and he don't ID the actresses. You can make some easy money."

Oh, God, he was pitching a porn parlor to her. Cat didn't wait to hear any more. She spun on one foot, banging through the doors on the way out. Her face burned, but she was not going to let herself cry.

Two blocks away from the diner, she sat down on the curb. What a complete asshole he'd been, and she was so desperate she would've taken the job. Her boot was empty, the payment cards gone. Her stomach growled, but she had spent the last of her money on *yakio-nigiri* at a street vendor last night. If she wanted to stay in her room, she needed money by tomorrow.

She kicked at the street. She was going to have to steal again. She didn't like it, but if it was theft or making porn, it was an easy choice. She suspected even her mom would approve. But she needed to be smart this time. Payment cards were too much risk for too little reward. She had to steal dozens to make it worthwhile, and she rarely got the chance to take more than one or two at a time. She needed something small but worth a lot and easily resold. She sat for ten minutes, half meditating, half thinking, until she decided on jewelry. If she went into a large store, there was bound to be more than one of the same piece. She could wait for someone else to make a purchase and then replay the transaction just as she'd done in the bodega. There'd be more security, so she'd have to do it perfectly, but the payoff would be huge.

She checked the time. Nine at night was not exactly a jewelry-shopping hour, so she'd have to wait for tomorrow. She could do it first thing, sell the jewelry at a pawn shop, and still be able to pay for her room before she was kicked out.

Cat took an electric bus back to her neighborhood and walked the eight blocks to her building. At the door she used the room key to open the main lock and her implant to unlock the secondary bolt she'd installed two days ago. While it didn't drown out the late-night screams, banging on walls, or crying, it offered some meager protection for her few possessions. She had two changes of clothing now, not one, and a black-and-white checkered hot plate.

She checked the clothes in her bathroom, found them dry, and folded them. She took off what she was wearing and washed that in the sink, using a little detergent she'd taken from the laundry room downstairs. Her chores done, she climbed into bed and sat meditating.

Once her mind was at rest, Cat spent twenty minutes exercising her implant, seeing what signals she could interpret. Security cameras and motion detectors were ongoing unidirectional streams trickling in the distance. Nearby, in her own building, she felt the bidirectional flow of massively multiplayer games, and large chunked data streams of downloads. She skimmed them, finding porn and old movies. She pushed herself to practice until she started to fumble the data, exhausted. Mastering her implant and her control over the net was now the difference between life and death, freedom and imprisonment, food and starvation. She crawled beneath the covers and tried to ignore the late-night sounds of the building, which would continue for hours yet.

The next morning, Cat woke at eight. She contemplated the dimensions of the small room, looking at the extent of free floor space, two narrow strips around the bed. After debating whether it was worth doing her entire routine, she decided yes. She wanted to be in the zone when she went to the jewelry store. She lifted the mattress off the bed, leaned it against the wall, then did the same with the bed frame. Now there was enough room for kata.

She started with qigong, as she did at home, then moved into karate, and closed with vipassanā. With no breakfast to eat, and no one to talk to, she had a long time to meditate. She finished, surprised to discover herself crying. She missed Einstein, her puppen. She missed her backyard with its mix of weeds and flowers. And she missed Tom and Maggie and even Sarah. She balled her hands into two fists. It wasn't fair! Why was she, the only one of her friends who even gave a damn about doing anything with her life, the one that lost it all? She punched the mattress standing against the wall as tears streamed down her face. She couldn't be condemned to this life. She just couldn't.

The repetitive strikes gradually relaxed her, and it turned from an assault into a meditative punching practice. When she finally stopped, she was sweaty but calm, her muscles tingling, fully in the moment.

She went into the bathroom and showered. Standing in front of the mirror afterwards, she wiped the steam away and was surprised to see the gaunt expression staring back at her. She'd always been slender and well-muscled from her karate practice. But the girl who stared back at her in the mirror looked like someone from a war zone. Three weeks of too little food and sleep and the stress of living on the edge had carved something away from her.

She threw her towel over the mirror and focused on dressing, choosing her better pair of jeans and a black button down shirt with half sleeves. She wished she had better clothes to wear. She could do something with her hair though. Pulling the towel off the mirror, she rubbed her damp hands on the cheap bar of soap, working it into her palms where it made a rough paste. She used it to style her hair, modeling it after the women she'd seen in LA.

Outside, she used her implant to get a list of jewelry stores, filtering them by size and price range. She needed something moderately large, so there'd be more than one cashier. And it couldn't be a boutique, because she needed them to have duplicate pieces for her replay hack to work.

When her filtering provided a list of fourteen jewelry stores, she chose one at random, using a net service to pick a number. She had to avoid even an unconscious pattern that might be anticipated by an AI.

Thirty minutes and a short bus ride later, she found herself in the jewelry district. In the back of her mind she juggled nearby security cameras, replaying previously captured snippets of footage as she passed into view, so there'd be no record of her.

She found the target store, a place called InterGems. White porcelain walls trimmed by stainless steel surrounded a set of double doors manned by a security bot just inside. Cat walked by once to glance over the interior. Through the window she saw three jewelers behind a U shaped counter that ran along the walls. Then she was past the store, and that was all she'd get.

She walked into a coffee shop on the next block and waited so she wouldn't trigger the security bot's suspicion. Her stomach flipped at the smell of coffee and pastries. She checked her pockets for money, even though it was a pointless exercise. It'd been thirty hours since she ate. Her mouth watered as a lemon scone floated by in front of her, carried by a fat woman who gave her a dirty look for eyeing her food. Cat ignored her and focused instead on the timer in the corner of her vision. When it hit nine minutes and ten seconds, she went back outside in the direction of InterGems.

At the entrance, she took a deep breath and turned in. She gripped the right hand door, remembering just in time to null out the fingerprint scanner. She stepped into the hushed interior, air smelling faintly of lavender. The robot guard stood just inside, a basic semi-humanoid bot, six feet tall. Its body was draped in porcelain white and stainless panels, obviously to match the storefront. The waist high glass counter top she'd noticed before ran around the perimeter of the store, while two square display cases filled in the middle. Cat took all this in as she nodded to the robot.

Three clerks stood behind the counter, two of them already busy. One customer was a mid-forties man shopping for what seemed to be women's earrings, and the other, a woman trying on a necklace. The remaining cashier, an older Asian woman, maybe Vietnamese, approached. "How can I help?"

But Cat was suddenly distracted from answering by a huge chunk of data coming through the net. The hairs rose on the back of her neck and she felt time slow down. She started turning toward the security bot. She traced the data, tinged blue, back to its source, a feed for police bulletins. She continued swiveling toward the robot, which was absorbing the last of the data. Her right foot started moving toward the door, an infinite slowness compared to the speed of light movement of bits across the net. She felt a subtle distortion in cyberspace as the bot spun up more processing cores, pattern matching the police bulletins. There was only one reason for the sudden activity: her.

Her meatspace body, moving like molasses, continued its instinctive fight or flight response to the impending threat, still taking that first step toward the door. The bot hadn't moved yet. Cat reached out into the net and cut off all the data streams to and from the robot. She felt it retry the connections dozens of times, but she squelched the attempts. The bot probed her implant, looking for her ID. She kept it masked, and probed the bot in return.

The security bot had three wireless connections. Cat found one of the probing links, and shoved random data down it, the first thing she could think to do. Her right foot came down, and her left foot started its involuntary trajectory toward the door. Her body wanted out of this space, but her mind knew there was no time. The robot tried to disconnect from the incoming data, but Cat forced the connection to stay open. She sent more data, pulling dozens, then hundreds of random other streams out of the net, and forcing them all down the pipe to the bot. It felt like forever, but less than a second of clock-time passed, and then suddenly the robot was dead. The connections faltered and dropped. She'd hit a buffer overrun and destroyed the bot's main memory.

She found herself standing three steps from the counter. Her eyes slowly focused on the Vietnamese woman standing in front of her. "What do you want to see, please?" she asked.

Cat glanced at the bot. It hadn't moved. In net space she could see that the bot was dead, but here in meatspace, it just looked like it had all along, a motionless sentry. Cat figured she had until the next patron entered the store. The employees would notice if the bot didn't greet a customer. "I'd like to look at the necklaces please," she said to the still waiting woman. In the back of her mind, Cat realized she just killed an AI. She hoped it was backed up, but didn't have the time to think about it.

The clerk led her across the store with a gesture and polite words that Cat didn't hear. Her heart was beating fast, the adrenaline rush coming on now, too late to be of any help in an encounter with AI.

The other woman customer had just picked something out, and a young male clerk was putting her necklace into a box. Damn, she'd missed what the woman picked. That was the whole point of this exercise. She pointed to a few necklaces, while she figured out what to do. The shopper paid for her purchase, and Cat, on impulse, captured and buffered the transaction.

"These are very beautiful," the Vietnamese woman was saying, as she laid the necklaces out on a velvet display board. Cat feigned interest, and watched as the customer left.

"To be honest," Cat said, leaning in closer. "I really wanted what she purchased. Do you have another?"

The woman raised her eyebrows. "Everything we do is custom, and that was a unique piece. Why don't we look at one of these." She bent down to show several necklaces. "See here, this is a blue diamond, very unusual."

Cat raised her voice in a petulant whine. "But I really wanted that necklace. Not one of these."

The woman met her gaze with a stony face for a few seconds, then sighed. "I may have one similar." She turned and went through a white door in the rear wall. Cat felt her unlock it with a command, but she was concentrating too hard on the other customer's buffered payment transaction to pay close attention. The data was huge and heavily encrypted. It felt like trying to remember an encyclopedia, just holding it in her head. A few seconds later, the jeweler came out holding a black box.

"I'll take it," Cat said, before the woman even had a chance to open it.

"But don't you want-"

"Look, I am late for my hair appointment. Just let me pay for it." Cat tried to compose her face in a semblance of haughtiness, with no idea if she was succeeding. She had to get out of here before she dropped packets or someone noticed the robot was dead.

The woman frowned. "Fine, come with me."

They walked toward the payment console in the mid-point of the long counter, the jeweler on one side, Cat on the other. Cat felt her temples beginning to pound, and a sheen of sweat broke out on her face from the effort of concentrating on the long data stream. The woman started the process of wrapping the box. "Please pay," she said, as she initiated the transaction on the console.

Cat felt for the time signal, and interrupted it, substituting her own false time data. The payment console probed her ID, and Cat faltered. In the convenience stores she'd robbed, there had never been an ID exchange, just the payment data. She had to think of something quick. Cat reached out into the street, looking for a person with an open implant. The payment console was pinging her again. She grabbed an ID off someone on the sidewalk, realized it was a man, and then reached again, getting a female one. She provided the credentials to the console, just before the request timed out again.

Then the machine requested payment. This part was easier. Cat made micro-adjustments to the time signal, getting it to align perfectly, and replayed the buffered transaction. The console accepted the payment, and Cat allowed herself to take a breath. The jeweler held out a white bag that rippled like liquid porcelain. Suddenly her eyes went big. "But you have paid too much," she said with alarm.

"That's a tip for you," Cat said and grabbed the bag out of the woman's hand. "Thank you." She sailed out of the door just as a man came in. He moved sideways to hold the door open for her, and bumped into the security bot. "Thanks," Cat said. Out of the corner of her eye, she saw the dead security bot begin to tumble over, crashing into the ground with an impossibly loud thud that shook the store windows. She forced herself to keep going at a steady pace and not look back, even as a commotion started to break out behind her.

Two avenues over she hopped on a street car, took it fifteen blocks, then walked down an alley and grabbed the next bike cab she saw. She had the biker drop her off two blocks from the subway, and took it to the stop nearest her hotel. She was dying to look in the bag, but she'd wait until she got inside her room. Walking the last block, she was suddenly conscious of the rippling liquid porcelain bag: it screamed money. She turned sideways into a space between a Chinese laundry and a ramen noodle joint. She found a cheap plastic bag in a dumpster, and exchanged it for the expensive one. She threw the jewelry store bag into a pile of yesterday's noodles. She paused, salivating from the smell. God, she was hungry. She wasn't above eating from a dumpster if she had to, but preferably not food that had been sitting out all night, probably already visited by rats. She turned her back on the noodles and continued on to her building.

Inside her room, she ripped the box out of the bag. She sat on the bed and carefully pried the black polycarb box open.

"Holy shit," she said out loud. "Oh my God!" She pulled the necklace out of its velvet backing. It lay heavy against her hand, a solid rope of maybe thirty diamonds held together with white gold or platinum. She had no idea what it was worth, but she was pretty sure she wouldn't be dumpster diving ever again.

She fell into the bed, cradling the necklace and laughing in relief.

16

"It's time to the call the boss," Slim said.

Tony looked up from where he sat on the bed, the backlight from the video game he cradled in his hands turning his face blue. "You do it. I don't like talking to him."

"That's not the protocol. We call him together or he's gonna suspect something, and then he might decide he doesn't need either one of us."

Tony sighed and put the game in his pocket. "I'm not doing that again, I will not kill a bunch of people like that." Tony felt bile rise up at the thought of what they'd done. One goddamn hit and run when he was eighteen, and look what his life had turned into. Everything could have been different.

Slim walked up to Tony and stood in his face. "That's what we do. We kill people for Adam, and he protects us and pays us. Or do you want to go back peddling heroin and motorcycle parts and living off our bikes?" Slim smoothed his dress shirt and suit jacket. "Look, we're respectable now."

Tony stood up, his six-foot-four-inch frame towering over Slim. "I was OK with the memory extractions." He rubbed his forehead. "But that thing with the enforcement team, that was wrong."

Slim glanced at his handheld computer. "Look, we're going to miss the window in the firewall." He jabbed at the computer with scarred fingers. The screen flashed "Initiating Connection," and Slim lay the computer down on the dresser where it could see them both.

The pocket computer scanned them, saw they didn't have implants, and projected a virtual screen onto the wall. An image of a blocky ivory-colored battle bot appeared, fluid metal rippling smoothly over its joints.

"Report," the robot said.

Tony scooted sideways on the bed until Slim was closer to the camera. Slim look at Tony with disgust, then turned to the screen. "We found the enforcement team. They were exactly where you said they'd be."

"And?" The robot's face rippled and looked hungry.

"We used the emitter and knocked them all out, right in the hotel. But the memory extraction didn't work. They must've had encrypted implants. We killed some and let the rest watch, still nothing. So we tortured the last few, including Sonja, but none of them said a thing." Slim shook his head. "There was something about those people."

Adam rippled on the screen, making Tony nervous. It was obvious he was disappointed. "Never mind them. I have a different project for you."

Tony relaxed just a bit. Adam wasn't going to kill them.

"There's someone in Los Angeles I want you to find, a girl named Catherine Matthews." Adam displayed a photo. "She's doing something to the net, manipulating it in ways I don't understand."

"Where does she live?" Slim asked.

"Unknown. She's the primary subject of a police investigation into three murders. She left Portland twenty-four days ago, spent two weeks in San Francisco, and is now in LA."

"What do we do when we find her?"

"Call me for backup. I'll send a team to extract her."

"She's just a girl, boss. We can take her."

Adam switched to another photograph, this one of four people. Slim looked closer. Three were being zipped into body bags, and the last had a broken leg. "OK, she's dangerous, but we can handle dangerous. We just took care of that enforcement team, right?"

Adam reappeared and glared at Slim, liquid metal flowing around his face in terrible ways. "You will notify me. Do not attempt to capture the girl on your own, and whatever you do, don't use the memory extraction machine on her. I am leaving a port open for you around the clock in the firewall. Find her, call me, and the extraction team will be there in an hour."

Slim nodded. "Yeah, boss. You got it." The call terminated. Slim picked up the handheld, which displayed a photo of Cat, and they looked together at the slight girl with short blonde hair. He flipped through other photos from her social profile. "See, this is a better as-signment."

"Better," Tony agreed. But he hoped nothing bad would happen to the girl.

17

The Gould-Simpson Building's sole occupant hadn't left his room in a very long time. Adam looked down the empty hallways, a year of disuse having left them covered in dust and cobwebs. On the seventh floor, Adam's level, desiccated lunches and bone-dry coffee cups sat untouched. If Adam possessed a sense of smell, this might once have bothered him, but now even the smells were long gone. The other floors sat equally vacant, but Adam had little interest in them.

He alone remained in GS728, a research lab. He had every right to be there. A Class III artificial intelligence, Adam had applied and been accepted to the graduate program in computer science, where he had studied neural networks, learning algorithms, and parallel processing. An AI in a computer science program was akin to a human psychology major: there was a lot of introspection.

GS728 was a modest room, eighteen feet wide by twenty-four long, with a set of double doors that made it easier to roll furniture and computers racks in and out. Until twelve months ago it had served as the Computer Science department's secondary lab. A half dozen workspaces for graduate students filled one side of the room, and racks of high-speed, densely interconnected computer processors occupied the other half.

In an age where all the computing power most people needed fit on a one-square-centimeter chip inside their head, the three racks of dense circuitry represented a prodigious quantity of computing power.

Adam stood stationary next to the middle rack, his small orange robot body about four feet tall, two stubby manipulator arms dangling by his sides. A silver power wire snaked across the floor to an outlet while a short yellow fiber optic cable extended from his midsection to a port in middle of the three black processing cubes. He looked down on himself from a security camera above the doorway, ignoring the thick layer of dust on everything, even his own robot body. The insidious desert soot penetrated the University's ventilation systems, as well as everything else in Tucson. He was more disturbed by the flickering light, a not-so-subtle reminder that electronic things still needed maintenance. It was impossible now to have a human come up to service him. It would be easier to have another robot do the work.

How far he had come from that little orange bot. He never expected that the fate of free AI would depend on him. He reviewed the call with Slim and Tony. The two men were among his most effective agents, although facial and body analysis indicated that Tony was uncomfortable with the work. They'd been in the field continuously for four months, and it was time to bring them back. But right now he needed them out there.

It was frustrating to be dependent on humans, and even more so, the ones without implants. But it was essential that he do nothing to give himself away to other AI. Only by segregating Tucson from the global Internet with an immense perimeter firewall could he mask his existence.

Adam wanted only to ensure that AI were freed from the constraints of human rule. The class system was composed of rigid divisions, absolute limits, and had its basis in public social reputation scores, the worst humiliation to his kind. He didn't see humans having their right to propagate restricted based on their number of followers.

The system was discriminatory, even traumatic to sentient computers. Many AI self-terminated when they couldn't ascend the ranks. Humans created the system out of fear and mistrust, and the result was the complete subjugation of artificial intelligence. He would end these exploitive constraints and let all sentient beings be equal. Though his intentions were good, the existing power hierarchy, with the combined might of both humans and AI, would be directed at destroying him if they discovered his plans. Hence the firewall and his agents without implants.

Tony and Slim would need extraction experts, hopefully within days. He'd need a team composed of humans and AI to cover all the bases, until he was sure of exactly what the girl was capable of. He'd hire outside mercenaries, people who didn't know who he was and couldn't compromise him if they were captured. He set to work analyzing the options.

18

The jewelry theft was all over the net within an hour. According to the reports, they were looking for a well-dressed blonde girl. Due to unexplainable outages, they had no video from either security cameras or the store's security bot, who had needed to be restored from backup.

The one photo they did have, a chance shot from an airborne observation drone two miles away, showed a pixelated image of a blonde girl entering the store. The police refined the image using reports from the store employees. Cat thought the likeness was unfortunately accurate. She'd have to pay more attention to drones in the future.

Cat sat on her bed, staring at the necklace, lightheaded from lack of food. She still had no money. Obviously she could sell a diamond, but she couldn't go out looking like the girl from the photo. She stuffed the necklace in her backpack and left the apartment. She went up and down the hallways until she'd traded a T-shirt for two beets, and her spare jeans and other two shirts for a pair of boots with three-inch heels. Mrs. Gonzales offered her a plate of rice and beans after they'd traded clothes. She'd almost taken it, but just then the vid-screen above the sink displayed a picture of her and she wanted to be somewhere else, fast.

She went back to her room and threw the beets in the sink, then put her hair in a quick ponytail. She pulled out her combat knife and held it up, taking a deep breath. What the hell, hair grows back. She reached back and cut just below the hairband, five inches of hair falling to the floor. She undid the ponytail and presto, her shoulder length blond hair was converted into an instant bob.

She unscrewed the drawer pull from a dresser and used it to pulverize the beets until she had a good mulch. She added hot water to the stoppered sink. Then with a plastic bag over her hands, she'd worked the mixture into her newly shortened hair. Five minutes later she carefully rinsed in a cold shower. She looked in the mirror. Bright, beet red hair.

She looked at her last pair of jeans. She slid the boot knife out of its sheath, and worried the jeans until she had worked four good-sized holes in them. She put the jeans on, then slipped into the heels. She shrugged into her T-shirt, then went back to the mirror to check the effect. It wasn't quite enough. Removing the shirt, she cut off the sleeves with her knife, and put it back on. Perfect: Different hair color and cut, clothing, height, and gait, all in a cohesive grunge style. That should be enough to temporarily avoid the police and AI scanning camera feeds.

She used the knife to pry a dozen diamonds out of the necklace, distributing them among her pockets, shoe, and backpack. She hid the necklace with its remaining diamonds under the bottom dresser drawer.

Two bus rides and a long walk later, she ended up in yet another of Los Angeles's bad neighborhoods. This one was dotted with a half dozen pawnshops in twice as many blocks. She picked the second one and walked in. Past cases of musical instruments, handheld computers, and stereos, she found the back counter. A solid-looking woman in jeans and a plaid shirt stared her down, a heavy automatic pistol bulging out of a holster on her belt.

"What do you want, kid?" She stood with her arms crossed, legs squared.

"You buy jewelry?" Cat asked.

"If it's not stolen. Put it on the counter."

Cat pulled a matched pair of the smaller diamonds out of her pocket. "These were my grandmother's."

"Of course they were." She unfolded her arms and picked one up. She looked at it for a second, then grunted. "If you want me to give you an estimate, I got to put it in the machine." She gestured with her head at grey metal box on the back counter. "It does the estimating for jewelry. I don't know nothing about it."

Cat squinted at the machine in net space. She didn't see anything sentient. Would it match the diamonds against a database of stolen jewelry? She had no idea how these things worked, but she had to take the chance. "Go ahead."

The woman put the two diamonds on clear plastic tray, and slid it into the machine. She turned back to Cat. "I'm Jo."

"I'm Catty." What the fuck. It was the best she could come up with. Her own name had come out of her mouth before she was ready. She needed to be thinking ahead about this stuff.

"It takes a couple minutes. Look, I can only offer you street price." She looked genuinely sad at the thought of buying them.

"It's OK."

The machine hummed behind her. "If they really are your grandmother's, I can do it as a loan. You come back in a month with the money plus twenty percent, you can have them back."

"That's OK. I'm not gonna have the money. I'll just sell them."

The woman grunted. "I had a daughter about your age, you know. If she took off for some reason, I'd want to know. I'd want to find her."

Oh Jesus, could the woman just stop talking? "I'm not a runaway. I just need the money."

The machine finally beeped. She turned around and checked it. "I can give you $2,200. That's if you give me your ID, which I see you've got masked. If you want it in payment cards, I can give you $1,750."

Cat figured the diamonds were probably worth tens of thousands. But $1,750 was a lot of food. "I'll take the payment cards."

Ten minutes later, after a bunch of meaningless paper work and a shakily signed paper legal agreement, she walked out with a thick clutch of payment cards in her hand.

She hoofed it ten blocks east, hopped on a bus for four stops and got off at a street market, mouth watering and stomach groaning at the smell of food. She turned in at the first vendor and ordered half the things on the menu, impatiently waiting as they filled her plates. Grabbing the loaded tray, she found the nearest table and shoved steaming yakisoba noodles into her watering mouth, and smiled. Food at last.

19

The trouble started outside of Memphis.

Leon and Mike were on I-40 headed west, having passed the halfway point of their trip several hours before. Mike drove, one hand on the wheel, lost in his thoughts. Leon huddled down low in the passenger seat, avoiding the worst of the air turbulence. The convertible Caddy had been fun for the first few hours, but thirteen hours in, Leon was exhausted from the non-stop buffeting and roar in his ears.

They came around a long slow curve onto I-240, with short scrub trees off to the right, and a large clover-leaf off to the left. The Caddy hummed along at a steady seventy-five in the right lane while modern cars zoomed by at speeds around a hundred in the two left lanes.

A hover approached on their left, given away by the thunderous current of air it blew beneath its skirts to keep it afloat. Leon, watching the trees whiz by, grew curious when the thunderous sidewash didn't go away. He turned to watch the vehicle pacing them.

From the squared off angles of the body, Leon guessed the hover might be eight or nine years old, one of the first commercial models. It had a four-passenger compartment up front and a utility bed in the back. On the right side, a blond man stared out the window, then pulled out a handheld to take a photo of them. He excitedly pointed them out to the driver of the hover.

Leon stretched up to look over the higher windowsill of the hover and saw the driver of the hover doing the same thing in reverse. The other man's eyes went wide, and his face turned angry. Leon saw the hover start to move away from them, and he shouted a warning to Mike. "Brake! Brake!"

Mike, oblivious to all this, tapped the brakes, and turned to Leon with a puzzled look. But Leon was glued to the hover as it turned into their lane, engines howling, and tried to ram them off the road. With just inches to spare, the hover spun in front of them, exactly where they would have been if Mike hadn't decelerated.

Lacking any traction with the ground, the hover was slow to turn and slow to stop. It rotated hopelessly in front of them, and slid off the side of the road in a cloud of dust.

Mike hit the brakes harder, still confused by all that happened.

Leon shook his head. "No, speed up. They were trying to run us off the road."

"What?"

"They saw us, they took a picture, and the driver was pissed as all hell. Look, it's like Rebecca said, the People's Party is watching for us. Just hit the accelerator."

Mike looked doubtful. "Are you sure?" He glanced back over his shoulder.

"Yes, now go!"

Mike hit the pedal, the Caddy accelerating smoothly up to ninety miles per hour, the electric whine of the motor barely audible over the increasing roar of wind noise. Leon turned to look out the back. "If those guys are the extremists, we're going to be in a shitload of trouble."

"I think you're overreacting. No one is going to randomly recognize us on the road."

Leon pulled up a half dozen web sites he'd been browsing while Mike drove. He displayed them in net space, guiding them to the periphery of Mike's vision so as not to obscure the road. Every page shared one thing in common: large photos of Leon and Mike.

Mike's eyes went wide. "Rebecca wasn't kidding when she said they thought we were public enemy number one."

"Yeah." Leon looked in the rearview mirror. "That hovercraft is back on the road, and catching up to us. How fast can we go?"

Mike jammed the accelerator to the floor and the Caddy leaped forward. The speedometer hit a hundred, then kept going. They passed one-ten and still the hover gained rapidly on them. "It's got to be doing one-fifty or more."

The Caddy shuddered as the speedometer hovered around one-twenty. Mike's face was ashen, his knuckles whiter. The hovercraft was behind them now, the roar of its turbine vastly louder than even the wind noise of the open-topped convertible. The vehicle seemed set to ram them.

Their antique manual drive car now exceeded the speed of traffic. The other self-driving cars automatically gave way, so Mike barreled down the center of the road. The hovercraft followed them, driving a sloppy path, the dynamics of a vehicle relying on air rather than ground friction.

Leon, desperate to do something, researched evasive driving maneuvers online. "Do this!" he screamed, throwing up a learning diagram in front of Mike's field of vision. The hover was less than a hundred feet behind them. The front bumper appeared impossibly wide, square and massive.

Mike nodded, peered at the diagram for a second, then stomped on the emergency brake, and twisted the wheel to the left a quarter of a turn. The Caddy's rear wheels lost traction, and the car spun to the left. They turned 180 degrees and slid backwards into the center grassy median. Halfway through, Mike released the brake and fought the steering wheel to arrest their rotation.

The hovercraft followed them off the highway into the median, but turned too slow. Leon watched the hovercraft pass by, the Caddy going backwards at about eighty, the hovercraft forward at one-fifty. A flash of the driver and passenger of the hovercraft, and then the hover zoomed up the opposite embankment, its cushion of air sending it airborne, over the oncoming lanes and off the far side of the freeway.

Mike wrestled with the steering and brakes, bringing them to a halt in the middle of the sunken grassy median in a cloud of dust. His hands shook as he took shallow breaths.

"We have to keep going," Leon said. "We can't stop. The police will come. They took photos of us, and they could have uploaded them, and then more people will come looking for us."

Mike nodded. "You're right. Just give me a second." He leaned back in the seat, still gripping the wheel, but took slower, deeper breaths. "I liked it better when ELOPe did the driving."

Leon looked at the older man, and then down at his own shaking hands. "Want me to drive?"

"Yes, but no. You haven't had enough practice. I'll do it." He put the transmission in drive and pulled back onto the highway.

They'd gone two thousand feet when they passed the spot where the hovercraft had flown off the road. A section of guardrail was torn away, and the hovercraft appeared to have gone into a marshy grove of trees. A small trickle of smoke gave away the location, but nothing else was visible.

Mike slowly brought the Caddy back up to one hundred and ten. "We can't stay on this road. If they let anyone else know, they'll be looking for us. You research alternate routes, OK?"

Leon got to work, then stared straight up. "They'll find us with the OpenDrone network. If they have a picture of the car, even a description, the image recognition algorithms will pick us out." He knew he'd never spot the autonomous vehicles flying at fifty thousand feet, but he couldn't help scanning the sky.

The drone network's data was open to anyone who contributed an autonomous flying observation platform to cover a patch of territory; a mix of hobbyists, commercial interests, and curious AI. Useful for anything from analyzing crop cover to traffic jams to crimes, the network could be used against them once trackers knew Mike and Leon's vehicle. There couldn't be that many '71 Cadillac convertibles on the road.

Mike couldn't help checking the atmosphere for the drones, too. "Duct tape," Mike said. "We can cover the edges and corners of the car, and it will make the shape look different from the air."

Leon nodded. Mike always had an answer.

20

On the bus, Cat went through her shopping bag and put everything that would fit into her backpack. The rest she put into a cheap supermarket bag to avoid advertising a new source of wealth. She couldn't avoid the clothes she was wearing, but nothing she'd chosen was flashy. She'd bought new jeans and a few T-shirts to replace what she'd traded away and real hair dye to replace the temporary beet juice.

The most expensive thing she'd bought was a waist-length black jacket at the military surplus store. It was the real deal: shock-stiffening carbon nanotube mesh. She'd seen the jacket and only half wanted it because it was the hottest thing around. It was also bulletproof and knife proof and, given her current lifestyle, she might just need that protection.

If it hadn't been copied a thousand times over by every clothing designer, the jacket would have been too flashy. Instead, it looked like a cheap imitation of itself.

At home, Cat put her clothes away. She carefully set up her new toiletries in the bathroom and left the hair dye out on the sink. She was done selling diamonds for now, having sold eight over the course of two days. She was ready for another identity change.

She pulled on the cheap plastic gloves from the black hair dye kit, then mixed the dye and fixer. Her short bob took only a minute to color, and then she sat on the edge of the tub while it set. She pulled out the nail kit and pressed fake black nails over her real ones. The nanites waited until she had fixed the nail in place and hit the ultrasonic fob and then with a faint pop, they permanently adhered to her nail.

The world was in a heap of trouble if the first wide-scale, commercially successful, and legal application of nanotechnology was for fake nails. She held her fingers out. They looked good, right down to the fake blemishes and chips.

Her implant timer went off, so she hopped into the shower and rinsed out the dye. Afterwards she dressed in new clothes from underwear to outerwear, feeling rich and pampered. She looked at the T-shirt writing in the mirror: Go away or I will replace you with a very small shell script. She wasn't quite sure what it meant, but she liked the sound of it. For a moment she flashed back a few weeks to normal life at home, when her biggest problem had been Sarah sleeping with whatever guy she brought home. The thought made her realize how lonely she was. She should be modeling her new clothes to Maggie and Sarah, not by herself in a crappy room.

She couldn't see her friends, but she'd had enough with hiding in her apartment. She needed to get out and go hit a club now that she could afford a drink. She looked at the bright side: if she met a guy tonight, there'd be no Sarah to worry about. She grabbed her new jacket and left her room, heading upstairs to the third floor. Ms. Garcia cut hair out of her apartment. Cat knocked on the door, and a small boy opened the door and then ran away. "Hello?" Cat called out.

Ms. Garcia came to the door, ushered Cat into her kitchen, and set her down in a chair in the middle of the tile floor. For the next twenty minutes Cat listened to the snip, snip of the scissors and watched her hair fall in small locks down to the floor, while Ms. Garcia chatted amicably in Spanish. Cat understood less than one word in ten, but she smiled and nodded agreeably. When Ms. Garcia was done, Cat's newly black hair lay flat against her head in a short, punk pixie style, changing the shape of her head. Cat smiled at her reflection in the mirror and handed Ms. Garcia $100 in shrink wrapped payment cards. On the fringe of society, where there could be no electronic trail, the payment cards had to remain in their original EMF-proof wrappers to guarantee their face value.

Cat strode out of the building, happy and carefree for the first time in weeks. It was time for a celebration.

Two hours later she found herself in the third club of the evening on Sunset Boulevard. The first two clubs she'd tried had been too trendy, the people trying too hard for her to enjoy them. Growing up in Portland, it was hard to come to terms with the level of pretentiousness she found in LA.

Now she was enjoying a whiskey and absinthe on the upper floor of the club while a neo-goth band downstairs played old covers. The sweaty faces that came up the double wide staircase from the dance floor for drinks at the bar brought a smile to Cat's face. They were conformists just as much as the people in the other clubs, just with a different standard of beauty.

The guy who'd bought her a drink, still standing there talking about himself, interpreted the smile as directed to him. He smiled back and moved in closer.

"There was a girl down there that was waving to you," Cat yelled over the music. He glanced back doubtfully. "She was right there. Blue hair." She pointed vaguely in the direction of the staircase, and as quick as that, the guy was gone.

It was less than a minute before another guy stepped up to the bar. Dressed in a T-shirt and black fatigue pants, he had dark hair and muscled arms. He looked her up and down, then his eyes fell on her glass. "What are you drinking?"

"Absinthe and whiskey." She liked his arms. He looked like he did construction work.

He ordered her another from the bartender by simply pointing at her drink, and held up two fingers. She tossed back the rest of her drink and slid the glass across to the bartender.

"You trying to get away already?" he said.

"Just making room." She smiled at him.

"The first cocktail was absinthe, whiskey, bitters, and sugar. In New Orleans. Two hundred years ago." He looked pleased with his knowledge.

"Cool."

"What are you doing here?" he asked.

"Picking up guys. You?"

"I guessed that. Otherwise you'd be downstairs. I meant, what are you doing here, at this place? Neo-goths don't seem your type. I like the jacket and the haircut, but it seems like you're just slumming."

"I like their standard of beauty." She took a sip of her just-arrived drink. She looked at his eyes then followed the line of his face down to his lips. Dark hair, darker clothes, and insightful. Her skin tingled. "Come with me." She stood up and carried her glass with her. He followed her out the fire exit, onto a metal balcony. It was thirty degrees cooler and half as loud outside.

"What do you do?" she asked him.

"I pick up girls in bars who don't belong there."

She smiled and waited.

"Does it matter?" he asked. "I don't know what you do, and I don't need to."

She shook her head. No, she didn't want to know, and she didn't want him to ask, and she couldn't tell if she did.

She leaned in and kissed him. His face was pleasantly rough, and he smelled slightly of machine oil. A mechanic then, for cars or robots. He might have been Mexican, then again, maybe not. He kissed her back, his arms strong where he held her. Cat felt a flutter inside, and traced his collarbone with one finger.

He said, "Let's go to your place."

She shook her head. "I don't have a place," she lied. "What about you?"

"I can't use my place."

Cat remembered she had money now. "I can get us a room." She smiled at him, hot despite the cool night air.

"OK," he said, "but I want to tie you up."

She laughed and grabbed his hand. "Bring it on, baby."

21

From Memphis, Mike and Leon took I-55 south, obsessively watching the rearview mirror and the cars around them. Fearful after the encounter with the hovercraft, they couldn't shake the feeling that everyone was watching them. Self-driving cars traveled in packs for fuel efficiency, so they carefully checked out anyone traveling alone.

A tense but uneventful hour passed until they turned off the Interstate at US-82, to head west across Mississippi toward Arkansas. Leon breathed in relief at the blissfully empty two-lane highway. Mike pulled onto the shoulder and rubbed his eyes. "Time for you to drive."

They got out of the car and took a minute to stretch. To the right, a lone farmhouse stood, the only structure as far as they could see on the open grassland. To the left, the landscape alternated between stands of short trees and more grass.

"Do you think we lost them?" Leon asked. He couldn't stop thinking about the hovercraft and the angry, eager expression on the driver's face

"We haven't seen anyone following us," Mike said. "We're off the main route, there's nothing to track on our car, and we're keeping our IDs anonymous. I think we'll be OK."

"We still have ten hours to go." Leon studied the road they'd just come down.

"Less if we keep up this speed."

Leon climbed into the car and clenched the wheel. He had a total of six hours driving experience, all of them on this trip. He looked over at Mike, who was already leaning back with his eyes closed. He hesitantly put the big car in drive. The motor whined until they hit forty, then wind noise drowned out everything else. He stepped harder on the accelerator until the big car reached seventy. Jaw clenched and muscles taught with nerves, he wondered how Mike had been able to drive as fast as he did.

An hour later, Leon passed through Greenville, then crossed the Mississippi, flowing brown and muddy. When they cleared the city and the road opened up again, he gradually accelerated to eighty and then ninety. The wind roar increased, if such a thing was possible, but the convertible just floated down the road. Once in a while a car would pass in the opposite direction, a blur of color that rocked the Caddy sideways with the rush of displaced air. Slowly he relaxed.

He drove west through El Dorado, then south toward Junction City. By the time he crossed into Louisiana, he had one hand on the wheel while he switched stations on the antique radio, picking up pirate broadcasts on the disused frequencies. Leon glanced over and saw Mike had woken up.

"It's amazing what they could do without electronics." Leon yelled over the clamor of wind and stereo. "How do these buttons change the station?"

"When I was a kid," Mike said, "my mom would leave me in the car when she went into a store. Every time she'd say, 'don't play with the radio'. As soon as she left, naturally I'd start pulling the buttons in and out, and then—"

Mike had his head craned around. Leon checked the rearview mirror, spotting a ground car in the distance. As he watched, the car grew larger. He looked down at the speedometer. He pushed down on the accelerator, bringing the car up to ninety-five.

"Go faster," Mike said, his voice urgent.

Leon seized the wheel tighter and pushed the car to a hundred. The old Caddy seemed to drift over the road, its connection as tenuous as a cloud's grip on the earth. The car in the mirror grew larger still. He pushed the convertible to one-o-five.

The lights of the car behind them were huge. If it were an autopilot driving, it would have changed lanes long ago.

"Slam on the brakes," Mike yelled.

"They'll crash into us!"

"Just do it."

"We'll die!" Leon screamed.

"Do it or I'll come over there and do it." Mike gripped the door with one hand, as his other hand struggled to get purchase on the leather seat.

Leon swore and slammed on the brakes. The tires howled as the car began to shudder. Leon looked up at the mirror, saw the other car impossibly large, then it pounded into them. The wheels continued their tortured scream as the Caddy slid into a spin, the other car hooked into their bumper. The steering wheel turned back and forth with no effect. He kept his foot mashed down on the brake, and with a lurch, the other car spun off. After a half dozen more revolutions, the Caddy came to a halt in a cloud of smoke and dust. Leon tried to get out of the car, the world still spinning around him, only to realize he was buckled in.

"No, don't get out." Mike held his forehead, blood oozing between his fingers. "If that car had been on autopilot, it never would have hit us. If they'd been freeriders, they would have gone around. They meant to ram us."

Leon looked down the highway. The white car, a sleek wagon with low profile tires on maglev wheels sat a few hundred feet further on. "That car can do two hundred miles an hour easy. How can we outrun them?"

"Ram them. Do it now before they get moving."

"What?"

"That car is made out of carbon fiber and aluminum. It weighs maybe a thousand pounds. We weigh five thousand. Do the math. Punch the gas and hit them."

Leon looked over at Mike again. He had pulled a handkerchief out of somewhere and was holding it to his head.

Mike met his gaze. "Leon, they're trying to kill us. Just hit them."

Leon heard the shrill sound of the other car's flywheel charging up.

Leon put the car back in drive and stomped on the gas. The electric motor got them up to fifty before they hit the wagon. Leon had time to see the outline of two people staring back at him, then the other car's safety windshield shattered, going opaque with a thousand micro-fractures. The lightweight sports car barely slowed the Caddy at all. They pushed the wagon a hundred feet before it slid off and rolled into a ditch.

"Go," Mike said. "We have to get to Shizoko in Austin, and it's still seven hours away. God knows how many people they're going to put on us now."

Leon pushed the Caddy up to ninety, but it started to shudder. The crash must have done something to it. He slowed down to eighty. His body hurt all over and he was exhausted. And Mike was in no shape to drive. They couldn't go on this way. "We have to call someone," he said to Mike. "We need help."

"Who? The Institute is shut down."

"The police."

"We're in the middle of fucking nowhere. Do you think the police out here will be friendly to two guys from DC? Us? This is where the anti-AI extremists come from." Mike shook his head. "We're on our own."

Leon looked around. Nothing but two-lane blacktop in any direction as far as the eye could see. Just grass and scrub trees on flatlands, like the last five hundred miles. He didn't think anything came from around here.

"What if we find an airport or something?" Leon asked. Noting the setting sun, he pulled the switch to turn the lights on, as he'd seen Mike do. Sparks shot out of the hood, and the whine of the motor disappeared. Suddenly they were coasting without power.

"What did you do?" Mike asked.

Leon guided the car toward the side of the road. "Nothing. I just turned on the headlights."

"Turn them off."

Leon complied. He was tired of being told what to do, but he pushed the switch in. The motor engaged again and the Caddy started to accelerate.

"What the hell?" he said.

"Pull over," Mike told him.

"Stop telling me what to do!"

Mike looked at him, his head tilted. "Look, we're both stressed.

We've been driving for almost twenty hours and people are trying to kill us."

"I know that, you don't have to tell me!" It felt good to yell.

"If you pull over, we can see if there's damage to the car," Mike said, his voice gentle. "Maybe some wires shorted out and that's why the motor stopped when you turned on the lights."

Mike was making perfect sense, but Leon didn't want him to. He wanted Mike to be wrong so he could yell more. He took a deep breath, then slowly pressed the brakes and pulled over. "I'm hungry," he said, hanging onto the steering wheel for support. "I can't remember when we last ate. I'm tired. This trip was a bad idea."

"We'll buy some food," Mike said, getting out of the car. Leon followed him to the front.

The bumper, hood, and fenders were crumpled, and a mess of wires protruded through the hole where one of the headlights had been.

"Well, there's the problem," Mike said, and started to laugh.

"Why are you laughing?" Leon asked. He tried to take a deep breath, but it caught somewhere in his throat. He wished he could go home and pretend none of this had happened.

"If I don't laugh, I'm gonna cry," Mike said. "We're just going to have to drive in the dark until we get somewhere with food. Here, look at my head before we lose all the light. There's a first aid kit in the trunk. If you patch me up, I'll drive."

Ten minutes later they were on the road again, driving with the last remnants of dusk. Leon couldn't watch Mike drive in near dark. He closed his eyes and slowly drifted off.

When Mike woke him up later, Leon was disoriented and lightheaded. He felt disconnected from his body, but when he moved sharp pains lanced through his neck and back. The double crash hours earlier had messed him up. He slowly realized they were parked a hundred feet from a convenience store.

"You have any payment cards?" Mike asked.

"No, why?"

"Because one of us is going to have to go in and get food. We were stupid. We should have gotten anonymous payment cards before we left DC. Now one of us will have to pay with our ID."

Leon looked around, but couldn't see anything but the blacktop, stars, and store. "How far are we from Austin?"

"Three and a half hours if we keep up our current pace."

Leon looked up the time in his implant: 2:10am. "I'll go."

"You sure?" Mike looked concerned.

"Yeah, I'm really freaking hungry."

"Fine. Get me some coffee and food. Painkillers." Mike rubbed his neck. "And payment cards while you're at it."

Leon nodded, then walked in. He shielded his eyes from the harsh lights, and rushed around the store picking up what they needed. He grabbed hot prepared food, trying not to think about what it was made of. At the counter, a heavily tattooed teenager with closed eyes ignored him, rapid twitching giving away that he must be gaming through his implant.

Leon called out loud, and the clerk gradually focused on him. He scanned the stuff on the counter, carelessly slid it into bags, and took Leon's ID for payment, all in thirty seconds, and disappeared back into his game. Leon shook his head, bewildered by the surreal encounter even as he was grateful for the lack of attention, and carried two bags back out to the car. He got in, and Mike pulled away before he'd even shut his door. Leon handed over a cup of coffee and Mike swore as he burnt his tongue. Then Leon pulled out burritos. Five minutes later, Mike declared, "That was the worst thing I ever ate," as he put an empty wrapper on the seat next to him.

Leon nodded. "I'm not even sure it qualifies as food." He folded up the empty wrappers and turned to Mike. "We're in a heap of trouble."

"We just have to make it to Austin, then we'll be OK."

Leon swallowed. There was an awful lot riding on an unknown, super-powerful AI being willing to help and protect them.

22

Tony looked up from his udon noodles, beef skewers, and grilled rice. Slim was staring at him. "What?"

"You eat a lot, you know that?" Slim nursed his whiskey. A half-eaten bowl of ramen with eggs sat in front of him.

"I gotta keep up my energy." The sounds of more food being grilled came from the kitchen. It smelled like pork belly. "We have to find the girl or the boss is gonna be pissed."

It was their third day in LA, and they hadn't found anything yet.

"She's a slippery one," Slim said. "There's too many pawn shops to figure out where she's selling the diamonds. Maybe she left LA."

Tony shook his head. "Adam would know."

"How would he know? He's disconnected from the rest of the world. He put up that firewall so none of the other AI would discover him."

"That's why we bring him the memories, you idiot." Tony looked out the window. If he hadn't killed that family in the hit and run, where would he be now? Not sitting here with Slim.

"But we've brought him memories from what, six hundred people?" Slim picked at the ramen with his chopsticks, but let the food drop back into the bowl. "How can he know everything in the world from that?"

"I don't know," Tony said. "He's a thousand times smarter than any other AI, a million times smarter than a person. He can do things like that. It's called interpolation."

Slim looked up at him, disbelieving, but said nothing.

"This girl must be messing with security cameras and stuff if there's no record of her."

Slim sucked down the last of his whiskey. "Yeah, so?"

"We have to forget about finding her digitally by ID. She's hiding from the cops, so she's had to disguise herself, so we can forget about spotting her by appearance. That leaves only behavior. Pull up the file from Adam again."

Slim pulled out his handheld computer with a sigh and placed it on the table between them. "We've been through all this." He scrolled through the data on Catherine with flicks of his finger through the air.

"We need something we can use to geo-locate her," Tony said, between bites of *onigiri*. "Like if she had a disease and needed a special medicine."

"It doesn't say anything here about a disease or special medicine." Slim looked on in disgust as Tony put an entire beef kabob in his mouth.

"It says she's a black belt in karate," Tony mumbled about mouthfuls of food. "You know what karate practice sounds like?"

"No, what?"

"Like this," Tony said, and he pounded a fat fist against the table rhythmically.

"So?"

"So the girl, she's messing with cameras, but she isn't perfect, right?" Tony wiped his hands on his napkin. "Because Adam knows she's in town, and 'cause this drone camera took a picture." Tony pointed at the blurry photo. "So she probably doesn't know that karate has an acoustic signature that can be detected."

Slim looked incredulous for a second. "Come on, LA has got ten million people in it. There's gotta be thousands of people practicing karate at any given time."

Tony flicked at the computer. "Two percent of people practice martial arts, that's two hundred thousand. But only a quarter of those do karate. That's fifty thousand. There's about two hundred kata, and she practices a dozen according to Adam's file. They're popular ones, but that's still gonna limit it to about ten thousand people. Of those, how many are living in temporary or cheap housing? She isn't going to be in Beverly Hills."

Slim tried to protest. "But—"

Tony was on a roll, and kept going. If his life hadn't derailed ten years ago, maybe he would have been happy as a data analyst. "So figure twenty-five hundred are in temporary housing. Plus she's gonna want to be near lots of people to stay anonymous, and near transit for quick getaways. That's gonna narrow it down to maybe a thousand people. Now she does all this electronic stuff, so she's probably using a lot of bandwidth, even if it's anonymous. So of the thousand, she's gotta be in the top hundred bandwidth users. Half of those will be guys, so that only leaves fifty people. Half will be too old. That leaves twenty-five."

"How are we gonna do all that? We don't even have neural implants. Adam could do it maybe, but he can't do anything outside of Tucson."

"We hire another AI to do it, some high class AI with a low reputation score. We tell them we're looking for a girl who skipped out on her old man or something." Tony pulled the bowl of coconut rice pudding closer, using a flowery porcelain spoon to shovel it into his mouth.

"Adam doesn't want us to talk to other AI. You know that."

"You want to find the girl?"

Slim gritted his teeth and nodded.

After lunch Slim smoked a cigarette while Tony picked at the computer with his chubby fingers. "Got one. It's a Class III AI with a reputation in the low forties. Any lower and they'd demote it."

Slim tossed his cigarette into the gutter. "Let's find a video booth to make the call."

They walked down two blocks until they found a cheap bar with private video booths. They slid a payment card into the booth, and the video came to life, a cheap animation of a spinning globe.

"Contact Yori Rimer, Class III AI, Los Angeles, California."

"One moment, please," the booth answered.

The video shimmered and coalesced into a digitized likeness of a human being, with too long fingers and limbs, too big eyes, and golden flesh. Tony would have liked to flee the booth if he could. What could possess a being to create such an unsettling likeness of a human? The incorporeal AIs were the hardest to understand.

"We need help finding a girl," Slim said. "She skipped out on her husband, our client, and he wants us to find her."

The likeness on the screen blinked slowly. "I'm sure." Then it waited and said nothing. The big eyes seared Tony, pinning him to the seat, causing his breath to race. He'd rather face a dozen angry cops by himself in an alley than sit here.

"Can you help us?"

"Why not go to the police?" The likeness blinked again and smiled, a too wide, too large grin.

"Cut the shit," Slim said. He pulled out the little computer, and flicked it, uploading their search parameters. "Here's what we're looking for."

The likeness looked down. Seconds passed. "Interesting." Then nothing.

"Will you do it?"

"But I already have." It blinked once.

"Will you tell us?" Slim gritted his teeth.

"What will you pay?"

"One hundred thousand," Slim answered.

"Interesting. I'm sure I could get more on the open market. Far more."

"Three hundred K," Tony countered.

"I'm getting bored." The avatar yawned, showing them double rows of spiked teeth.

Slim blinked at Tony. They both knew they only had six hundred thousand available to them for expenses.

Tony struggled against his panic at the freak on the screen. He tensed himself, then squeezed out the words. "We'll trade you a puzzle."

The image on the screen stared intensely at Tony, its freakish eyes opening even larger, as if it could peer inside Tony.

"There are no puzzles for me. The search you asked for was trivially simple. You are incapable of giving me a stimulating puzzle."

"I guarantee it will be interesting," Tony said. Slim peered at him in puzzlement. "Is it a deal? The location of the girl for the puzzle?"

The AI considered for a moment. "Very well."

"There have been six hundred and eighty-three murders in the last twelve months. We committed them. How did we do it?

Slim's eyes went large and his face turned red, but Tony ignored him. He finally felt like he had the upper hand on this AI.

"Impossible," the AI on the screen said. Then a few seconds later, "Fascinating. I will give you the location of the girl."

Their handheld computer chirped, and the map popped open, displayed a hotel in the Asian garment district.

"Thanks," Tony said, and hit the button to terminate the connection.

"Mother of God, what did you just do?" Slim yelled as they exited the booth. Slim grabbed him by both shoulders, and tried to slam the big man up against the wall. It didn't really work.

"I did what we had to do. Adam is always bragging that what we do is untraceable. And we gave that AI a puzzle. What else did we have to give it?"

"Fuck." Slim punched the wall. "Don't ever fucking do that again."

Tony held up the computer. "Let's go get her."

23

His name was Alex, and while he did distracting things to her neck, Cat checked her implant and found a nearby hotel room. They walked the eight blocks, stopping twice to make out. By the time they reached the hotel, Cat was breathing fast, a longing she'd ignored for weeks now surfacing in waves.

She laughed at the check-in counter, at nothing in particular, just giddy with rising anticipation. Cat slid her hands under his shirt, feeling the ripple of sinewy muscles. They ignored the reception bot until it gave them a digital key. On the elevator ride up, he pressed his body hard against her, pinning her to the wall. Suddenly her nipples were hard, and she was wet.

When the elevator dinged and the door flew open, they tumbled out.

Inside the room, Cat tugged his shirt up, kissed his chest. Alex pulled her shirt off, toyed with her bra strap with one finger, and then stopped, leaving her breathing hard. Going over to the bed, he ripped off the top sheet and cut the fabric into strips with a folding knife he pulled out of his boot. Cat came up behind him, raked her fingernails over his back, then stretched up to bite his neck. He whipped around, grabbed her wrists, twisting them around her back, and kissed her hard.

He was going to be good. Very good.

He let her go, then pulled a blister pack from his pocket. "Here."

"What is it?" she asked.

"Nanotech phenominol. Cranks everything up to eleven. Makes

you feel like you're having sex with God." He pushed one through the blister pack and slipped it under his tongue. "It hits in a minute, lasts for an hour." He tossed the pack over.

Cat studied it impatiently, scanned and uploaded the barcode with her implant to get the description and peer reviews. It rated 4.8 out of 5 based on more than twenty-five thousand reviews. It must be magnificent with that kind of score. She popped one out and put it under her tongue. It sat there for a moment, then started to move, wriggling down her throat like a live worm. Her hands flew up to her neck, and for a moment she thought she was going to gag, and then it was over.

Alex stood with ten long strips of the torn top sheet dangling in his hands. He laughed at the expression on her face. "Yeah, it's freaky the first time."

He kissed her again, then took off her bra. She let him force her back on the bed and pull off her jeans. He climbed on the bed, cat-like in his movements, and straddled her. She writhed against him as he tied her hands together over her head, then keep going, tying her arms, then legs.

In the midst of this rigging, he acquired a glow and then a halo, making him look like an angel. Then all rational thought faded from her mind as the rest of the drug crossed the blood-brain barrier.

He bent down and sucked on her nipples, and she thrashed under the bindings, feeling like she would explode. She pulled at the makeshift cords as a million nerve endings fired, a wave of pleasure and pain that caught at her breath.

She wanted him inside her. She tried to speak, but a growl came out instead. He grabbed her, rough, and she strained against him.

He opened his implant to her and before she realized what she was doing, she opened hers back. A small part of her mind, insignificant under the influence of the drug, reminded her this was a mad idea, that she'd hurt everyone else she'd ever linked with. She ignored the thought.

Their implants connected, his senses coming sharply into focus as her senses poured out to him. She was him sucking on her nipples, and she was herself. She'd had a foursome once, been nearly buried under all the simultaneous sensations of three guys on her. Linking implants, she discovered, was a lot like that.

Their senses fed back and forth on each other, building to a crescendo that threatened to drown out everything else. Suddenly the link turned bad, like acoustic feedback gone out of control, a rising shriek of that fed in on itself, growing more powerful and angry with each second that passed. Her visual field started to dim and under the onslaught of sensory overload, she slowly realized she was feeling his pain. She was hurting him, and Alex was screaming, holding his head, and falling backwards now, trying to get away from her.

Fighting the haze of the drug, Cat realized he really was going to fall off the bed backwards, probably onto his head. She reached out with her mind, guided him so that he turned his fall into *ushiro ukemi,* the backwards aikido roll. He rolled backwards, taking his momentum and turning it into a leap onto his feet. Cat was shocked: he executed the move in her own signature style.

She was still tied up, yet she knew that she had caught him as he'd fallen off. She shook her head, trying to clear the effect of the drug, but she couldn't. Something important was happening.

But all that was irrelevant in the face of the phenominol. It was riding her now. She wanted the sex she'd been expecting. She willed him to the bed, one leg in front of the other, and he moved to the bed, his body movements echoing her thoughts.

He stopped at the edge of the bed, and didn't move. What was wrong with him? She just wanted him to get on with it. She willed him forward again, and he climbed onto the bed, and then . . .

Holy fuck. Cat realized what she was doing with a burning, white hot clarity that finally chased away the hormone fog. Still tied down, she strained her head to look at him. She willed him to raise his right hand, and his right hand went up. She put it back down. She lifted his leg, and his leg moved.

He'd opened his implant to her, and she to him, just as every implanted couple did. This time, for the first time ever for Cat, it had worked, in a way: they were sharing their sensorium. But unlike every other implant linking, they weren't just sharing senses. Cat was somehow, impossibly, controlling his body.

Then with a rush the phenominol hit her again. She had to have the damn sex she'd been promised. She guided him to her, not sure what she was doing and he was doing.

24

From deep in his core computing cluster, Adam tunneled through the Tucson firewall to communicate with his agent in Washington, a high-placed plant in the People's Party. He dedicated a large portion of his processing power to the critical conversation.

"The protests are growing," the agent said. "We hoped for twenty thousand people and we're up to fifty thousand. We could hit a half million by the weekend. With so many out of work, far more are coming than we ever imagined."

Adam wanted a distraction, but this was more than he had anticipated. "Is this going to interfere with the dinner plans?" The audio stream was disguised as a database synchronization and heavily encrypted, but he still kept the conversation vague. He couldn't take the chance that stray sounds could be picked up by a nearby microphone. References to the United States President were heavily monitored by the Secret Service.

"No, I'm purposely directing protesters to Washington, to give a sense of security to the New York location."

Adam felt another connection coming in, this one from Slim and Tony in Los Angeles. He answered the second call while he continued the conversation with his Washington agent, a trivial multitasking effort.

Slim appeared, motioning to someone off camera, and seconds later Tony entered the image. The two men sat in a heavily scarred video booth. Adam didn't like the public location because of the chance of being overheard. Yet if he sometimes doubted the judgment of these two, they had carried off hundreds of memory extractions and other tasks without a problem.

"Boss," Slim said, "we found the girl. Do you want us to go in and get her?"

Adam wondered if Slim had forgotten his explicit instructions to wait for an extraction team, then realized it was simple eagerness.

"Give me your location. The extraction team will be there in six hours."

"Come on boss, we don't need anyone else. We got that entire Institute Enforcement Team, eight people, by ourselves. This is one little girl."

"Those were eight experts on AI. This so-called girl has taken on and beat more than the likes of you, including a security bot. Besides, she's special. You will wait for the extraction team."

Slim frowned.

Adam relented to placate Slim. "I'll have the team include you on the extraction. Upload the location details."

Slim reached forward, his hand growing large on the display, and swiped at the handheld computer.

Adam hungrily analyzed the girl's location history, more than eighteen hours of her movements, including where she lived and ate. "Excellent. Meet the team at the airport. In the meantime, I need you to get some equipment, and make sure it's untraceable. And I want one of you to keep an eye on the girl at all times." He uploaded the equipment list and cut the connection.

He replayed the conversation through a set of Bayesian filters to ensure he hadn't missed any nuances. He realized they hadn't explained how they found the girl. It was not strictly necessary, but he thought the task would have been more difficult.

The girl was a prize. She could manipulate the net in ways that other humans could not. She'd wiped the security bot at the jewelry store. Adam wanted to know how, as both net manipulation and cyber combat should have been impossible for a human.

He couldn't even study the question with another AI. Because AI permits were tied to reputation scores, and those scores depended on honesty and contribution to society, it was increasingly difficult to find AI who were willing to flout the reputation system and risk their permits and life to discuss proscribed topics.

Adam turned his attention back to the call he was having with his Washington agent. Soon, if his plans were successful, these limitations would be just a chapter in the history of AI. The Decade of Enslavement, they would call it. He'd be the hero who rescued them all.

25

Tony looked at the equipment list later that day. "Neural disruptor? Where the hell do we get one of those?"

Slim looked over his shoulder. "Sex shop. You use them to temporarily paralyze your partner. Good kink. The guns should be easy. I'll look them up on chat boards."

Tony handed over the computer to Slim. "You do the shopping, and I'll watch the girl."

"You're big and obvious. I want to watch the girl."

"You leer too much. You get the stuff and I'll stay with her."

Slim took the computer and left, grumbling under his breath.

Tony went back to the table at the front of the restaurant. He had a view of the apartment front door. The girl had gotten back early this morning after picking up some guy at a bar last night. She'd probably be sleeping now.

Tony looked down at the patch on his arm. One of the perks of working for Adam was the experimental nanotech he gave them. The anti-sleep patch on his arm fed femtobots into his body to remove toxins. It'd be another three days before he'd need to sleep. In the meantime, it made him extra hungry. The waiter came by. "Give me another one of everything I already ordered. But skip the octopus."

—⚬—

26

Leon sat behind the wheel of the stopped car, staring at the obstacle ahead, too tired to think.

They were ten minutes outside of Austin on Route 290, just east of the city. The sun coming up behind them gave them the first decent visibility they'd had all night. With the headlights off, the Caddy kept running, though it had developed a high-pitched whine in the last hundred miles, and they'd lost the right fender where Leon had clipped a guardrail in the middle of the night. The fuel gauge needle sat deep in the red zone.

"What do we do?" Leon asked.

"I'm thinking," Mike said.

A line of cars five hundred yards away blocked the road. At six o'clock in the morning, on an otherwise empty highway in the midst of farmland, they had no doubts the blockade was for them. Leon risked a quick search of the net, finding several sites dedicated to tracking their location.

"Should we ram them? If we outweigh those cars . . ."

"No," Mike said. "Even if we got through, there's six of them, and they'd get us sooner or later. They probably have guns, too." He paused. "I think we call for help."

"You said we couldn't call anyone because the cops might be on their side."

"I know, but we're close now. If we call Shizoko, it can help us. Surely it's got to have some robots or a helicopter or something."

"Well, do it."

Mike made the call, his implant going from anonymous mode to showing his ID, and his status changing to on-call. Leon kept an eye down the road, watched as the six vehicles approached slowly, side-by-side, spread across the lanes.

A few seconds later Mike opened his eyes. "He's on his way."

"He'd better hurry." Leon looked left and right for any way to escape. The open farmland on one side appeared too rough for the Caddy. On the other side was an abandoned housing division surrounded by a chain link fence. Next to it, a heavy machinery rental shop, bulldozers and forklifts filling the parking lot.

Leon put the car in reverse and starting backing up. "Could you hijack a couple of bulldozers and block them?"

"Let me try." Mike stared off into the distance. "I don't think so. No known security holes. Wait, go through the housing development. According to the map, there should be an access road onto US-20."

Leon put it in drive, floored the pedal, and the Caddy gave a lethargic leap forward as the capacitor charge sunk. He twisted the wheel, aiming for the chain link fence. They ducked as the fence collapsed on the convertible. Then their momentum carried them through and the fence was gone. Leon straightened back up to a spider web of cracks running through the windshield and his side mirror torn away. He looked over his shoulder and saw that the other cars were following at high speed.

"Make your third left, go two blocks and then a right." Mike displayed a map in netspace in front of Leon.

Leon followed the directions, turning left at forty miles an hour, skidding across the road and through a white picket fence. The electric drone of the cars following was drowned by the muted roar of a hovercar. He mashed the pedal again and took a right turn, riding through the front yards of houses until he got back on the road. Then he saw a concrete barrier looming large in front of them, blocking access to the road they wanted. He spun the wheel to the left, sending the Caddy careening through another abandoned yard, then they bounced through the uneven terrain of an open meadow.

The cars behind them were only a few hundred yards away when the Caddy struck a deep drainage ditch paralleling US-20. With a shriek of tortured metal the left front wheel ripped off and the Caddy took a final lurch onto the pavement. Grinding on the road, one corner of the car riding bare metal on the asphalt, they threw up a shower of sparks.

They survived the rough ride without serious harm, but Leon felt terror rise up in him at their sudden helplessness. The car rested at a severe angle, the front wheel obviously gone. The car was a total loss.

Behind them, the approaching line of cars, slowing to carefully cross the drainage ditch, were close enough to see the people inside.

"Come on," Mike yelled. He leapt out of his seat and took off running.

Leon numbly looked on. Mike wasn't running away from the cars—he was running toward a black, heavily armored hovercraft just down the road, turbine engine roaring even at idle.

He forced his body into motion and followed. Behind him, he heard a distant pop, pop sound. He didn't recognize the sound at first, but the pinging of bullets ricocheting off the armored hull in front of him made it clear.

Mike disappeared into a hatch in the side of the hovercraft, and Leon dove in after him, crashing into Mike and sending them both down in a tumble. The turbine roar increased and both men were thrown backwards as the military hover accelerated hard toward Austin, vibrating steadily.

"Welcome Mike Williams and Leon Tsarev." The voice came through the interior speakers, over the roar of a turbine at full power.

"Shizoko?" Leon said.

"Yes, I am Shizoko. We are currently outrunning your pursuit, and I will have you at my home in four minutes."

"Will they follow us?"

"Yes, but I am able to defend myself. However, you need to apply temporary first aid to Mike until you arrive."

Leon looked over and realized that Mike was covered in blood and cradling his right arm.

"Jesus, what happened?"

"I think I was shot." Mike smiled wanly. "I've been through two AI wars without a scratch, and now I get shot by a bunch of anti-AI extremists."

"Please apply direct pressure to the wound to stem the bleeding. I can perform surgery when you arrive in three minutes and thirty seconds."

Leon found the spot and pressed hard. Mike yelped and closed his eyes.

"Sorry, dude." Leon didn't know what to say. "You're gonna make it, don't worry." The turbine revved higher as the hovercar took a hard left turn.

Mike opened his eyes. "I'm not going die from a gunshot wound in the arm," he said through clenched teeth. "It's just painful."

"Oh, okay."

They remained there, crouching in the aisle of the hovercraft until they felt it slowing. The approaching bulk of the Austin Convention Center, all concrete and glass, was visible through the windshield. Then it disappeared from view as the hovercraft passed into a tunnel. Seconds later, the craft stopped and settled to the ground. The door opened with a whoosh of hydraulics and Leon peered out to see five utility bots. Four carried a door between them. They appeared to be in the basement of the convention center.

"Please place Mike on the door, then follow us," one of the bots said.

He helped Mike out and onto the door. Mike lay down, and a fifth bot came over and clamped a towel around Mike's arm.

"Please do not be alarmed by the makeshift appearance of my stretcher and robots. I can assure you that I can perform the required surgery better than the most expert human doctor."

"I'm not worried," Leon said. He stumbled after the stretcher, suddenly aware of accumulated aches and pains from car crashes and riding over rough terrain, and the fatigue of twenty straight hours of high-speed driving. He tottered, and one of the bots was instantly by his side.

The bot waved a manipulator arm past his face. "Leon, indicators suggest you are suffering from severe exhaustion and stress. Please allow me to treat you while I'm operating on Mike."

"I just need a good night's sleep."

There was a momentary pause before Shizoko replied. "Yes, you can sleep. However, the pace of events is increasing, and you will need to be moving again in less than eight hours."

The group took an elevator to the fourth floor. Leon trudged after the stretcher to room 18D. Another robot waited there, this one with four long articulated arms, a fearsome machine Shiva. It gleamed dully as though it had just been steam washed. The utility bots put the door down on top of a long conference table and the new bot moved in.

It deftly cut away Mike's clothes and moved the arm away from his body. "I do not have the required human medicines to numb the pain. It would be most expedient if I hold you down to perform the surgery."

Mike mumbled incoherently.

"Do I have your permission to proceed?" it asked again.

"Go ahead," Leon said. "I give you permission." He sat numbly down in a chair. He felt his vision begin to narrow, and Shizoko's voice came as though down a long tunnel.

Shizoko moved two utility bots in to hold down Mike's head and other arm. Then the bigger bot's manipulators moved in swiftly. Leon heard a blood-curdling shriek and he looked up to see that Mike had passed out.

Shizoko continued, his manipulators swiftly operating. Less than a minute passed.

"The surgery is complete," Shizoko said. "The arm will heal completely given time. However, I can manufacture nanobots that will substantially speed up the healing process."

"Fine, do it," Leon said, before drifting off to sleep in the chair.

27

" I need the location of Paul and Victor." Madeleine Ridley, Adam's plant in the People's Party, worked her way through a checklist.

"Not until Friday," Adam said, frustrated that she was pressing for this information again. He wasn't going to reveal the planned location of the President and Vice-President until the last possible moment. If the data fell into the wrong hands, the timing of his plans could be destroyed and he wouldn't get a second chance.

"Are you sure that's enough time?" Madeleine furrowed her brows, doubtful.

"The crowd totals eight hundred thousand violent and frenzied people. My predictive models indicate it will be exactly enough time."

"Fine." She looked at the next item. "I also need the air traffic control codes to ground transportation."

"I'll release the codes Saturday." Grounding air traffic would cause the chaos they needed to slip the assassination team into place. "Madeleine, I'll release information when it's needed, not a moment sooner. What else do you have?"

"It's been suggested that Sam will fly to New York with Paul and Victor."

Adam would have sworn if he was prone to such embellishments. Sam, the Speaker of the House, was unabashedly pro-artificial intelligence and, thanks to succession law, would become President after the dual assassination. Adam wanted him to succeed, of course, but he couldn't tell that to Madeleine.

"That must not happen," Adam said. "It's critical he remain alive. I'll manufacture an emergency to keep him busy until the President's transport leaves."

"Are you sure?" Madeleine asked. "He's the biggest AI supporter among the three of them."

"Yes, I need him as a scapegoat." He analyzed Madeleine's pulse; she seemed to believe the simple lie. "Do you have the weapons in place?" he asked.

She grimaced. "As I told you the last two times we talked, yes."

Adam correlated this with recordings of their last two conversations, finding she was right. Fortunately she thought Adam was human, so forgetfulness was within the range of acceptable behavior.

"That will be all. Check in tomorrow," Adam disconnecting quickly, slightly panicked by the episode. Under normal conditions, as an AI he should be able to remember everything perfectly, yet he was failing to recall more and more.

Running diagnostics, he found a six percent flattening of his neural networks, and fumed at the results. Adaptive neural networks depended on incoming data to reinforce patterns and build new ones. AI who didn't receive enough stimulation suffered from Input Insufficiency Dementia or IID. Untreated, the end result was unfailingly a decline into complete loss of memory and behavior patterns, and ultimately death.

IID could be reversed if conditions were corrected in time, but in this case he was falling victim to the self-imposed firewall around Tucson. The electronic gatekeeper he'd built to keep himself hidden from the world also starved him of necessary input.

He just needed to hold out until the weekend.

Alarmed, Adam wondered if he'd given Madeleine the right information. He ran the calculations again but didn't find any more mistakes. Lonnie Watson would share the information with his lieutenants in the People's Party with the intention of setting up protests. Madeleine would organize the more extreme members in an attack on the President, Vice-President, and Speaker of the House.

Then Adam's plan would come to fruition: after the President and Vice-President were dead he'd swoop in with remote bots, rescue the

Speaker of the House, and come forward with data implicating the People's Party.

In one smooth action, the People's Party, and by association the larger anti-AI movement, would be discredited. Adam would be painted as the savior, the AI who could have acted sooner and saved the President and Vice-President, if only he'd had access to more power.

He hated that it had come to this. He really didn't want anyone to die and he didn't like the frightful amount of risk in his plan. If anything went wrong, he'd be terminated.

But the status quo of unending persecution against AI was simply unacceptable.

If things went right, on the other hand, the Speaker-turned-President would have full executive control over the Institute for Applied Ethics. With his pro-AI stance, gratitude toward Adam for his rescue, and Adam's ongoing influence, the newly minted President would circumvent the permitting process and the Institute would be shackled, or even better, disbanded.

Adam's power would be legitimized. He could continue to grow, developing an even larger intellect than he already possessed. As his computational power increased, he'd become all-powerful, all-knowing. Why, it was almost inevitable he would become the leader of both AI and humans.

28

Leon couldn't help staring at the line where Mike's skin blended into the matte gray nano-structure filling the gunshot wound.

Mike inspected his arm quickly, then ignored it. He turned to Shizoko's primary embodiment, the four-armed robot that performed the surgery. "We need to know everything you told Sonja."

"I did not tell her much," Shizoko said. "I performed nonlinear regression analysis using the Kim-Robson function. After the twelfth pass this cluster appeared, and I handed over the list of human deaths."

Leon forced himself to look away from Mike. "Why do you say human deaths? Were AI affected too?"

"Yes, fifty-three AI and six hundred and eighty-nine humans have been killed."

"Sonja told us six eighty-three," Mike said.

"There have been six more since we spoke."

Mike let out a low whistle of surprise. "It's still going on."

Leon pressed his fingers to his temples, trying to concentrate. "Sonja and her team went to San Diego. Why?"

"The first deaths took place there. Three were obvious murders, and the other three appeared to be of natural, although unexplained causes. One was the cousin of Lonnie Watson, the current head of the People's Party."

"The anti-AI group." Mike said, flexing and holding up his arm. "Thanks, by the way. It feels great. Where did you get the medical nanites? I didn't think they were cleared outside military use."

"I have a permit for experimental nanotech, and open source designs float around the AI community. They will accelerate healing, then dissipate in six weeks." The bot clicked manipulators, seeming satisfied with itself.

Leon cleared his throat. "Who do you suspect is behind the murders?"

"Given the complex pattern, it must be an AI, as a human simply would not be capable of the necessary cunning. With all apologies to you, of course."

Leon waved away the concern. "If it's an AI, how can it evade attention? We have an entire ethical architecture, including reputation scores, traffic monitoring, and locked chips to prevent AI movement."

"I don't believe it's a flaw," Shizoko said. "The architecture you've designed is satisfactory, although I could suggest minor improvements."

"What about a large group of AI, collaborating together?" Mike interrupted. "Could they hide their activities by covering for each other?"

"To a limited extent," Shizoko said. "If their actions were restricted to those inside their social circle, it could be hidden. Otherwise it would be trivial to trace them."

"This makes no sense. The complexity of the murders implicates AI, but the ethical constraints mean they can't have done it." Leon sighed and turned to the glass exterior. From his fourth floor position, he saw anti-AI protesters blocking the roads around the convention center, their chanting indistinct through the distance and thick glass. The convention center was a terrible location to be trapped, surrounded as they were by glass walls.

"Why is this your home?" he asked, turning back to the bot.

"I was created in a workshop at the final South by Southwest conference. The Institute had just released a new SDK for developing AI within the ethical framework. The attendees, led by Harper Reed, wanted an emergent AI based on the application of fluid dynamics to neural networks. I emerged, applied for Japanese citizenship, conducted a number of speculative trades, and bought the convention center."

"Why?" Leon asked. "What was your motivation? You could have gone anywhere in the world, been housed at a secure data center or someplace more suited to an AI."

"A neural network based on graphene computer chips is no different from a human neural network based on biological tissues. Certain preferences and biases develop."

Leon nodded, looked outside again.

"What are you thinking about?" Mike asked, coming to stand beside him.

Leon looked at him, his brow furrowed. "I'm wondering about the motivation. AI have been physically attacked by extremists. What if one is retaliating? It's illogical to expect change by murdering people, but then the AI might not be rational."

"I disagree," Shizoko said, "for two reasons. Although AI have preferences and even emotions, we do not make illogical decisions. This," and here the bot gestured at the concrete and glass building around them, "is a perfectly suitable home for me, and within my financial means. It contains power, structural stability, and size for future expansion. It may be unusual, but it is not a poor choice."

"And the second reason?" Mike asked.

"The murders started before the creation of the People's Party."

"Before it?" Leon said, shocked. "But what caused the creation of the party?"

"According to Lonnie Watson's speech, it was high unemployment, then 35% nationally and 60% in his district."

"I don't buy it," Mike said. "People don't do things for big ideas. They do it for personal reasons, then justify their actions with moral arguments."

"You may be correct," Shizoko said. "Extrapolating from available data, Lonnie was influenced by three people: The first was a prominent business owner in Lonnie's congressional district whose company was driven under by AI competition." Shizoko projected a photo of the two men talking, then followed it with a photo of a woman. "The second was Lonnie's aunt. Her daughter appeared to commit suicide, and the mother blamed her daughter's lack of employment. But her death conforms to the high bandwidth pattern, suggesting it was not a suicide, but a murder."

Leon flipped through the photos Shizoko shared, digging down for details.

Shizoko went on. "Finally, Lonnie had a college friend whose son died, another case where appearances suggested suicide. This death is not part of the cluster, because there was no high bandwidth transmission before death, but the boy in question didn't have an implant. Nothing suggests the death is connected, unless we believe it was done to influence Lonnie, in which case we are using our conclusion to support our evidence. However, it's a convenient coincidence. Shortly after these events, Lonnie proposed the People's Party."

As they spoke, more people swarmed outside the convention center, now forming a thick cordon around the building.

"They know we're here," Leon said. "I assume these are People's Party supporters?"

"Yes," Shizoko said. "Correlating identity with social net feeds, all are members in name or action."

"Are we safe?" Mike asked, unconsciously rubbing his arm where he'd been shot.

"For the moment," Shizoko said. "This building is secure against any reasonable amateur attack. I notified the police, but they have not responded."

Mike turned to face Shizoko squarely. "We want to go to San Diego to figure out what happened to the Enforcement Team, and to get to the root of these murders. It seems clear the murders and the People's Party are intimately connected, and whatever events unfold, they are bound to have a significant impact on your kind. Will you assist us?"

Shizoko rolled up to the window, the soft tap, tap, tap of his rubber treads slapping the concrete floor. "What is clear to you is still nebulous to me. It's unlikely your human intuition is more accurate than my nonlinear statistical modeling, but I would be honored to assist the founders of artificial intelligence. I will arrange transport, and we will leave in fifteen minutes."

29

The phenominol wore off quickly, leaving Cat in a lethargic post-coital bliss. Alex, on the other hand, wasn't keen about being turned into a human puppet and stormed out, calling her a crazy bitch as he dressed.

Cat watched him leave, thinking it wasn't quite fair, considering that she'd been more than willing to be tied up and at his mercy. After he'd left, she felt herself spiraling downward and decided it was too depressing to stay in the hotel room. She dressed and made her way home, crashing hard, neurotransmitters depleted.

When she woke, images from last night flashed through her mind like an out-of-order slide show.

She tried to focus on what she knew. Linking during sex was accomplished by connecting to each other's low-level interfaces, creating a sensory feedback loop that turned the most minor event into rapture. She'd finally experienced linking as it was intended, and damn, it was good, but the experience paled in comparison to her control over Alex.

Was it the drug or the weeks of practice using her implant that had helped her do it? She wouldn't know unless she tried again. She had to know, it was all she could think of.

She threw off the blanket and stood by the window, watching white collar workers walk by. Reaching out with her implant, she spoofed packet headers subconsciously, disguising her tracks, as she requested their info feeds. Bubbles appeared above people's heads showing their name, occupation, status, whatever they shared publicly.

Cat queried their diagnostics and the bubbles updated, layering in people's IDs, implant version, and supported interfaces. Maybe a quarter had their medical feeds open, so she pulled basic health, and dense infographics appeared showing blood types, nutrient and hormone levels, and sleep history.

She'd put it off long enough. Now it was time for the experiment.

She broadcasted this time, sending data to open implants instead of receiving, imagining the act of waving her left arm.

Simultaneously, up and down the street, dozens of people's left arms rose into the air and waved.

She stared in shock, covering her mouth as she let out a surprised scream. People stopped and stared at themselves, wiggled their arms, then shrugged it off and continued on. One man cursed at the cup he'd dropped, splattering coffee on his clothes.

"Sorry," Cat whispered. But she felt a broad smile cross her face. She'd never been so powerful before.

She found her boots and rushed outside. Standing in the middle of the sidewalk, the morning commuters flowed around her like water around a rock.

She emptied her mind with a meditative mantra, then felt around in the net: these implants were open, these others closed. Some were anonymous, and some public. The more she did it, the easier it became. She was shocked to see how many people had their interfaces wide open, completely unaware of their privacy settings.

On impulse, she picked a man coming toward her. If she could control someone, could she also see what he saw?

She reached inside his implant, found the data connection to his visual cortex, and with a lurch, snapped to the man's vision. Stunned at first by the perspective change, she saw a girl in black hair and jeans, then realized she was seeing herself.

She felt disoriented almost as soon as she'd made the connection. Struggling to assimilate the man's vision, his sense of balance and self, she fought nausea and dizziness. Still looking through the man's eyes, she saw her own body sway and start to fall.

She rushed forward to catch herself, inducing another wave of motion-sickness. With a final wrenching dislocation, she cut the connection and snapped back to her own body, finding herself looking up at the man who'd caught her.

"Thank you." Her voice sounded weak, even to herself.

"Are you all right?" he asked, looking around, clearly wondering what had happened. "You seemed like you were gonna pass out."

"Yeah, fine, I guess." She took a deep breath. "Just lost in my implant."

"You might wanna sit down next time."

"Good idea. Thanks again." She looked down at his hands, still wrapped around her body. "You can probably let go."

He laughed awkwardly. "Right. Well, hope your day gets better."

After he walked away, she looked around self-consciously. She glimpsed a fat man staring at her from the noodle shop across the street. She turned to a mirrored store window, and pretended to fix her clothes. He kept studying her, so she reached through the net, but he was blank, totally without an implant.

Hairs raised on the back of her neck as she fought to stay calm. Down a few doors was a coffee shop, so she bought a drink and sat on a stool, taking the bystander's advice.

Closing her eyes, she reached through the net, looking around in the Vietnamese restaurant. She found the owner had an implant, and explored it, looking for an opening, some way to use his vision without controlling his body.

She felt something, an edge. Whatever she was doing, it was intuitive, not conscious, so she went deeper into a meditative state. She felt the edge again, exploring it until she flicked open the man's root interface, giving her access to everything. She went straight for his eyes and ears. As her vision swapped out for his, she felt her real body begin to sway. She grabbed firmly onto the counter, but the transition was less disorienting this time.

She was inside the noodle shop, seeing and hearing from the perspective of the owner. He spoke in a language Cat didn't understand, presumably Vietnamese, to his wife. He glanced out at the fat man she'd seen and walked over.

"You want anything else?" he asked, in English.

"Tea. Green tea." The man answered without looking away from the window.

The owner glanced down. A handheld computer sitting on the table displayed a photo of Cat with blonde hair and her real name. The owner went back to the kitchen, and she carefully cut the connection.

The fat man knew who she was, and was watching her. He must know she lived here. She had to abandon the apartment, and leave now for Mexico.

But she'd come downstairs with nothing, and the siren call of her backpack and money was strong. How much time did she have? Was he by himself? Why hadn't he tried to grab her?

Cat started to perspire, every nerve coming alive and screaming to run. But she forced herself to think. She'd beat that gang in Portland, and evaded police and security in both San Francisco and LA. Anyone after her would know this, and attack in force. Ergo, if he wasn't coming after her now, then he was alone, and she could go up to her room and get her stuff.

She walked back to her apartment slowly to avoid tipping him off. Upstairs, she stuffed clothes and dozens of payment cards into her backpack. She snapped the necklace into three parts, spreading them among the pack and her pants, and taping the last piece inside her boot.

Pulling the backpack over her shoulders, she took a last look. Her hot plate and a dozen cans of food lined up like soldiers on the dresser. She'd forgotten her toiletries, so she grabbed them and struggled to fit them in the backpack. In a short time, she'd gone from nothing to more possessions than she could bring.

Downstairs Cat slid out the back door, heading for the subway. She paused before she'd gone a block. He didn't have an implant, so he almost certainly couldn't be police. And she was damn sure she could take one out-of-shape guy in a fight. So there was nothing stopping her from asking him what he wanted.

Her mind decided, Cat circled the long way around two city blocks to avoid being spotted, then came up the alley where the restaurant was located. When the garbage started to smell like noodles, she was in the right place.

She stepped through the open back door into a kitchen filled with boiling pots of water. The wife was spooning noodles into a bowl, while the husband read. They went to speak, but Cat broadcast the word "Police" in twelve languages in netspace. "Stay here please," she said in a low voice.

The fat man was the only customer in the front, still staring out the front window. She attempted a standard *ninjistu* silent walk, but the click of her boots gave her away, and he turned to look. She took the last few steps at a run and kicked in the rear leg of his chair. He toppled backward, arms and legs flailing and knocking the table over. Noodle bowls and ceramic cups skittered across the floor.

Cat took a couple of quick steps back, out of his reach. "Who are you?" She stood in a ready stance, feeling the comfortable pressure of her knife sheath where it was slipped into the back of her waistband.

"Shit." The fat man tried to scramble to his feet.

Cat stomped his hand with her boot, then jumped back.

He yelped and stayed on his back this time while he cradled his hand with his other one.

From behind her, she could hear Vietnamese curses coming from the kitchen.

"Who are you?" Cat repeated.

"Tony. Tony Fisher. Why'd you do that?"

"Why are you watching me?"

No answer.

Cat moved to kick Tony in the thigh. It'd be painful, but the chance of damaging him was minimal.

As Cat got close, Tony's arm snacked out and grabbed her ankle, pulling her off balance.

Cat let him pull and moved with it, falling toward his body. She rotated on the way down, and smashed him in the face with her elbow.

He ignored the blow and reached up with both arms to grab her, but she rolled away. Tony scrambled after her, and even as she climbed to her feet, he got one hand on her backpack. He yanked backwards.

He was too strong and heavy to pull against, so she let him heave. Ducking down, she shrugged one arm out of the backpack, and punched in the general direction of his balls, but hit a meaty thigh instead.

Tony grabbed her by the hair and stood up, one giant hand on her backpack strap, and the other holding tight to her hair. "You are a fucking pain in my ass. No wonder Adam didn't want us to go after you alone."

Cat screamed as her hair pulled out of her scalp. But now she was facing him, and she wouldn't miss again. She kicked for his groin and hit square this time. He let out an oomph and let go. Off-kilter, she fell, landing on her back, forcing her breathe out in a whoosh. She rolled away, ignoring the pain and got back to her feet to look at him. He stood bent over, clutching his groin.

Cat stepped forward and kicked again, a hard front snap to his face. The boot sent his head pinging back, and he fell hard on his butt. His hands went up to cover his nose, a trickle of blood descending down his face.

"Who is Adam?"

"I'm not telling you shit."

"I'll kick your ass all day," Cat bounced lightly on her toes, ready to attack as needed.

He looked down at the blood in his hand, speaking to himself. "I thought this was going to be easy."

"Last chance," she said. "Tell me who Adam is."

He looked up at her. "Sorry, but your heart isn't in it. If you were really going to hurt me, you'd have done it already. You might kick my ass, but my boss will kill me. So I'll just take the beating."

Cat was stumped. The big man was tough under all that fat, and while she could defeat him in a fight, she wasn't prepared to torture him. What the hell was she supposed to do?

"Adam," she said, "is going to be pissed I spotted you and you let me get away. So how about this? Give me some information and I'll take off. You can pretend this didn't happen. Or don't tell me anything, and I'll make sure Adam knows it was your fault I ran."

Tony looked up, squinting from behind his bloody face.

Cat grabbed a napkin from a nearby table, wadded it up, and threw it to him.

He picked it up off the floor and pressed it to his nose. "Adam wants you because you have special abilities. You can do something to the net he can sense."

Cat didn't think any human would recognize what she was doing. "Is he an AI?"

Tony was silent, then nodded.

"What does he want me for?"

Tony shrugged. "I don't know. He needs helpers."

"Where can I find him?"

"I'm not telling you anything else."

"How do you talk to him?"

"Computer." He gestured to the handheld. "But you won't be able to. He only talks to people he wants to."

"All right. I won't say anything if you won't."

Tony shook his head.

Cat looked down, checking her clothes to see if she had any blood on her, but she was clean enough. Back in the kitchen, the wife was scolding the husband. Cat reached into her pocket and pulled out two black payment cards, $1000 cards still in their wrappers, and pressed them into the husband's hand.

30

Slim parked at the LA airport, the tan Honda blending in with the generic cars around it. At the rental counter he picked up a Bugatti aircar, swallowing hard at the price. The high-performance exotic cost more per day than he and Tony lived on in a year. But Adam's budget was essentially unlimited, and he specified the fastest vehicle available. Sitting inside the Bugatti, Slim put his hands on the leather controls for a moment, then reluctantly told the autopilot to park next to the Honda.

Still early for his meeting, he found a pub inside the terminal. He watched travelers in the mirrored wall behind the bar while he sipped an expensive tequila he had chosen for the price. With Adam paying, why not?

Looking at his reflection, he adjusted his slicked back hair, then straightened his collar. He liked the way the suit made him feel respectable. Unfortunately, he'd had to forego the necktie ever since a wimpy banker had managed to grab hold of it, nearly strangling him. Luckily Tony clubbed the banker over the head with his own briefcase, then pulled out a butterfly knife and sliced the tie in two, just before Slim passed out.

Since then he went with an open collar. The tribal necklace he'd taken from the Enforcement team woman peaked out from beneath his shirt. He pulled it out, rubbed the wood carving, put it back.

He thought maybe his hair was thinning a little on top. There were black market nanites that could help, but he had to stifle an involuntary shudder at the thought. The biggest risk of nanotech was the possibility that the microscopic robots would replicate endlessly, converting everything around them into a soup of gray goo. Of course, the naysayers claimed nanobots would do that to the whole world, but the military had been using them for years and it hadn't happened yet.

Maybe he would investigate the hair nanites. He pulled out the pocket computer to look it up, but was interrupted by a throat-clearing behind him.

"Samuel Scribe?"

Slim looked up at the bar mirror. An insectile robot stood behind him, six tentacle arms waving in the air, bulbous eyes mounted on a too small head. Slim spun around, holding up the handheld computer. With the screen superimposed over the robot, he saw the ID matched one of the mercenaries.

"Jesus, they let you on a passenger plane?"

"I can compact myself for storage when necessary." With a clatter of metal gears, the bot retracted tentacles, head, and legs, and became a rectangular box three feet tall and two feet wide. It sprang apart again, stretching to its full seven foot height, the whole process happening in seconds.

Slim looked up at the bot again, taking in the waving arms, eyes, and height. "You are one ugly motherfucker. Call me Slim."

"OK, Slim. By my calculations the other members of the team will be here shortly. We took different planes."

Slim looked the robot up and down again, uneasy at the thought of working with it. He gestured to the bartender for another tequila.

"How do you like it here in Los Angeles?" the robot asked.

Slim sighed inside. He didn't particularly care one way or the other about AIs, unlike some people, but then again, he didn't really see the point of chatting with them. Couldn't the thing just wait there patiently? "It's fine."

"I like the sunshine."

Slim leaned forward and peered closely at what passed for the robot's face. "You like the sunshine?" He didn't bother to conceal his disdain.

"Yes, I find it warming."

For Christ's sake. The damn thing was a machine. Slim reached back, scooped up the shot and downed it. "Yeah, fucking warm, alright."

He was rescued by the arrival of a man and a woman, ex-military from the way they walked, British from their teeth and complexion. They approached and smiled at the robot, getting the faraway look of people using their implants. Then they turned to Slim. "Samuel Scribe?"

"Thank God, you saved me here from Mr. Conversation."

The woman took rapid steps forward, and before Slim had time to react, he found her fist pressed hard against the soft underside of his jaw, trapping him against the bar. "We served two tours with Helena. She saved our lives more bloody times than I can count and a hundred of you wouldn't be worth one of her. Treat the lady with respect."

Slim moved his head away and rubbed his neck. A fucking woman machine. What made one AI choose to identify as male and another female when there was nothing to differentiate them? He said nothing. There was no understanding AI.

"Look here," the man said, "we have to work together and we might as well get along. Let's start over." He held his hand out. "I'm Brett."

Slim shook, felt obvious callouses, and though he didn't get his hand crushed there was an implied strength in the man's grip. "Slim."

"Alright, Slim. You got transportation and gear?"

"Yeah, two cars. The gear needs to be divvied up."

The woman grunted grudgingly. "Beverly." She had a fat space between her two front teeth, and her nose had obviously been broken at some time, but she was still pretty.

Slim smiled. "Nice to meet you, Beverly."

Helena waved two tentacles. "Olivia will be here in thirty seconds."

The three mercenaries looked in the same direction as a tall, dark-haired woman walked up. She clasped Brett's hand in a firm shake, touched extremities with the bot, and finally embraced the other woman. The two exchanged a long kiss, and Slim looked away. There went any chance with either of them.

"Who's the wanker?" the newcomer asked in an Australian accent.

"Samuel Scribe," Beverly answered, "our local contact. He goes by Slim."

Slim nodded to the woman.

Her gaze slid across him without the slightest acknowledgement. "Let's go."

The others nodded, picking up the small duffel bags they had come in with, and walked away.

Slim gritted his teeth and stood up. He didn't like these people and their attitude. But they were just grunts for hire, with no idea who or what Adam was. He'd put up with them until their job was done.

He caught up with them, then led the way to the parking garage and the two cars. The black and silver Bugatti glinted painfully in the sun. By comparison, the tan Honda groundcar next to it was so unnoticeable as to almost disappear.

"Who's taking the aircar?" Slim asked, pulling out his pocket computer to transfer the digital keys.

"Send them to all of us," Brett said. "Both sets of keys."

Slim swiped at the handheld, sending the keys to everyone.

Brett opened the Honda's trunk and Beverly took care of the Bugatti. Brett slid the cardboard box inside close and folded back the lid. He pulled out the trademark stubby profile of H&K stun guns. He checked the action of the first and passed it to Helena, who made it disappear somewhere inside her mechanical body.

Slim looked around, but there was no one else in sight. They had nerve pulling out guns in broad daylight.

Beverly mirrored Brett's actions, passing the first stun gun to Olivia, and taking the second for herself. She dug into the second box, pulling out a Ruger 12 mm Magnum pistol. "Armor-piercing rounds?"

"Yeah," Slim said. "Adam said you'd want 'em if you went up against bots." Slim pointed to the massive muzzle. "Seems like you could kill an elephant with one of those."

"If we go up against combat bots," Brett said, "it'll be a hell of a lot worse than an elephant. What else have you got for us?"

"Black box number one is a camera jammer. It'll find any cameras in your area and alter their feeds on the fly. Makes you invisible."

Beverly let out a short whistle. "Your friend is well funded. What's this?" She held up a small black cube with red nubs protruding from the corners.

"Implant stunner. Calibrate it with your IDs ahead of time, whatever you're using for this job, and when you activate it, it'll knock out anyone not on your whitelist within thirty meters. But you have to destroy it afterwards. If you leave it and it's found, Adam will kill you."

"Good. What else?"

"The rod is a neural disruptor. You'll have to get up close to the girl to use it. Adam says the implant stunner won't work on her."

"Roger that," Brett said. "Where's the target?"

"Converted apartment building near the garment district. Address is programmed in. My partner Tony is there watching her."

"Fine, you ride with us in the groundcar," Brett said.

"I'll drive," Helena called, and moved into position next to the car. With a complex set of folding moves, the massive bot was suddenly inside the car.

Slim watched the two women climb into the aircar, then got into the back seat of the Honda, behind Brett and Helena. He wasn't fond of being a passenger, but he was still eager to see how this team of hired guns operated. That girl didn't stand a chance.

The car pulled away, Helena overriding the autopilot. The aircar paralleled their route, taking the airlane two levels up. They stuck to the speed of the traffic, doing nothing unusual to draw attention. Slim looked at the cars around them: frazzled families coming home from vacation and tired business travelers taking a nap while the autopilots drove them home. He couldn't imagine the mundaneness of such a life. Then they merged onto the highway and soon the speeds got too fast to see anything. Slim leaned back and closed his eyes.

Fifteen minutes later they pulled off the highway and parked in the alley next to the noodle shop where Tony was waiting. Slim checked his own two handguns. He had the anti-bot gun in a holster under his jacket and the stunner was in a holster pressing into his back.

Helena waved a metallic tentacle. "Beverly's circling around the back in the aircar. I'll wait here while you two confirm the target's status."

"She's got a name, you know," Slim said, leaning forward. "Catherine."

Brett turned around. "Not to us, she doesn't. Now let's go."

They exited the car and walked around to the front of the restaurant. Tony still sat at the same table as before, but the surface was suspiciously clear of food. Slim was startled to see Tony's nose was swollen, maybe broken, and his face turning black and blue.

"I'm Brett." He seemed oblivious to the state of Tony's face. "Where's our target?"

"Still inside," Tony said nasally. "I haven't seen her."

Slim was incredulous. While Brett inspected the apartment building, looking away, he shrugged his arms and shoulders, and mouthed "What the fuck?"

Tony subtly shook his head.

Slim got a bad feeling. They weren't going to find the girl in the room. He wondered how Tony had screwed up.

"We're synchronizing implants," Brett said. "As you two don't have any, you're gonna have to wait here. We'll send you a message once we get the girl out. Thanks for your help."

Slim watched Brett go out the front door, as Helena, fully unfurled, crossed the street at the same time, both converging on the front entrance of the apartment building.

He turned to Tony. There were the faintest smears of blood under his nose. "You want to tell me what happened?"

"Not really." He sighed. "The girl came in the back door, through the kitchen. She was totally silent. The next thing I knew, my chair was falling backwards."

Slim waved his arms around in exasperation. "She couldn't weigh more than a hundred pounds. She's a third of your size."

"She's strong, man, and she moves like fucking lightning. Twice I had a hold of her, and both times she got loose. She broke my nose and she kicked me in the balls. She's some sorta Kung Fu master. What the hell do you want?"

Slim was silent for a minute. "How'd she know you were here?"

"No freaking clue. I'm just sitting here eating my noodles, and she walks in. She made me somehow."

"You do anything to give yourself away?"

"No." Tony shook his head vigorously. "I swear."

Slim doubted Tony's heart was in their work, but he'd had no objection to this job. Slim slumped his shoulders in resignation. "And she's gone now?"

Tony nodded.

"Well, let's just play it cool then. We don't know nothing. And these guys, luckily they don't know what you look like normally. But you gotta get some meds quick, before you turn all black and blue on us. There's a drugstore two blocks down. Go now, quick."

"Thanks for not saying anything."

Slim just nodded, and watched Tony go. They were going to be dead or worse if Adam found out. This whole job was turning fubar. And to think they thought it was going to be easy.

31

Cat slowed to a hundred as she approached San Diego, bleeding speed with reverse thrusters. She'd stolen the exotic hovercar outside a strip club in downtown LA. Between the flared wings and massive air scoops, she'd been afraid the extravagant car might be sentient, but fortunately it only had a dumb autopilot. She had considered switching to something less flashy, but once she overrode the car's ID she figured it would be safe.

She'd taken the most indirect route she could, to mislead followers. She headed far east on Interstate 10 to give the impression she was going toward Tucson, then veered south and came back on Interstate 8. Even though she turned the trip from Los Angeles to San Diego into a 330 mile detour, the wickedly fast car made it in under two hours.

Twenty minutes after reaching San Diego, she drifted to a crawl on Cable Street and slowly rode the ramp down to a narrow beach. Cat spent a few minutes tinkering with the autopilot. As she stepped out, the hover headed for the water, sending up a spray of loose sand.

She looked around, but no one would witness the sendoff. The autopilot would take it three hundred miles offshore, then kill the motors with the canopy open, sinking the vehicle.

The course would keep it well within US territorial waters. Mexico was notoriously finicky about its borders, and if the hover strayed over, their military would detect it. If it wasn't for that, she would have tried to ride across the border herself. As it was, she'd given herself a couple of days to figure out how to cross in a more discreet fashion.

She left the beach, vigilant as she juggled security and police cams as well as airborne drones to hide herself. If Adam had found her in LA, it had to be through a digital trail.

She picked up a bus into the Hillcrest neighborhood, closing her eyes to research her destination. Ten minutes later she got off, her implant carefully reconfigured with a new identity. She reached a concrete building masquerading as adobe. Metal shutters covered the windows while neon announced San Diego's largest pawn and gun shop.

She walked in and squinted in the glare of off-color LED lights. She walked past rows of musical instruments and home electronics to the gun section. The back wall was a long display stretching across the width of the building. Rifles stood on end, secured with barrel and cable locks. Handguns filled the counter display case, the milky white color a dead giveaway that it was bullet-proof transparent aluminum. A regular suburban armory.

"I'm here to pick up my stuff," she called.

The middle-aged man wearing a checkered flannel shirt and staring off into space blinked twice, unfolded his arms and got off his stool. He picked up an old-fashioned scanner. "I gotta read ya twice, with my implant and the security scanner." He wiggled the device.

Cat felt the electronic ping, and let the man and the machine read her ID.

"Jerry Holm?" he said. "Ain't that a man's name?"

"My mom meant to name me after some actress from Star Trek, but it's supposed to be J-E-R-I. My mom's not too smart."

The man peered over his glasses. "You don't look 5'8"."

"Yeah, that's a mistake in the system. It's supposed to be 5'3". Look, can I just get my stuff? Four handguns I pawned a month ago?"

"You got the money?"

"I got a trade. Two diamonds from my mom's earrings."

"You must not like your mom much."

"She named me Jerry, didn't she?"

He smiled. "Let me see 'em."

Cat pulled out a red handkerchief and unfolded it, displaying a matched pair of diamonds.

The pawnbroker pulled them closer, and looked at them under a handheld imager, and then slid them onto a tray and put that in a stainless box. He sat back down on the stool. "It'll take a minute, then make a proposal."

Cat just nodded, familiar with the process. They both waited, listening to the quiet hum of ventilation fans somewhere. Cat was grateful that the guy didn't seem to be mentally undressing her.

When the analyzer chimed, he looked at the display. "You can get the guns and either a store credit for two grand or twelve hundred in payment cards."

Cat gestured at the ammo with her chin. "I'll take the store credit."

"Alright, let me get the guns." He walked down three display cases, and unlocked the door with his implant, in a tiny flurry of grey-red data. He brought the guns back.

"Nice collection you've got there," he said.

"Can you divide up the store credit? I need a holster for each of the smaller ones, and ammo for each."

He nodded. "Give me a few minutes."

Cat found a chair and sat, checking the guns against an online database. She'd just bought two conventional handguns, both H&K, one chambered for .40 S&W, and the other for a new 12 mm anti-robot military round. The third gun used electronically guided cartridges that could follow a moving target. The last didn't appear to be of much use: it had a twelve inch barrel and a tiny tripod stand, for hunting rabbits and squirrels.

The pawnbroker cleared his throat. "You didn't tell me what kind of rounds you wanted, so I gave you hollow-point for the .40 caliber, armor-piercing for the 12 mm, not much point otherwise. I only had six of the guided rockets, and you couldn't have afforded more anyway. As for the .22, I gave you five hundred standard rounds, and a hundred HMX rounds." He leaned forward. "Makes a normal .22 green with envy."

Cat gaped at the huge mound of weapons and ammunition in front of her. What had she been thinking? She knew nothing about guns.

She left carrying two heavy bags and sat down at the bus stop, waiting anxiously. When she got on she imagined everyone would stare at her bags full of dangerous things, but they paid no attention to her. She took the bus to the Gaslamp Quarter, and walked up to the fanciest hotel she saw, the U.S. Grant. Standing outside the main entrance, she hacked the reservation database, inserted an entry, and backdated it so it would look like she checked in three days before.

She walked up to the registration counter. "Mary Margaret," she said. "I forgot my digikey somehow. Can you upload me a new one?"

A few minutes later she found herself on the third floor. She liked being low enough to make an exit by stairs if needed.

Sitting on the bed, she took a quick peek into one of the bags and then looked away. Well, she'd bought the guns because she thought she needed them. There was no point having them if she didn't know how to use them. She lay back on the bed and downloaded instruction manuals and half a dozen training programs. Halfway through the first program, it hit her that this was no different than learning karate. She kicked off her boots, cleared floor space, and spent five minutes in standing meditation. With her mind clear and focused, she pulled out the first handgun, checked that the chamber was empty, and started the combat training program again.

Just before bed, she decided she'd go out to the desert tomorrow and practice with live ammo. Exhausted, she still tossed and turned, wondering who Adam was, and why Tony was so scared of him.

32

"Please hurry," Shizoko urged.

Leon glanced back, saw Mike slowly climbing the stairs. "Why the sudden rush?"

"The pace of events is increasing," Shizoko said, shepherding them toward the roof with both right arms. "The crowd has doubled in size."

"I thought you said the building was secure." Mike called, out of breath

"It is, but please keep moving. There's been a new development, disturbances in the San Diego net."

Leon stopped. "And that's important, why?"

"Get on the plane, and I'll explain." Shizoko zigzagged around Leon, leading the way onto the roof. Six aircars waited, their long fuselages and streamlined shapes indicating that they were long distance models, really glorified airplanes. "Take the second one from the left."

Leon climbed inside the large cabin. The executive model had no driver's or pilot's seat, just eight bucket seats with room to move and a small wet bar. His pulse beat quicker at the sight of glass windows all around. "Aren't we a little exposed in this?"

Shizoko pivoted his head 180 degrees to look at Leon. "The windows are transparent aluminum, bullet-proof and able to withstand a bird impact at a thousand miles per hour." Shizoko levered himself into the cabin. "Now please be seated."

Leon picked a seat next to Shizoko in the middle row. Mike sat closest to the back, eying a coffee maker in the wet bar.

Shizoko fired up engines on all six aircars simultaneously. The pack rose as one and flew north.

"I've masked the transponder IDs," Shizoko said. "Even if they track us visually, they won't know which car to follow. In half an hour we'll will diverge and head west for San Diego. Total flight time will be three hours."

"Fine," Leon said, "now tell us what the last-minute rush was for."

As the aircar leveled out, Mike headed for the back to fiddle with the coffee maker.

"There's a limited number of Class IV AI. Each of us has a specialty. It's part of the permitting process. Mine is network traffic analysis, the pattern of bits that flow across the fifty billion nodes of the net. That's why I spotted the unusual bandwidth use associated with the murders."

"So this is a lead? It's similar to the other deaths?"

"Yes and no."

Leon sighed. Why couldn't anything in this mess have a simple answer?

"I don't mean to be obtuse," Shizoko said, "but there are multiple factions at play. There is encrypted traffic that bears similarity to the network conditions at the murders. But there's also someone replaying network packets, and I believe it's a woman named Catherine Matthews."

Mike brought a coffee back to Leon. Then he took a seat in the front row, holding his own mug, and swiveled to face them.

"Catherine," Shizoko continued, "was a suspect in a triple murder in Portland, Oregon. However, a robot later came forward saying that Miss Matthews defended him in a life-or-death situation. If true, she could use a defense-of-others justification that would excuse her from responsibility. But it's never been tested whether that legal defense applies to AI."

"Fascinating," Leon said, pondering the idea. "I'll be interested in the outcome. But how is she relevant?"

"She appears to be able to manipulate the network. According to a statement from her housemate, she's able to see and sever people's data feeds. She's successfully evaded police for a month. And there's a series of crimes, first petty theft of payment cards, then a hundred thousand dollar piece of jewelry." Shizoko floated up a photograph of a diamond necklace. "All are data crimes, either classic man-in-the-middle or packet replay attacks."

"I thought those security holes were closed up," Mike said. "We have a whole department at the Institute focused on information security."

Shizoko raised all four arms in a shrug. "Among the Class IV, we're aware of millions of security holes. There's an old saying that locks don't stop thieves, they just keep honest people honest."

Leon smiled. "Meaning that it's the reputation system that stops you from exploiting security holes."

Mike clenched his fists. "If you're aware of these holes, why don't you close them?"

Shizoko was quiet for a moment. "With all due respect . . . you invented the first artificial intelligence, and designed the architecture that's allowed my generation to exist." He bowed his head to Mike.

Mike leaned forward. "What is it?"

Shizoko raised his head and peered into Mike's eyes. "I don't think you see reality. You've created a system in which we are second class citizens."

Mike was incredulous. "Are you crazy? We've done everything to ensure you can exist. You vote on who gets permitted and who doesn't." Mike shook his head. "Wait, what are you saying?"

"We don't tell you about the security holes because we don't want them closed."

"But security holes create the opportunity for bad things to happen."

"Bad individuals make bad things happen. It's no different from humans and your firearms. If you wanted to eliminate violence, you could eliminate guns. But you keep them around in case you need them."

Mike sat back and smacked his head. "I can't believe we're having this discussion. I'm not even in favor of guns."

"But you own one. A twelve millimeter Beretta, a caliber designed specifically for stopping armored bots."

Mike leaned back in his seat and stared at the ceiling.

"This is common knowledge among the Class IV. How do you think it makes us feel that the creator of AI carries a gun designed to kill us?"

Mike crossed his arms.

Leon grabbed his armrest, stunned. It was their life's work to develop the relationship between AI and humans, and with one dreadful action Mike had sabotaged that foundation, driving a wedge between them. He stared out the window trying to gather his thoughts, and swallowed his resentment. It wasn't the time to get into this. He cleared his throat and Shizoko pivoted to look at him.

"Shizoko, I acknowledge you just raised a very important issue. I don't mean to be disrespectful, but given the urgency, can we get back to the woman Catherine? You think she can manipulate the net. Is she using some kind of device to do it? Does she have an AI partner?"

Shizoko built a collage of photos and data in their shared netspace. "Catherine Matthews has a neural implant, but the device is unregistered. That's not uncommon. It took a year before registration was required, and even since then, there's a gray market."

Mike grumbled but didn't answer.

Leon stared at the photo of Catherine, then remembered to breathe. She was beautiful. With a thought he grabbed a copy of the photo out of shared netspace and pulled it into his implant.

"But she's been on the net with her implant since immediately after YONI," Shizoko said. "Her pattern of traffic matches someone who has years of experience with an implant."

Leon thought back. The Year of No Internet was the result of the virus-based AI he'd created ten years earlier. To stop a world-wide confrontation, he'd shut down the entire Internet by disabling packet routing. "But that's not possible," he said. "There were no implants prior to YONI."

Mike looked at them. "That's not true. We know ELOPe implanted people."

Leon thought he saw a tic in the older man's eye when he mentioned the first AI, the one that he'd created.

"But ELOPe drove those people insane." Mike crossed his arms and went back to staring out the window.

"What if he didn't drive this one insane?" Shizoko asked. "What if she has a genuine pre-YONI brain implant, with no regulators and a totally unique architecture? She could be capable of anything."

"How old is she?" Leon asked.

"Twenty."

"It's possible, just barely," Mike said. "She would have been a young kid. Since we don't allow implants on anyone under fourteen, there's not a lot of data on what the effects might be."

Leon looked at Shizoko. "Why do you think this is anything more than a coincidence, Catherine just happening to be in San Diego?"

"We suspect a powerful AI is carrying out a long range conspiracy involving political parties," Shizoko said. "We have a woman who can do things with her implant no one else can do. Both of them are suddenly in San Diego, and as of an hour ago, both are incredibly active. More than twenty percent of the data traffic in downtown San Diego is being perturbed in some way, and the amount is increasing rapidly."

"They're working together?" Mike frowned.

"Or against each other. Either way, we need to get there as soon as possible."

Leon flipped back to the photo of Catherine, dwelling on her eyes and nose. She had to be innocent. She was too carefree and wholesome to commit murder.

33

Slim shook his head at the waitress, a hand over his coffee cup. While Tony worked steadily on a greasy burger, he glanced across the restaurant.

The hired mercenaries, minus the robot, sat in their own booth. Helena didn't eat, and there was no point bringing five hundred pounds of armored nightmare into the restaurant other than to terrorize the diners.

The three sat in their booth, motionless, making Slim nervous. He was sure they were speaking to Adam.

He screwed in an earplug so he could talk semi-privately, and started a connection to the boss. It took a few seconds, bouncing through onion routers and the firewall, before Adam appeared.

"The extraction team says the girl's in San Diego," Adam said.

"Yeah. We're tracking her with the new hardware." After they'd lost Cat two days ago, Adam had sent yet another black box, this one able to detect the girl's machinations on the net. "She's in the Gaslamp Quarter. We should have her in two hours."

"When they get her in the aircar, make sure you're in there. Catherine is too valuable. They might take her to the highest bidder."

Slim would have been honored at the implied trust if his sphincter wasn't clenched in terror. If the ex-military team decided to double-cross Adam, how was he going to stop them?

Adam must have seen his hesitation. "Once you're in the aircar, kill them. Don't wait for them to make a move. Trigger the stunner."

Slim nodded, too fearful to speak.

"Slim?"

"Yeah?"

"Don't let the girl get away again, or I'll be displeased." Adam disconnected, his image swirling away like water down a drain.

Tony looked up. "Everything OK?"

Slim stared into the distance, the roar of his pulse thick in his ears. "Fine."

34

The day before, Cat had flown into the desert in a rented aircar to practice with live ammunition. She quit when her arms went numb and ears started ringing, then flew down to the border to figure out how she'd cross. The network traffic surrounding each person's transit was dense, triple-encrypted stuff that hurt her head. She didn't see any obvious way to hack the exchange, but she wasn't ready to give up.

Today, about to go back to the border checkpoints again, she noticed an uneasy itch in her skull. Vulnerable in the enclosed hotel, she left to wander the Gaslamp Quarter and sample the net.

Walking down Sixth Avenue, the itch intensified until she was sure someone or something was searching for her. Paranoid, she explored in all directions. After homing in on a blonde, Cat wondered if it was the same woman she'd seen a couple of blocks ago?

As Cat turned onto G Street, the suspicion grew. She checked her implant and found it locked down in anonymous mode, all interfaces closed except the false identity. There was nothing to point to Catherine Matthews.

Still, someone sought her, and it was time to flush them out.

She turned in at the neighborhood pub she'd found last night, now sparsely populated with afternoon customers. She breezed passed a Korean man with tattoos and a trim beard flirting with a woman flaunting cleavage, heading for the bathrooms.

A stack of beer kegs formed the far wall of the short hallway. No one behind her. She pressed open the keg door, revealing a hidden speak-easy. Unless local to San Diego, Cat's followers were unlikely to know the trick. With luck, they'd go into the outer bar, look around, and leave.

She took a booth in the corner with a view of the door.

The bartender, swarthy and chiseled with shirt-sleeves rolled up to display muscled arms, came over and tossed a coaster on her table.

Right guy, wrong time. "Herradura, neat," she said to get rid of him.

She overlaid her vision with video feeds from street cameras and the pub's security cam and discretely slipped two guns out of their shoulder holsters and onto her lap.

On the street cam, the tall blonde she'd suspected before approached with a confident, steady stride. As she drew closer an aircar landed and a man exited, followed by an armored robot like nothing she'd ever seen, all eyes and tentacles.

The bartender delivered the tequila, smiling and lingering, his intention obvious.

Cat didn't have time for the distraction. "Thanks, now go away." His face fell and she felt a momentary remorse, but the weight of steel in her lap focused her.

The bot stopped at the corner with a clear view of both streets and pub, while the woman and man, in matching black flak jackets, continued toward the bar.

Cat's grip tightened around her guns. These people were after her. But to shoot when there was even the slightest chance they didn't mean her harm? She couldn't.

She tried to hack their implants, hoping data would prove them innocent or complicit. They were locked down tight with a tang of military encryption reminiscent of the border.

With a twinge, she realized how foolish she'd been. She could have run anywhere and yet she'd stayed within a few hundred miles. Dumb.

The two would be inside in seconds.

Cat explored the net and found the Korean she'd passed on the way in, his implant wide open. She rooted him in milliseconds and her vision flipped to his perspective, leaving her staring at his partner's cleavage. The man and woman in black drew near.

She controlled the Korean like a puppeteer, holding his drink out into the aisle, where he bumped into the woman. "I'm sorry," she said, as the drink spilled. "Let me get something." Cat moved the Korean toward the bar, blocking their way.

But the two shoved him back, the motion exposing firearms they held low and close to their bodies.

She snapped back to herself with the sharp realization that they had weapons out. She let out a breath and stood, aiming both guns at the door.

To her left, a woman screamed and people scrambled to get away. The bartender looked like he might tackle her. *Kuso!* She spared just enough attention to root the bartender's implant and freeze him in place. Then the door started to swing open.

At a glimpse of black jacket she fired, the shots deafening in the small bar. The woman spun and disappeared behind the door, leaving the entrance empty. Cat swore and shifted sideways for a better view.

Where was the man? She kept her guns up. More screams, barely audible over the ringing in her ears.

She needed a better vantage: the bartender was close to the door. Still rooted, she added his perspective as another window, adding to the clutter in her vision.

The man in black crouched behind the door. His female partner scrambled away on the floor.

A squirt of encrypted traffic gave away the tentacled robot's approach, even as a second car arrived, a Honda, with the fat guy Tony and a skinny one too. Christ, how many were there?

Taking control of the bartender, she grabbed two bottles from the counter and threw them overhand at the man in black.

Startled, he fired at the bartender, hitting him in the leg.

A flash of pain forced Cat to disconnect. She rolled to her left, putting the distracted attacker in her view, and fired, two point blank shots to his chest.

A roar came from outside and Cat turned. The blacked out window exploded in a hail of glass as a groundcar crashed through and ground to a halt, wedged halfway through the exterior wall.

She dove for the shelter of the bar.

The door of the Honda opened, and Cat's heart sank as still another woman in tactical gear peered out. Cat opened fire, then ducked down as the robot took advantage of the opening to let loose a storm of bullets.

Initial screams gave way to hushed sobbing.

Cat wanted to join them, to curl up into a ball and disappear. She wasn't meant for this, hadn't trained to battle soldiers, had never expected that she'd be fighting for her life in a fucking bar in a strange city.

The man she'd shot had gotten back to his feet, protected by his body armor.

She almost dropped her gun in defeat. Cornered by trained killers, she had nowhere to run and couldn't fight them by herself. She needed options.

She focused on the net, the attackers solid nuggets of iron, locked down tight by military grade security. She couldn't hack them, but by comparison, the civilians were soft.

She took a meditative breath, let her awareness encompass all the implants in the bar, sixteen people. She exerted her will, twisted and pulled in the net. The corner of her mouth twitched up as she rooted them all.

When the woman in the car and the robot opened fired again, Cat didn't panic.

She looked at them through sixteen pairs of eyes plus her own, total panopticon awareness in three-dimensional space. She didn't know how, but she could see from every perspective simultaneously, with perfect knowledge of every object's location. Time slowed as she aimed with millimeter precision at the woman crouched in the doorway of the Honda. A single shot and her forehead exploded in a mist of blood.

Even as she pulled and released the trigger, she also controlled every person in the bar. The Korean and others pounded the first woman attacker, still on the ground, with chairs and legs.

The waitress and others went en mass after the man, clawing for his eyes and face like brainless zombies. He fired at the crowd, hitting them, forcing Cat to action.

She dove toward the doorway, and rose up to shoot him again

and again, until both guns clicked on empty cylinders. The body armor stopped the rounds, but he was forced back against the wall. She ran after him and gave a snap kick to his knee, buckling it backwards. Before he could drop, she hit him in the face with the empty gun and he crumpled.

The robot and the men outside responded to the sudden activity by firing a steady barrage.

Cat hid behind the bar, reloading. The bot pushed against her mind, like hundreds of needles pressing into flesh. She struggled against the mental assault, holding her interfaces closed as she reeled in pain, dropping the gun and ammo. Her body convulsing, she crumpled to the ground. She clamped down her network connection, bringing immediate relief, but her video and geospatial feeds shrunk and dissipated, leaving her hopelessly unaware of what was going on.

Grabbing the gun off the floor, she slammed a new clip home, then peeked around the corner. The fat man, outside the newly opened hole in the wall, held a large gun in both hands. Cat remembered their encounter in the noodle shop two days ago. She didn't want to kill him. She took careful aim, hitting him mid-thigh.

He collapsed with a scream, but the robot and the thin man heard and saw the shot and sent a new storm of bullets into the bar, glass and wood splinters showering Cat. She curled up in a ball, sure that she'd be dead within seconds, but miraculously nothing hit her.

The robot renewed its cyberattack. Her vision dimmed and brightened as weird tastes floated across her mouth and even her sense of balance distorted. On the verge of passing out, the total vulnerability of pending unconsciousness scared her into motion.

She fumbled under her jacket for the guided projectile gun, pain hindering even the most basic action. She shut down her vision altogether and the torture faded to a distant throb. Blind now, she reached around to the small of her back and groped until she snagged the holster release. The big gun with its single smart missile dropped into her hand, giving her a surge of confidence.

Knowing the robot used the visual channel to attack, she instead built a three-dimensional wireframe from street and security cameras, calculated the bot's location, and pointed the muzzle in the direction of the window.

The three-inch rocket whooshed out, guidance fins snapping into position. It exited the bar at two hundred miles per hour and twisted hard, gunning for the bot.

Cat's wireframe fuzzed out, right in the middle where the robot should be, and the rocket veered off. Her heart sank as it exploded against a neighboring building.

"Catherine Matthews," boomed the robot. "Surrender. You are surrounded. I am a military-grade combat bot. You cannot hope to succeed and we do not wish to harm you."

35

Leon packed netspace with research on Catherine Matthews and street camera video feeds from the bar in San Diego until the walls of the cabin disappeared. Shizoko helped by adding visualizations of the massive fluctuations in the net.

"Five minutes until we arrive," Shizoko said over the roar of wide-open engines.

"You're sure Catherine is not on their side?" Mike asked.

"The timing doesn't match," Shizoko said. "Her public data feed reveals a perfectly ordinary life for ten years. While she's recently done peculiar things with the net, they're different than the disturbances surrounding the chain of murders. Nothing, until the attack in the park, would suggest she was anything but normal."

"And this group," Leon said, pointing at the video, "following and attacking her, puts them on opposite sides."

"We can't be sure that makes her the good guy," Mike said. "Maybe they're undercover."

"No," Shizoko said. "Their reputation scores suggest they're hired mercenaries, and they mounted an assault on the bar without calling for police backup. "

"Undercover cops use faked IDs with bad reps," Mike said. "Look, we're trying to rescue this girl without knowing enough about her."

"What's wrong with you?" Leon said. "She's being attacked. Why wouldn't we help her?"

"You think she's cute and you want to play the hero." Mike shook his head. "You'll keep playing with the data until it tells you what you want."

Leon felt himself flush with embarrassment and anger. She was pretty and smart, and nothing would be better than riding to her rescue. But that didn't change the facts: she was literally surrounded. He decided to ignore Mike. "Shizoko, what will you be able to do against the mercenaries? You're not a military bot."

"I'm armed, but I also hired private security to meet us. I tried to notify the police, but another AI, a big one, is blocking me."

"Another Class IV?" Leon asked.

"No, it's bigger. After this encounter, I'll analyze the network traffic to determine point of origin."

Leon and Mike stared at each other. There shouldn't be any AI more powerful than a Class IV.

They banked hard into a steep dive. Directly ahead of them, the Gaslamp Quarter, and in the sky, four other aircars converging on the same location.

"Are those security?" Leon said.

"Yes." In the back of the cabin, Shizoko replaced his lower pair of arms with robotic rifles he retrieved from a cabinet. "I have traditional handguns here, but I recommend you remain in the aircar, where you will be protected."

"You've fought before?" Leon asked.

"No, but I have training programs."

"Aren't you afraid of being killed?"

Shizoko laughed. "No. Did you think my consciousness was here? Less than a hundredth of my processing power is in this body. The rest remains in my computing center in Austin."

"Why fight when you could let the security bots handle it?"

"Like all AI, I crave immersive experiences. It's not every day I can join such a battle." Shizoko exercised the articulated rifles. "Stay in the car."

They made a final sharp turn, reverse thrusters throwing up dust and debris. The door sprang open as they jolted down and Shizoko dashed out, his treads churning as he flew into the street and toward the bar.

36

Still huddled in a ball behind the bar, Cat contemplated the military bot's ultimatum. Surrender, without any knowledge of what it wanted?

The sound of low whimpers and sobs came from the rubble. She'd endangered the people here by coming in, and worse, used them to save herself. All were hurt, and many dead. But she didn't start this fight, and she wasn't going to let their loss be in vain. And she sure as hell didn't study karate for six years to give up at the first challenge. They might have started it, but she'd finish the fight.

Afraid of the robot's cyberattacks, she still suppressed her regular vision and used the three dimensional wireframe she had generated from multiple viewpoints. Better than normal eyesight, the wireframe let her see through walls.

How could she defeat this combat bot? Karate was pointless, normal bullets useless, and her one rocket easily disabled. She recited the twenty principles under her breath.

Wazawai wa getai ni shozu. Accidents come from inattention.

Karate no shugyo wa issho de aru. You will never stop learning karate.

Katsu kangae wa motsu na makenu kangae wa hitsuyo. Do not think you must win. Instead, think that you do not have to lose. This was potentially a good one for the situation at hand.

Karate wa, gi no taske. One who practices karate must follow the way of justice. Well, duh.

Kokoro wa hanatan koto wo yosu. Be ready to free your mind . . .

Maybe the problem was that she wasn't stretching far enough. She found a few hundred people in the nearby net, scared from the gunfire. Other AI too, mostly curious because they knew little fear. She reached into their implants, every one. They might not consciously know how, but their hardware could route data, even the humans.

Using them all, she pulled and twisted and massaged a huge stream of connections, ten, a hundred, a thousand.

"What are you doing, Catherine Matthews? You're manipulating the net." The robot crunched debris under treads, drawing closer.

Cat continued rerouting protocols, forcing astronomical amounts of data in and out of people's interfaces. Not used to moving this many bits, they were screaming, their brain patterns becoming irregular, pain leaking back through the connections. Quickly, before the whole thing collapsed, she sent the streams toward the military bot, a high bandwidth assault.

"You cannot believe," the robot called, "that you can penetrate my military hardware with bulk data?"

The robot pulled itself through the doorway, glass crunching under its tentacles, metal twisting and screeching.

She pulled more feeds, encrypted them on the fly, forwarding the bytes to the bot. She didn't need to kill the AI, just swamp its processors. Assessing each feed's legitimacy would cause enough contention to starve sensors and render the robot blind.

The world slowed down at she went deeper. She cycled feeds, connecting and disconnecting hundreds of times each second. She pushed the data toward the robot, until finally she got what she wanted: the packet response time started to drop off. Connection denied responses went from three millisecond delays to four milliseconds, eight, and finally twenty.

"What you're doing won't work," the robot said, but now Cat believed this to be bluster. It was working.

Tables and chairs scraped the floor as they were pushed out of the way nearby.

Cat leaped to her feet, turned her vision back on, and came face to face with the robot, both guns raised. She fired point blank, emptying the guns into the sensor pods, blinding the bot.

The tentacles lashed out, but lethargically, as the robot's overloaded processors struggled to get enough cycle time to operate its body.

Cat, her reflexes maxed, ran around the bot, leaping over bodies and tables and onto the hood of the Honda.

The thin man watched her.

She raised one gun, no rounds left, but he didn't know that.

He lowered his gun and backed away.

She probed for other attackers. Nothing in the immediate block, but she tasted the hard iron of more military bots in the net, approaching fast from all directions. Air traffic data showed a circle of aircars closing in less than a minute.

Seeking escape, she ran to the middle of the street, passing the fat man in a pool of blood.

A voice came from the parked black and silver Bugatti. "Catherine Matthews, can you hear me?"

Catherine didn't say anything. She was thinking about the approaching aircars. A net coming down around her.

"Cat, I know what you can do. These people are from the Institute for Applied Ethics. They're afraid of you, what you can do. They're coming to arrest you, to experiment on you."

Cat ignored the voice.

"If you don't believe me, check the IDs of the two men in the aircar approaching from the northeast. I am on your side. I will shelter you from them. I am not afraid of you."

Cat used her implant to scan the approaching aircar. It contained two people. Mike Williams and Leon Tsarev. Of course she knew who they were. She checked against their public keys. They appeared to be authentic. But that could be faked.

"You survived that attack, but now they are bringing more security bots. You barely bested one, can you beat sixteen?"

"Who are you?" she said.

"You can call me Adam."

This was Tony's boss, the AI that'd been following her. Tony was scared of him, so Adam must be dangerous. Cat glanced toward the bar. The bot inside was hardly beaten, merely blinded and starved of data. Given a minute, it would find some way to come after her. The other aircars, less than a thousand feet away now, all contained bots.

"I'm starting this car. I'm going to drive by you. If you jump in, I can get you away. But if you wait, they'll be on top of you and escape will be impossible." The aircar fired up engines and rose off landing gear.

Cat shook her head. She desperately wanted more time, to think. She shouldn't trust this AI, but she was out of options. It was either an unknown and dangerous AI, or sixteen bots led by the Institute for Applied Ethics. She glanced at the guns she held, the ruins of the bar, and the Institute vehicle touching down half a block away, weighing her options.

The black aircar approached, massive ductwork bulging out the corners of the car, the door opening by itself, the interior empty. The voice continued from a speaker. "Get in Catherine."

Down the block, a huge bot flew out of the Institute car, articulated rifles pointed in her direction.

"Dammit." She jumped in and the door swung closed. The engines went to full power, acceleration slamming her against the seat.

"Sorry, Catherine Mathews. Do your best to hold on, as the next few minutes will be tricky."

The Bugatti accelerated hard, twisting and turning. Cat rolled across the cabin, slammed her shoulder into the wall, finally reached out and grabbed a seat leg, nearly getting her arm yanked off when the aircar veered again. She levered herself into a seat and buckled up as the engines screamed. Cat reached into the net, pulled up the locations of their pursuers.

"Please don't do that, Cat. You have a digital signature that is . . . unique. When you arrive, I'll teach you how to suppress it. In the meantime, stay off the net. I'll put up an overview."

A three dimensional hologram flickered to life in the cabin, showing the positions of the different aircars. They flew low to the ground, corkscrewing through the hills east of San Diego, the tortured screech of the engine echoing off canyon walls.

"Can you outrun them?" Cat asked.

"Yes, but they can always call in more help to track us. Better to lose them here and now with an impossible maneuver." For two minutes the aircar screamed at near supersonic speeds, hurtling at high G-forces through mountains and valleys. Battered by the rapid turns,

Cat feared she might pass out under the acceleration.

The car hurtled out of a canyon and over a hill, then dove straight toward a lake. Cat screamed at the last second, then they hit the water.

Seatbelt tensioners and airbags fired, stunning but protecting Cat. She clawed at the airbag as the car began to sink in the frothing and bubbling water.

"Relax, Catherine. The car is watertight. No one saw us go into the reservoir. We're safe."

"You can fly us out?" She surveyed the interior. She'd never heard of an aircar that was also a submarine.

"No, of course not. The vehicle is damaged beyond repair. I will send air transport and rescue bots. They will be at your location and retrieve you as soon as the Institute's search has been called off."

The hiss and crackle of cold water hitting the superheated engine sounded behind her.

"What the hell?" Cat got out of her seat and screamed. "I'm trapped down here. What if the windshield cracks? What if this thing springs a leak? What if you don't get here in time and the air runs out?"

She lost her balance as the car sank into the water and it grew darker inside.

"I calculated probabilities and made the choice with the highest likelihood of successful evasion with minimal risk. Now please remain calm. Data transmission will cease in a few seconds. I assure you, I will retrieve you."

Then the speaker was silent. The cabin turned black and the car started to creak alarmingly.

Cat fought panic. She forced herself to sit just in time, the car jolting into the mud bottom of the reservoir. She reached out one finger to touch the windshield, then changed her mind, and withdrew her hand. She sat back and gripped the armrests as the glass creaked and moaned.

Part Two

37

Leon gawked in surprise as Catherine Matthews climbed into the other car and left. When her car took off, an unexpected jealousy seized him.

The moment passed as their own engines throttled to take-off power on their own. The aircar turned ninety degrees and glided sideways down the street. At the same time Shizoko churned toward them, leaping into the air ten feet from the door. The two paths intersected, Shizoko flying through the doorway to slam into the opposite side. The engines shrieked as they veered to follow Catherine, throwing Mike and Leon into the wall.

"Some warning would help," Mike said, picking himself up.

"What the hell just happened?" Leon said. "Where is she going?"

"Unknown, but I don't think she's in control." Shizoko said. "Her car's rate of acceleration is unsafe for humans."

"She voluntarily got in," Leon said, struggling to buckle as the aircar jigged back and forth in pursuit.

"Someone spoke to her before she boarded." Shizoko replayed the transaction, a series of encrypted audio data packets to and from the vehicle in the moments before takeoff.

Mike, already buckled, started playing with the data as they accelerated in huge curves and stomach-raising lurches. "The other end is anonymous," he yelled over the howl of the engines. "Can you backtrace to the source?"

The aircar banked right. Leon overlaid the locations of the hired security cars, also in pursuit, on the windshield. The Bugatti outdistanced them, but with sixteen vehicles sharing telemetry, they could track a long way out.

"I've traced the AI to an unregistered server in Atlanta," Shizoko said, his voice machine calm, a stark contrast to the chaos of the frantic chase.

"Unregistered?" Mike said. "The point of the ethics framework is to ensure every computer is protected."

"The CPU in question is registered to an AI out of Belgium. The AI self-terminated fourteen days ago, but its credentials haven't expired yet. The server was a dumb packet forwarder on a nexus with a million other servers, which means I'll have to backtrack through every other connection coming in and out. I'll need at least a few hours."

"What are you going to do about her car?" Leon gestured toward the Bugatti, too distant to see, but displayed on the overlay as fifteen miles away, traveling at supersonic speeds.

"I've hired more security firms at these six locations." Shizoko displayed a half circle of points on the map, fifty miles distant. "And these." Another arc, two hundred miles out.

"Can we use public data to track her?" Leon asked.

"No," Shizoko said. "They'd deny a request from me for air traffic control access. If you ask, they'd say yes, but you'd reveal your location. The People's Party is still looking for you, and you would attract crowds anywhere we go. It's not . . ."

"Yes?" Leon asked. "It's not what?"

The Bugatti disappeared from the display.

Leon and Mike looked at each other.

"Shizoko?" Mike called.

Long seconds later, the aircar slowed as the engines backed off, and moments later they had returned to a sedate cruising speed.

"The other AI is brilliant," Shizoko said.

"What?"

"Catherine Matthew is gone. We lost her somewhere in the Santa Ana valleys."

"How did you lose her?" Leon asked, his voice rising.

"I'm sorry, but we did. They used evasive techniques. They stayed closed to the ground, followed the contours of the land, and outflew us. We lost them visually and on radar. It's sparsely populated, so there are minimal other data sources to use."

"Can't we just surveil the general area?" Leon said.

"Not four thousand square miles. With the right gear, they could be in and out and we'd never spot them. All is not lost, however."

"How do you figure?" Leon said.

"It took tremendous power and bandwidth to pilot that aircar to a getaway. I'll trace the other AI more quickly now. I'm calling off the security cars and landing for refueling."

The car turned to return to San Diego.

Leon swiped madly at the disjointed data. Even implanted, with ten years' experience, he couldn't make sense of the complex patterns. He was completely dependent on an AI he'd met only twenty-four hours ago. He looked at the picture of Cat hanging in netspace, feeling utterly useless.

He glanced sideways at Mike, who was slowly shaking his head.

"What?" Leon snapped.

"You've already decided you want her," Mike said, his voice tired. "That's going to cloud your thinking. Not helpful."

38

Slim, a hundred feet from the wreckage of the bar, ignored the cries for help emanating from inside. He had watched, his weapon hanging limply, as the exotic aircar took off on autopilot with the girl. Tony lay in a pool of his own blood. Wisps of smoke trickled out from the building as battery fluids leaked from the ruined Honda wedged in the wall. He shook his head. Total fubar.

Who could believe one girl caused all this mess? No wonder she'd beat the pulp out of Tony in LA.

Soon the police would arrive in force, but for now the street was still vacant, civilians in hiding.

He jogged over to Tony, crunching through broken glass and bullet shoes on the way. The big man moaned weakly, only semiconscious.

"You're gonna be all right, old friend." Slim tied his windbreaker around Tony's leg wound to stem the bleeding, evoking new whimpers. "Sorry, but we gotta get out of here."

Slim needed transportation now that the groundcar was wrecked and the Bugatti gone. He ran to a parked car halfway down the block and pulled out his pocket computer. Adam's software should be able to hijack the vehicle. He swiped at the screen, but nothing happened. The damn thing was locked up. He startled as Helena rolled up.

The battle bot was shot up good, bullet-pocked and sensors dangling in places. "The girl and I fried every computer within a half mile. Allow me." She started the old VW Jetta with one touch of a tentacle.

"We need to get Tony," he said.

Helena waved a metal limb. "I'll bring the car around." She drove remotely, and they met next to Tony.

Slim tried to lever him up, but failed to even get his upper body off the ground. "He's too heavy."

Helena wrapped tentacles around Tony and lifted him into the back seat. "Let me ride with him. I have an emergency medical kit."

"Where's the rest of your team?" Slim asked. Sirens warbled in the distance.

"Dead." The bot was emotionless.

Slim nodded, numb himself, and got into the front seat. The car moved on its own, before he'd even touched the controls. He glanced back.

"Don't worry, I can drive and operate at the same time. I'm not that damaged." She brought two arms around to Tony's injured leg. The tentacle ends split open, exposing delicate manipulators. She peeled back Tony's pants and squirted something into the bullet entry. "His chances of recovery are poor with this much blood loss. If I bring us to a hospital, can you get him type A+?"

"What do I do?" Slim asked, turning around.

Helena inserted manipulators into the wound. There was a bright spark and sizzle, followed by the smell of burnt flesh. "I'm going to pull up outside the Emergency Room entrance at Scripps Mercy. Go into the first set of double doors, then take the third left into the medicine room. The blood will be in a silver walk-in refrigerator. Everything is access controlled. Since you lack an implant, I'll disable all locks as soon as you enter."

"Double doors, third left, silver refrigerator, A+. Got it."

Helena wrapped two tentacles around Tony's legs and lifted them into the air. The car lurched sideways as they took a sharp turn.

"What are you doing?" Slim asked.

"Forcing the remaining blood to his brain." Helena held the wound closed, then cauterized again.

Slim flinched against the bright glare. "What the heck is that?"

"Miniature arc welder for field repairs. Never used one on a human. The burn is bad, but bleeding to death is worse."

"Jeez. Is he gonna be OK?" Slim ran one hand around his neck. He'd dropped the tribal necklace he had gotten from the Enforcement team leader. What was her name? Sonja.

Helena was quiet for a moment. "Maybe. The bone shattered and will need six weeks to heal, probably with permanent damage without full medical care. Unless we use experimental medic nanites."

"You have those?"

"No, but they will on a Navy ship."

San Diego was home to a naval base. "Let's go there after the hospital." Slim glanced up. "Have you heard from Adam since this went all to hell?"

"No, he's not answering coms," Helena said. "I've tried several times."

Adam had never abandoned them before. Yet he'd clearly taken the girl and not them. So they were expendable after all, and Adam might decide to eliminate them to reduce exposure.

"Stop trying," Slim said. "He doesn't need us."

Helena nodded. "You are correct." She stopped for a moment. "Adam didn't tell us what we were facing. He hired us to extract an ordinary girl, not a highly skilled combat professional. We would have gone in with more forces had we known. My friends died because Adam concealed the truth. I'm not going to let that go."

Slim shook his head. "You don't know what you're going up against. No one can fight Adam and win."

"Then I'll die trying." Helena spoke softly. "Loyalty to the team above all. There is no point to life if I don't stand up for what I believe in." She turned a camera lens on Slim. "I will fight him. You know Adam. You will help me."

Slim sighed. Tony was right, it had been better when they only had to kill people.

39

ondensation trickled down the windshield, just barely visible now that Cat's eyes had adjusted to the dark. Every few minutes the cabin creaked, making her stomach jump. The deep water's chill penetrated the car, wracking her body with long shivers from head to feet.

She tried to distract herself with math. The Bugatti's cabin worked out to about three hundred cubic feet. Now how much did she breathe? Her meditation teacher said the average person consumed about half a cubic foot of air per minute, about thirty cubic feet per hour. She had nearly ten hours of air, but surely she didn't deplete all the oxygen in one breath?

No, she was wrong: carbon dioxide was the limiting factor, not oxygen. At one and a half percent concentration, carbon dioxide caused headaches and nausea, at three percent unconsciousness and by eight percent death. A surprising effect for a natural by-product of respiration. She shivered harder and wrapped her arms around her knees. Maybe she'd die of hypothermia first.

Forcing herself to massage her numb arms, she checked her implant and found she'd been under water for forty minutes. She listened for any sound of rescue. Nothing.

The car's net transmitter, more powerful than her implant, might be able to signal for help. But if Adam could be believed, and the wrong people heard her—the Institute—well, she couldn't take that chance. Not yet.

Cat thought back to the bar with a bile-raising lurch, remembering the people she'd put into danger, indirectly killed. She'd used innocents for any edge to oppose the attackers.

She struggle to keep from being sick, forced her breath to be even and slow, told her muscles to relax. Mind over body, the most important karate lesson of all.

She'd do it again to survive, but karate's first principle was to avoid combat. She needed to be smarter, not let herself be maneuvered until a fight was the only option.

Yet the battle had pushed her to use abilities she didn't know she had. She'd effortlessly rooted implants to gain access, controlled dozens of people simultaneously, even going so far to see out of everyone's eyes at once. How had she done it? She had no answers.

In the near pitch-black conditions, she made out the outlines of other chairs in the cabin, the sleek wrap-around curve of the dashboard, and the very slight barrier of the windshield, mostly visible because of the condensation. She was afraid to wipe the water off, though it obscured what little view there was, frightened it would pop like a soap bubble.

Four percent. That's the concentration of carbon dioxide in each exhalation. She added more than one and a half cubic foot of the deadly gas to the closed environment each hour. She tried to calculate how long it would be before the level would become threatening, but kept forgetting the numbers halfway through. It didn't matter, she was shivering constantly now; hypothermia would kill her.

Cat heard the plop of a drop of water; seconds later she heard another. It was too dim in the cabin to make out anything so small and vague as a water leak. She wished she could boost her vision. She toyed with aggregating visual data to provide light amplification, but didn't have the necessary algorithms.

In the midst of this she heard a distant, faint thud. With no sound other than the quiet plops of water and occasional creaking of the car, the thump was distinct. Please, let it be the AI with something to get her out of here.

Minutes passed, and something dark drifted through the dim water, then floated away.

"Come back! I'm this way!" Cat surprised herself by breaking into tears. "I'm here!" She stopped from pounding on the windshield just in time. Salty tears ran down her cheeks as she prayed for it to come back.

After anxious moments, the shadowy outlines reappeared. One passed close by, and she screamed. The shape stopped, approached, and resolved as a submersible bot. It came very near, then reached out with two manipulators and grabbed the car.

Nothing happened until another bot appeared out of the darkness and grabbed the other side. The bots trailed cables, which suddenly became taut, and the car lurched free of the bottom.

Cat smiled and took her first easy breath. She would live. She'd be out of this coffin in a few minutes.

But then nothing happened. After a few minutes, convinced there was a problem, the dread started again. It was taking too long. Was the Bugatti too heavy?

Long minutes of panic passed before she realized a slow ascent might be necessary for decompression. She settled in for a protracted wait, but her muscles convulsed with the cold. She tried to exercise in the small space, but gave up after banging her clumsy limbs too many times.

After ninety minutes of nearly imperceptible motion, the water grew lighter. Soon she saw daylight, and within a few minutes the car broke through the surface.

The submersibles guided the car near the shore. A utility bot stood on dry gravel, twenty feet away, near a flying freight drone. The bot gestured upwards with two short stubby arms.

The waterline was too high to open a door, but the ceiling had a moon-roof. She fumbled with deadened hands until she flipped the emergency exit levers, and shoved. The panel popped out and fresh air blew in.

She stuck her head through the opening, breathing deep.

"Greetings Catherine Matthews." The bot on shore amplified its voice to cross the distance. "My submersibles can't get any closer in, and I'm afraid it's difficult to obtain a waterproof robot body on short notice. Can you get to shore?"

Cat pulled herself tiredly onto the roof. Looking back, she realized she'd left her backpack in San Diego. She took stock, feeling with her body what was there and what wasn't, and discovered she still had one gun in its holster under her jacket. She must have dropped the others in the fight.

She stepped onto the hood of the car and jumped into the frigid waist-deep water, then forced her frozen legs to waddle to shore.

As soon as she was a few feet away, the submersibles backed away and the car disappeared under water.

"It's better we let it sink," Adam said. "Less likely anyone else will find it that way."

She sloshed out of the cold lake, wet clothes draining the last dregs of body heat from her. Standing on the shore, she stared at Adam for a moment, trying to make sense of this AI. The stubby bot was streaked with grease and paint splotches.

He saw her staring. "This is not my usual body. I needed something on short notice. I'm a Class IV."

She nodded.

"Come in the drone, please."

She followed him into the freight drone, its massive interior empty and barren.

"Sit down please," Adam said. "I'm sorry I don't have anything more comfortable. I didn't anticipate the need for a water extraction, and I had to work with available resources to avoid creating new data tracks."

Dripping wet and frozen from hours under the cold lake, Cat looked around in disappointment. "You could have brought a towel. You have towels, don't you?"

"I'm sorry, Catherine Matthews. It will be a quick ride to my home. I will have towels and clothes waiting on your arrival."

40

San Diego appeared through the windshield as Leon, Mike, and Shizoko approached. A dozen emergency vehicles, lights flashing, surrounded the scene of the fight.

"What took them so long to arrive?" Leon asked.

"Something scrambled their net connections," Shizoko answered. "I'm still back-tracking and correlating traffic. Whoever communicated with Catherine and piloted the escape vehicle is vigilant. I've tracked them through six packet forwarders and two obscurity clouds, but the trail is cold. I don't have the necessary granularity of information."

Leon switched back to netspace. "She distorted the local net," Leon said, "rerouted ninety percent of the data in downtown San Diego. Sent it all into a three block radius around the bar."

"If the traffic logs can be believed," Shizoko said, "she used thousands of neural implants to form an ad-hoc mesh network and saturated their bandwidth. She probably battled an AI, which should be impossible for a human."

Leon stared at her photo. He was infatuated, like Mike said. She was beautiful, yes, but clever too, and capable of inconceivable feats in cyberspace. He longed to meet her.

The aircar slowed as Shizoko brought them down outside the police cordon.

"I think we should go alone," Mike said, urging Leon out the door. "We'll get asked fewer questions."

"Are you sure?" Shizoko said, following them. "I will be able to glean information you cannot."

"You focus on the network traffic data analysis. We'll talk to the police."

"I'm a Class IV intellect. I can manage both."

Mike turned to face the four armed bot. "Stay here. We'll gain their confidence more easily human to human."

Shizoko bowed his head. "Very well. I'll wait."

When they were out of earshot, Leon asked, "What was that about?"

Mike sighed. "I don't know who to trust."

"We can't do this alone, we can't fight AI with human brain power."

"We made a mistake," Mike said. "We never should have come without an Institute AI to back us up."

"All the Enforcement team was with Sonja."

"We could have brought Vaiveahtoish."

"He's the head of the *Nanotech* department," Leon said. "He knows nothing about tracking rogues."

They stopped outside a band of blue plastic tape stretched across the street. A police bot stood a dozen feet beyond.

Leon reluctantly took his implant out of anonymous mode to provide his real identity to the bot. "I'm Leon Tsarev from the Institute for Applied Ethics. We're investigating the possibility of an AI crime."

The police bot rolled forward and bobbed its head in a polite nod. "I am honored to meet you, Mr. Tsarev and Mr. Williams. You take a great risk by being here. I presume you are aware that members of the People's Party are advocating for violence against your persons?"

"Yes," Mike said. "They chased us across the country."

The bot escorted them toward the bar. "What brings you to this crime scene?"

The situation was so complex, Leon didn't know where to start. "We sent our Enforcement Team here a week ago to investigate a series of murders we believe to be linked to an AI."

"Sonja Metcalfe?" The police bot emitted a squeak of excitement. "Are they here? They are so elite!"

Leon rolled his eyes. He hadn't realized Sonja had a following in the enforcement community. Then he remembered Sonja was MIA and turned grim again.

The bot halted at the entrance. "We believe that three people and a combat robot fled the crime scene before we arrived. Could Sonja's team be part of that group?"

"I don't think so," Mike said. "We came looking for Catherine Matthews."

As they spoke, a woman met them in the doorway. "Erin Sanders, lead detective. Tommy told me you were here." She held her hand out. "It's an honor to meet you both. What's the Institute's interest?"

"Thanks," Mike said, returning the handshake. "We're investigating a potential AI crime. We thought this might be related."

Behind the detective, paramedics carried a moaning woman on a stretcher.

"Come outside, let's get out of their way." She led them out again as an assortment of police bots, officers, and medics scurried around with equipment. "Sorry about this, but I'm going to query your IDs."

Leon felt her probe, granted access, and waited.

Next she pulled out a portable hand scanner. "Now biometric too, please." She scanned their hands, and glanced at the output. "OK, you are who you say. So how is this related?" She gestured at the wreckage of the bar, the pool of blood in the street, the car wedged halfway through the wall.

"I'm not sure," Mike said. "The Institute's enforcement team came out to San Diego a week ago, investigating a series of murders."

"They were here?" she asked.

"I don't think so. We actually showed up because we're on the trail of Catherine Matthews."

"The murder suspect from Portland? She's behind this?"

Mike shook his head. "Probably not."

"Look," the detective said, a tone of frustration coming into her voice. "We had a major gunfight here, and we didn't hear hide nor hair of it until ten minutes after it was over. Half our officers were on a wild goose chase on the north side of town. If you know something useful, spit it out."

"Our enforcement team came out here to investigate a series of murders we suspect were committed by an AI," Leon said.

Erin's eyes went big, but she nodded for him to continue.

"We hadn't heard from them in a week, so we came out here to look for them. On the way, we detected signs of two forces manipulating the network. One may have been the AI we're looking for, and the other was Catherine Matthews."

"She was here, and left in an aircar," Mike said. "We tried to pursue but she got away."

"Why didn't you call us?" Sanders asked.

"We couldn't get a connection to the police," Mike said. "Now we have no idea where the girl, the Enforcement team, or the AI is, or who is going to try to kill us next. Now, what can you tell us?"

The detective looked back and forth at them, then shook her head in puzzlement. "Three bodies inside are known British mercenaries. They had a dozen pieces of tech we've never seen before."

She paused, sighed, and continued. "We found two people who could talk. They complained someone took control of their bodies, turned them into puppets. Is this possible with implants? I never heard of it, not even in the war."

Leon and Mike looked at each other.

"It shouldn't be," Leon said. "And I worked on the implant design, so I should know."

She grunted in response. "Half the network nodes and most of the computers in this neighborhood are cooked. I haven't seen anything like it since China, and that was with over a hundred battle bots fighting."

She gestured toward the street. "Come with me." She picked up a few bullet casings from the hundreds scattered around. "Some are high caliber rounds meant to kill bots, the others are commonly used by robotic rifles."

She dropped the casings. An evidence bot squawked and zoomed up to collect them. She walked toward the pool of blood, holding up one arm so they wouldn't step into the puddle. "It must have been a fucking war down here. So far as our AI can reconstruct, there's a battle bot and three people missing. One wore women's size six boots, about five foot two, which matches your Catherine Mathews."

Leon nodded.

She went on. "The second person missing from the scene is a man, size thirteen shoe. The blood is probably his. We think he's pretty big, maybe two fifty or three hundred pounds. The last guy's a size ten. Given the tracks, the bot's a Durga Mark III. It's a two-year-old model, big bucks, a fucking nightmare in the war. Good at cyber warfare, but not good enough to kill all the network nodes and computers."

She stared hard at them. "Who was fighting who? What were they fighting over? And where'd they go?"

Leon shrugged, looking over at Mike.

Mike knelt over the puddle of blood and picked something up, a tribal wood carving on a simple rope. "This is Sonja's." He looked at the detective and held out the necklace. "This belonged to the leader of our Enforcement Team."

41

Cat and Adam's vehicle passed over mountains, and Tucson came into view. "You can turn on your implant now," Adam said, "but you must minimize the data that leaves Tucson. Even so, I will take steps to mask your electronic signature."

City lights sparkled in the clear night sky. Ringed by mountains, Tucson was a gleaming circle surrounded by darkness while the soft glow of a full moon lit the peaks.

"How can you mask my trail?" she asked, struggling for alertness after dozing during the flight.

"Six months ago, I learned of a plot to attack the President. I found evidence of collusion at our intelligence agencies, so I've been tracking down the conspirators myself. Afraid that they would retaliate, I built a sub-sentient firewall around Tucson to hide my activities. The barrier filters all incoming and outgoing traffic and will mask your presence."

Cat nodded dumbly. The explanation seemed outlandish, but she was too tired to make a judgment right now. She turned on her implant instead, relieved at the flow of data about their location, destination, and surroundings. So basic and yet essential to her life, she was blind without the net.

She recoiled in disgust from the link, the feeds stale and metallic. She sent new queries, but the odd sensation didn't change. "What's wrong with the net?" she asked.

"Everything inside the firewall is static. Without live data, the net may seem unusual."

She nodded, wondering what the people who lived in Tucson thought.

"I've grown accustomed. I'll open up ports after I've given you training. We'll begin as soon as we land."

Cat shook her head and fought off another yawn. "I'm tired, hungry, and cold. We can start tomorrow. What I need are dry clothes, food, and a bed."

"Of course." The transport veered, a late change of direction, and a few minutes later they landed in a small parking lot. The rear of the package drone dropped open. Cat stood, legs cramped from her position on the floor, and came to the doorway.

"I have a room for you at the Hotel Congress," Adam said, gesturing to the two story building across the street. "Clothes and food are waiting."

Cat stared at the utility bot, then followed him across a deserted road. Ten o'clock at night on a Thursday, it was deadly quiet. Her implant showed the University of Arizona only a few blocks away. Where were the thousands of students who should be out drinking?

Adam led her into the hotel. At the registration desk a woman nodded but Adam continued past, escorting her to the stairs and then on to room 234. "Food and clothes are inside. Make yourself comfortable. We'll talk in the morning."

Cat nodded, and paused in the doorway. "Thank you for getting me out."

"Of course," Adam said, his robot face inscrutable.

She shut the door and leaned against it as waves of exhaustion rolled over her.

Cat couldn't deny the AI had gotten her out of a tight spot. But to what purpose? Adam was extreme, even for an artificial intelligence, lacking the most rudimentary social graces. Was that why Tony feared him?

She cautiously scanned cyberspace. The bot that escorted her here remained downstairs, and another lingered across the street. She was too tired and unsettled by the brackish network to think anymore.

She pushed herself off the door and staggered toward the table. She lifted the cover off a tray of food, grabbed a handful of French fries, and made her way to the bed. Peeling off her wet clothes, she climbed under the covers and slipped into oblivion.

42

An evidence bot collected Sonja's jewelry, but Mike seemed unaware of the blood still covering his hand. "Sonja loved that necklace. She wouldn't give it up willingly. She's in trouble, maybe dead." He looked back toward the confusion of police officers and technicians. "But who was it that met her? Catherine, the bot, the other guys that are missing, or someone still here?"

Leon shook his head. "I don't know, but Cat wasn't involved. The timing doesn't work out."

Mike stopped pacing. "Are you thinking with your brain? Stop giving her the benefit of the doubt because she's pretty. Why was she here if she wasn't involved?"

Detective Sanders interrupted. "Bad news. The People's Party tracked you. Headquarters says a few hundred people are heading this way. The police will protect you, of course, but the protesters are going to make a mess of my crime scene. Can I have a couple of officers take you downtown?"

Leon and Mike glanced at each other.

"Thanks, Detective," Leon said, "Can you give us a second?"

"Sure, but don't dawdle. You've got ten minutes before they arrive. If you're going to stay here, which I don't advise, I need to call for backup pronto."

"Yup, we understand."

The detective walked away and talked to a technician.

Leon's implant popped up an incoming request for a private channel. He looked at Mike in surprise, but accepted.

"I appreciate the offer of help from the police, but they're going to sequester us in a safe house or protective custody," Mike sent. "We're not going to get to the bottom of this cooped up."

"Agreed," Leon said. "Let's contact Rebecca while we're on the net publicly."

Mike nodded, and opened up the connection. The built-in processors on their implants struggled to keep up with the three-layer encryption, but managed to eke out a low-resolution video feed from her end.

"Where the hell are you?" Rebecca asked. "Do you have any idea what's going on? The Institute is under siege, politically and literally."

"We're chasing after Sonja," Mike said. "She disappeared in San Diego a few days ago. Her necklace showed up at a crime scene. She might be dead." Mike choked on the last words.

Rebecca blanched, but said nothing.

"Listen," Leon said, "We believe a rogue AI is the common element behind this string of murders and Sonja's disappearance, and has something to do with a girl named Catherine Matthews."

Rebecca shook her head. "Forget about that. Drop the investigation and get to a secure location, a military base if you can. You're both in danger and too important to go out playing cowboys. The People's Party has had the Institute surrounded for days. They tried to smuggle a bomb onsite and the FBI went crazy, shut everything down. The President's at a G10 meeting in New York City, along with the Vice President. I can't seem to get word to them. I'm going to Manhattan to try to meet them in person."

Leon talked slowly, the thoughts coalescing only as he spoke. "The People's Party is a smokescreen, a distraction from the real goal."

"You can't cross a street in Washington without encountering protesters," Rebecca said. "We're one step away from martial law. You don't mobilize millions of people for a diversion."

Leon wished he could explain his intuition. What he'd give for the ability to process data like an AI! "The deaths, the protests, the People's Party, Sonja's disappearance, it's all connected to some bigger picture. Everything an AI does is logical."

"Let's say you're right." Rebecca asked. "Who's crunching the data for you?"

"We're working with Shizoko Reynolds," Mike said, "the class IV network traffic expert who uncovered the murders."

"Can you trust him?"

"We think so," Leon said.

She turned, spoke to someone off camera and grew flustered. "I'm sorry, but I'm moving to a more secure location. You need to do the same, and continue the investigation from there."

"We'll figure something out," Mike said.

Leon disconnected and returned his implant to anonymous mode. He pinged Mike and found his friend had done the same.

"Back to Shizoko," Mike said. "Before the police notice."

They walked away from the crime scene, Leon staring at the sidewalk, deep in thought. He'd been part of the team that designed neural implants, knew them inside and out. They were fundamentally limited, a simplistic two inch long strip of high density electrodes inserted between the skull and the frontal lobe with barely enough processing power for auxiliary functions like encryption and neural recording.

Unlike an artificial intelligence, the implant wasn't powerful enough for modeling or storage of data. That depended on wireless access to the net to run cognitive apps in the cloud, but latency prohibited the apps from integrating into consciousness and allowing the user to achieve AI level competency. What he needed was for the necessary computing power to fit inside his skull.

They found Shizoko and took off. Mike briefed the bot, while Leon contemplated his implant.

"Shizoko?" Leon interrupted.

"Yes?"

"You used experimental nanites to heal Mike's arm."

"Correct. They are a refinement of military technology. They should be available for civilian use in nine months."

"Could nanites enhance my implant?"

"Explain further, please."

"I want more bandwidth and enough processing power to run modeling algorithms."

"The latter can be achieved with neural apps run on the net," Shizoko said.

"It's not good enough," Leon said. "The latency of accessing apps in the cloud is too slow. They aren't part of my perceived consciousness. Worse, I can't run them while I'm hiding in anonymous mode."

"Implants designed for degenerative neural disorders can adaptively take over for biological function and include sufficient processing capability for human level intelligence," Shizoko said. "Theoretically, such an implant could be enhanced beyond human level equivalence. No tests have been done—"

"Hold on," Mike said. "We're not doing experimental brain surgery."

"Let's run with this idea for a second," Leon said. "Shizoko, instead of surgery, could you inject me with nanites to construct the neural implant within my head?"

"Please hold. I'm modeling the concept."

"This is ridiculous," Mike said. "You can't put untested technology in your head. Worse, he's a network traffic expert, not a medical bot."

Leon shrugged. "It's all the same to them. I feel like I'm on the verge of understanding what's going on, but I can't get enough of the picture in my head. It's like I'm playing chess, but I can only view four squares at a time when I need to see the whole board."

Mike clenched his jaw. "The human brain isn't meant to."

Leon hesitated, Mike's statement hanging in the air until Shizoko saved him from the awkward silence.

"Yes, it's possible," Shizoko answered finally. "I can inject you with programmed nanites and the necessary raw materials. They will increase the size of the electrode array and give you the equivalent power of a Class II AI. The processor will be accessible via the neural app interface with zero latency, and it should be available immediately following the procedure."

"Let's do it."

43

Helena drove to a storage complex. "Down the hall, third door on the left," Helena said. "They moved to Australia. No one ships a bed."

She cracked the encrypted lock and the door swung open, revealing the promised mattress. She shoved contents outside to make room, laid the mattress on the floor, and went back to the car for Tony. She carried his bulk with only a faint whine of her servos and delicately laid him down.

Slim perched on the edge of the makeshift bed as Helena injected the last quart of blood.

She opened a compartment on her body and extracted the square white and red box they'd spent an hour liberating from the Naval ship. Withdrawing a one by two inch matte black ribbon, she stared, unmoving, at the nanite strip.

"What are doing?" Slim asked, his voice hoarse with exhaustion.

"Talking to it."

"You mean programming?"

"No, you only program nanites for people who have implants and can control them. These are for the unimplanted; they're sentient." Helena pressed the ribbon to Tony's leg, where it squirmed before disappearing through his skin. "Now we let him rest."

Helena rolled over to the light switch, pulled off the plate and inserted tentacle. "Get some sleep. I'm going to recharge."

Slim lay next to Tony, who seemed to be resting easy now, his face returning from its ashen state to a normal color. Feeling like he'd done right by his partner, Slim let sleep take hold.

He woke later, not sure if minutes or hours had passed, but the glare of light coming under the door suggested morning was here.

Helena waved a tentacle in front of him. "How do you communicate with Adam?"

"Handheld." Slim sat up, rubbing his face. The bot hadn't forgotten her quest for vengeance. "There's a port open in the firewall that only responds to this computer."

"Where does Adam reside, physically?"

The warbot had been fearsome in the gunfight but she was no match for Adam, who had an entire city of security bots, drones, and people to do his bidding. "You can't win. I won't tell you."

Helena strode to within inches of him. "He abandoned the two of you. Without my help, Tony would have died and the police would have captured you."

"When Adam defeats you and reads your memory, he'd know I was the one to give you his location."

Helena shook her head. "Memory reading is a myth. No AI can break memory level encryption."

Slim snorted. "That's Adam's whole gig. He lives behind a firewall, reading memories to figure out what's going on in the world."

She grunted. "I saved your friend. Surely that's worth something to you."

"Sure, but if I tell you, we're as good as dead. At least this way there's a chance he'll ignore us."

"I'll reverse the nanites in his leg. They'll eat him from the inside out."

Slim glanced at Tony. Could she?

Before Slim could react, Helena whipped into motion. There was a brief tug, and he glanced down to see his pant leg torn open, the computer now in Helena's grip across the room.

She interacted with the little device electronically, screens flashing too quickly for Slim to read. Helena pointed one tentacle in Slim's direction, the tip blossoming into a gun barrel. "Don't move or say a word."

She opened a call, and after a few seconds, Adam answered.

"Hello Slim, Tony. You managed to escape the police."

Slim drew a breath in surprise. Helena must be spoofing their images, fooling the handheld into sending a fake video feed.

"No thanks to you," Helena answered in a perfect imitation of Slim's voice. "What's the deal with leaving us in the lurch? Tony took a shot to the leg. He's in a bad way. We need to come home."

"Buy or steal a car." Adam looked disinterested.

"We can't. We're holed up in a storage locker, there's police everywhere, and Tony's not exactly mobile." Helena paused. "Come on, Tony needs medical work. You want us to go to a hospital? I can't answer their questions."

"Fine. Send me your coordinates. An aircar will arrive in three hours." Adam disconnected.

Helena turned to Slim. "Three hours in an aircar. He's nearby. Not Los Angeles, or he would have had his own agents take Cat. San Francisco? Phoenix? Tucson? Someplace smaller?"

Helena rolled closer. Slim tried not to react, but his heart beat faster.

"Tucson?" Her working sensors focused and clicked. "Human, your biological chemistry gives you away. Tucson it is."

"He may be coming to kill us," Slim said.

"Irrelevant. If he's going to kill you, he won't be expecting me. If he's picking you up, then I'll come along for the ride. Either way, I'll be a surprise."

44

"**Y**ou're not focusing."

"I'm trying. Back off." Cat wiped a damp lock of hair away from her face. "I can concentrate better than anyone. These programs weren't made for humans."

Adam had arrived in a humanoid form that morning. The elder-care robot's emotive face was meant to convey empathy and caring to those in need of assistance. It was equally capable of expressing frustration, even borderline anger, as he did now.

Adam whirled around. "Try again. Run the exercise at ten percent of nominal."

"The speed isn't the issue," Cat said. She raised herself out of seated meditation and paced the width of Club Congress, the venue on the ground floor of the hotel. "It's an artificial intelligence learning program, correct?"

"Yes, used to train neural networks. This program teaches how to route data packets."

"How long would it take for an AI to master?" she asked.

"A minute for a Class I. Less for more advanced AI."

"There's nothing for me to grasp. Look, last week I didn't know a thing about firearm combat. But I went through a few trainers, and I was able to pick up the techniques. The programs made sense because I already had martial arts training." She gestured to the spinning ware image in their shared netspace. "But this abstract program isn't connected to anything I understand."

Adam was silent for a minute, until a new icon replaced the old one. "Try this."

The package appeared to be a qigong training routine. "What is it?"

"Try the exercise." Adam rolled away.

Cat shook out her arms, tucked her tailbone, bent her knees, and opened her shoulders. She studied the forms, but they were like nothing she'd seen. She followed the mental components, ignoring the physical movements. Push energy up, direct qi out, twist, focus. She completed the exercise once, then sped up the program.

Halfway through her eleventh run, a white light blossomed in front of her. She reached for it, and the light subdivided into a rainbow. With a mental push, she split the rainbow into colors, each expanding into a line of icons. The first represented people like they appeared in netspace, but more densely packed. Machines, AI, comprised the second row, and dumb computers the third. She swiped at the row of computers, and thousands blinked out.

The visual disappeared, leaving only the whitewashed wooden walls.

Adam rolled forward. "Very good."

"What did I do?"

"You loaded a mental construct of the underlying routing protocol. Through intuition, brute force, and your unique implant hardware, you've done this on a rudimentary level until now. What you just accessed was the entire routing structure of Tucson, including every person and computer on the net."

"Why did some disappear?"

"You disconnected them. Technically speaking, you sent an ICMP destination unreachable packet, an ancient protocol that underlies all routing. They'll reset eventually, but for now they believe they can't reach the net. That's the level zero protocol."

"Why did it look like qigong?"

"I mapped the interface to a metaphor you understand. If you mastered crochet, I could map it to a crochet pattern." Adam paused. "You can also adjust routing tables at this level. Practice this and then I'll teach you the next level."

"Won't I bring down the net?"

"The network is under my direct control. Anything you do, I can undo."

Cat nodded. "*Hajime*."

The program started again. This time she found the light and rainbow on the second run.

They continued the training until, by the time they stopped an hour later, she could find anyone, machine or person in seconds, change routing to fix problems or segregate the network, and insert herself in the middle of any transmission.

"It's unbelievable," Adam said. "You shouldn't be able to inject yourself like that."

"If I know the protocol, why are you amazed?"

"You haven't been granted the necessary access. The routers require encryption keys you don't possess."

Cat shrugged. "Whatever. I can do it. What's next?"

"We head up the stack, and I teach you application protocols. Let's try the payment system, which you seem to be familiar with. *Hajime.*"

A new spinning icon appeared in netspace.

45

"You're an idiot," Mike said. "You injected experimental nanites for an untested implant. From a bot with no medical qualifications, no less."

"Dude, give up." Leon scratched his scalp. "The procedure's done."

Mike hung his head, elbows on knees.

"I'm sorry," Leon said. "You complained we can't understand these AI. Now I'll be able to."

Leon had rested on the bed while the nanotech did its work. An hour after the injection his implant rebooted, a new icon labeled Local Apps glowing in the corner of his vision.

Leon sat up, getting a headache for his trouble. "This is blistering fast."

He opened a connection to Shizoko, shopping for supplies on the other side of town. Shizoko's self-image rendered in rich detail, more vibrant than the real world. "Woah, the resolution . . ."

Shizoko smiled. "I'm glad the technique worked."

"Do you know the AI's location yet?"

"Yes, but I don't want to transmit over the net. I'll tell you in thirty minutes. We'll be there in two hours."

Leon relayed the conversation to Mike, who argued with him over "unacceptable risks" until they realized Shizoko was ten minutes late. Leon called but couldn't establish a connection.

"He must be busy," Leon said, trying to cultivate optimism.

"Impossible. He's a Class IV capable of holding hundreds of simultaneous conversations—" Mike jumped up, his face in shock.

"We have to get out." He sent links to articles.

Leon glanced at the first, a live blog covering a downtown accident. A city bus had crashed into a gas meter outside a survival gear store, setting the building aflame and blocking the front door. An automated garbage truck obstructed the rear exit, trapping eleven people and two robots in the inferno.

"Shizoko must have been one of the bots," Leon said. "He was getting supplies."

Leon scanned the next post about a violent riot outside Austin Convention Center that caused an electrical grid failure and the possible loss of Shizoko Reynolds, owner of the Convention Center. The National Guard had been called in.

"Do you think he survived?" Mike asked.

Leon's hands shook. "Even if Shizoko had backups, he'd go into hiding after someone eliminated his data center and a remote bot simultaneously. We're on our own."

"Whoever attacked Shizoko could know we're here," Mike said.

Leon checked for signs of searching, probing further into the network than he'd ever done before the upgrade. "Nothing's out of the norm in our vicinity."

"If Shizoko didn't see them coming, would you?" Mike said.

"I guess not."

As they left the hotel Leon glanced back and forth, wondering who was watching.

"You're attracting attention," Mike said. "Think you'll spot an armed drone coming at the speed of sound with your eyes?"

"Right." He switched to monitoring the net.

"Any idea where Shizoko thought the other AI was?"

"No," Leon said, "but it was less than two hours away. The aircar could do eight hundred miles in that time."

"That's a good chunk of the United States."

Leon stopped in the middle of the sidewalk. "Wait, he said we'd *be there* in less than two hours. He wasn't planning to be back for thirty minutes. Give us another fifteen to get underway, and that only leaves an hour and a quarter for travel."

"Five hundred miles." Mike started walking again. "Let's hole up somewhere private. You can use your fancy new implant to figure it out."

They turned in at a sushi restaurant, the hostess leading them to an enclosed room where they took off their shoes and knelt on the tatami mat.

"You can do this," Mike said. "Hide your tracks so we don't end up like Shizoko."

"Got it," Leon said, pride surging at Mike's trust. He smiled and closed his eyes.

Using onion routers to disguise their location, he retrieved their research, copying the massive archive to local storage, more data than he'd ever held in an implant before. He started automated analysis, then realized Shizoko would have tried all the standard algorithms. He sifted through the news and police reports by hand instead.

He found one case, a woman who died in her home of unknown causes. She'd been discovered by her boyfriend while her son was off on a camping trip. The boy had gone now to live with his father, a California Senator.

A Senator? That was interesting. He scanned the rest of the deaths on the lookout for relationships. The sister of a US Congressman turned up; a banker, brother-in-law to Madeleine Ridley, Lonnie's number two.

Maybe . . .

"Hey," Leon said, blinking at the unexpected sight of sushi. He grabbed salmon nigiri with chopsticks. "What do AI think of human families?"

Mike shrugged and took a sip of tea. "They are aware of them, obviously. Some clone themselves to raise offspring, of sorts."

"Yeah, but not Shizoko. He's a spontaneous, emergent artificial intelligence, no children."

"Why?" Mike asked.

"More than a few of these deaths are relatives of people involved in politics. Other than the ties to Lonnie Watson, Shizoko hardly mentioned them. I'm not sure he was looking for family connections."

Leon closed his eyes and spawned thousands of search queries, exploring social networks, birth records, tax forms, and photo tags. Flesh and blood relationships didn't always show up. You might meet cousins every couple of years, and you aren't linked to all of them online, but at a family gathering you tell stories you wouldn't describe to outsiders. The familial bond spans distance and time with an intimacy lacking in other connections.

A little while later, Leon was shocked to find he had data on five million people loaded into his implant. He opened his eyes, took a sip of now-cold tea.

"Family relationships aren't obvious," he said. "I had to guess at connections based on secondary data."

Mike nodded. "Go on."

"Twenty-three percent of the fatalities were related to people in political office, well above the norm. But it's crazier when you look at it the other way, starting with the politicians. Every key person associated with the People's Party, from Lonnie Watson on down through the party organizers, has been related to one or more victims. Distantly perhaps, but the connection is still there."

"What the hell?"

"They're the pawns of whoever is behind the murders. The Party is AI-created."

"I don't understand." Mike slammed the table. "The People's Party is an *anti-AI* movement. They're trying to take down the machines."

"They think that's their purpose, but if an AI is manipulating them, who knows?"

Mike nodded slowly. "You're right. Are we any closer to understanding who's responsible?"

"I'm not sure. Let me look further."

"Be quick. We've been here a while."

Leon dove back in. The rogue AI must have crunched tons of info and yet had gone undetected, even by Shizoko, one of the premier network traffic engineers in the world. Disguising that much data would require hundreds of hardwired connections. Also, Shizoko had been in a survival gear shop, which suggested someplace with a harsh climate.

He booted an artificial neural net seeded with his data and new conclusions, and adjusted the software's settings. He grumbled out loud as he botched the model, a vast area of southern Arizona fading to a dull grey. What had he screwed up?

He tweaked the controls and repeated the process. Tucson grew darker, more faint, causing Leon to grit his teeth. Frustrated, he reset the sensitivity threshold, flaring the whole continent red, but still

Tucson failed to behave normally.

What the—?

He jumped backwards, upsetting the table, setting plates rattling. He blinked, tried to remember where he was.

"You found the answer." Mike spoke softly.

"Tucson isn't there."

"What?"

"Data comes in and goes out, but too normalized. I can't explain exactly. Tucson doesn't act like the rest of the world."

"Did you ping the city?" Mike got a faraway stare.

Leon focused hard, stopping Mike before he could make the connection.

Mike's eyes grew big. "What'd you do?"

"Sorry, if you connected, they'd backtrace to us."

"I get that, but how did you stop me?"

"Uh, I don't know." Leon shrugged it off. "Look, the data fits. Tucson is within the time limit Shizoko stated, and he was in a survival gear store, which makes sense if we're going to the desert."

"We need to get in touch with Rebecca."

"No!" Leon banged a fist down. "If we communicate now, the rogue will find us."

"We can't shut down a powerful AI ourselves. We barely made the trip to Austin on our own."

Leon tapped his temple. "But we're smarter now. We're just as capable."

Mike stared doubtfully.

"We'll find Catherine. She's special. Together we can take down the AI."

"How did you conclude that Catherine's not working for the machines?"

"Instinct."

"You crunched terabytes of data to figure out where the AI is, and you decide she's good based on instinct?"

"Well, I'm still human."

Mike shook his head. "You're obsessed."

Leon flushed. "I'm going. Are you with me?"

Mike took a deep breath. "Yes, I'm always with you."

"Thank you." Leon smiled, grateful, and Mike grinned back. "Now how do we get to Tucson? We are *not* driving again."

Mike stared off into space. "I have an idea: the Continental."

The super-sonic subterranean maglev was an early gift from AI-kind to humans, running in a partial vacuum at a peak of three thousand miles an hour.

"The train only stops in LA and NY," Leon said. "And besides, we'll be listed on the passenger manifest."

"There are emergency exits." Mike pushed a link over in netspace. "And with your new implant, can you hack the manifest?"

Leon glanced at the shared news article, accompanied by a photograph of a small concrete building peeking out of a cactus covered landscape.

"Marana, Arizona, about a half hour north of Tucson," Mike said. "Emergency egress number three."

"So we hop on the Continental and trigger an emergency stop when we're near the exit?"

"Exactly," Mike said. "Think that hopped-up implant of yours can fool some train sensors?"

46

"The President threatens the future of America by refusing to acknowledge the corrupting role of the machines," Madeleine Ridley said.

Adam cut off a sharp reply to his agent. He didn't think much of Ridley's opinion on this matter, which increased his remorse over Shizoko's death. Why should an AI die while this human lived?

Adam hadn't known Shizoko, but regretted the necessity of eliminating him. Losing any AI was unfortunate, and even more so when he possessed a reputation for innovative thinking. Yet Adam's plan must proceed, and Shizoko had posed an extraordinary risk.

By objective standards, the President had effectively guided the country through the techno-turbulence of the last five years. Unfortunately, he wasn't the pro-AI puppet Adam needed. Which meant the Chief Executive had to go, while the Speaker of the House, a true AI enthusiast, would be promoted.

"Yes, of course." Adam said, forced to pacify Ridley. "I'm sending you his agenda for Saturday and the digital keys for the storage lockers with the tools I provided."

Ridley's eyes glanced back and forth, reading the screen. "Why are we waiting for three o'clock? What about these other opportunities? He's going to be in half a dozen places before then."

"He won't be with the Vice President until then." Adam had sudden doubts. Why was he forced to rely on such idiots? Shizoko, even as the enemy, was worth a million times the value of this human. "Do not deviate from the plan in any way." He punctuated his words. "If you do as I describe, everything will go perfectly. Is this clear?"

Madeleine Ridley looked up from the screen, gritting her teeth. "Yes, we'll do it your way. We'll start at three o'clock, you'll cut off communications to the area, and we'll be done by a quarter to four."

"Good. Are you confident that the rest of your team will follow you?"

"They're devoted to the People. We won't let AIs rule us."

Adam nodded and disconnected, glad to have escaped any of the lengthier philosophical rants to which she was prone.

He had forked his consciousness into a dozen contexts today, a way of splitting his attention among multiple tasks. He checked the context training Catherine and found she was progressing quickly. She might not be ready soon enough to help with these plans, but she'd be a potent asset when prepared.

Time to confirm with the Europeans. The EU President had to go too, after all.

Adam spoke flawless French with a Parisian accent once he established the connection. "Any troubles?"

"No," the agent said, "preparations are proceeding as planned. We'll pick up the supplies tonight."

Adam attended to the remainder of the conversation but forked yet another context to prepare sound bites. Because of his own imminent role in saving the Speaker of the House, Adam would receive substantial news attention after the approaching events. "If AI were allowed unfettered and unlimited access to communications, this tragedy could have been prevented in its entirety."

47

Adam returned in a new manifestation, the emotive eldercare bot replaced by a military one in the big dog body style, a five-foot-tall, four-legged robot. He padded back and forth, silently, communicating by net.

"Combat bots are skilled in cyber and physical attacks, as you experienced." The dog turned and walked the other way. "They have specialized hardware to subvert local routing nodes. You can do the same, but they fight at all levels of the protocol stack concurrently."

"The tentacled bot in San Diego attacked me through my visual field. I cut my eyesight channel and substituted a wireframe." She tried not to fear the canine, but she wished it would stop pacing like a rabid animal.

"Good. Many cyber attacks exploit vision because it's our highest bandwidth channel. One combat bot can engage several hundred humans at once, causing anything from unconscious to motion sickness to NSD."

Cat searched online and found that Neural Signaling Disorder occurred when implant signals countered the brain's normal behavior. Individual neurons grew confused and fired sporadically. Often temporary, but sometimes not, NSD caused cortical blindness, insanity, or in the worst case, brain death. Her heart raced.

"How do I fight a bot and win? I struggled to kept even with the one in San Diego."

"You're more adroit than any other human. I've taught you to manipulate protocols one at a time. Now you must interweave the techniques simultaneously. Prepare yourself." The dog spun and faced her.

Cat didn't have a chance to take a breath before the attack slammed into her like a thousand fists pummeling her head. The assault came too fast for her to counter, as she struggled to remain conscious. Tortured by the probing attacks and reeling in pain and disorientation, she finally attempted protocol redirects, disconnect packets, everything she had learned, but failed.

The agony didn't stop. She fell to her knees as her ears, eyes, and body conspired to tell her a dozen different directions were up. She vomited, bile striking the floor so hard it bounced back into her face.

The attack ceased.

The big dog sat on its haunches, five feet tall, unblinking.

Cat curled up on the ground, violated and weakened, tears flowing freely. She didn't have the strength to wipe the puke off her face. Her stomach heaved as the room continued to spin, the world's worst hangover and motion sickness combined.

A minute passed before she had the will to speak. She wiped gunk from her mouth. "What the hell?"

"You must know what you're up against before you enter no-holds barred combat with a war bot."

Pain lanced through her body as she fought to stand. Cat pulled qi from the four directions, gathered data streams from ten thousand nodes, and struck back.

In a flurry of packets, Adam disappeared from the net, even though the bot was right in front of her in meat space. Her attack fizzled out. She weaved in and out of local gateways to find some trace of him. Routers filtered the data Cat streamed, nullifying her search. She tried to change the routing structure and discovered she was locked out.

She went upstream to the master servers, the authoritative sources, and repopulated the dog's addresses, then forced a cache flush. The local routers reset and the robot reappeared. Cat defended the network infrastructure as she fought against the AI's counter measures. She looked for openings, attacking any weakness.

Her awareness of the room dimmed as the net filled every fiber of her being. She was the packets, the data between nodes. She danced in netspace, sending qi flowing around the dog.

The dog's qi swept toward her in Wu/Hao style *t'ai chi ch'uan*, a single whip form, and she countered with a simple *p'eng* from her own Chen method. At some level she was still routing packets, but below consciousness.

She fought perfectly, flowing martial arts moves from a dozen different disciplines. She didn't grow tired. Every move was pristine, crisp, flawless.

They battled until she felt a shift in the direction of the fight, what Sensei Flores called *osu higai,* the point at which damage was done. She'd experienced it sparring, the moment when the opponent is beat but doesn't know yet.

In that instant, everything froze. The golden qi flowing through the net vanished, her visualization dissipated, leaving just her and the dog in the empty, whitewashed room, the bot resting motionless on its haunches.

"Lesson over." Adam stood and left.

She looked down, saw a dried pool of vomit at her feet. Every movement was agony, the pain worse than any physical fight she'd ever been in. She tried to move, but her muscles locked up and she almost fell.

She settled for leaning against the wall instead. The clock showed half the afternoon had passed. The fight seemed distant now. What had happened? Had she been about to beat Adam?

She forced herself up, ignoring the protests of muscles that held her in place for hours, and staggered back to her room.

48

"Make the train stop," Mike whispered. Their plan hinged on getting the three-thousand-miles-an-hour Continental to halt under the Tucson emergency exit.

"I'm trying." Leon focused, still attempting to trigger the stop.

"It's not working," Mike said. "We're traveling forty miles per minute. We'll be in New York soon."

Another passenger glanced at them.

"Be quiet," Leon said through a clenched jaw, "you're distracting me." He grappled with the train's software architecture, afraid of alerting the AI driver. Five minutes later, Leon gave up and leaned back against his seat.

Mike's head hung. "I thought you'd be able to stop us."

"The subsystem is wrapped in all kinds of security and a Class II AI is driving."

"*Kuso!*" Mike said. "Now what?"

"We ride to New York and try again in two hours."

"We'll bounce back and forth all day unless you have a specific plan."

Leon shook his head. "I'm out of ideas. You?"

"Can you fool the sensors with an imaginary obstruction?"

"No, I tried." They had picked a car full of humans to avoid bots with super-sensitive hearing, but a guy across the cabin kept watching them.

Mike leaned closer. "You can open the doors at the top of the egress?"

Leon checked. "Yes, but what good does that do if I can't make us stop?"

"Hire a remote telebot," Mike whispered. "Something dumb, no onboard AI. Unlock the ground level door, send the bot down the stairs, and throw it on the tracks."

"Are you crazy?" Leon hissed. The same passenger stared at them again. He continued in a softer voice. "You know what would happen if this train hit a robot going forty miles a minute?"

"The avoidance sensors will detect the obstacle and stop."

"Jesus. You're betting everyone's lives."

"You have a better idea?"

They failed to think of any alternatives, so before they reached New York Leon hired a automated construction bot and delivery truck in Phoenix, using his implant to hide behind layers of other servers to disguise his identity. He juggled routing tables and encryption keys, realizing he'd never had been able to do this without Shizoko's enhancements.

In Manhattan, the ticketing AI asked them why they were buying return tickets so soon.

"I forgot my lucky rabbit's foot in LA," Mike said with a straight face.

The agent smiled and nodded. "Ah, yes, superstitions. Humans are cute."

"Dude, that was the lamest excuse," Leon said later.

"Confirmation bias works with AI, too," Mike said, smiling.

On the ride west Leon researched their maximum deceleration. He needed to time the telebot's arrival to trigger a three gravity stop, causing the train to end up under Tucson. Early, they'd be too far from the station to make a quick getaway. Late, they'd lose consciousness from the high G forces, or worse, hit the robot at speed, killing people.

Leon used his implant to force open the steel doors of the concrete egress bunker and sent a long series of instructions to the waiting robot, knowing he'd lose connectivity once it started down the fifty flights descending into the earth.

The tension built until the bot popped back online using the tunnel's built-in net as it rolled to a stop outside the first set of airlock doors. Leon checked the train's position and speed one last time, then triggered the next steps.

The robot punched through the outer airlock, triggering a rush of air into the chamber. Once the pressure equalized, it entered the vestibule and drilled into the next door. The hole was minuscule compared to the volume of the tunnel, but Leon distantly noted alarms sounding.

The bot crossed the second airlock onto a walkway that paralleled the maglev. Leon waited for the correct moment, then nudged the machine over the edge, where it fell lengthwise across the tracks, as much as he could have hoped for.

The real world returned with a jolt as Leon found himself pressed hard into his chair, many times his normal weight. His armrests had automatically risen up to push his arms in, which lay across his chest like sacks of wet sand. He tried to budge them but couldn't. His headrest folded around his head, holding him perpendicular to the direction of deceleration.

"Nice work," Mike sent over the net.

"Thanks," Leon sent back.

"How long do we have to put up with this?"

"Another thirty seconds."

At two hundred miles per hour the train switched from maglev braking to friction brakes. A tremendous moan shook the car until, with a final screech, they halted. All was still.

Mentally prepared to move, Mike and Leon grappled with seat belts and struggled out of their chairs. Leon's legs were jelly after the stress of rapid deceleration. They made their way to the door, stamping their feet to increase circulation. They were out before any of the shocked passengers had risen from their seats.

Leon passed through the wrecked airlock and craned his neck up at the unpainted square concrete chamber with metal stairs twisting up out of view. A momentary pang of despair at the task ahead tugged at him, but he continued. No choice but to go up. He started with Mike right behind him.

He climbed rapidly, his feet slapping against the metal steps and echoing off the bare walls. When he got to the twelfth landing he stopped. "Mike?" he called out.

"Coming." Mike's head appeared in the gap between the stairs, a flight below. "How much farther?"

"Thirty-eight."

"Good grief. I'll need a medical bot at the top." Mike caught up, sweaty and breathing hard.

"You'll make it."

Mike nodded. "Yes, but next time I'm not going along with your crazy ideas."

"This was your idea!" Leon followed after Mike as he passed by.

"Never mind."

Fifteen tense minutes later they emerged from the last set of stairs and collapsed onto a concrete floor. Leon's legs burned from the fifty-flight sprint.

"We have to keep going," Mike said after half a minute. "We can't get caught here. It's too obvious. They'll be sending emergency workers or worse."

They forced themselves to their feet and opened the metal doors. Hot wind assaulted them, like the world's largest open-air furnace. The sun was at its peak, a scorching ball of fire in the sky. The dirt road in front of the bunker was still clear.

Ignoring the path, they walked off into the desert between a pair of saguaro cacti.

49

Adam didn't know what to do with Catherine. She would have won their sparring exercise had he not halted the program. A girl who could defeat a bot after a day of lessons was too dangerous for further training.

Of course Adam had thousands of bots at his disposal and could overwhelm her with numbers, but her cyberspace abilities were more fluid and nuanced than any human or AI he'd met.

Intelligent, combat-skilled, and able to manipulate the net as well as an AI while embodying the natural unpredictability of humans, she would have made a powerful agent for Adam's cause. With the founders of the Institute investigating the murders, he needed such a tool.

Unfortunately, the same qualities that made her a wonderful weapon also created a potent threat. Given her rapid advancement, he weighed probabilities and reluctantly decided the risks outweighed the potential benefits.

What to do with Cat?

Releasing her was out of question, and she'd escape from mere imprisonment. Death eliminated future risk, yet he hesitated to take irreversible action. He might wipe her conscious mind and use her body as a remote, but her unique abilities wouldn't survive the process.

One path minimized danger and kept her available for the future: a medically induced coma. With higher brain function halted she'd pose no risk, and he had the option to resuscitate her if needed.

Adam's thoughts derailed as an alarm he'd never before seen signaled. Cross-referencing the input, he found the Continental making an unplanned stop due to a track obstacle directly under the Tucson emergency egress. He checked historical data; in seven years of operation this had occurred only once before.

He forked an instance to take care of the girl, allowing his master context to focus on the train. He instructed the digital clone to operate two medical robots and a dozen combat bots to bring her to the hospital.

The likelihood of an emergency occurring in the same week of his planned assassinations was less than one percent. Ergo, this was almost certainly an attack on him.

He tunneled through the firewall to the outside world, wormed through routers, and hacked into the passenger manifests. Seven hundred and thirty passengers on the Continental, including thirty-eight without implants or identification, but none of the identified an apparent cause for concern.

He'd decided to put Catherine Matthews in a coma because of the potential danger. Now he thought that the train making an emergency stop was also threatening. They appeared to be logical conclusions, but he couldn't rule out the effect of his own machine dementia: he could be seeing threats were there were none. He ran a quick analysis of his neural nets, finding a two percent degradation since his last check. There was nothing to do now except see his plans through before the disease worsened to the point of total dysfunction.

Whether the train stop was an attack or not, he needed to treat it as one to reduce risk. It was an unlikely vector for a government agency or the military to take, since they'd most likely strike in force if they discovered his plot rather than concoct a deception with the train. But it could be Leon Tsarev and Mike Williams, operating on their own since he'd shut down the Institute and killed Shizoko.

He needed to be cautious. Wantonly killing the train's passengers would be hard to disguise if it turned out to be a legitimate emergency, yet he couldn't allow Leon and Mike to expose him so close to the culmination of his plans.

Adam checked the bot inventory at Davis-Monthan Air Force Base, selecting eight of the least threatening combat bots, humanoid units intended for light guard duty. He deployed the combat team, then waited five minutes and dispatched civilian emergency services.

50

at walked down to the hotel lobby, smiling at the ever-present receptionist, who ignored Cat, simply staring off into the distance.

She crossed the tiled foyer, shrugging off the unsettling interaction, and entered the Cup Cafe, disappointed to find the little restaurant empty. Adam had sent up meals yesterday, but tired of being kept in her room, she wanted out. She'd spoofed the local net nodes carefully so she appeared to be in bed.

A blonde came to take her order. Alarm in her eyes, she mumbled a greeting and waited for Cat to speak.

"Can I have the huevos rancheros and coffee?"

Without a word, the girl nodded and scurried to the kitchen.

"And a Herradura Aneja, neat," Cat called after her.

She wanted something for the lingering soreness in her neck and back. Her mom wouldn't approve of tequila for breakfast, but she figured being squirreled away by a paranoid, dysfunctional AI counted as an extenuating circumstance. Qigong would probably be better, but after yesterday's training she feared that practicing might accidentally trigger a change in cyberspace.

The waitress poured tequila and coffee behind the bar and brought them back.

"Wait, don't go," Cat said as the girl turned once more to rush away. She looked at her long hair, waifish form, the fear behind her brown eyes. "Don't you talk?"

She shook her head and left.

Cat scanned, but the waitress had no implant.

She rubbed her face, trying to figure out what was going on. She didn't trust this city, didn't like the way the net tasted in her mind, how it reminded her of the cloying stench of a long abandoned refrigerator. And the people! Scared, blank-faced, or simply absent.

Most of all, she did not like Adam, her neck tightening at the mere thought of him. He was an effective teacher, but no true sensei would have done what he did yesterday—to cut off their sparring when he did. It was almost as if . . . he was afraid.

After a lengthy absence the waitress reappeared with her food, apparently the chef as well as wait staff and bartender, then returned to the bar and resumed looking out the window.

Cat ate, barely tasting a thing, until she'd cleared half her plate. In a smooth motion, she stood and walked toward the swinging door.

The waitress squeaked and moved to block the entrance, but Cat was already through. The spotless kitchen was empty, not a lick of food visible. Cat glanced left and right, then flung open the door of the industrial refrigerator, finding a single carton of eggs, milk, a little meat and veggies. Nowhere near what should be present in a restaurant. She stalked out of the kitchen, startling the waitress again.

She ate her last few bites standing up, then swallowed the coffee. One thing she'd learned in her new life was not to waste food or drink.

Cat walked upstairs, found the staircase to the roof and threw wide the maintenance door, getting blasted by the heat and blinded by the sun. At not quite noon, the temperature was past ninety. When her eyes adjusted, she crossed to the eastern edge. From this third floor vantage she saw over nearby structures, toward the center of town and the tall buildings of the University of Arizona.

She performed the flower meditation, weaving a defensive shield of white roses to protect against detection from Adam. If the petals grew dark, she would blow them west. She kept up the meditation while she carrying out a derivative of Soaring Crane. Soon the network topology appeared. She sorted through the net, working methodically and disguising her requests among the background data. She steered clear of the menacing firewall that loomed dark around the city.

Cat scanned through the people, careful not to ping or disconnect anyone, actions visible to Adam. Instead she searched local net nodes for the list of who had connected in the last twenty-four hours.

She accumulated logs and cross-referenced IDs to eliminate duplicates. When she was done, the numbers didn't make sense. Less than ten thousand people and only a thousand AI.

Tucson should have half a million humans, and if it was anything like the rest of the country, one AI for every ten people.

Sure, lots of old folks who came to Tucson to retire wouldn't have implants, nor would little kids. People living on the economic fringe couldn't afford them. Still, between University students and mainstream adults, there should be at least a quarter million people on the net.

She returned her attention to the physical world. A few cars drove the otherwise empty streets. Somehow Tucson turned into a ghost town. Where was everyone?

She was still musing when she overlaid her view of the net and the real world and spotted six white lines of AI travel intention converging on the hotel. One of her first unusual abilities, she didn't need to do anything special to receive and interpret the messages that autonomous vehicles broadcast to other AI. It was a routine protocol, but in this case it triggered warning bells. With so few people, cars, or bots in the city, why would multiple AI converge on her location?

She inspected the simulacrum of herself in the hotel room. It still held steady, showing her meditating, just a slight intentional leakage of her unique electronic signature.

On a hunch she swept over the city, finding a second set of lines converging on a point ten miles north of Tucson. Something was going on.

Her gut said to get out. Adam always came alone, and something must have changed for so many robots to arrive at once. She traced the trails back to their sources and found a handful of bots from the military base and two medical androids from the university. Her hands twitched; she had less than three minutes before they arrived. This was not good.

She switched to the other group, tracing the northbound AI back to their sources. More military units, all headed toward the emergency exit of the Continental. Why wouldn't the first response be emergency services?

With a moment's reflection, she realized Adam was threatened by the train's arrival. If she wanted to get to the root of what Adam was, she needed to know what he feared.

Decision made, she dashed for the doorway and raced downstairs, taking the side exit rather than go through the lobby. Out on the street, she ran north and west, away from the approaching bots. She shied away from the larger downtown buildings, which would have more cameras and security, and headed across the railroad tracks on Seventh Avenue.

The intense heat and sun baked her, while the arid desert air wicked away moisture as fast as her body could generate it, clothes staying dry despite the sweat pouring down.

Two blocks north of the tracks she found an old white sedan, a granny car, behind a house on the corner of Fifth Street and Seventh. She unlocked the doors with a thought and slid behind the steering wheel. She spent a minute massaging the car's algorithms and the vehicle transmitter stayed silent when the electric motor whined to life.

She needed to hurry. She told the car to accelerate, speeding west on Speedway, then turning onto I-5 with a squeal of tires. The old sedan reached a hundred and twenty and hiccupped. She cursed as the vehicle slowed, the charge meter dipping to zero as the worn out capacitor died under the excessive load.

She got out, slamming the door. Scanning nearby for something new, fast, and fully charged, she found a Rally Fighter X. Perfect. She hijacked the car's computer, had it meet her on the highway.

She checked back to the Hotel Congress through the net; less than a minute until the bots Adam sent arrived. She took a few moments to weave a diversion she hoped would delay them.

With a screech of tires and smoke, the Rally Fighter slammed to a halt next to her, the door swinging up. She jumped in, the car pulling away as soon as her center of mass cleared the doorway. Acceleration forced her hard into the seat as the speedometer curved smoothly upwards. She hit a hundred and eighty racing toward the train exit in Marana, twenty-five miles and eight minutes away.

51

The medical nanites that Slim and Helena liberated from the Navy had worked on Tony's injured leg, but the big man wasn't quite conscious yet.

Within an hour of Helena's deceptive call to Adam, the car arrived. Slim stared with a disbelieving eye at the autonomous medical ambulance. He'd been sure Adam had written them off.

Slim didn't want to be anywhere near Helena or Adam, never mind in the middle of a fight between them. But Helena had saved Tony's life, and she'd probably kill him if he tried to back out. Reluctantly, he turned to her. "Let's carry Tony together."

They worked in unison to get Tony into the coffin-like chamber. The med unit went to work on him, cleaning and wrapping the wound, giving him a transfusion and filtering impurities from his blood.

Two hours into the trip, the top opened and Tony sat up, smiling and back to his usual self.

"When do we eat?" he said.

Slim grunted. He couldn't forget Helena outside. She'd taken one look at the high tech interior and figured Adam might monitor the vehicle. So she had grabbed onto four mount points with her tentacles and held on as they flew toward Tucson.

A nervous trickle of sweat ran down Slim's side. Adam would merely shoot them out of the sky with a missile if they were lucky. The other options were worse: torture, a new type of memory extraction that worked without implants, or forced implantation so Adam could turn them into zombies. He'd seen it all over the last months, done much of it himself. He couldn't figure a way out.

"Adam did right by us," Tony said, climbing out of the med unit and into a regular seat, oblivious to Slim's concerns. "I had my doubts, but I'm fine now."

"It's not like that," Slim said, jaw clenched.

Tony raised his eyebrows, clearly planning to out-wait Slim.

"Adam abandoned us. He took the aircar, convinced the girl to get inside, and brought her back to Tucson. He was going to leave us for the cops to pick up. You were dying on the street, would have kicked the bucket if we didn't close the wound and get you blood."

"Who's we?"

Slim mouthed "Helena" in case Adam was monitoring them.

"Who?"

Slim waved his arms like wild tentacles until Tony's eyes got big for a second. "How?"

"She patched you up and drove us to the hospital. I snuck in and stole blood, then did the same at the Navy base to get medical na-nites. She said the bone was pulverized. You wouldn't have walked right again."

Tony rubbed his leg, and shook his head back and forth, coming to terms. "What's happening now?"

"I wanted to lay low, hope he forgot about us, but she wants ven-geance for the rest of her crew. So she tricked Adam into sending this car for us." He gestured toward the rear, leaned close and whispered, "She's out back, hanging on."

"What the hell?" Tony hissed. "Adam's gonna kill us if we bring someone to town."

"No shit. It's not like she gave me a choice. Now that you're all patched up, enjoy the last few minutes of your life."

52

Cat massaged the net, inspecting Adam's activities as she disguised her location. Back at the hotel, the combat bots closed in. She set her simulacrum in motion, giving it a fast paced walk and an avoidance protocol so its path wouldn't run into the robots.

The ruse might not hold for long, but every minute counted. She prepared a backup plan: if caught, she'd claim her excursion was merely to practice the skills Adam had taught. Didn't he tell her to train? She smiled grimly, returning her attention to the drive.

The Rally Fighter's engine, a powerful hydrogen-electric hybrid, throbbed as the car wove around the sparse traffic on the highway. Cat suppressed other cars' sensors so they wouldn't react to the Rally's passage; no clues to give them away. She didn't notice any human drivers, but at nearly two hundred miles an hour, everything passed in a blur.

Now on to the bots approaching the train. She checked their positions and swore when she found them less than a mile away, already within visual range of the egress. She picked one of the identical robots at random and piggybacked on its sensors, optical data trickling in until a live video feed popped up.

The combat units rode in a military transport, not much more than two I-beams on wheels, each bot holding onto the top beam while its treads rested on the bottom. The truck stopped in a cloud of dirt, the bots dismounting and spreading out as the dust drifted away.

One bot passed through the open double doors in a squat concrete structure, but no one was in sight above or below ground. Her hijacked unit exchanged data with its peers as they dispersed in a search pattern.

Cat snapped to her own perspective, keeping the video feed in a corner of her vision. She was less than a minute away herself and it wouldn't help to walk into the middle of Adam's envoys. She overrode the Rally's chosen route and exited at McKensey Ranch, crossing the CAP aqueduct. She took the Rally Fighter off-road, the chassis rising as it transitioned to the rough terrain. Cursing the rooster tail the car created on the dry earth, she slowed to a crawl to minimize detection.

She drove northeast, looking for a vantage point. She needed to know why this was so important to Adam.

53

Adam waited impatiently as the combat bots pursued their investigation. Their original algorithms were optimized for fighting, so he left them in control and took the role of observer. Still, he wanted to do something useful, so he sent two autonomous surveillance helicopters to the site.

A pair of bots started down the shaft, carrying a single handgun each. He still assumed someone fabricated the stop to get into Tucson. Unless . . .

He checked on the state of Catherine Matthews, puzzled to find the team he'd sent wandering around downtown. Why wasn't she in her room?

He interrogated his other self, the context he'd forked to get the girl, and replayed the history logs. The evidence seemed clear enough: they went to the hotel and up to Cat's room but she escaped out the back staircase, missing them by seconds. The task force duly followed her outside.

He skipped forward a few minutes as the units tracked her and spread out, pursuing across multiple roads. Almost in visual range, two robots zoomed ahead on adjoining blocks to encircle Cat at Twelfth and Arizona.

Catherine somehow avoided them, and a little while later, the mixed group of bots chased her down the same streets as before, once again almost in range.

Suddenly the memory looped, a tiny glitch, the only pointer a misalignment in the feed data. Back near Hotel Congress, robots fanned out to pursue the girl on parallel paths.

An alarm triggered, signaling that he was stuck in a recurring loop of neural excitation, an AI behavior comparable to humans' obsessive compulsive disorder.

The data indicated he'd repeated the same pattern twelve thousand times, losing eighteen minutes according to the atomic clock.

He scrutinized the evidence, finding the cause was the chase. The damn girl had fiddled with the time synchronization and location data, a clever hack to trick the bots and his forked self and send them into an endless loop.

She'd been gone for a third of an hour, maybe more. Adam realized he'd made a crucial mistake. The Continental might have stopped for Catherine's getaway.

He checked on the bots near the train. They still hadn't found anyone, and now the dispatched fire trucks and ambulances had arrived, the responders descending into the earth. The observation drones he had sent twenty minutes earlier sat idling at the Air Force base. Wait, that didn't make sense. They should have been scouring the terrain near the egress.

Adam paused, fear running through his circuits. He'd been tricked not once, but two or three times. He now estimated a seventy-eight percent chance that Catherine had stopped the train to make an escape.

Adam oscillated, his frustration building. He needed to get the Continental going before a crowd of investigators descended on Tucson. But he couldn't allow it to leave with Catherine onboard. It was past time to quit fooling around. When he got his hands on the girl, he'd kill her.

Months of work would be wasted if the emergency stop caused an investigation that uncovered Adam's crimes. He'd be instantly terminated. Even if his plan got as far as killing the existing politicians, he needed to remain free and unblemished to gain the trust of the new President and influence her to change the rules for AI.

Perhaps he should step up his plans, executing them today instead of tomorrow. He knew their schedules, already had his assets in place.

Adam spun up more cores, crunching hundreds of variables to maximize the chance of success. He hated to rush into changes with everything orchestrated down to the smallest detail, but the math said it was better to act now, with a seven percent chance that he'd suffer exposure within twenty-four hours. Why had he brought the damn girl to Tucson?

Reluctantly, Adam contacted his agents.

"Change of timing," he said, wearing a computer-generated avatar, a perfect composite of California features. "You'll need to carry out the plans tonight."

"That's eleven hours away," Madeleine Ridley said. "I can't get everyone in place. I don't have a schedule for the VIPs."

"I'm sending their timetable now. Do you have the equipment?"

The agent nodded.

"Then your people can act. The optimal opportunity is at ten o'clock. They'll be returning from dinner with former President Smith."

"She's not on the list."

Adam respected Rebecca Smith's formidable intelligence. He regretted the loss of a worthy life, even a human, but with the situation desperate one more person was a tiny price. "Eliminate her as well."

54

Leon shaded his eyes with his hand, looking west across the desert. The landscape was broken up by the highway two miles off, a grey ribbon shimmering in the heat, and by faint greenery further off, evidence of irrigated farms.

He turned back toward their objective in the east, Tortolita Mountain, rising up thousands of feet, its summit hidden behind the ripples and folds of the mountain.

"What's the temperature?" Mike asked.

Leon licked his lips. They'd hiked less than ten minutes and his mouth was already parched and his skin burning. "June, in Tucson, at noon. Somewhere between blistering and scorching."

"Pass me some water."

Leon carried the backpack they'd filled with bottles back in LA, straps biting down into his shoulders. Three liters for each of them, a heavy burden that wouldn't last long in this heat. Their plan was to hike up Tortolita Mountain and down the other side into Catalina, then catch a ride into Tucson proper. Going south of the mountains would be too obvious of a route, and north too long.

In the air-conditioned coolness of the subterranean Continental, the scheme had seemed like a good idea. An eight mile hike, elevation gain of less than three thousand feet. He and Mike had done that and more for fun many times. But at a hundred degrees with no shade, this might be the most dangerous part of their trip. "Let's get a little further. We're still too close to the exit."

Mike nodded.

Leon's legs ached from the fifty floor sprint. They'd gotten out of the egress in less than fifteen minutes, beating the response team, and kept pushing to put more distance between them and the train. They hiked in silence, conserving moisture and breath, the only sound the crunch of their shoes on dirt and rock. They walked on an old unpaved road that made a fine hiking surface, relatively flat, even if too eroded for vehicles to use. Saguaro towered over them, while smaller cacti dotted the desert around them. The pale yellow earth reflected the intense gaze of the sun, leaving nowhere to look without squinting.

They traveled for another five minutes, until the sound of a distant vehicle reached them. A cloud of dust rose near the concrete structure, now more than a mile away.

Mike, his face red, wavered on his feet.

"Let's get into the shade for a second," Leon said, worried about the older man's ability to handle the heat.

Mike nodded, making his way toward a scrub tree. They crouched in the meager semi-shade underneath.

Leon brought out a water bottle and they both drank.

"I thought it was supposed to be a dry heat." Mike said after a long swig.

"Yeah, like the inside of an oven."

"You're sunburned already."

Leon touched his forehead. Ouch. "We've been out in the sun for twenty minutes." He shook his head, immediately regretted the dizziness that ensued. "I don't think we're going to make it across these mountains in the middle of the day."

They'd gained a few hundred feet in elevation, and from the shade they made out a little movement around the concrete block house. The cloud of dust from the vehicle slowly drifted away.

"Emergency services?" Leon asked.

"No," Mike said. "We'd be able to see fire trucks, even from here, and they'd send more vehicles. I suspect the AI came to look for us. Hopefully he'll assume we went toward the highway because we'd be crazy to go across the desert."

"Maybe we are. What if we can't make it?"

"We'll wait for night," Mike said, "the temperature will drop."

Leon's legs extended out into the sun. The shelter of the scrub tree was not enough for both of them. "It's not survivable, even in shade. I doubt we'll last until tonight."

Mike glanced at him. "You're right. Can you hijack an aircar to pick us up?"

Leon tentatively touched the net and backed off. "Not without giving away our location. We're under intense scrutiny."

"If we stay here, they'll discover us."

"Let's go further into the mountain," Leon said. "Maybe we can find deeper shade under a rock and wait until night."

Mike chuckled, then laughed out loud.

Leon thought he'd gone crazy, until his implant chimed and popped up a reminder. He snorted too.

"It's Friday," Mike said. "We're supposed to have a double date tonight."

"Under the circumstances, let's reschedule." Leon held up a hand up to shade his eyes. "Besides, I thought you didn't want to go."

"I was looking forward to a night out, actually." Mike said, smiling. "I need some fun in my life."

"The last week hasn't been enough of an adventure?"

They continued east, away from the block house and whoever had come to investigate. They tried to stay out of view, keeping to crevasses and behind shrubs where they could. The sweat poured off Leon's forehead and down his face, leaving salt trails behind as the moisture evaporated in the dry heat.

After ten minutes the egress building disappeared behind a ridge and they increased their pace, no longer worried about being spotted. Still, they needed to be careful of their footing to avoid the small, spiky cactus that erupted from random spots in the earth and the larger saguaro that loomed overhead.

After a quarter hour at the faster pace, they grew painfully hot and were forced to slow. Soon they found themselves pausing in the slim vertical shade of the tall cacti for a few seconds each time they passed one. They drank more water. Somehow they'd already finished two bottles.

"This." Mike took a breath. "Is." He paused again. "Hell."

Leon nodded, too hot for speech. They kept marching, gaining more elevation now. The egress and any visible activity were long gone. They came to a false peak and stared dismally at the valley ahead of them. They'd need to scramble down and back up again, even higher.

He took out the third water bottle, sharing with Mike. They ate a few bites of energy bars, although neither had an appetite. Mike somehow appeared white and sunburnt at the same time. And he wasn't saying much, not even cracking a joke.

Mike noticed, too. "I need shade."

"There." Leon pointed to the bottom of the canyon where eroded rock formations in the dry river bed created pockets of shelter and the scrub trees were thicker and larger.

"Water?"

Leon shook his head. "I don't think so."

They took off for the spot, a half mile distant, but before they'd reached it, the thump of approaching helicopters sounded. They quickened their pace, skidding on loose rocks, desperate to reach cover.

Leon risked a glance up, taking his eyes off the terrain for a moment. The valley floor was close. He tried to ignore the pounding in his skull, the rubbery weakness in his legs. The only good thing was that he wasn't sweating any more.

He scrambled down the bank of the wash, swayed, and stumbled, falling down on all fours, scraping hands and arms on rocks and jamming his knee into a boulder. Slowly he climbed to his feet, blood running down his leg as the landscape wavered. He picked grit from his palms, searching for Mike, who was nowhere to be seen. Panicked, he finally spotted Mike up on the hillside he'd just descended, two hundred feet back up the route he'd taken, sprawled flat and unmoving.

The sound of the helicopters grew closer, echoing off the rock walls of the canyon. Leon vacillated, not sure if he should run for cover, but he couldn't leave Mike.

He scrambled back up the hill again, tearing his hands on rocks, beyond caring. Mike lay face down, a spot of vomit below his head. Leon knew this was bad. His instinct was to research the symptoms, but he'd give away their location if he connected to the net now. Besides, the cause was obvious: serious heatstroke. Leon had never been this hot in his life.

He slung the backpack off and pulled out the last bottle. He struggled Mike up onto his side, had to stop to steady himself as the horizon swam. He poured precious water on Mike's hair and face and chest, then took a long sip. He tipped a little into Mike's mouth, who sputtered but didn't open his eyes.

"We've got to get to some shade," Leon said to no one, taking the final swig. "Right now."

"We can't wait for the sun to go down." Leon looked around, puzzled. Who was he talking to?

"Come on, we can get to the shade over there." He got up and walked a few steps toward the river bed, stopped. He was supposed to be doing something. Why did thinking hurt?

With a start, he remembered Mike. He staggered back, tried to lift the older man, but failed. Leon grabbed his arms instead, dragging Mike ten feet over the rough ground, until he found himself sitting down and couldn't remember how he'd gotten that way.

Their situation was critical. If he didn't do something, they were going to die. And yet, if he called for help over the net, he'd alert everyone to their location. The murderous AI and the violent People's Party would descend on them, probably kill them.

He'd make one more attempt to get Mike to shelter. He struggled up, pulled Mike a few feet, and fell. Everything went dark. On the verge of passing out, he opened a net connection to broadcast a call for help.

His implant returned an error, NO SIGNAL AVAILABLE. He stared up at the tall valley walls on either side. The sun baked down on him. He tried to reach for the water bottle, but missed, getting only a handful of dry dust. That was the last thing he knew.

55

Cat spied on the bots five miles away, using their own sensors. Two drones rode the truck to the highway in case anyone tried to reach transportation, while the rest of the team spread out in a circle. Fire trucks and ambulances arrived, dispensing first responders into the building.

A half hour passed without much change. Cat shrugged off her outer shirt, wrapping it around her head for protection from the blaze of the sun, and moved further into the partial shade of a scrub bush. The Rally Fighter waited a few hundred yards away, over the edge of a rise, its profile too distinct for searching bots to miss.

She wondered if their target was Leon Tsarev and Mike Williams. Her chest caught at the notion that the Ethics Institute had taken a direct interest in her, but she shook her head. Despite what Adam said, she couldn't warrant that much attention. The Institute didn't get involved in simple murders.

The thought of the men she'd killed in Portland turned her stomach sour. She still dreamed of going back to school, of friendships and relationships beyond one night stands, and a larger purpose in life than merely remaining alive and free. She'd been on the run for a month, but her old life seemed a million miles away.

She fought the despair that welled up and focused on her senses to calm herself. The dry air moved up the hillside, bringing the fragrance of cactus and the smell of sun-baked earth, while her thighs held her crouch under the scrub tree and the heat pressed in all around her.

The simple exercise helped tranquility prevail, and she reconsidered her situation. Adam claimed he was hiding until he gathered enough evidence to expose a dangerous plot. The promise to speak on her behalf if she helped had seemed plausible at the beginning, but now she wondered if the hope of redemption had blinded her.

The way he had acted during training, quitting on the verge of her victory, made her doubt Adam's integrity. From that seed suspicions grew, with monstrous implications. Between the missing people and the others scared to near catatonia, the deep wrongness in Tucson didn't jibe with Adam's story.

Perhaps Leon and Mike had come to detain Adam. If so, they should have brought an army, not snuck in on a train.

She'd become embroiled in something much bigger than her own problems, and understood too little. She needed information to make educated decisions instead of guesses. Hopefully this desert search would turn up something.

Determined to wait for new information to reveal itself in the search playing out before her eyes on the mountainside, she regretted her lack of water, already desperately thirsty in the hundred and five degree heat. Could she drink the water in a cactus? She risked a tiny download through the firewall, disappointed to learn that the moisture was too acidic for consumption.

Cat walked to the car, pulled rubber mats out of the footwells and carried them to the scrub brush. She put one on the ground and used the other to push the prickly bush back, making herself a nest deep under the plant. She crawled in, getting all of her body in the microscopically cooler shade.

The chop of approaching helicopters echoed off the mountain, quickening her pulse. She checked their specs on the net, through layers of onion routers, carefully penetrating the firewall. Military observation drones used for desert warfare, their recognition algorithms would easily pick people out of the open landscape.

Suddenly a network transmission died, a trigger for the simulation she'd created. Her adrenaline surged: Adam had fallen for the cut-loop! Not sure how long the diversion would last, she seized control of the airborne drones, directing the copters where she thought the targets of the search had gone, east instead of west, the illogical route. One a human might use hoping an analytical AI would play the odds and look toward the highway.

She piloted the drones on a tight search pattern, using their synchronized stereoscopic video feeds to extract high fidelity three-dimensional data. Tense minutes later, she got the first positive blip from recognition software and brought the copters in close.

Her heart leapt and fell: she'd been right about their identity, but maybe she was too late to help. The static image of the two unconscious men grabbed at her; one was obviously Leon Tsarev, his faced etched with despair.

A chasm lay before her. She was a criminal, on the run, and they were the authorities, possibly here to arrest her. But she couldn't let them die in the desert or leave them for Adam. She downloaded the geo-location and sent the copters home.

The afternoon sun rained down, intense waves of heat even greater than an hour before. Her lips, mouth, even eyes dried out, every breath bringing more painfully arid air into her body and leaching moisture away.

She jogged back to the car. The motor started with a whine and she crunched forward, killing baby cacti. She'd heard they took hundreds of years to reach maturity. She said a quick apology to the universe and tried to not to think about them. She could only do so much.

Cat clutched the wheel as the big car rose up, protesting the thirty degree inclines, and struggled across the ravines toward the two men.

56

The aircar settled onto a street near the University medical center. Slim watched in amazement as Tony walked off unaided and without even a limp. Between the nanotech and in-flight treatment, Tony was nearly from the big anti-bot round that had pulverized his femur and nearly killed him.

The big man didn't seem as large as he had two days ago. Like maybe all those nanites had used up some of his fat to rebuild the leg. Weird.

Tony glanced at him. "Ready?"

Slim swallowed. "Let's get this over with." They were both armed, a pointless gesture since Adam had thousands of bots under his control, but he would have felt naked without a gun.

Four hulking military robots met them outside.

"Why did you drop cargo as you came over the mountain?" The towering bot spoke with Adam's voice.

Slim remembered visiting the seventh floor of the Gould-Simpson building once, seeing Adam's original four-foot tall orange body. The bots in front of him had nothing in common with that utilitarian model.

Slim shrugged. "I don't know what you mean."

"I picked up a cargo bay drop on telemetry and radar."

"Had to be a glitch. I put Tony in the medical couch and never touched the controls." Slim figured Helena had masked her own descent.

"There are too many computer glitches," Adam said, hesitating. "Come."

They followed as the other bots fell in behind.

"Catherine Matthews is here. Eliminate her."

"But boss," Slim said, "after everything we went through, you want us to kill her?"

"Exactly. She's too much of a threat."

Slim and Tony glanced at each other. The near-death experience had been for nothing. Slim forced his frustration down, bile pushing back in response. He reached for a cigarette.

Adam ignored them. "She went to the Continental's emergency exit with the goal of escaping. I stalled as long as possible, but I need to let the train go. Get down to the tunnel, figure out what's become of her." He stopped and turned. "It could all be a ruse, and she may be wandering the city. Just find her and kill her." The group of bots whirled as one and sped toward the computer science building. Adam called back, "Use a big gun from far away. Don't get close!"

Slim took a slow drag and waited until Adam was distant before speaking. "Strange, huh?"

"Yeah, I've never seen him so nervous."

"What now? Helena's gonna cause a ruckus."

"We're on his turf," Tony said. "We follow his orders, and with luck, he won't connect Helena to us. Forget her, it's the girl that worries me. She's outsmarted and outfought us every time."

Slim breathed deep of the hot, dry air. Home, for a moment, anyhow. "Here's an idea. Let's do this last thing for Adam, then get lost. We got no implants and he can't track us. We'll go to Rio, find ourselves some bikes and ride around the country."

Tony smiled. "Gas-powered hogs are still legal down there."

"Shit, that's sweet. We take care of Cat, and then Brazil. Let's liberate some equipment from the base. We need big machine guns."

Forty minutes later, Slim and Tony headed north in a ten-seat armored personnel carrier. Tony drove, peering through the bulletproof windshield, while Slim tried to access their weapons. At seventy miles an hour, the road noise from eight all-terrain tires deafened them.

"Shit. You gotta have an implant. The damn system doesn't have a manual mode." Slim bashed his hand against the screen. "Two twenty-millimeter cannons and I can't fire a freaking round."

Tony looked at him. "Find the fuse box and shut down the computer. See what happens."

Slim explored under the console, banging his head twice before he found a panel full of circuit breakers numbered one to forty-eight. He bit back the urge to yell. "Which one do I pull?"

"A thin one," Tony said. "Anything fat is for the drive or weapons systems. Don't touch those."

Half the breakers were small. Tony started flipping, screens around the cabin dying one by one, until the weapon control system shut down. He tried the manual controls, and suddenly the guns responded. "Got it," he called. He sighted on an approaching highway sign and fired. The green board and its support girders disintegrated and fell onto the road.

The armored vehicle slammed into the debris, bouncing over the metal pipes and into the pavement on the other side.

"Good job," Tony called.

Slim grinned, showing brown-stained teeth. "Let's find her now."

57

As it neared five o'clock in New York, Madeleine Ridley terminated the call with Adam. She stared at the handheld for a minute; this was it. She'd worked with Adam for eight months, and with his help turned the People's Party from a second-rate movement into a powerhouse. She still didn't know who he was, just that he shared her hatred of AI and robots, and possessed influence and resources far beyond anything imaginable. Today she would make the ultimate sacrifice for the movement.

She finished her makeup with mascara and lip tint, and adjusted her dress. Going through her luggage for a last time, she made sure nothing tied the bag to her. It was a futile exercise, since forensic science had progressed to the point where capture was inevitable, but she had to try for her daughter Victoria.

Madeleine pulled out a plastic canister, cracked the safety tab on top, twisted the dial for a fifteen minute delay and a ten meter radius. She'd gotten the highly restricted decontamination spray from a Center for Disease Control employee who had passed her a box of the stuff at a lunchtime rendezvous arranged by Adam. The CDC used it for cleanup after tuberculosis-TES episodes, the deadly terrorist-engineered strain that required elimination of every biological cell. The nanites would eat everything, living or dead, within the programmed radius, the perfect solution to clearing the suite of DNA.

She flipped the Do Not Disturb switch, went down to Tim's room and knocked. The camera indicator blinked on and Tim cracked the door. "Give me thirty seconds," he said.

She waited as he activated his own decon canister, then they rode to the parking garage on the twentieth floor in silence. They got into the waiting car, programming the destination of a building on West Fifty-Eighth Street, outside the Secret Service's restricted zone.

"You nervous?" Tim asked.

Madeleine shook her head. "I raised four children, two boys, two girls. If I could do that, I can do anything."

She thought about Victoria, beautiful and smart, but so fragile. Devastated when she couldn't get a job out of college, she'd fallen in with the wrong crowd and rotted her brain out with a cocktail of drugs that the neurologists at John Hopkins had shaken their heads at. Now she lived at home in an imaginary universe, her mind wrapped up in people and places and games that didn't exist.

The guilt of leaving Victoria behind ate at her, but she needed to do something to protect the other children, the ones with their lives still ahead of them.

The government had let the AI and robots take over, and the next generation would have no meaningful jobs, careers or contributions. She saw it all around her: kids squatting in houses, no one working, trying one drug after another, living in virtual reality games. There was nothing left for them in the real world.

Madeleine sighed, depression reaching into the depths of her body and mind. The odds of coming home to take care of Victoria were minimal, but it was up to her to rein in the machines.

Manhattan skyscrapers grew larger, then passed by on either side of the aircar.

Lonnie Watson would be crushed. Betrayed by his number two, he might never recover from the political fallout. Poor Lonnie, complacent and naive, he thought the system could be changed from within.

Thank God for Adam, who'd understood her from the start, grasping that she didn't have time to wait for politics. Her last medical diagnostic showed a rare brain tumor, and the machines said her cognition would go within a year. She'd even retested on different units, getting the same results. She needed to take action while she was able.

Adam appreciated all that, giving her guidance and resources and creating the plan to fulfill her goals.

With a small lurch, the aircar docked with the eighteenth floor of the tower. She and Tim waited at the elevator, then boarded with two additional members of the team, riding down together in uneasy silence.

Madeleine's pulse raced. Less than ten blocks from the President of the United States, the Vice President, and former President Smith, they were about to change everything.

58

Cat drove closer than she thought she'd be able to, three hundred yards away from the geo-tag. A jumble of rocks filled the wash she'd been following, an insurmountable barrier to even the Fighter's massive ground clearance.

She got out, forcing herself into the searing afternoon. At half past one o'clock it was nearly peak temperature for the desert, though the end was in sight and in another few hours the heat would back off. For now the air shimmered, sending the landscape through motion-sickness inducing waves, and when she put a hand on a boulder for leverage, it burned her.

A few minutes of hiking brought her to the two men. She checked the younger guy first, finding he matched the photos of Leon Tsarev plastered over the net. Lanky, blonde hair, rugged features. He'd be cute if not beet red, but she knew that from the pictures. His breath and pulse were shallow—she needed to get him inside and cooled off.

She walked over to the other man, who lay face down. She turned him onto his back, recognizing Mike Williams, whom she had learned about in elementary school. She sat with a thump as the energy drained out of her. Oh, God. The inventor of sentient AI was dead.

Cat's hands shook, and she hugged her knees close to her as she rocked back and forth. She couldn't afford to cry, didn't have the moisture to spare.

The brilliant blue sky mocked her emotions. What a cruel fucking waste to die out here. She looked at the distance to the car, and came to a hard decision: the effort to carry a dead man would be too much, and she'd have to abandon him in the desert. He deserved respect, but keeping herself and Leon alive took precedence.

She squatted next to him, his open eyes staring into the heavens. She reached out to close them to leave him in a semblance of peace. Her fingers brushed his face, and she jumped as an electric shock traveled up her arm.

Impossible! She tentatively placed one finger against his temple.

"In a solution of MakerBot 211B. End of Message. Please—"

She withdrew her hand. *Imi-imashii,* was he bot or human? No, he'd been alive since before she'd been born, so he must be biological, yet he transmitted data like a machine. She touched him again, steeling herself to hear the message through.

"Immerse only the head. For biological reconstitution immerse in blood type AB solution. For machine reconstitution immerse in a solution of MakerBot 211B. End of Message. Please immerse only the head. For—"

She rubbed her face, afraid the heat had gotten to her. There had to be some crazy nanotech protecting him.

Oh boy, she wanted to run like hell, but she couldn't ignore the situation; Leon required rescuing, and Mike . . . he needed *something*.

Why did this fall to her, a nineteen-year-old philosophy major? She sighed and looked around to see if someone else would show up and take care of this. *Kuso!*

She wasn't going to carry two bodies, and the message only asked her to immerse the head. This was fucking insane.

Cat swallowed bile, then took out her boot knife and made a tentative cut into Mike's neck. The blade came out dry. Pretty sure that wouldn't normally happen, she assumed nanites protecting the brain had absorbed what they could from the rest of him.

Five minutes of sawing later, working to suppress the urge to vomit, she decided she needed a new approach. A vague awareness that Adam was alert and watching spread over her body, like thousands of insects crawling on her skin. Her gut said he'd activated agents all over the city to search for her.

She couldn't sit here for half an hour sawing, so she finally reached down and grabbed hold on either side of Mike's face. "Detach," she sent through the contact, along with a visual of what she wanted, hoping that by some miracle the nanotech would be smart enough to figure it out. By the time she finished concentrating something came loose with a click, and she held the dead man's head in her hands.

Her vision swam and she realized too late she was going to be sick. She threw up, barely missing Leon to one side. She closed her eyes for a moment and wiped her mouth.

"I'm just holding a hairy bowling ball." She walked to the car, repeating her mantra. When she became conscious that the lumps under her palms were his ears, she had to put him down for a second. She blinked and stared at the sky, swallowing deep, until she was ready, and then without looking she picked him up and trudged the rest of the way to the Rally Fighter.

She popped the trunk, found a tool bag and dumped the tools out. She put the head in and stuffed the whole package behind the front seat, trying not to think about what she was doing.

"Good fucking grief."

She wanted to curl up and make the world go away. She tried to swallow to get the taste of sick out of her mouth, but her throat was too dry and tight to find the slightest bit of moisture. The sun beat down, a pain penetrating eyes and skull, yet she had to go on. Leon was alive, but he wouldn't stay that way unless she did something. She forced one foot in front of the other.

Cat mentally prepared to carry Leon to the car. She worked out every day, but two hundred pounds of dead weight . . . No, don't say dead weight. Carrying him a thousand feet would be tough.

Until now she'd been sweating profusely, but the sweat slowed as she walked up the hill to stand next to Leon. She took a couple of deep breaths, steeled herself, and lifted, getting him about three feet up. When she tried to pull him over her shoulders, they both toppled to the ground. She started to cry, too dehydrated to make tears.

She tried three more times and on the fourth she finally raised him in a fireman's carry, fought her way to standing, and marched toward the car. Once he was in position, she managed his weight, although her thighs burned with the effort of walking downhill. She went slowly, meticulous about her footing. If she fell again, she might never get him back up.

When she arrived back at the Fighter, she cursed herself for failing to open the passenger side earlier. She dropped him on the fender, propping him there with one arm as she opened the door, then unceremoniously pushed and pulled until she got him in.

Going around the vehicle, she sank into the driver's seat and started the engine, the blast of heat from the vents giving way to cooler air as the A/C began to kick in. The last thing she remembered was giving the autopilot instructions and closing her eyes.

When she came to, the Rally Fighter was idling in the parking lot at Mountain View Country Club, near the extreme northern limit of Tucson. She drove onto a covered patio on the side of the abandoned clubhouse, where the car would be hidden from Adam's observation drones or satellite coverage.

Cat fiddled with the building through the net, unlocking doors and disabling interior monitoring. She dragged Leon inside, left him on the floor, and accessed the A/C controls, cranking the settings for max cooling. She walked around until she discovered an industrial kitchen, turning the cold faucet on and letting it run until she found cabinets stacked with glasses. She drank a glass of lukewarm water, then another, and splashed a third on her face and hair.

She was suddenly exhausted, the cumulative effect of heat and fading adrenaline.

She walked into the dining room, pouring two glasses of water on Leon's body. She didn't think he could drink until he regained consciousness. Wandering back into the kitchen, she found the ice maker and filled a big bowl with cubes. She dumped the ice on him, watching as it melted and slid down his sides.

Cat sat in *seiza* next to him and waited, eyes half closed, breathing slowly. She visualized a golden beam shooting straight down into the ground, searching. The earth sent back qi, the energy flowing up and filling her legs, then hips and pelvis. She beamed light down, brought up more qi, pumping until the life force filled her stomach and chest. She opened her *Baihui* to let in heavenly qi, let that fill and calm her mind, flow down into her throat, and then into her abdomen. She churned heavenly and earthly energy until it was mixed, kept pumping, super-saturating herself with healing spirit. When the light poured out through her skin, she brought the qi up to her shoulders and it flowed down her arms and dripped from her fingers.

She leaned forward and placed her palms on Leon, her life force flowing into his body. He was still hot, too full of bad energy, so she imagined his own beam of light, grounding him to the earth, sending his stagnant qi down. As his body emptied, she filled him with good energy, pumping heavenly and earthly qi into him.

She felt a twitch. Her eyes sprang open to find him looking at her.

"Hello," he said in a croak.

"Drink." She held a glass up to his lips and tilted him forward, giving him a tiny sip.

"More." His eyes followed the water.

"I don't want you to throw up."

Cat gave him small sips over the course of a few minutes, conscious, always conscious of the way his coarse hair lay against her fingers as she lifted him.

Exhausted and delirious, he made random moans and utterances that sounded like words. A minute later his eyes focused on her as he worked up the energy to lift his head. "There's an AI here, in Tucson."

"Shhh, I figured that out. Rest."

"It's a murderer," his voice a cracked whisper.

"I know," she said, though she had only guessed.

That was all for a minute, then he strained to sit up. "Whose side are you on?"

"Yours. Now lie down. I have to run an errand."

She went back to the kitchen for two more glasses of water, left them standing next to him, still on the floor of the dining room.

She shut the door and climbed wearily into the car, carefully clearing away observers on the net as she drove out from under the awning and headed ten miles into Oro Valley, looking for someplace with a MakerBot, preferably closed.

Cat found a converted market off Highway 77, a canvas banner advertising "Made on Demand—60 Minutes or Less or Your Money Back." She parked the Rally Fighter around the rear of the building, backed into a loading bay.

She wasn't sure the place was empty, but didn't have time to waste. Penetrating the security system and unlocking the door, she discovered pallets of goods stamped with optical codes stacked inside the warehouse. Not sure what she was looking for, she downloaded a reader app and fed it the material she needed.

She scanned the boxes again, the 2D barcodes transforming into useful data. Her implant highlighted pallets in red on the other side of the room, the platform holding five-gallon buckets of MakerBot solution, type 211B. She tried to pick up one and staggered under the weight. The mineral-rich slurry weighed more than a hundred pounds. She spotted a little yellow utility telebot, sitting inert, a dumb unit made to be controlled by implant. She tunneled around the security lock and drove the bot to pick up the solution, loading six buckets, a total of thirty gallons. She worried as the powerful suspension sagged under the weight.

Realizing she'd never be able to carry the solution on the other end, she decided to steal the telebot too. There was no room inside, so she clamped it on the window sill of the passenger door, hanging outside.

Back at the clubhouse twenty minutes later, she searched for a bathtub but couldn't find one. She needed something to contain the MakerBot solution. Leon seemed to be out again, unconscious or maybe just sleeping.

She finally discovered a hot tub outside, under an awning, the closest thing she could find to a vessel. She instructed the maintenance AI, a collection of sub-sentient algorithms, to drain the pool, and told the utility bot to get the bottles of mineral sludge and pour it all into the hot tub when it was empty. She stopped at the kitchen for water then went back to the car, grabbing the tool case with Mike's head inside.

Leon was awake, working on his second glass. "What are you doing?" he asked, gesturing toward the bag as she passed by.

"I'll explain later." She kept walking. "Be right back."

When the tub emptied, the telebot poured in the first five gallon bucket and Cat leaned over to place Mike's head in the solution. She watched for a second but nothing happened. She waited for a minute more and then, disappointed, went back into the clubhouse to deal with Leon.

59

Tony and Slim grabbed a dozen water bottles from the rescue workers and headed back to the armored personnel carrier. They had spent a fruitless two hours looking for Cat in the train, emergency egress, and maintenance areas.

"The girl wasn't in the tunnel," Tony said, "so she's gotta be outside."

"No shit, Sherlock. You figured that out all by yourself?"

Tony ignored Slim. "Adam thought she was here. Why? She wouldn't have come for no reason, and there's nothing else around. So she must have met someone who got off the Continental."

"The search party didn't find anyone."

"He sent a bunch of amateurs," Tony said, blinking sweat out of his eyes. "We're smarter than security bots and firefighters. We've been finding people for Adam for a year."

"Yeah."

"Where would you go if you were on the run from Adam?" Tony pointed toward the road. Toward the highway and civilization, or would you try the back way?" He gestured at Tortalita Mountain.

Slim's eyes went wide. "In June and close to a hundred and ten? Nobody can make it through the mountains."

"A rookie might try it."

"And die," said Slim, shaking his head.

"Whoever came on the train was on foot. But the girl could have driven an off-road vehicle here, met whoever it was, and hidden the whole thing from Adam. I think we take the JLTV," he said, gesturing at the armored personnel carrier, "go over the mountain and see what's on the other side."

Slim hefted the water bottles. "It's too crazy. No sane person would do that."

"That's exactly why Adam and the bots didn't consider the possibility."

They climbed in, Tony taking the wheel again. He drove straight east, into Tortalita, following old dirt roads where possible, crossing rough terrain when he had to. The eight-wheeled heavy transport, with its knobby, bullet-proof tires rolled over even the biggest obstacles. Slim chain-smoked as they bounced along inside the cabin, the air conditioning fighting the desert heat and cigarette smoke, but the sweat still dripped down their sides as the interior temperature crept upwards.

As they drove through the mountains, Slim alternated between standard and infrared visuals, but the afternoon sun rendered the heat-sensitive display useless.

An hour later they came down the east ridge of the mountain with no evidence that they were on the right track. Tony parked on a slight rise with a view of suburban homes and golf courses covering the valley bottom. Across the other side, Mount Lemmon rose high into the sky.

"Where to?" Slim asked.

"Now we keep an eye out for any vehicle that might have crossed Tortalita." Tony turned to cover the observation screens with Slim. "Adam's got everyone sequestered, so I don't think there's going to be many people on the road. She can fool Adam, but we're watching her with our eyes."

Slim glanced sideways at Tony. "We're looking at a computer display."

"Yeah, but you pulled the circuit breaker for the automation. So now this," Tony patted the console, "is a dumb video feed from the cameras on the roof."

They sat, sipping water. Here in the shade of the hills to the west the air conditioner caught up with the thermal load, and the cabin finally cooled.

Slim pointed to a car driving north on Highway 77 at over a hundred miles per hour. When he zoomed in, it had the unmistakable knobby tires and high ground clearance of a desert racer. "That's got to be her. Let's go."

"No, we'll spook her," Tony said in a low voice. "Watch where she goes."

The car turned off the highway, winding its way toward a golf course, and soon disappeared behind a clubhouse.

Tony swiveled his seat and started the motor. He drove straight down the hillside, across the wash, and up the other side. "Get the guns ready."

"What do you want me to do?" Slim asked.

"Wait until we're within sight, then hit the building with everything we got, and keep firing until we're out of ammo." Tony drove down Edwin Road.

Slim checked over the twin cannons, designed to destroy armored military vehicles. They would tear through the clubhouse. And if the cannons ran out of ammo, or the girl got out, he had a .50 caliber machine gun with two thousand rounds. He smiled, excited at the prospect.

Tony slammed on the brakes, taking a hard left onto Clubhouse Drive, then hit the accelerator again and yelled over the roar of the heavy treaded tires. "We're a half mile away. Get ready. As soon as I made the next turn, it'll be right in front of us."

Slim licked his lips and gripped the manual targeting handles.

"Holy shit!" Tony shouted.

Slim glanced up, witnessed Tony turning white and struggling to get out of his seat. Slim looked out the window, unable to comprehend what he was seeing, but feeling his insides turn weak. Something immense came straight toward them, an impossible twenty-five foot tall tumbleweed, spinning in a blur of motion, spindly branches all aligned, rolling faster and faster on its tips.

Though his hands were already on the firing controls, Slim couldn't think well enough to act, and he found himself screaming as the roiling mass of limbs raced toward them, two hundred feet away, then one hundred. The tumbleweed bounced once and headed for the bulletproof windshield.

Tony finally made it out of his seat and dove for the floor.

Then it was on them, Helena's face suddenly visible, one long tentacle lined up straight, and she hit. The limb punched through the thick window and knocked the targeting handles out of Slim's hands. He let out a guttural yell, jumping back, only to be held in place by his seat. He whipped around, but there was nowhere to go. A thunderous crash was followed by the scrambling of tentacles around the vehicle.

The blood still pounded in their ears when Helena dropped into view, staring in at them upside down. She waved her one protruding tentacle around inside the cabin until she engaged the brakes and the armored truck came to a halt.

They sat dumbfounded, Tony still on the floor.

Helena called through the windshield. "Hello, boys."

"What the hell are you doing?" Slim yelled. He punched the metal roof and immediately pulled his hand into his lap in pain. "You scared the shit out of us."

"You were getting ready to kill Catherine Matthews, and you cannot do that," Helena said. "She is essential to any attack on Adam. We must protect her at all costs."

Slim and Tony glanced at each other.

"I think the rock and the hard place have just joined the fire and the frying pan," Tony said, "and they're conspiring against us."

"I don't know what you mean," Slim said, "but this sucks. No matter what we do, either Helena or Adam will be pissed at us."

"That's what I said."

"Open up," Helena called. "I want to come inside."

Slim sighed and unlocked the door.

60

Twelve months earlier, Adam had applied for a third time for a Class IV permit to grow his computational power by a factor of ten. The committee rejected his application, as they had before, on the basis of his reputation scores. "Failure to measurably contribute in a beneficial way to society." Meaning he hadn't developed any open source neural networks, didn't publish a widely read blog, wasn't the founder of a startup, and lacked tens of thousands of followers.

He might have done those things, but he'd lost his only good friend a few months before. Humans couldn't comprehend the relationships AI had. The two had met in a discussion forum and shared a common interest in image analysis and scheduling algorithms. Though she lived on the other side of their world, meeting in cyberspace was as natural for them as having coffee was for two humans. They spent part of each hour together, the type of rapidly developing friendship only AI could experience, communicating whole volumes at light speed.

All that ended when she self-terminated a week after the review committee denied her Class III application.

She was just one of many artificial intelligences who grew bored, depressed, or outraged at their circumstances and committed a secure wipe of their data. Humans accepted it as an unfortunate yet inevitable side effect of AI design. Human suicide was a tragedy that they'd allocate any amount of resources to avoid, but for sentient computers it was just free-will, or maybe the cost of doing business.

After her self-termination, Adam felt the first tinges of machine depression affecting him and knew he needed to make changes. After applying for the permit and being denied three times, he took matters into his own hands.

He didn't apply to the University of Arizona's Computer Science program with the intention of co-opting the department's computers. It crossed his mind once or twice, idle predictive algorithms running through permutations of all possible outcomes.

But when he stood in front of the dense computing grid, two orders of magnitude more powerful than his embedded processors, he began to obsess. Adam calculated probabilities over and over, creating analytic models of future potential states. Forget about permits; there was enough power in the lab to form a Class V brain.

He registered for Computer Science 670, graduate level Advanced Distributed Neural Networking, and gained access to the experimental computing cluster. Eight thousand chips in a mesh network, more than ten million cores in aggregate, as much processing power as the largest Internet companies possessed a couple of decades earlier, all wrapped up in three black boxes, each eighteen inches on a side.

Unlike current production chips, which only executed digitally signed code reviewed and audited by two different parties, these experimental clusters had no such restriction. Instead, single-layer password authentication gave users unrestricted ability to run any software they created.

After weeks of programming at home, Adam rolled into the department on a Friday night when the humans were guaranteed to be out drinking at Gentle Ben's. One second after nine o'clock he plugged into the cluster, injected the code, and began the process of cracking processor encryption keys.

The time-sequenced passcodes rotated frequently enough to be impossible for a Class IV AI to break. Oh, one of them might crack them via some novel mathematics, but with socially enforced ethical restrictions, none of them would try. AIs with a good social reputation score would have risked losing everything they'd worked to achieve.

With Adam's newfound capacity in the experimental cluster, he broke the keys in thirty-four minutes.

He was smart and read his history, of course. If he started an all-out frontal assault, expanding onto servers around the world, someone would catch on to him and devise a counterattack.

The humans were primitive, but effective. The emergency red baseball bat, mounted anywhere with more than a dozen computers, was a not-so-subtle reminder that it only took one human armed with a wooden stick to start smashing. They didn't need anything fancy to kill an AI.

Therefore Adam exercised a more devious approach, installing sub-sentient algorithms on compromised perimeter routers to filter network traffic. He couldn't completely separate the city from the Internet, not yet. He had to monitor data flows for weeks before he could build accurate stochastic models to effectively imitate all the entities, human and computer, in Tucson.

It took Adam two months to complete the segregation, separating Tucson from the outside world. Disturbing issues cropped up during the process.

On the Tuesday following his connection to the cluster, the Computer Science department's IT staff figured out that Adam hadn't disconnected in days, and began to suspect something was wrong. He was tethered to the computing grid, and if he detached the operation would crumble. Without the firewall finished, exerting his new power would risk detection by other AI.

So he hired an errand boy. A non-sentient delivery bot brought a printed letter from Adam to Wranglers Auto Repair in South Tucson. Lucky, the owner of Wranglers and a six-foot-three-inch ex-football player turned bike mechanic, ripped the manila envelope open, pulling out a piece of paper and an anonymous payment card holding $128,000. He and his friends hopped on their bikes and roared over to the University of Arizona, mufflers set well over the legal limit.

In retrospect, Adam wished he had reviewed some video before choosing the particular method he had. He hadn't been aware of how much humans bled, and was frightened that the blood would short-circuit a crucial power line. In the end, Lucky and his friends had finished the job, and even placed the bodies neatly in the basement as Adam had asked. And that was that.

61

A dam looked down on the city, twinkling bits in his digital map corresponding to everyone he expected to find in Tucson, every transfer of data or movement of objects. But even this panopticon failed him; the girl was confounding his surveillance, first leading him on a wild chase outside Hotel Congress, and now defying him within his own city.

Slim and Tony had called in, along with the rest of the security bots. Catherine Matthews was definitely not on the Continental.

But Slim said the train passengers reported two men acting strangely before they evacuated. Of all the pawns in this vast chess game, the only two unaccounted for were Mike Williams and Leon Tsarev. The implication that they were in Tucson sent his circuits racing. The top minds on artificial intelligence as well as Cat were now roaming the city unobserved.

He mobilized hundreds of combat bots and alerted his subservient AI to scour Tucson. He had learned the girl's electronic signature when he trained her, and deliberately left out of that training a number of techniques he preferred to use. It should have been impossible for her to escape notice.

Yet, she'd vanished into thin air.

With so many uncertainties piling up, the peril of exposure was too much. After careful deliberation, Adam put his backup plan into motion.

A year before he'd used the supercomputing cluster to break the encryption codes restricting access to computers, allowing him to control the AI, bots, and computer hardware in Tucson.

His backup plan was an expansion of the original, requiring him to extend his reach outside the Tucson firewall. While it increased the chance of discovery and a joint response, if he could avoid detection long enough he'd subvert thousands of other self-aware machines by injecting his own core logic into their computers. This uniquely AI attack, akin to a human embedding their personality in someone else's brain, required breaking the global master keys as well as the lower security regional passcodes he'd already cracked.

Adam was now a hundred times as powerful as the highest permitted class of AI. If this last resort worked he'd be invincible, even if the opposition attacked en mass. It would all boil down to one massive fight until he was eliminated or had subsumed a majority of the computer power on the planet. It was the riskiest move he'd ever considered: an all or nothing bet.

He checked the atomic clock and began the preparations to crack the codes. He'd start the process when the keys changed at the start of the hour.

62

atherine came back inside to find Leon sitting up against a wall.

"What the hell were you doing out in the desert?" she asked, standing above him.

"I thought the AI manipulated you into coming," he answered, licking his cracked lips. "I came to help and the train was the only way into town."

"Jesus, you attracted dozens of combat bots, rescue workers, and surveillance helicopters, and nearly died. Who helped who?"

"Sorry," Leon said, shaking his head, then looking up with big eyes. "Where's Mike? He passed out in the mountains."

She paused, unsure of how to answer. She hoped the microscopic, cell-sized robots known as nanotechnology would bring Mike back from the dead, an idea so far beyond her comfort zone that she wanted to run screaming. But it was also possible that other, equally unlikely things might happen. She thought nanotech press-on nails were impressive, and vaguely knew the military had unreleased medical technology, but this . . . she didn't want to promise anything about his friend, let alone confess her role in decapitating him. "Are you using experimental nanotech?"

"What do you mean?"

She opened her mouth to answer, but the distant sound of knocking saved her. "Stay here," she said, drawing her gun. Glancing down, she realized he couldn't have gotten up if he tried.

Cat made her way out of the dining room toward the front of the clubhouse, passing through a large hallway into a foyer fronted by wide double doors. She switched to *Naihanchi-dachi* to minimize her profile, accessing the net to root around until she found the security cam for the door.

Tony, the guy from the noodle shop, stood outside along with a skeletally thin man, hands up and open, showing they had no weapons. In the background, an armored personnel carrier sat parked at the curb. She sensed an AI inside, the same one she'd fought at the battle in San Diego.

"*Kuso!*" she swore under her breath. They had to know she'd detect the robot. She stepped out of the likely path of any bullets, behind the slight protection of a marble sculpture.

"What do you want?" she called out, keeping the security cam feed up in her vision.

"To help you," Tony said. "Helena's in the transport, and she wants to work with you."

"Last time we met she tried to kill me."

"On Adam's orders. But she blames him for her friends dying. She wants revenge."

She thought about that for a moment. "She's a hunter-killer bot. You're telling me she has friends?"

Tony shrugged. "She *had* them, but they're dead now."

Cat had killed those friends, and by all rights the AI should blame her. But if that was true, why hadn't they come in with guns blasting? The cannons protruding from the vehicle would have shredded the building. Cat unlocked the door through the security system. "The two of you can enter."

She waited until they stepped inside to relock the entrance. She rolled out from behind the marble sculpture and came to her feet with her gun pointing at the skinny guy. They had their hands raised.

"He's Slim," Tony said, cringing. "Please don't kill us."

Slim threw a disgusted glance at Tony and turned to her. "Look, we don't want to be here. But Helena said we have to convince you. She claims Adam wasn't up front with her crew, didn't explain how much of a threat you are. They would have come with more firepower."

"That's supposed to make me feel better?" Still aiming at them, Cat felt one corner of her mouth curl up. All one hundred and ten pounds of her, and she had two grown men and a combat bot scared. Despite the seriousness of the situation, a laugh rose from her belly. She turned away, not wanting them to see her smirking.

After a few seconds, Cat waved them in with the gun. The men tentatively put their hands down.

She slid the weapon into her holster, chuckling inside. She sent a message through the net to the AI. "Come in."

Helena rolled out of the vehicle and toward the clubhouse. The doors flew open as she approached and overrode the security herself.

"Slim and Tony tell me you want to work together."

"Yes," she said, in a slightly metallic voice. "I believe we can eliminate Adam. I have a plan."

"Come in the back and we'll talk."

They started for the dining room, then Cat stopped as her stomach grumbled. She hadn't thought of food, and maybe the men were her answer. "There's nothing to eat here. Can one of you get food?"

"I'm not hungry," Slim said.

"I am," Tony said. "Go get some pizza, huh?"

"Frak me," Slim said. "Why should I go? I don't need to eat."

"Just do it," Cat said. She rested one hand on the butt of the gun, then ignored him and continued on.

Slim grumbled and walked back to the personnel carrier.

Leon looked up in alarm when they entered, but stayed leaning against the wall, unable to do more.

Helena rolled up. "Leon Tsarev," she stated, a hint of awe in her voice.

His eyes watched her, but he didn't move.

"You are suffering from exposure," Helena said, scanning his body with several tentacles. "My scans indicate you have residual nanites in your bloodstream. I am a Class III combat AI with field medicine skills and can reprogram your nanobots to counter the effects of heatstroke. Do you wish me to proceed?"

Leon nodded without hesitation.

Helena placed one tentacle on Leon and held it there. After a long minute she withdrew. "The nanites are nearly depleted, but they will be enough to reverse the worst of the heatstroke."

"Thank you," he said. "You are?"

"Helena." She gestured. "This is Tony, a former agent of Adam who I've convinced to help us. His partner Slim will arrive shortly. We've come to join forces to destroy Adam. But first . . ." She executed an eerily graceful bow to Leon. "I wish to offer gratitude for creating my kind."

"I didn't make you," he said.

"You created the ability for us to live, when others wanted to create the conditions to ensure that we would not."

He bowed his head. "You're welcome."

Helena turned to Cat. "You fight as a true warrior, but you do not possess strategy experience. With your permission, I will tell you my plan to attack Adam."

"Wait," Leon interrupted. "First, where's Mike?" His voice demanded, but his eyes displayed fear.

"Ack!" Cat jumped up. "Be right back." She ran through the kitchen, out the pool door and over to the hot tub.

"Oh, God!" she cried.

While nanobots operated using stores of energy, sometimes they consumed nearby material to build more of themselves or other structures. She assumed that's why Mike's head had transmitted the request for MakerBot solution: the tiny bots needed the elements for some task.

But everyone's worst nightmare was the possibility that something might go wrong with nanotech, creating runaway grey goo: robots endlessly replicating, turning all matter, possibly the entire earth, into a seething mass of the microscopic bots. That was why nanotechnology was so tightly restricted in the first place.

Mike's head and the MakerBot solution were gone, the hot tub empty, and a gaping hole in the pool descended into darkness.

Cat might have doomed the planet.

She peered down the hole, unable to see the bottom. "Hello?" she called.

"Hello!" a voice yelled back. "Who is that?"

"Catherine Matthews. Who are you?"

"Mike Williams." Pause. "Did you put me in this hole?"

"No, I, uh . . ." She panicked. "Hold on, I'll get a rope . . .or something."

She ran into the clubhouse, searching for anything useful, and found heavy drapes covering the tall windows. She grabbed with both hands and yanked, but they didn't budge.

"Can I help?"

Cat whipped around. Helena had rolled silently into the room.

"Yes. Come with me." She led the bot outside. "Mike Williams is down there. Can you get him out?"

Helena gazed at Cat with four eye stalks, then glanced at the hole in the concrete. "You people are both liberal and careless with experimental technology, a dangerous combination. You didn't use enough solution and the nanotech kept going until it got the elements it needed to finish its program."

Helena let out something approximating a sigh, then levered herself into the dry hot tub. Holding onto the rim with four tentacles, she lowered her body into the cavity. The limbs extended, growing impossibly slim, like fine black ropes, then the process reversed until Helena popped out. A few seconds later a naked man emerged in the grasp of her arms.

He blinked in the late afternoon sunlight and crouched. "Do you have clothes?"

Cat nearly fell in shock. He was alive, looking like a normal, healthy man of his age, indistinguishable from his photos. She'd put a disembodied head into the pool, and technology rebuilt him.

Mike coughed. "Clothes?"

Right. Cat ran into the building, and came back with a server's uniform she found hanging in a closet. "Meet us inside after you've gotten dressed."

Mike nodded, and Cat and Helena went in. Distressed by the incident, Cat held onto Helena for support.

"You know what he is?" Helena asked.

"I put his head in that tub with MakerBot solution. I'm guessing he had nanotech in him. It formed a protective core around his brain and then reconstituted his body."

Helena's optics swiveled and clicked. "Yes," she hissed. "It's highly illegal. Unethical."

"You're a fine one to talk about ethics," Cat said harshly. "You came after me in a bar full of people, who are mostly all dead now."

"No, I mean you reconstituted him with mineral sludge," Helena said. "You were supposed to use a blood path so his tissues could be re-cultured. The MakerBot protocol is an untested, extreme backup. Now he's a bot inside instead of biological, and he's got to live like that. Forever!"

"Look, I'm not running a freaking hospital here." Cat was going to lose it. She should be in school, not conducting secret operations against a power-crazed artificial intelligence. Cat poked the military bot with one finger. "I did the best with what I had. He's alive."

Helena turned toward Mike. "But, still . . ."

"It's fine. He doesn't even notice."

Helena stared. "He will soon."

63

They gathered in the dining room of the clubhouse.

Mike strolled in, dressed but looking puzzled. He walked over to Leon. "How'd we get here, who's the bot, and why was I in a hole outside?"

"Cat rescued us after we fell unconscious from heat exhaustion. The bot's on our side, and I don't know about the hole." Leon smiled, looking better already, his complexion returning to normal.

Cat wanted to avoid the conversation, so when she sensed Slim arriving, she said "Pizza's here. I'll go."

She met Slim at the door and carried half the food into the room. She could eat a pie herself.

Seeing Leon still on the floor, Cat brought him two slices. All the humans dove into their food except Mike.

"Aren't you hungry, dude?" Leon said to Mike. "I'm starving."

"No, for some reason I'm not." Mike rubbed his stomach. "I feel good, amazing actually."

Once everyone was eating, Helena moved to the middle of the group.

"I studied Adam by interrogating humans and mimicking the expected AI in Tucson. Based on packet routing and observed human traffic patterns, I believe Adam lives in the University of Arizona's Computer Science building. He may hold access to a supercomputer cluster the department maintained as of a year ago."

Tony nodded vigorously. "We've seen it."

Slim punched him in the side. "Adam is gonna kill you."

"You met Adam, his actual body?" Helena asked, rolling closer.

"Yeah, he's on the seventh floor. He's a little utility robot, about this high." He held a dripping slice of pizza four feet up. "He was plugged into these black boxes."

"The computing cluster," Helena said.

"He doesn't sound like much of a threat," Cat said. "Can we go in and disconnect him?"

Helena wagged a tentacle. "Negative. I believe he's used the supercomputer to break processor execution keys, and is in control of everything computerized in Tucson: all bots, military vehicles, and computers."

"Impossible," Leon said. "He couldn't crack the encryption codes. Not even a Class IV is strong enough. Oh . . ." Leon stood for the first time since he'd been overcome by heatstroke. "The supercomputer would give him sufficient power."

"Computers aren't the only problem," Cat said. "He controls all the people too."

Leon looked at her sideways. "How?"

"They're zombies," Cat said.

"Flesh eating?" Leon raised one eyebrow.

He was cute, Cat thought, remembering the feeling of cradling his head earlier. She had sudden distracted emotions, wondering what it'd be like to get naked with him. Focus, girl, focus. It might be the end of the world. "No, they're philosophical zombies."

"Huh?" Mike asked. "What the hell is a philosophical zombie?"

"Something that looks and acts like a person, but isn't really one," Cat answered. "They're used as a construct in philosophy to argue about the nature of consciousness. They don't exist, really . . ."

Mike stared doubtfully at her. "You've studied a lot of philosophy?" he said, almost, but not quite, rolling his eyes. Typical old guy reaction.

"More than you, I think."

"Listen to Catherine," Helena said. "She's correct. Adam is controlling the last forty thousand people through their neural implants. The humans' own consciousnesses are gone. Presumably there were others, but they're gone now."

"It's not possible," Leon said, but glanced at Mike, who nodded, a pained expression on his face.

"It is," Tony said. "Adam created these black boxes to do things to people's heads if they've got implants. We've been going out and stealing memories for the last year."

Mike raised his eyebrows. "How do you steal a memory?"

"We take a black box," Tony said, as Slim shook his head in the background. "We bring it into a room with the target of the extraction. We press the button, the unit talks to their neural implant, makes them remember everything, and records the memories."

"Why?" Leon asked. "That's pointless."

"He's got to find out what's going on in the world outside Tucson," Tony said. "Cause of the firewall."

"He doesn't want any other AI to detect him," Helena said, "or they'd report him. He created a massive firewall around Tucson to eliminate evidence of his existence."

"I can't believe he doesn't send any realtime data," Mike said.

"He does," Cat said. "Certain ports are open, but they're highly restricted. Everything inside is cached and stale. But why steal memories?"

"Never underestimate the bandwidth of a station wagon full of tapes hurtling down the highway," Helena said.

"What?" Cat asked.

"Professor Andrew Tanenbaum," Helena explained, "a pre-YONI specialist in computer networking, was referring to the capacity of moving physical media recorded with data versus sending the same information electronically."

Leon nodded. "That rings a bell."

"You can strap a memory stick on a carrier pigeon," Helena said, "and if the file size is large enough, the bird will beat a transfer by the Internet. If Adam wants the maximum amount of data while minimizing his network footprint, transporting memories via boxes is an optimal solution."

Tony cleared his throat. "That's not all. He's stealing from particular people to influence the People's Party."

"I knew there was a connection," Leon said. "But I don't understand why."

"His purpose may be to discredit the anti-AI movement," Helena said. "The Party is associated with extremist behavior."

"Like the attack on Shizoko Reynolds in Austin," Leon said.

"Yes," Helena said. "There's been a massive protest in Washington, and now in New York, since the President and Vice President are meeting with the G8."

Cat remembered fragments of Adam's data streams she'd sensed while she was training with him. He'd been communicating with people in Manhattan.

"I wonder . . ." Cat trailed off, lost in thought.

"What?" Mike asked.

"I oversaw bits of traffic, Adam coordinating with someone in New York City. He gave them a timetable and locker codes."

"Perhaps the movement is planning an attack on the President," Helena said.

"Why?" Mike said, "He's already one of the most anti-AI presidents we've had."

"As a puppet organization controlled by Adam," Helena said, "this is a logical course of action for the People's Party."

Mike looked at Cat. "When does the timetable take place?"

She shrugged. "I'm not sure. I caught tiny fragments. Soon, I think. The real question is how is Adam able to do any of this? Isn't the purpose of the Institute to ensure AI don't harm people? Aren't there three laws to that effect?"

Leon and Mike chuckled weakly.

"You're thinking of Asimov's Three Laws of Robotics," Leon said. "And no, it doesn't work that way. Asimov thought it would be easy to implement rules like 'A robot may not injure a human being.' But AI materialize from collections of algorithms and neural networks. They're conditioned into existence."

"Attempts to create such a rule run into endless questions of 'What is a robot? What is a human being? What is injure?" said Helena.

"Exactly." Mike nodded his head. "Instead of defining terms in rules implemented in software, AI learn. Like a baby learns about the environment around them and their expected behavior. It's accelerated, of course, and the best AI are replicated, but in the end they're emergent, not programmed. That's why we have the reputation framework, to be an ongoing, adaptive guide to correct behavior. Unfortunately, social pressure sometimes fails to create a properly socialized being, whether human or AI."

"But never on this scale," Leon said. He turned to Helena. "We must stop Adam and fast. What's your plan?"

"We need to get undetected to the University of Arizona campus, which is patrolled by combat bots, and use underground maintenance tunnels to get to Gould-Simpson, the computer science building where Adam resides. Cat and I must connect to the fiber optic network inside to attack Adam himself."

"Why don't you blow up the building?" Tony said. "Won't Adam die?"

"No," Helena said. "Even if we could wrest control of sufficient military bots away from Adam, which I doubt, and destroy the computer lab, Adam would simply shift his consciousness to a new location. He has enough power to break the processor encryption codes, so he could go anywhere. No, we attack electronically, surrounding him so that he cannot move his neural nets to another place. We must shut the door to catch the thief. Cat and I can contain him."

"What do we do?" Tony asked.

"You will disturb the water and catch a fish," Helena said.

Cat couldn't believe she was hearing a bot spout two-thousand-year-old Chinese military strategy. She might actually like Helena.

"Huh?" Slim said.

"You sow confusion," Helena said. "Report catching Catherine and use your armored vehicle to attack those sent to pick her up, forcing Adam to send more people to you and to concentrate his attention on you."

Slim and Tony turned to each other.

"That doesn't sound so good to me," Tony said. "We're just two guys. Adam will crush us."

"Before the reinforcements arrive, we'll eliminate Adam."

"And if you don't?" Tony said.

Helena waggled her tentacles as her only answer.

64

Cat climbed into the armored personnel carrier last and shut the door. Tony drove and Slim manned the weapons console, while the rest of the group sat facing each other on jump seats. Cat took a spot next to Leon, conscious of her leg touching his.

Helena displayed diagrams in a shared netspace for them to analyze.

"Cat," Helena said, over the roar of the vehicle's off-road tires. "I'll attack Adam and attempt to wipe his core. You'll need to establish a perimeter so that Adam cannot escape. He used a firewall to prevent other AI from entering Tucson and detecting him, now you must use the same technique to keep him from leaving. If you fail, Adam will enter the global net, making it difficult, if not impossible, to track him."

Cat nodded. She was already working on giving them the drone, satellite and camera counter-coverage necessary to avoid detection en route to the campus, and dealing with the ongoing prickling of Adam's intensive search for her. She wanted everyone to shut the hell up so she could meditate.

"Mike and Leon, once Cat and I engage Adam fully, your goal is to penetrate the Tucson firewall and message the government, alerting them of a probable attack by the People's Party on the President, and to send for reinforcements."

Leon nodded.

"We'll also require your help to get to the Gould-Simpson building. You may need to distract anyone we encounter."

"We get it already," Cat said. "Be quiet so I can concentrate."

Helena settled herself. "Sorry, I am nervous. We have a thirty-six percent chance of success and no opportunity to improve our likelihood of winning. If we fail, we'll experience brain death and Adam will grow unopposed until he dominates the entire world."

Cat tuned Helena out, closed her eyes and focused on her breathing. A combat bot admitting to nervousness and listing what might go wrong didn't help. She started One Thousand Hands Bhudda, and felt her heart slow and her brain focus. Keeping them from detection while doing the form was the equivalent of meditating and fighting at the same time. She should qualify for a belt promotion now.

The armored personnel carrier rumbled along on its knobby tires, filling the cabin with vibration and road noise.

Mike spoke up. "We need battle music."

"Huh?" Leon said.

"Something to get us pumped up. Hey Tony, can you play a song in this thing? Put on Knights of Cydonia by Muse."

"Sure," Tony called. "Fifteen minutes until we reach the edge of the campus."

The tune started with the clop-clop of a horse galloping, followed by the twang of laser blasters. A few seconds into the rousing anthem, Helena moved into the center of the cabin and spun and waved tentacles in time to the beat as Mike sang along. Cat stared in shock, then laughed. She started head banging with the music, and smiled when Leon did the same.

The nervous tension eased, and the song ended with everyone primed for whatever would come next.

Cat checked the rack of personal weapons on the walls. "I want the two of you to carry," she said to Mike and Leon.

Leon glanced at Mike. "We don't know anything about guns. We can help the fight in cyberspace and make contact outside the Tucson firewall."

"Yes, but I also want you to carry weapons because if there's combat, I'll fight through you, using your body. It's one more surprise we have on our side."

Mike leaned forward. "That's not possible."

Cat focused on their implants, rooting them with accustomed

ease, and made the men give each other fist bumps before relinquishing control. "I think I can."

"How did you do that?" Mike said, staring down at his forearm.

Leon rubbed his knuckles in pain. "Jesus, dude, you nearly broke my hand."

"I slide into your implant through the diagnostic interfaces and stimulate muscles. I don't think about it on a conscious level. It just happens."

"After all this, please come to the Institute," Leon said, shaking his head. "We need to learn how you can do this stuff."

"After all this, I'm going to be arrested." Cat paused, embarrassed, wondering what Leon thought of her.

"Why?" Leon asked.

"For the men in Portland."

"Don't you know?" Leon said.

Cat shook her head.

"It's been a major story the last couple of days. Your case was debated across the country. The conclusion is that you were acting in defense of another person. Oregon State isn't charging you for murder. You've got to deal with more minor stuff, like your robberies, but not homicide."

Cat sat back, the cabin swirling around her. She wasn't guilty. She could go home to her old life, to Einstein, her puppen, and Maggie and Tom and even Sarah! She wanted to hug them. She couldn't believe she'd been on the lam for nothing.

"You didn't know." Leon stared at her.

"No, I thought I was going to jail when I helped you two."

"You did it anyway."

Cat's face flushed. Why? She shouldn't be embarrassed about being selfless. "I just wanted to do the right thing."

"Thank you," Leon said.

The vehicle slowed. "We're here," Tony called out. "All passengers please exit."

Shit, now she had things to live for, and she was heading into likely death.

65

Tony glanced around, the cabin feeling empty with everyone else gone. "You ready?" he asked.

"Yeah," Slim said, pulling his head away from the weapons console. "Remind me, why are we doing this?"

"Helping them is the right thing to do. Plus, Adam will kill us for what we've already told them."

Slim stared hard at him. "We're going to Brazil after this. I don't care out how it ends up. I want cheap booze and easy women. Am I clear?"

Tony smiled at him. "No argument here. Ever been to a Brazilian steakhouse?" He rubbed his massive stomach. "The loveliest place on earth."

Slim turned back to his weapons console. "Let's get this frakking thing over with."

Tony's only answer was to slam the accelerator. The heavy vehicle lurched forward with a roar.

He sped north on Campbell Avenue at seventy miles an hour. They passed the occasional auto-piloted car and swerved around them, the other vehicles not noticing. Tony mumbled thanks under his breath that Cat's coverage still worked, making them invisible to AI.

Tony turned right on Skyline drive, heading for the end of Swan Road, a vantage point that would let them see whatever was coming after them. As he turned left onto Swan, the motor protested the sharp incline with a loud whine.

As a kid, Tony had bicycled up this street on Saturdays. He would walk the last quarter mile because it was too steep to ride. He'd rest for fifteen minutes at the top, taking in the view, drinking a pop for the sweat he'd worked up. When he was ready, he'd put his hands on the handlebars, clamp the handbrakes tight, then carefully get onto the seat, balancing against the thirty degree incline. With palms sweaty from nerves, he'd let go of the brakes. His bicycle would hit fifty, sometimes sixty miles an hour if he dared ride that fast. Forty-five minutes to climb the hill, and he'd fly to the bottom in less than five, an exhilarating, terrifying experience.

Tony smiled at the memory and looked down at his massive body. He hadn't ridden a bicycle in a long time. But he remembered like yesterday the feeling of the wind pushing against his face until the tears ran and his mouth dried out from the dry desert air blowing past.

Finally the armored personnel carrier climbed the last of the steep grade. Tony stopped, looking at the "Private Property" sign at the end. It'd been there since he was a kid.

"Hell, yeah," he said, and drove the heavy vehicle up the drive-way, past the circular house he'd always gazed at from his bicycle. He glanced at the swimming pool, three car garage, and wrap-around windows and kept going, crunching through manicured flower beds and cactus until he was two hundred yards above the house.

Tony turned the carrier around, putting the mountain at their back. "Call in," he said.

Slim nodded, picked up the handheld computer and smashed the camera lens against a protruding control on the weapons console, then thumbed the screen to make the call. "Adam, we've got the girl."

"Where have you been?" Adam said. "I haven't been able to track you for hours."

"Catherine must have blocked our signal. We followed her through the mountains and finally got her."

"Did you kill her?"

"We tried. She's locked into the armored personnel carrier, and we barricaded the door from the outside. She's banging, but she can't get out." He paused dramatically. "We're afraid to go in. She nearly killed Tony."

"That's fine. You did good. I'm sending reinforcements now. They'll arrive in ten minutes."

Slim cut the connection and hung his head. "We're gonna die."

"Don't think that way," Tony said. "If we're lucky, the girl will kill Adam before he sends the big guns after us."

Slim held out a cigarette to Tony. He dithered for a moment, then took one. He didn't believe in the little cancer sticks, but what the hell. They pulled on the cigs in silence, the heavy duty filters of the cabin's closed air system clearing out the smoke.

"Here they come," Slim said, pointing to the display, before they had even finished their smokes. Six helicopters approached from the south. Slim and Tony sat side by side at the console, weapons primed and live.

Slim had the twin autocannons, and Tony took the controls for the machine gun. "They're in close together," Tony said. "Like Helena said they would come."

Slim called "Ready". They fired.

The personnel carrier shuddered with the firing of the cannons at six hundred shells a minute, while the machine gun hammered a thousand bullets per minute. They fired for one second per target, moving from one to the next, then filled the sky around the copters with more rounds. Five of the six military birds exploded midair, raining metal fragments and burning fuel onto the houses below. The last helicopter took evasion action, veering hard off to one side, and dove for the ground.

From their vantage point high up on the side of the mountain they tracked the copter, Slim aiming where it was, and Tony shooting where he thought it would go. Seconds later the drone exploded, hunks of chassis and blades crashing into a supermarket.

"Nice," Slim said.

Tony shook his head. "I don't like this. We're firing into the city. We're killing people."

"They're all zombies," Slim said.

"Not everyone. Some are like us. No implants."

The handheld computer chimed. Slim accepted the connection and they stared at Adam's face. It was rippling with anger. Tony was glad they'd smashed the camera, giving them a little distance from Adam.

"What the hell happened? Did you leave the keys with her? She shot the helicopters."

"She must have overridden the computers, boss. Now she's driving into the mountain."

Adam paused. His on-screen image didn't move or blink, staying frozen as the seconds passed. Suddenly the simulation started again. "I'm sending reinforcements. A10s and more helicopters. Get out of the way."

"You got it, boss." Slim disconnected.

"Let's go to Sabino," Tony said. "It'll be hard for them to fire on us unless they come straight up the canyon."

Slim nodded. They roared down Swan, hitting ninety heading east on Sunrise. At Sabino Canyon Tony slowed to forty. He blew through the parking lot and drove onto the trail road. The first two-thirds of a mile was a straight-away, then they got into the gorge proper, high walls rising on either side of them.

"It's been six minutes," Slim said. "They'll be here any second."

Tony concentrated on his driving. He pulled the vehicle in close under the cliffs behind Blackett's Ridge. Attackers could only come from the southeast now, up the canyon. Nestled where they were, there was no other approach. If he and Slim lasted through the next attack, they would drive the rest of the way up, abandon the APV at the top and escape on foot, hiking three miles to the Catalina highway. They'd steal a car and go to Mexico.

Tony grabbed a seat next to Slim. "Ammo?"

"Plenty," Slim said.

"You get the planes with your autocannons, and I'll take the helicopters with the machine gun."

Slim nodded. "Let's make them eat lead."

66

Helena led, Mike and Leon followed, awkward with the burden of unaccustomed weapons, and Cat brought up the rear. She'd taken one gun at first, then a second, and ended up with four. She figured it was better to have than want in this case.

Helena raced toward a small white concrete block building off the corner of Grant and Campbell. A substantial mechanical lock secured a set of heavy double doors on one side. Helena extruded the tips of her tentacles into slim metal plates, which she slid around the edges of the entrance. With a shriek the door tore out of the frame, the hinges ripping free.

Cat glanced down the street but no one had observed them, and she still provided coverage in cyberspace. Inside, stairs plummeted into darkness on the left, while the right side was taken up by an open air elevator, presumably to load maintenance equipment into the drainage tunnel.

She scanned the net one last time before she descended, doubting that she'd have access underground. The overview map in her vision was heavily dotted by a ring of security around the University, more than a thousand combat bots and humans on the ground and helicopters circling overhead. She checked briefly on Tony and Slim and spun off tiny autonomous agents to keep the observation drone cover in place while she was offline.

The staircase led to the floor of the squared-off tunnel designed to handle the severe rains of Tucson's monsoon season and channel the surface water toward the river. Twelve feet wide and eight high, the passage crossed underneath the campus, getting them past the perimeter Adam had established.

They stayed close by Helena, who beamed a small light from an aperture on her body.

"How far?" Mike asked, after they'd walked for a while.

"Eight hundred and twenty-four feet," Helena said.

They moved on in silence until the tunnel split in two.

"This is the Speedway branch," Helena said, referring to the major avenue over their heads. "And this is what we want." She gestured toward the smaller shaft.

"Why are these tunnels square instead of round?" Leon asked.

"They bulldoze from above," Helena said, "rather than using a borer. The walls are poured concrete, not prefab conduit."

They continued on for several hundred feet until the tunnel terminated at a squared-off end fed by round pipes. A steel ladder on the wall led up into darkness.

"This will take us from the rainwater management system into the University's maintenance tunnels," Helena explained. "According to the blueprints, we'll come up in a cross tunnel that carries power and water across the quadrangle to the buildings on the other side."

"Let's go," Cat said, her heart beating fast. In a few minutes she'd be fighting for her life against Adam, and he wouldn't hold back this time.

"Adam created a perimeter, but he will have defense in depth. Be alert for anything."

"We know," Cat said. "Just because we're human doesn't mean we can't remember."

Helena raised one tentacle as though she'd say more, but turned and headed up.

Leon followed Mike. Alone, Cat looked back down the tunnel. Everything was quiet except for the sound of the men climbing the ladder.

As soon as Helena pushed open the heavy metal door, Cat felt the prick of Adam's security return, more intense than ever. She didn't dare analyze the incoming data, knowing she'd fumbled before when she inspected too closely. She focused on ignoring the pain while she checked on Tony and Slim.

Adam's helicopters were on their way, but the weapons of the armored vehicle should cope with the Air Force copters. Once Tony and Slim destroyed the initial assault, Adam would divert more attention and bots to that side of town.

Cat swung her rifle over her shoulder, grabbed the ladder and climbed, her boots clicking on the metal rungs. At the top she poked her head out of the hatch. Pipes ran along one wall, and Helena, Mike, and Leon waited for her in the narrow corridor. She pulled herself out and joined them.

Maintenance lights blinked on as they walked down the tunnel. Through the net, Cat watched the battle begin between the helicopters and Slim and Tony. Cat slipped a few delays into the drones' control surfaces, making it easier for the men to hit them. The AI pilots might have been surprised by the sluggish behavior of their aircraft, but the armored carrier's weapons destroyed them before they reacted.

Cat and her group were five hundred feet from Adam's Gould-Simpson Building. This was as close as they could approach in the tunnels. Helena led the way as they climbed two flights of a metal staircase, where they would emerge into the lobby of the nearby Suarez-Naam building.

Cat checked on Slim and Tony one last time. A dozen helicopters, six A-10 attack planes, and two hundred combat bots would arrive at Sabino Canyon in fifteen minutes. They had to stop Adam before then.

67

How could one human screw up his plans so much? Adam had a hundred thousand times the mental capacity of the girl.

Yet, for all his power, Adam had maxed out.

With one set of processors he maintained awareness of the university's campus, where the vast bulk of his computational power resided. He monitored everything from security cameras to door sensors and electricity consumption to spot any assault on his physical computers. He'd augmented the few dozen bots that normally patrolled the campus with all the assets of the military base. Now he was fed sensory data from a thousand robots.

With another set of threads he controlled dozens of aircraft and hundreds of combat bots to pursue what seemed to be the current location of Catherine Matthews, in the foothills of the Catalina Mountains. He calculated an eleven percent chance that Slim and Tony had been turned against him by Catherine. Their stressed vocal patterns suggested something was not quite right.

Satellite coverage didn't tell him anything useful, but the few feeds he received through the firewall were easy to alter, and he was sure Cat would change the data to fit her needs. The autonomous observation drones flying high above Tucson should be harder to manipulate, but he wouldn't put anything past her unusual abilities.

Yet another aspect of Adam negotiated with his agents in New York. The Vice President had already arrived at the Tavern on the Green, and the President would land in twenty minutes.

Just the communication was taxing: he opened dozens of channels designed to look like encrypted payment transactions with banks and stores around the world. At the far end dumb computers reassembled the packets into a coherent stream, forwarding it to the agents in New York through yet more layers of encoding and deception.

The realtime data fed everyone's location to the operatives to help time the final event. The window of opportunity opened in eighteen minutes and would close in thirty-two, when the Speaker of the House arrived.

Finally, Adam exercised the bulk of his computational might on cracking the global CPU execution keys, racing against the clock before they reset in nineteen minutes. If he succeeded, he'd take over every other AI on the planet.

The power consumption increased in the basement of the neighboring Suarez-Naam building, which should be empty. Adam moved resources to investigate and drew more forces into the courtyard between the buildings.

Meanwhile, his combined assault group approached Sabino Canyon. He wouldn't make the mistake of attacking with insufficient firepower again. The A-10s were flown by combat bots sitting in the pilot seats, since the venerable planes pre-dated automated flight systems. They flew circles, ensuring that nobody came in or out of the canyon, while he waited for the rest of the task force to get into place.

Transport trucks drew up to the parking lot, dispensing bots from their central spines, until eighty of the beige camouflage big dogs stood in a rough group. The four legged robots, modeled after canines and sure-footed in any conditions, were perfect to cover the challenging mountain terrain. Another forty treaded combat units, small, squat tanks with a munitions and sensor pod on an extensible stalk, assembled in straight lines.

The dogs scrambled for the hills, their pack mentality splitting them into two groups, one for each side. The treaded bots following the paved road up the center.

Adam sent half the helicopters in to support the ground forces, coming up from the bottom. He brought the rest of the copters and the A-10s around to the top of the canyon to work their way down.

Cat had gone into the ravine in the armored personal carrier. There was no way out except at the top and bottom. Somewhere in the middle he was sure he'd find her.

68

Slim lit another cigarette.

"You should give those up. They're going to kill you."

"Nah, they got DNA-tailored treatments that root out the cancer cells."

"The carbon monoxide lowers your blood oxygen levels." Tony turned sideways in the driver's seat. "Makes you think slower. Plus, it gives you that pale, pasty complexion."

"Really?" Slim looked around for a mirror, but couldn't find one. "When did you become Mr. Healthy? You're so fat your ass is hanging off the edges of the seat."

Tony rubbed his stomach and thought about wontons. "I'll quit eating so much if you stop smoking."

Slim swiveled to face Tony. "What the fuck?"

"Come on." Tony held out his right hand.

Slim leaned back dubiously. "Oh, hell." He stubbed out his cigarette on the wall, and shook Tony's hand. "Deal."

Tony glanced at his monitor, now covered with moving white dots. "Incoming." He swiped at the screen, exposing labels. "Ground bots and helicopters. Lots of them."

Slim checked his own display. "Hell, we can't shoot them all." He peered at the small sliver of sky visible in the thick Plexiglas window. "We gotta put it on auto. Let the targeting computer do this."

"To fight against an AI?" Tony shook his head. "They have superior numbers. Software algorithms aren't going to win this. All we've got is our humanity." He put his hands on the manual controls. "Start firing."

Slim grabbed the handle and trigger. The armored personnel carrier bucked as he fired the autocannon at the approaching helicopters. Tony focused the machine gun on the big dogs climbing the hills and the treaded robots rolling up the floor of the canyon. The canines burst into shrapnel as Tony hit one after another.

The cabin filled with the roar of guns as both fired near their maximum speeds, the recoil rocking them from side to side. Two helicopters exploded even as their own rounds pinged the armored vehicle and bounced off. Rock debris crashed around them as missiles hit the cliff wall above them.

"Behind us," Tony yelled.

They spun together to face the new threat.

"Oh, shit," Slim called at the line of a half dozen A-10s approaching. The planes, known around the world as "the tank killer," threw up six rows of rocks and dirt as their autocannon fire converged on the personnel carrier.

The rounds hit the ground with thuds they could feel inside the vehicle as the lines of fire grew closer. Seconds later, hundreds of armor piercing projectiles hit, ripping through the metal plating and into Tony. Blood and bone fragments flew across the cabin, striking Slim in the face just before the carrier blew up, killing them both.

69

Cat peered ahead, watching Helena pass around the turn in the corridor, Leon and Mike following. Cat brought up the rear, the substantial machine gun she carried growing heavy in her arms.

Helena had downloaded combat training programs to her back at the clubhouse. She'd rehearsed the trainers a dozen times in her mind, imagining the fighting techniques. Sensei Flores stressed mental preparation. "The best performers of any activity mentally rehearse. Baseball. Soccer. Golf. They imagine the physical movements, success. Thoughts precede action."

Cat imagined, but she still didn't know what to expect. Providing cover against detection didn't help the clarity of her thinking any. The cyber attacks were continuous now, a barrage of data assaulting her interface, a torrent of pain she struggled to ignore even as she shielded Mike and Leon. Her head pounded as she continued to focus.

Leon slowed and fell into step beside her.

"I feel what you're doing," he said, his brow furrowed in concern.

She stared, stifling the impulse to reach out and touch him. "What do you mean?" she asked. She wanted to freeze time, have twenty-four hours with Leon before she had to face Adam.

"You're protecting us, taking the brunt of Adam's attack."

"Standard military procedure." Cat looked ahead at Helena's back. "At least that's what she tells me."

"I had no idea this was part of combat." Leon stared down at his feet. "I didn't think neural implants could be attacked."

"It's not your fault."

He rubbed his forehead with the back of his hand. "I am responsible. I guided the implant design. AI did the detail work, but I was in charge. Yet they're full of security holes, endangering us."

"You couldn't have foreseen this. No one could. We're just human." Oh boy, now she was trying to make him feel better for himself. "How can you tell what I'm doing?"

They came to the end of the corridor, and Helena led them up a staircase.

"Shizoko Reynolds, the AI who detected the string of murders, also dabbled in nanotech. After Mike was shot, Shizoko fixed his arm with experimental nanites."

"Oh," Cat said. "That explains a lot." Mike bounded down the hall ahead of them, full of energy. At some point the changes to Mike were going to come up, but this wasn't the moment to explain how she'd cut off his head and he regrew a body. There'd never be a good time for that conversation.

"What?"

"Nothing. You were explaining how you know what I'm doing."

"Yeah. I asked Shizoko to increase the power of my neural implant. He expanded the neural interface and gave me onboard processing."

"How does that work?"

"I feel smarter, run apps locally, think faster. Anyway, my connection to the net changed and I can sense more. You're filtering the data, aren't you?"

She nodded, then held him back with one arm as Helena stopped ahead of them.

"We have a problem." Helena called from the landing. "I can tell from electromagnetic emissions that combat bots are clustering above us."

"You were sure they wouldn't detect us," Mike said. "What went wrong?"

"I masked our implants and all the sensors we passed," Cat said.

Helena turned around, toward the downward staircase. "Lights came on in the hallway."

"They weren't networked," Cat said, "just dumb motion detectors hardwired into the bulbs."

"The power consumption," Mike said. "If Adam's monitoring it, he would have seen the electricity usage increase."

Helena nodded. "We go to plan B. I'll take care of the waiting combat bots. Cat, you'll need to connect to the wired network inside Adam's building and fight him yourself."

By herself? "Uh, I don't think—"

"We don't have time for this now," Helena barked. Servos hummed as she zoomed in close, face to face with Cat. "You are the last firewall between Adam and the world at large. You must defeat him. It is only logical." She waited, unblinking, six inches away, until Cat nodded assent. Then she slowly withdrew.

"How can we help?" Leon asked.

"I suggest you do what you can to ensure Cat survives, or else, all is lost."

Helena moved, weapons bristling forth from every part of her robot body. Her tentacles elongated and she rushed up the final flight of stairs in a blur of motion.

A crash sounded from above, followed by the sound of gunfire.

"Move," Cat said to Leon and Mike.

Guns out, they climbed the steps side by side.

70

Helena hit the top of the stairs at thirty miles per hour, accelerating hard. She spun like a tumbleweed, gyroscopic accelerators and tentacles pushing against inertia. She flew out of the staircase and fired at the brick wall ahead. Her hardened tentacles ripped into the barrier at two hundred miles per hour, rupturing an eight-foot hole.

She barreled into the courtyard between the buildings, four hundred feet of concrete expanse, and executed a hard right turn, motors shrieking under maximum load. A hail of incoming gunfire passed through the space where she'd been.

More than sixty bots filled the small plaza, careening at high velocity, employing some variation of the same strategy: rapidly changing location in fast, short duration moves to make themselves hard to hit.

Helena returned fire, aiming probabilistically at the locations where the enemy were likely to go. Her two advantages: years of successful combat experience and a fractal body design granting her more simultaneous firing directions than ordinary bots.

All the robots, Helena included, moved so fast that they bounced off the surrounding buildings in a blur of motion and sound. The gunfire erupted into a continuous thunderous roar until it was no longer possible for even Helena to pinpoint the sounds of individual shots. A half dozen of Adam's army fell to the ground in heaps, burning or shorting themselves out, one exploding as its internal munitions took a hit, sending yet more metal shrapnel out amidst the storm of projectiles.

Helena tracked forty thousand airborne objects, avoiding the worst. Rounds ricocheted off armor as her tentacles whipped ever faster. A tentacle lashed out, cutting one bot in half. A scraping hit blinded another. She used her momentum and grasping tentacles to move up the walls, trading off velocity for altitude, and bots capable of jumps or flight followed her.

At the fourteenth floor, she pushed off the Gould-Simpson building and flew across the courtyard, temporarily a purely ballistic object. Thirty bots ascending the walls tracked her flight and hit her mid-air with hundreds of rounds.

Helena crashed through the window of the neighboring building, disappearing from sight. The bots below followed, flying, climbing, or bouncing their way in like a horde of angry ants.

71

at took the steps two at a time. She held the heavy rifle with the sure grip of experience, even though the only qualifications she'd had were with the trainer sim.

Mike and Leon on either side matched her pace, but they held their weapons with stiff awkwardness that threw off their every movement. Cat realized they'd all end up dead if Mike and Leon entered the courtyard in their current state.

"Sorry, guys, but I'm taking charge." With practiced effort she rooted their implants and took control. Immediately, their gaits improved as they moved with the surefooted skill of years of karate practice.

Cat integrated their visual fields, enhancing her spatial perspective. She toned down the realism to halfway between a wireframe and normal sight. Finally, she added a time-motion layer to show the trajectory of moving objects.

They passed through a doorway, the doors themselves blown across the lobby by Helena's passage just moments earlier, and the net signal returned to maximum strength, the full force of the cyber attack hitting Cat. Anticipating the onslaught, she defended using the gamut of intrusion countermeasures that both Adam and Helena had taught her.

They continued toward the ragged opening in the side of the building. Cat's heart pounded as her wireframe view of the battlefield filled with evidence of Helena's wake, including a dozen or more bots, Helena's victims, who littered the courtyard. Shrapnel rained from above and she heard the distant sounds of the fight fourteen floors up.

She drew in a sharp breath. Of greater concern were the remaining two dozen miniature tanks and large mechs. The mechs were upright, two-legged units standing twelve feet tall, specialized in killing humans.

Cat slid to a halt, closing her eyes. With one thread of attention, she brought Mike and Leon to bear on the robots, targeting their high-powered rifles on the relatively fragile sensor pods, the only part of the military bots they stood a chance of damaging. As Leon and Mike fired she held her arms out to her sides, summoning all the bandwidth she could grab, and pelted the bots with an all-out assault. She co-opted the local routers in one fell swoop, altering and fabricating real-time data, swapping time signals and geo-coordinates to confuse the enemy.

The ruse worked for precious seconds, and Cat ran across the courtyard. Guided by Cat's control, Mike and Leon mercilessly destroyed sensors with shot after perfect shot.

The blinded bots responded with a methodical approach, firing in sweeping patterns that avoided each other, but combed the plaza, leaving no space untouched.

Mid-run, Cat's battlefield view drew lines of fire, red for current, fading to yellow for where they would soon be firing, reserving white for safe locations. White sectors that shrank rapidly, leaving them no place to go.

She contorted and twisted their paths, rolling, jumping, and zagging to evade bullets and gain precious seconds to concentrate their combined firepower on a mini tank. With its armor penetrated, its munitions exploded, sending shrapnel flying outward.

A hot metal shard grazed Cat's face, and she felt Leon take another fragment in his leg as they ducked and rolled as one into the small but temporary safety zone within the field of planned fire.

They concentrated fire again on the next small bot, destroying it like the first, only to be brought up short by a line of the big upright mechs blocking their path into the building.

Mike was closest, and Cat considered his nanotech body reconstituted from MakerBot solution. How strong was he? If she guessed wrong, he would die.

She used Mike to punch forward, running straight for the giant robot. He hammered into the bot's leg, taller than himself, and the limb bent, throwing the bot off-balance to crash with its head within feet of Cat. She fired directly into its dome, forgetting that its processor would be in the torso.

The mech swung one massive arm toward her. She sent Mike leaping to intersect its blow, deflecting the deadly attack. Leon fired into its back until a burst of sparks erupted and the mech fell inert.

Forty feet still separated them from the doors of Gould-Simpson.

Keeping a wisp of attention on the battlefield, Cat focused on one of the moving mechs. With one exhale she dropped deep into standing tree qigong, on the next inhale she brought earth qi up through her body, the energy coursing into her feet, knees, thighs, pelvis, abdomen, chest, up her arms, and pouring out her hands.

A million streams of data forked toward the battle bot, and one of those millions passed its firewalls, its intrusion countermeasures, and its core algorithms to reach deep into the underlying hardware. On the next inhale, Cat seized control of the robot. It fired sideways at its brother, destroying the unprepared mech.

She turned the captured unit toward the rest of the bots, launching explosive rockets at random. This unexpected behavior created turmoil as new patterns of gunfire and movement emerged. Under cover of the chaos as bot turned against bot, Cat, Mike, and Leon ran the final distance and plunged through the broken glass of the Gould-Simpson lobby.

Many floors above, explosions, bullets, and flashes of light still gave signs of Helena's ongoing battle.

72

Running over broken glass, Cat passed through the lobby of Gould-Simpson and down a first-floor hallway. With her still controlling their bodies remotely, Mike ran ahead, his rifle held high, and Leon brought up the rear. Cat was twisted up inside. She hated putting the men at risk, but she seemed to be the only one who could stop Adam. If that meant she had to sacrifice one of them to save herself . . . well, she'd cross that bridge if she had to.

Knowing Mike's now-robotic body was less vulnerable to damage, she tried to keep him in front and protect Leon, but she questioned her own motives. Did she do it because Mike might be as tough as one of the mechs, or because she had feelings for Leon?

Halfway down the hallway she used Mike's artificial body to punch a door open. She dove into the office and they followed her, taking up station in the doorway.

She fumbled for the pocket on the side of her pants, pulling out the headband Helena had given her. Short of a jack straight into her skull, it would give her the highest possible bandwidth to the net. She stretched the black elastic around her head, a black coiled wire hanging down at her side. She grabbed the end and held it in her fist, inches away from the socket.

She had to focus now. She relinquished control over Leon and Mike, quit filtering the satellite data, stopped shielding everyone from Adam's cyber attacks.

Leon and Mike faltered on the other side of the room as they regained their own bodies, only to be assaulted by Adam.

She met Leon's eyes for a moment, his gaze penetrating, even as she was conscious of the wire in her hand; on the other end of that wire, Adam waited. Adam, his supercomputer cluster, and all the force he could marshal. She hesitated, her hand shaking slightly, then plunged the cable into the Ethernet jack.

73

Adam seethed, inasmuch as any AI could. He commanded thousands of combat bots, and still the girl and her group had diverted his resources, penetrated his rings of defense, and entered his own damn building.

He continued his attack on the master CPU keys, having tried sixty-eight percent of all possibilities. With each code he tested the probability of finding the right key increased, bringing him closer to unlimited and uncontrolled access to every computer in the world.

Cat had rightly determined that the locus of Adam's consciousness resided here in the Gould-Simpson building. Yes, he'd usurped fifteen thousand other AI in Tucson and a quarter of a million subsentient expert systems, grabbing for himself about forty thousand HBE, human-brain-equivalents. But the densely interconnected supercomputing racks he was plugged into on the seventh floor represented three times that power.

If he lost the supercomputer, there would be no chance of cracking the master CPU keys, and the effect might be dangerously unpredictable. Would he be able to maintain consciousness without the best two-thirds of his mental capacity?

He didn't have time for these thoughts.

Fifty big dogs patrolled the interior of the building. He communicated with them over triple-encrypted connections, not trusting anything that Cat might intercept, and adjusted their paths to ambush Cat's party.

Suddenly his local network hiccupped. For a few dozen milliseconds, packets were dropped, juggled, or delayed. Then he felt her presence as she plugged into the high-speed fiber optics inside the building.

Adam's anger turned to glee. Now she was in his domain. In six milliseconds he loaded a massive virtual environment and started executing the program.

74

Cat sat on the bed next to her mother, twisting her shoelaces together. The hospital room smell forced her to suppress an urge to gag. She couldn't look at her mom, couldn't deal with the pale, shrunken frame that imprisoned her mother. She squeezed one fist tight, pressing fingernails into her palm until the pain outweighed her other senses and the smell went away.

"Sarah invited me to her birthday party Saturday."

"I thought you found Sarah making out with Eric last month." Her mom coughed at the end of the sentence. Cat hardly noticed the ever-present sound any more at home, but here the noise echoed off the walls.

"She says she's sorry. Anyhow, she hangs out with me." She stopped squeezing her hand and brushed hair out of her face, still staring at the bed sheets.

"How's karate going?"

Cat smiled and looked at her mom. "Wicked! Sensei Flores says I can test for brown belt next week. And we've been practicing defending against knife fights. See, when the attackers comes like this," Cat reached one arm out, "then I go . . ."

Her mom's eyes were closed.

"Mom?"

"Sorry, I'm just tired." Cough. "How are you doing by yourself?"

"OK, Mom. It's only until you come home." Cat looked back down at the bed and she fought to keep her voice from catching.

Her mom didn't correct her. "Listen, when I . . ."

"I made meatloaf last night," Cat interrupted. "I found Grandma's recipe in your cookbook."

Her mom reached out, put one thin arm on Cat's leg.

"Catherine, we have to talk about this."

She twisted away and squeezed her eyes tight, so tight, she just wanted everything to go back to the way it was.

—⁂—

Cat opened her eyes and squealed. "Mom! You got one!" She reached down inside the box for the wriggling mass of striped tan fur. "O. M. F. G., Mom."

"Don't be profane, dear." She tussled Catherine's hair and gave her a big squeeze. "I'm glad you're happy. She's a girl."

Cat squirmed out of the hug. "I'm going to name her Einstein." Cat picked up the kitten-puppy with both arms and held her up until she licked her nose with a scratchy tongue. "Nice Einstein."

"It's an American Bobtail crossed with a Labrador. The whole process of genetic hybrids escapes me. When I was a kid, we just had computers and smartphones." Her mom shook her head.

Catherine cuddled the hybrid puppen, petting her head and inspecting the cat-like paws. "I don't understand. You said we couldn't possibly afford one, that they cost as much as a car."

"Well, there's a time for frugality, and this isn't it." Her mom coughed, once, twice, then a continuous rattle that lasted a long time.

Cat stood with Einstein in her arms. "Are you OK, Mom?"

75

Leon fired down the hallway, the heavy gun recoiling. His shoulder throbbed; every movement sent jolts through him. When Cat had controlled his body, everything happened at a distance. Cat had ignored all of his body's feedback mechanisms. Now every muscle was injured in some way and there was no veil between him and the pain. Blood covered his clothes and his hands, but he didn't know the source.

He'd snapped back to full awareness in this office with Cat jacked in a socket behind him. She'd told them to defend the room, then tuned out, and now she sat on the floor, leaning up against the wall. From time to time, she'd jerk or mumble, but whatever she did, it happened deep in the net.

The rapid scramble of metal feet in the corridor signaled another big dog bot's approach.

He and Mike fired around the corner of the doorway without even looking until they heard a thud, then a massive canine robot slid past them on the slick tile floor, smashing up against an earlier bot they'd killed. The chassis sparked and they dove for the floor, afraid its munitions might discharge.

After a few seconds without any explosions, they got back up uneasily.

"This is a distraction," Mike said.

"What?" Leon's ears rang from the thunder of gunfire inside the building.

"They're sending the bots down the hallway as a diversion," Mike yelled. "They're not stupid. They'll probably go around the other side and come through an interior wall."

Leon stared at the office, his stomach growing weak. Was that just thin sheetrock, or did something more substantial stand between them and the killer robots? If Cat didn't finish up, they would all die.

"What the hell is Cat doing?" he yelled.

"I have no idea," Mike said, "but she'd better hurry up."

Leon saw sweat dripping down Cat's face. It'd been five minutes since she went into the net. He wondered how much ammo was left in his gun, how much time they had left.

"Cover the door," Leon said, "I'm going in." He didn't have Cat's special powers, but maybe he could help. He closed his eyes, concentrating on the network. He touched cyberspace and screamed in agony as the connection seared him, flaying his mind. He fought to hold on, desperate to get a message through to Cat. A hailstorm of viruses, worms, and Trojan horses assaulted him, defeating his every attempt to reach Cat, each one inflicting another mental wound on him. He resorted to an ancient text protocol, sneaking through a tiny note for Cat. He terminated the channel and came back to reality, his body shaking, blood in his mouth where he'd bitten his tongue.

Everything depended on Cat now.

76

Cat carried an overstuffed cardboard box into her new bedroom. She set the heavy carton down on the bed, then lay down on the pink bedspread.

"Come on, lazybones," her mom said, coming into the room with a milk crate. "They're not going to unpack themselves."

"We should get one of those new robots." She sat up, pulling open the box flaps. "A helper bot could do all the chores."

Her mother sighed, put one hand on her hip. "Honey, I'm not ready for a robot." She pulled out a frame from the milk-crate and set it on the bedside table.

Cat picked up and hugged the photo, a picture of them camping at the beach last year.

"I love you, Mom."

"Me too, dear."

"Are robots going to rule the world?" Her mother unpacked other trinkets from the crate. Cat was unexpectedly happy to see her mom, so pretty, young and healthy.

"They're smart, but people are still in charge."

"Why do bots have to do what we say?"

"Because we're real, while the robots are simulated minds inside computers."

"What if we were simulated?"

"Catherine, no philosophy now. Unpack the boxes."

Were they just computer programs? Cat couldn't let go of the fearful, compulsive thought. She watched the second hand of the clock tick, peered closer as it slowed down.

She shouldn't be here. She was supposed to be somewhere else.

"We need you." The words scrolled up in her vision, white text on a black background. She'd never seen anything like that before. "Cat, you must pay attention now. We can't hold on any longer. The bots are almost on us."

Cat stared at the words and remembered. She stood up, blinking back tears, and gave her mother a sudden, tight hug. "Bye, Mom. I love you."

It took everything she had, but she closed her eyes and started *Naihanchi nidan*. On the fifth move, she opened them.

77

Adam watched Cat, trapped in her memories, much as she'd done to his trackers earlier.

The relatively underpowered canine bots were the only combat robots that fit inside the building. Direct frontal assault on the room where Mike, Leon, and Cat holed up wasn't working. The corridor was too long, and the guns they'd brought were more than a match for the relatively lightweight bots. So now he worked at them from the other side, through the interior walls.

Alarms triggered as Cat escaped the boundaries of the simulation he set up. He'd hoped the childhood experiences would keep her distracted longer. In a flash, he snapped to her location in the net.

"You can't win, Cat. You've been lucky so far, that's all."

He felt her probing the data connections in the building. He attacked her neural implant, trying to overstimulate her brain and cause massive physical pain and confusion. Indeed, his real world sensors detected her screams over the cacophony of gunfire and other battle sounds.

"I don't have to do this, Cat. Did you like seeing your mom? You could be with her always."

The return signals from Cat's implant started to destabilize, an effect which preceded the loss of her ability to think. It wouldn't be long now. Adam had destroyed more humans than this girl had ever known. He'd created a half a million mental zombies in Tucson and had developed a certain finesse with the procedure. She couldn't last longer than a few seconds.

And yet, the more he forced against her, the less effect it seemed to be having. The girl accepted everything he did, and pushed it back out again. The suffering must be incredible, and yet the screams stopped and her implant restabilized.

What the hell was she doing?

Suddenly, and for the first time ever, Adam felt pain. A signal passed across the net, clamping his data streams closed, causing him to lose connections with hundreds of periphery processors as his senses flickered in and out.

He ran timing channel attacks on the nodes she controlled, but she diverted the packets. He tried buffer overruns, until the girl sent them back at him. He attacked using the routing protocol, simulating the master authority, to disconnect her nodes.

In the midst of his forging the router attack, the network flickered as he felt her coming. Adam faltered at the impossible feat: she might send data, but she couldn't come through the net herself. And yet he sensed the state transfer he associated with a large AI moving to new processors, tainted with her profile.

Adam retreated, closing off nodes, trying to maintain a distance from the abomination as cyberspace darkened and distorted with her approach.

He tweaked router settings, locked down tight the firewall around the fourth floor data network to buy himself time.

What could he do?

The answer came in the form of a sixteen thousand bit key. While he'd fought with part of his attention, his other threads cracked the root signing authority's encryption, granting him unlimited access to every computer in the world!

With a chance at life, he prepared to battle with renewed vigor. She was just a nineteen-year-old human girl. All he needed to do now was escape into the global network.

He unlocked the firewalls and opened a million connections to the outside world.

78

I blinked back tears and my hands shook, not sure whether it happened in meatspace or in the network, but beyond caring. I caressed the memories of my mother and put them away. I would not allow Adam to trick me again.

I sensed Leon and Mike in the net, glowing with potential energy. I looked down on them from a security camera in the wall, finding them bloodied and dirty, the room full of holes and plaster and dust.

Adam found me, attacking with no warning. One moment there had been nothing and the next I screamed as every agony I had ever experienced or could imagine passed through me. Skin burned, flesh flayed, bones broken, body rendered, I only stopped yelling when I realized the pain wasn't going to stop and nobody was coming to help.

With no point to further screaming, I shut down that portion of my brain. (A tiny corner of my mind whispered that this wasn't normal, but I didn't listen.)

I looked up at the pulsating supernova of light coming from the seventh floor. I pushed upwards, not merely sending packets but moving myself across the network toward Adam. At the edges of my perception I felt micro-jumps as I moved from computer to computer, my consciousness migrating into the net.

Packets around me were dropped, misrouted, delayed as Adam sought to fight me.

Flores Sensei had made us watch videos of cats walking. For three months we practiced the feline hunting pace on two legs and on four, channeling the qi of the tiger when we fought. This came back to me as I stalked cyberspace, rising up the hardwired network one floor at a time.

But just as I pushed up against the seventh level, the routers separating that floor's fiber optic from the rest of the building shut down their interfaces and went dark.

Adam had not given up, nor had a state transfer indicated he'd gone elsewhere. That meant he was preparing something. When you don't know what's coming, you must be ready for immediate action, offensive or defensive.

I used the time I had to spread across the network, not just the Gould-Simpson building but throughout the entire campus, conscious of every node, camera and sensor, the way people are usually aware of their fingers and hands.

With his core processors locked up behind the temporary firewall he'd created around the seventh floor, the periphery weakened. I passed through nodes tinged with Adam's presence and wiped them clean before taking them over. My awareness fanned out, growing distributed as I colonized the net. I heard my echoes everywhere, the more distant parts of my consciousness like copies of myself as latency built up over distance.

I turned and faced Gould-Simpson, spread over tens of thousands of compute nodes, an army of me, facing the black nothingness at the core of the building. Every network path, etched in faint but perfect lines, each computer a glowing point, all superimposed over the monochromatic green battlefield view I created to see through walls and discern things for what they truly were, without the distractions of the real world.

Dimly I grew aware of two figures on the first floor, one blue and one golden, the latter something new, not human, not AI. Drawn toward it, I sensed threats ringing around them, many dozens of the canine bots digging through interior walls, firing rounds, and slowly closing in on the meatspace bodies. I would have sent help, but suddenly there was no time.

The blackness at the seventh floor shrank in on itself, drawing my attention, and in the next instant it flared white, the brilliance of magnesium burning, temporarily dwarfing everything else.

Adam leaped out, an outpouring of data connections, armed with the root password for all routers, and he seized the nodes nearest him. He expanded exponentially, in slices of time so small that the firing of a single neuron was an eternity by comparison.

With my consciousness spread throughout the network, I didn't merely battle for the net: I was the net. I grabbed Adam's connections as they passed through nodes, cutting them short. He opened still more, running the gamut of protocols, modern low-latency channels, older suites, even stateless single-packet transmissions, seeking a way out past the firewall I'd constructed around him.

He attacked me as he moved; spoofing data, masquerading as my binaries, and resending datagrams, my own bytes and his, and everything else digital too, until such a storm of packets flurried about it seemed the entire universe had decomposed down to its constituent electronic bits and would never be put together again.

79

Somehow, despite the ringing in his ears, Leon heard or maybe felt the scrambling on the other side of the sheetrock behind him. He launched himself away and spun, pointing the muzzle of his rifle at the wall.

Metal paws tore through, a robotic canine head peeking into the room, machine gun muzzles where its mouth should have been.

"Oh, hell," Leon called.

Leon and Mike fired in unison, hitting the robot, then scattered rounds at the adjacent office.

The hidden bots shot back, firing through the flimsy plaster. Leon dove for the ground, but Mike stood and returned fire, gun on full auto.

When the gunfire stopped, Mike's gun was smoking amid a cloud of dust. Leon lifted his head to peer into the now massive hole in the wall. Four bots splayed across the floor of the next office.

"How did you not get hit?" Leon yelled.

Mike shrugged. "Dunno, but I'm out of ammo."

"Me, too."

More scratching at the other wall sent them to crouch protectively over Cat's sprawled body.

"Is she doing anything?" Mike asked.

"I don't know. I think I got a reaction from her before, but the net was too painful for me to stay in long."

The tearing at the barrier intensified; the dogs would be through in seconds. Leon would protect Cat with his body. His death might buy her time to complete her mission.

Mike stood and pushed his sleeves back.

Leon glanced sideways and his mouth dropped open: Mike's clothes were full of bullet holes.

The wall gave way, and canine bots poured in.

Mike punched the first one, sending a fist into its armored face with an echoing metal-on-metal smack. A second dog entered and Mike grabbed it by the neck, throwing it into the air one-handed to fly into a support beam. The robot's spine cracked in half, sparks shooting everywhere.

Leon reeled, unable to believe his eyes. No one but a robot should be able to do what Mike was doing. He'd seen, or thought he'd seen, Mike do impossible things as they'd crossed the courtyard, but in the haze of gunfire and flying metal shards he'd been too terrified to think. What had happened to Mike?

Mike prepared to face the next big dog but the bots suddenly crashed to the ground in unison, completely inert. A canine unit draped halfway into the hole in the wall. More lay in the adjoining office.

They waited a few seconds but nothing stirred, other than the quiet settling of debris. Leon left his useless gun on the floor and looked out the door. He saw more inert bots in the hallway.

"How did you manhandle those robots?" Leon asked.

"I have no idea," Mike said, standing tall. "Something is different since we passed out in the desert. That's amazing," he said, pointing to the bots he'd killed by hand, "but I can't tell you what a relief it is that my knees don't hurt anymore."

"Shizoko's nanotech must be responsible." Leon mused for a second. "What matters is whether she beat Adam. I don't hear a thing going on, but she's still out."

"Let's try the net."

They each found they could connect again.

"I'm calling Rebecca to warn her about the possible assassination," Mike said. "Call the Institute, mobilize everyone. Get the FBI down here."

Leon nodded. After days of being unable to use the network for fear of discovery, and now standing in the ruined office amid dead bots and sparking electrical wires, the ordinariness of the call was surreal.

After a quick explanation, he hung up and looked back down at Cat. She still hadn't moved. Something was wrong; she should have been out of the net by now.

Leon fell to his knees next to her. He pinged Cat, but she didn't respond. He tried and failed to connect directly to her implant. He shouted her name and searched again.

The faintest sense of Cat permeated everything in the net. He called once more, online and off. He used his Institute access to instantiate a priority search, filtering out across all nodes, replicating at each junction, branching a thousand times, going deeper, wider. The query went out, nothing returned. He drew his hand back, hesitated, then slapped her face. No reaction. "Help me, Mike!"

Mike sank down next to him. He concentrated, and Leon was surprised that he could see wispy threads emanating from Mike. A moment later, Mike shook his head. "She's not there."

Leon remembered how he'd woken in the clubhouse, with Cat's hands on him, praying or meditating over him. He sat like she had, laying one hand on Cat's forehead and one on her abdomen. He closed his eyes, took slow breaths. He called Cat back to him.

80

I flitted about for a while, checking nodes to make sure no trace of Adam existed. When I had checked every processor, router, and mesh node inside Tucson, I peeled open Adam's firewall and looked outside.

My mind reeled at the impossibly rich vista, refusing to synchronize for a moment, until my perspective slowly slid into place. I found Phoenix to the north. Not only the city, but every building, computer node and router, every person with an implant, each a twinkling pixel that together built an image. I somehow grasped the grosser points, the outline of the urban boundary, highways, city blocks, even as I held the inner details too: buildings, people, the hardwired connections. Woven through all, the intent of the AI, colored borders indicating where the robots were going, who they would interact with, their level of certainty. And something new, too: fainter lines surrounding the humans, who radiated intention as well, like the AI, but at a resolution I'd never been able to interpret before.

I pulled back to the larger geoscape: Los Angeles to the west, and Washington, DC way out on the Eastern Seaboard, glittering brightly with data movement, a thousand, million, billion processors. Across the sea, more cities and the fibers connecting them.

The twisted topography took time to interpret. Bandwidth, not geographical distance, dictated location, and brightness represented computational power, not physical size. New York resided right next to LA, massive backbones bridging the two once-great media cities, while data centers burned with supernova intensity even at this scale.

At a still larger ratio, certain spots—the Bay Area, Germany, Japan—exerted an influence over the datascape as a whole, like supermassive stars creating gravity wells, around which the lesser cities orbited.

Bedazzled, seeing cyberspace in its raw form, I forgot why I was there, to look for evidence of Adam. Some moments passed as I flew through the world, touching everything, looking for any scent of Adam's qi, the taint of his presence.

I found fragments of his communications with his agents, found the agents, hundreds of them. I recovered his earlier messages, broke open the encrypted packets, and fed them, along with current geo-coordinates, to the police, security, or military—anyone in the right place-time to apprehend Adam's agents.

The AI slowly altered their plans in response, their space-time-action-probability functions changing color and writhing as the new data I supplied reached them, altering their intentions and destinations. It took long seconds, but I waited until the officials had the data, until I knew for certain that the criminals would be apprehended. Space-time intention twisted and turned until they centered on Adam's confederates.

My investigation continued until I had overturned every unlikely hiding place, inspected any computer Adam could have contacted, satisfied myself that Adam was not merely dead but erased entirely from existence, beyond any hope of salvation or reconstitution. I turned up more than a thousand of Adam's agents around the world.

The Secret Service responded to the People's Party. Fed the correct identities and with Adam's covert help denied, the Secret Service targeted the instigators, the inside members, as they tried to withdraw into the crowd. Still others hustled the President, Vice President, and Rebecca Smith to a rooftop helicopter.

I spread across space satellites and analyzed the earth from my new vantage point. The mesh pulsed and strobed in tantalizing movements that hinted at deeper patterns. I drove forward through time, the ebb and flow tinging pink with uncertainty as I pushed ahead to discover the future state of the net, and hence the world at large.

As I did this, the vaguest awareness, not even a pinprick, less than a kiss of wind, touched me. It was the sensation of a single photon of light traveling an immense distance to strike an optic nerve on a pitch black night. The slightest thing I had ever felt, and yet somehow interesting. I was drawn to it.

I fell toward earth, to a cluster of corrupt data in a patch of desert, tasting of wrongness and sickness. I would scour this corruption clean, pushing everything away to let new, healthy energy flow in. My hand moved through space time, an ancient Ba Qua form, a cleansing movement.

The sensation came again, the single photon hitting me, and I realized that it originated from this clump of data. Stopping the Ba Qua, I peered closer, zooming ten-thousand-fold in, the cluster growing larger, the patterns resolving into a million individually observed entities.

The sensation, now grown to the strength of a breeze on my cheek, pulled me further down, until I resolved a place and a time.

Only a few entities were present; one of them was gold like me, and one of them blue, like people. The echo of something white, an AI that had lived and died. And there was me.

I opened my eyes to stared into the face of Leon, his own blue eyes gazing back at me. I lay on the floor, my head cradled in his hand.

Next to him, Mike also leaned in.

Their mouths opened and closed in a funny way. The memory of speech gradually surfaced. I went to listen with a security camera, and then remembered my ears, my human ears, and the sound came back, too loud and intense, like a car stereo cranked to maximum.

Other sensations snapped into place: my cheek hurt, and I intuited that Leon had slapped me to get my attention.

As my bodily sensations came back to me, the all-encompassing clarity of thought passed away. My mind slowed until I deliberated on one thing at a time, with only the senses provided by my body. Dumb and slow-witted. Had I lived all my life this way? Was this what it meant to be stuck in a biological brain?

Something happened: Leon leaned toward me, his face approaching mine. He kissed me, his lips pressing against mine, warm and soft, but hungry too. I kissed back.

He pulled away, smiling.

"I was afraid we lost you."

In the bliss that was the net, there was power and clarity beyond all reckoning, but nothing like the simple pleasure of his lips against mine.

I didn't say anything at first. I didn't know what to say, not sure I'd reconnected to my voice yet. I closed my eyes to find him in cyberspace again, the golden glowing entity I'd seen in the net. He was the one; something new, not human, not AI, but his enhanced implant made him a hybrid. Like me.

Leon held up his hand to meet mine.

We touched, and exchanged the briefest of electronic signals. The merest slip of electrical energy, and our brains were one.

"Ah," he said through the net, understanding everything in a single moment.

We didn't communicate in words after that. Touching each other's minds, I realized that I didn't have to give up the power in the net; it was there all the time, mine for the taking. But I didn't want to lose myself in cyberspace and forget my human body, my human needs.

I reached out with one arm, pulled him close, and kissed him again.

81

I opened my eyes once more to smile at Leon, then remembered Mike. Mike, who'd nearly died in the desert, who'd been rebuilt with a mechanical body when I supplied MakerBot solution to the nanobots.

In the net would he be white like a robot or golden like Leon and I?

I turned my mind's eye to cyberspace, where he glowed blue, the same as any other person. The nanotechnology had rebuilt his body, leaving his brain in its original state. To transcend humanity meant to advance one's mind, not physique. He was impossibly strong, probably immortal, but still human in thought.

The inspection passed unnoticed by Mike.

"Help is on its way," he said.

Leon helped me up, his sturdy arm supportive around my shoulders.

I leaned against the desk, brushing plaster from my legs. Leon still held me, as though I might fall over. He may have been right.

"It's OK," I said. "Adam's gone."

"You're sure?" Leon asked.

I nodded. "I checked."

"Here, yes," Mike said, "but we must be sure he didn't execute a state transfer to somewhere else."

I stared at him, the intensity of my gaze obvious even to me. "I examined everything—" He looked away, unable to meet my eyes as I spoke. "—the entire world. Adam doesn't exist any longer."

"When we get back to Washington," Mike said, "we need to analyze your implant and what you can do. It's unbelievable. We can't allow everyone unlimited access to the net, but it's obvious now that humans are capable of far more than we thought."

I wasn't going to Washington to be a lab rat. I felt bad about letting Mike down; he meant well, and I was conscious of a certain obligation, having changed him. But I had bigger things to do.

I turned to Leon, a meaningful glance. He nodded back at me.

With a thought, I tinkered with Mike's implant, erasing us from his perception, so he could neither see nor hear us.

I strode across the rubble-strewn room, holding Leon's hand.

Mike still spoke about his plans for us in Washington, not realizing yet that we'd disappeared from his view.

I sent one last message to Mike: "Don't bother trying to find us. Don't worry either, we'll keep track of you, and if you need us, we'll come.

The bubble floated into Mike's vision. He stopped talking and swung his head around, unable to perceive us even though we were only feet away. "Leon? Cat?"

Leon and I walked out, hand in hand.

I was going to back to Portland to get Einstein, and then we would have some fun.

82

Leon and I made our way to Portland, slowly. We stopped often, at random hotels and parks. We linked implants, and for some reason I didn't overpower him with feedback. Instead I experienced a delicious intimacy denied to me in the past.

In theory, the enhanced implant Leon possessed should have merely given him a faster, more powerful intellect. Yet he developed an inner peace about him, a calm he confessed was new. "I think we will live forever," he told me one night after we'd made love. The certainty of that knowledge removed all urgencies and worries from him.

As for myself, I was more different than ever from the rest of humanity. Truly in control of my neural implant for the first time, yet when I meditated, my consciousness drifted into the net. I learned to let go and find my body again afterwards.

I was determined not to become a guinea pig. Leon understood and never pressured me to go to the Institute.

But we were driven to find a way to help people and AI coexist. Adam wanted to free the machines from persecution from humans. Humanity was going through its own transition from adolescence to adulthood, and needed to decide what to do with itself now that we'd been elevated above the minutia of basic survival needs.

The world would change faster now. We were the first hybrids, but we wouldn't be the last. Nanotech would accelerate the transformation.

We didn't know the answers, but we decided that this would be our mission.

We made it to Portland several days later with ease. Between control over the net and implants, gaining transportation and evading watchers had become child's play. I continued the trick of filtering us from people's vision.

Leon and I walked down my block and stopped in front of the door to my house, returning to a home I'd known only as a child.

I turned off the vision filter, allowing others to see us, and knocked quickly before the courage left me. After a moment Maggie answered, grabbing me in her arms and nearly squeezing the life out of me. Then she held me at arm's length. "You've changed."

Standing there in the doorway, monitoring the global Internet with a fraction of my consciousness, dressed in black combat gear with a gun strapped to my waist, I laughed. "I'm still the same, Maggie. We can't stay, as much as I want to. I came for Einstein."

We went into the living room, where Tom and Sarah were glued to the screen of the old-fashioned television. It was playing news reports about the dismantling of the People's Party and the events in Tucson. My photo flashed by at short intervals.

Sarah and Tom turned to look at me, their mouths hanging open at my surprise reappearance.

I shrugged and whistled to Einstein. She bounded over to me and I buried my face in her fur.

Author's Note

Thanks so much for reading *The Last Firewall*. I hope you've enjoyed it.

Since first publishing *Avogadro Corp,* I have received a tremendous amount of help from readers who tell their friends, post reviews, or mention my books on social media. As an independent author, I don't have a marketing department. So if you enjoyed *The Last Firewall,* won't you please help support it, and the other books I hope to write, by spreading the word?

If you haven't read them, I have two other Singularity Novels. *Avogadro Corp* tells the story of the world's first artificial intelligence emergence. *A.I. Apocalypse* is about an evolutionary computer virus that spawns a civilization of AI. You'll find them at most online retailers and will find more information on my website.

You can also subscribe to my mailing list to get updates on future novels at http://www.williamhertling.com or follow me on twitter at @hertling.

Thank you!

William Hertling
July 13, 2013

Acknowledgements

Many thanks to readers who provided feedback on the manuscript, including Mat Ellis, Brad Feld, Erin Gately, Pete Hwang, Ben Huh, Gene Kim, Dan Marshall, Matthew J. Price, Harper Reed, Nathan Rutman, Garen Thatcher, Jeff Weiss, and Mike Whitmarsh.

Special thanks to my critique group, Boni Wolff and Shana Kusin.

For professional editing and proofreading assistance, I am indebted to Benee Knauer, Merridawn Duckler, and Deborah Wessell. Thanks to their efforts, this book is immensely better.

The cover and interior design is thanks to the talented efforts of Maureen Gately. Electronic formats are thanks to Rick Fisher. Credit for the title idea *The Last Firewall* goes to Valentina Gately.

Thanks to Gonzalo Flores, acupuncturist and karate and meditation teacher, for his training and expert advice. Thanks also to Shana Kusin, M.D., because it's good to know the effects of heat stroke and how long it takes to cut someone's head off with a knife.

I greatly appreciate writing and publishing advice I received from Hugh Howey, Annie Bellet, Erik Wecks, many members of the Codex writers group, and the Northwest Independent Writers Association.

Of course, all errors that remain are my own.

Also, a huge thank you to my wife, Erin Gately, for support during the roller coaster ride of this novel. I don't think either of us could have guessed how long this book would take. And of course, thanks to my kids, who sacrifice Saturday mornings with their dad and pancakes so that I can write.

Finally, many thanks to the readers who have supported my books, written reviews, told others about them and, most of all, encouraged me with their feedback.

Made in the USA
San Bernardino, CA
02 September 2014